The Disney Encyclopedia of Baby and Child Care

Judith Palfrey, M.D.
HARVARD MEDICAL SCHOOL AND
CHILDREN'S HOSPITAL IN BOSTON

Irving Schulman, M.D.
STANFORD UNIVERSITY
MEDICAL CENTER

Samuel L. Katz, M.D.
DUKE UNIVERSITY
MEDICAL CENTER

Maria I. New, M.D.
THE NEW YORK HOSPITAL AND CORNELL
UNIVERSITY MEDICAL COLLEGE

Genell Subak-Sharpe,
EDITORIAL DIRECTOR

Susan Carleton,
MANAGING EDITOR

ILLUSTRATIONS BY
Briar Lee Mitchell

VOLUME II

*A to Z Encyclopedia of Child
Health and Illness*

The Disney Encyclopedia of Baby and Child Care

HYPERION

New York

This book is based on current medical research and, to the best of the editors' knowledge and understanding, is accurate and valid. However the reader should not use information contained in this book to alter a medically prescribed regimen or as a form of self-treatment, without seeking the advice of a licensed physician.

DESIGNED BY BETH TONDREAU DESIGN

Printed in the United States of America. For information address Hyperion, 114 Fifth Avenue, New York, New York 10011.

LIBRARY OF CONGRESS CATALOGING-IN-PUBLICATION DATA
The Disney encyclopedia of baby and child care / edited by Judith
    Palfrey . . . [et al.].—1st ed.
        p.   cm
    Includes index.
    Contents: v. 1. Infant and child development—v. 2. A to Z
encyclopedia of child health and illness.
    ISBN 0-7868-8004-X
    1. Child care.   2. Child development.   3. Infants—Care.
4. Infants—Development.   I. Palfrey, Judith.
    RJ61.D58   1995   93-27905
    618.92—dc20   CIP

FIRST EDITION
10   9   8   7   6   5   4   3   2   1

DR. JUDITH SULLIVAN PALFREY is the Chief of the Division of General Pediatrics at Children's Hospital in Boston. She is also an Associate Professor of Pediatrics at Harvard Medical School and Associate Professor of Maternal and Child Health at Harvard School of Public Health. She is the 1995–1996 President of the Ambulatory Pediatric Association and former Chief of the Section on Developmental and Behavioral Pediatrics of the American Academy of Pediatrics. Since her graduation from the Columbia University College of Physicians and Surgeons in 1971, Dr. Palfrey has devoted much of her efforts to the problems of disadvantaged children. She has written on children with learning disorders and physical and mental handicaps, emphasizing their special needs for early identification and intervention. She has also worked to integrate children with complex medical problems into the educational system.

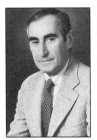

DR. IRVING SCHULMAN began his medical career in New York City, graduating from New York University College of Medicine, training in pediatrics at Bellevue Hospital, and then joining the staff of The New York Hospital–Cornell University Medical Center. He then became Director of Hematology at Children's Memorial Hospital and Professor of Pediatrics at Northwestern University Medical School in Chicago. In 1961, he became Professor and Chairman of the Department of Pediatrics at the University of Illinois College of Medicine and Pediatrician-in-Chief at University of Illinois Hospital. In 1972, he joined the faculty at Stanford University Medical Center, where he has served as Professor and Chairman of the Department of Pediatrics, Pediatrician-in-Chief at Stanford University Hospital, and Chief of Staff at the Packard Children's Hospital at Stanford. He is now the Marron and Mary Elizabeth Kendrick Professor Emeritus of Pediatrics at Stanford University School of Medicine.

DR. SAMUEL L. KATZ, the Wilburt C. Davison Professor at Duke University's Department of Pediatrics, is best known as the co-developer of the attenuated measles vaccine, now used worldwide and credited with taming this killer childhood disease. An honors graduate of Dartmouth and Harvard Medical School, Dr. Katz has spent most of his medical career at Duke, where he was Chairman of Pediatrics for 22 years. He is known worldwide for his research in infectious diseases. He has spent the past six years researching pediatric AIDS vaccines and caring for children infected with HIV. A past President of the American Pediatric Society, his many honors include the Distinguished Physician Award of the Pediatric Infectious Diseases Society, the Grulee Award of the American Academy of Pediatrics, the St. Geme Award for the Future of Pediatrics, an honor presented jointly by the seven American pediatric societies, and The Bristol Award of the Infectious Diseases Society of America.

DR. MARIA I. NEW, Professor and Chairman of the Department of Pediatrics at Cornell University Medical College and Pediatrician-in-Chief at The New York Hospital, is best known for her work in pediatric endocrinology, especially congenital adrenal disorders. After graduating from the University of Pennsylvania School of Medicine and training at New York's Bellevue Hospital and The New York Hospital, she launched her research career in 1957 with what became a series of fellowships funded by the National Institutes of Health. In 1964, she became Division Chief of Pediatric Endocrinology and Director of the Pediatric Metabolism Clinic at The New York Hospital–Cornell University Medical College. In 1980, she became Cornell's first woman Chair of Pediatrics. She has also held the Harold and Percy Uris Professorship of Pediatric Endocrinology and Metabolism since 1978. A fellow of the American Academy of Arts and Sciences, she has been President of the Endocrine Society and of the Lawson Wilkins Pediatric Endocrine Society. She is presently the Editor-in-Chief of the *Journal of Clinical Endocrinology and Metabolism.*

Editorial Advisory Board

Contents

Acknowledgments

The creation of a book this comprehensive is a lengthy, multi-stage process that draws on the work of scores of people and organizations. Without the help of our staffs at Boston Children's Hospital, The New York Hospital–Cornell University Medical Center, Duke University Medical Center, and the Lucile Salter Packard Children's Hospital at Stanford, the project would never have gotten off the ground. Special thanks are due to Lisa Menadue, Doris Lee, and Kathleen Dodd for providing invaluable support through three years of writing, editing, and revising via telephone, air couriers, and fax.

A hardworking group of writers hammered out the early drafts of each chapter and encyclopedia entry. They include Brenda Becker, Diana Benzaia, Cathy Carlson, Catherine Caruthers, Judith Dunlap, Philip Ivory, Rikki Lewis, Shelagh Masline, Emily Paulsen, Faith Paulsen, Luba Vikhanski, and Eileen Wallen. Manuscript editors Donna Goodwin, Susan Leon, and Susan Wensley were tremendously helpful in condensing and clarifying complex material. Judith Riven, Leslie Wells, Vicki DeStasio, and Laurie Abkemeier, our editors at Hyperion, provided timely guidance and encouragement. The illustrator, Briar Lee Mitchell, also deserves special thanks.

When the going got tough, Sarah Subak-Sharpe and Sharon Pestka were there to do last-minute typing, fact checking, and proofreading. Dushan Lukic cheerfully provided fast, accurate word processing on a very tight deadline.

A final word of thanks goes to Morton Bogdonoff, M.D., who helped recruit the chief medical editors and clarify the book's vision. Most of all, we thank our own children for always keeping us aware of the miracles involved in growing up.

—The Editors

Editor's Note

The Disney Encyclopedia of Baby and Child Care comprises two volumes. Volume I concerns Infant and Child Development, including the basics of first aid and a section on common childhood symptoms; Volume II contains an A to Z Encyclopedia of Child Health and Illness, with over 160 entries. Each volume contains an index for both volumes. Additional information for specific questions and special tips appear in boxes throughout the book.

A-Z Encyclopedia
of Child Health
and Illness

Abscess

An abscess is a pocket of pus that accumulates in the space left by tissue decayed from an infection. The yellowish pus consists of bacteria, white blood cells, and dead tissue. Abscess formation results from the body's attempt to contain an infection by walling off the affected area. An abscess causes pain when the associated swelling presses against nerves.

Abscesses can occur anywhere in the body. The location of an abscess determines its symptoms and severity.

How does an abscess develop?

Some abscesses develop after injuries allow bacteria to penetrate the skin. Others develop when an infection spreads from one part of the body to another through the bloodstream. An abscess can also arise as a complication of another disorder. Pneumonia, for example, can lead to a lung abscess.

When should I suspect an abscess?

An abscess just below the skin causes redness and swelling. Common sites of such abscesses include the anal opening, the skin alongside a fingernail, and the root of a badly decayed tooth.

Abscesses may occur also internally, with symptoms varying depending on location.

Is medical attention necessary?

Yes. Even a superficial abscess may need to be lanced and drained by a physician or, in the case of an abscessed tooth, a dentist. An attempt to open it yourself might cause the infection to spread. A course of antibiotics may also be required.

Getting Help

CALL YOUR DOCTOR IF YOUR CHILD:
- Has an unexplained, persistent fever.
- Develops localized redness, swelling, and pain in any area of the body.
- Sustains a puncture injury or a deep cut that could allow bacteria to penetrate.

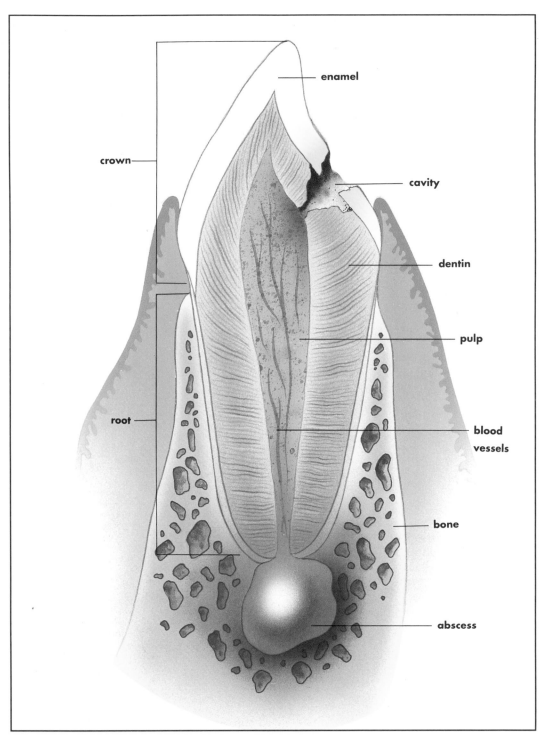

enamel

crown

cavity

dentin

pulp

root

blood vessels

bone

abscess

Dental caries (tooth decay) can lead to abscess formation in the bony socket at the root of a tooth.

Acne

Acne is a skin condition characterized by blackheads, whiteheads, and small, red bumps (pimples) on the face, back, and chest. Although the condition generally occurs during adolescence, a form of acne can also develop during infancy.

What causes acne?

Neonatal (newborn) acne develops when maternal hormones stimulate the sebaceous (oil) glands in the baby's skin. Boys develop this problem more often than girls. Outbreaks of neonatal acne generally appear on the cheeks, but in rare cases they also occur on the back and chest. The condition usually disappears two or three months after birth, when the effect of the mother's hormones subsides.

Infantile acne resembles neonatal acne in both appearance and duration. The main difference is that it appears at three or four months of age and is not due to hormones from the mother. The exact cause of this type of acne is unknown. In most cases, it disappears by the twelfth to eighteenth month of life.

How does acne develop?

The oil that keeps the skin smooth and supple is secreted by tiny glands connected to each hair follicle. (Hair follicles are microscopic, vertical canals out of which individual hairs grow.) When hormones stimulate the glands, they produce extra oil, which normally passes out of the follicle and onto the surface of the skin. Sometimes, however, dead cells clog the follicles, trapping oil inside. As oil and dead cells build up, the characteristic bumps are formed.

What distinguishes the acne that develops in infants from the type that occurs in adolescence is the absence of severe inflammation. In many cases of adolescent acne, bacteria multiply within the blocked follicles, causing them to rupture and creating large, purplish-red lesions. By contrast, neonatal and infantile acne usually consists only of pinkish bumps and plugged pores that rarely if ever get inflamed.

Is medical attention necessary?

It is a good idea to consult a pediatrician regarding any rash that appears on an infant's face, particularly if the baby is newborn. The doctor may want to examine the rash to make sure it is acne rather than cradle cap (which can also cause facial bumps) or some other condition.

What treatments are available?

Neonatal and infantile acne usually disappear over time without medical treatment. If a baby's acne is severe or persists for several months without much improvement, the doctor may prescribe a topical antiacne medication that removes the dead cells blocking hair follicles.

Getting Help

CALL YOUR DOCTOR IF YOUR INFANT:

- Develops any kind of rash in the first six weeks of life.
- Develops persistent acne, particularly with inflammation (redness and swelling). In children, this type of acne may be a sign of a hormonal disorder, a possibility the doctor should investigate.

Adenoid Disorders

Adenoids are the small masses of lymphatic tissue located above the tonsils. They sit in the part of the throat that meets the nasal passage (naso pharynx). Like the tonsils, the adenoids help guard against upper respiratory tract infections. Adenoid disorders—also known as *adenoidism* or *adenoiditis*—occur when the adenoids become swollen, causing difficulties in breathing and swallowing. Although adenoidism is common in toddlers and young children, no one knows why. It is thought that adenoids become enlarged as a result of frequent colds or allergies.

When should I suspect that my child has an adenoid disorder?

Children with adenoid disorders characteristically breathe through their mouths and have nasal voices. They also may snore. Development of these or any other characteristic symptoms should arouse your suspicions.

If a child has tonsillitis, her tonsils will appear larger and redder than usual. But adenoid disorders are much more difficult to detect. Adenoids, because of their location, cannot be seen by simply looking into the mouth. A special viewing instrument is needed.

When should I consult the doctor?

Don't worry about an occasional stuffy nose. Do consult a physician if symptoms such as runny nose, labored and noisy breathing, snoring, or unusual sleep patterns persist.

A generation ago, "T&A" (surgical removal of the tonsils and adenoids) was performed on an almost routine basis. Even today it remains the most frequently performed childhood operation.

Even so, alternative strategies are usually employed before the use of surgery, which always carries risk and may not reduce the number of respiratory infections a child has each year.

Is medical attention necessary?

A doctor may first suggest waiting to see if a child outgrows the problem. Children's adenoids grow primarily in the early years—usually up to about age five. Then the adenoids gradually shrink. By puberty, most children's adenoids have disappeared.

If the swelling persists, the doctor may recommend antibiotic treatment to eliminate possible bacterial infection, which could be the cause of an adenoid disorder. It is important to follow the doctor's orders about the timing and size of antibiotic doses and to continue the medication for as many days as the

---

SYMPTOMS OF ADENOID DISORDERS

- Stuffy nose.
- Noisy breathing through the mouth.
- Difficulty swallowing.
- A nasal voice.
- Loud snoring at night.
- Periodic cessation of breathing while sleeping (sleep apnea).
- Raspy cough after waking in the morning.
- Bad breath.
- Swollen glands.
- Repeated ear infections or sore throats.

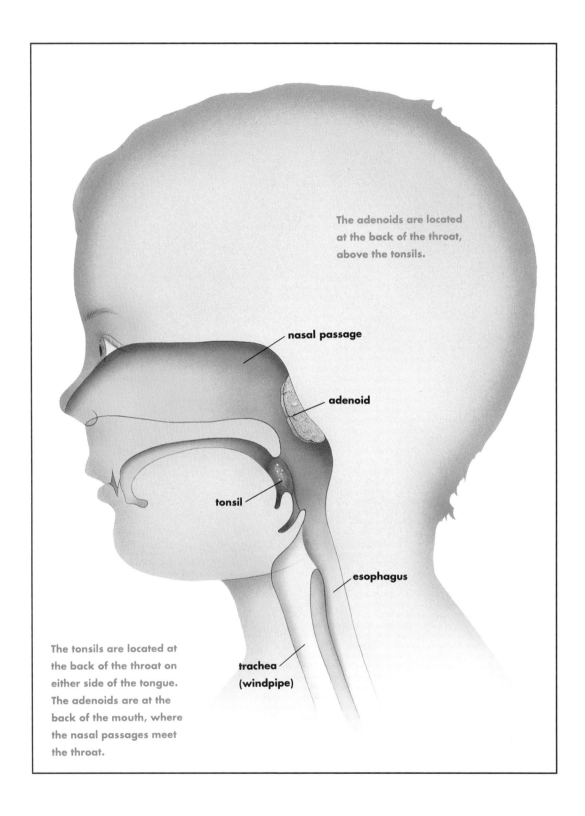

The adenoids are located at the back of the throat, above the tonsils.

nasal passage

adenoid

tonsil

esophagus

trachea (windpipe)

The tonsils are located at the back of the throat on either side of the tongue. The adenoids are at the back of the mouth, where the nasal passages meet the throat.

doctor prescribes, even if problems have disappeared.

If the adenoid problem is caused by respiratory allergies, treatment may be aimed at reducing allergy symptoms. Allergy control may gradually reduce swelling in the adenoids.

When does surgical removal of adenoids become necessary?

If all other treatments fail and a child continues to suffer from an adenoid disorder, the doctor may recommend surgical removal of the adenoids (*adenoidectomy*). The operation should take place only after careful evaluation by an ear, nose, and throat specialist (an *otolaryngologist*). In general, children should not have this operation until they reach school age. If a bacterial infection has occurred, surgery should be delayed two to four weeks after it has cleared up.

When should adenoids be removed?

According to the American Academy of Pediatrics, adenoid surgery is recommended if:

- Blockage from the adenoids interferes with a child's normal breathing.
- Swollen adenoids make breathing uncomfortable and severely impair speech.

In addition, adenoid surgery should be considered if:

- A child has had seven severe episodes of strep throat or some other type of sore throat accompanied by high fever, swollen lymph nodes, and pus in the throat.
- A child has had five serious sore throats (fitting the above description) in each of two

separate years or three serious sore throats in each of three separate years.
- A child has had swollen glands in the throat for six months or more despite antibiotic treatment.
- A child has recurrent ear infections that do not clear up even after treatment.
- The child has sleeping difficulties.

What happens during adenoid surgery?

First, an anesthesiologist administers general anesthesia so that the child sleeps through the operation. Then the surgeon—an otolaryngologist or a general surgeon—removes the adenoids using a small tool with a basket on the end. The adenoids are cut off and caught in the basket. Pressure is applied to minimize bleeding. Stitches are unnecessary. The surgery is usually over in less than 30 minutes.

CARING FOR A CHILD AFTER ADENOID SURGERY

- Stay with the child as much as possible during hospitalization, which may be needed for one to three days after adenoid surgery.
- Administer acetaminophen (brand names Tylenol, Tempra, Panadol, and others) to relieve discomfort.
- A soft, bland diet is recommended. Avoid hot, spicy, or coarse foods—chips, nuts, crackers—for about a week. Don't forget the ice cream!
- Most children are back to normal in two to three weeks, although they should avoid strenuous exercise for about a month.

Aggression

Almost all children display aggressive behavior at certain stages of development. This behavior usually appears by the latter half of the second year. Two- and three-year-olds are especially prone to aggressive actions, including temper tantrums, fighting, kicking, and biting.

For toddlers, physical aggression is a common way of expressing anger. While children under three are not mature enough to realize that hitting and shoving can hurt others, preschoolers may be aware of the effects of their behavior but unable to control their impulses.

Parents sometimes reinforce aggressive behavior by giving in to children's tantrums. Unfortunately, our cultural norms sometimes encourage aggression in boys (particularly against other boys) as proof of masculinity.

What causes aggression?

Over the years, the experts have held different views on the origins of aggression. Sigmund Freud saw aggressive behavior as an outgrowth of self-destructive impulses that are an inevitable part of being human. Another theory, developed in the late 1930s, held that aggression is a result of frustration. Later, however, psychologists concluded that frustration is not necessarily involved in aggression, although it may increase aggressive behavior.

GENERAL HINTS FOR PREVENTING OR REDUCING AGGRESSION

- If you know what situations trigger aggression in your child, try to avoid them.
- If possible, eliminate underlying stresses and anxieties that may cause aggressive behavior.
- Use of a time-out—briefly isolating the child immediately after the aggressive behavior occurs. Rather than scolding or physically punishing the child, place him in a quiet room or on a chair in the corner for a short period of time (many experts recommend one minute per year in age) in order to cool off.
- Try *not* to use physical punishment. It may stop aggression temporarily, but there is evidence that in the long run such punishment may actually increase aggressive behavior, probably because it conveys the idea that hitting is okay.
- Reward nonaggressive behavior.
- Reduce the time your child spends with playmates who engage in aggressive behavior.
- Limit the amount of violence young children watch in movies and on television.
- When children reach the age of four or five, talk to them about ways to express their anger without hurting others. Reassure the child that angry thoughts and feelings are normal and suggest a coping method, such as punching a bag or pillow to cool off.

- Make a colorful chart with a space for each day of the week; if the child is quite young, divide each day into smaller intervals to accommodate a shorter attention span. Hang the chart on the wall.
- For each period of time the child does not display aggression, give the child a sticker and help him place it on the chart. Say "Good, you didn't hit" (or bite or kick, etc.).
- Supplement the sticker with a snack or treat, or a few minutes of special attention.
- After the child has gone a whole week without aggression (or a shorter time for a younger child), show him the stickers on the chart, and say, "You haven't hit (or kicked, bitten, fought, etc.) for a whole week, now you've earned a special reward." This reward can be an outing with a parent, an extra period of time alone with mother, or anything you know your child would like. It should be unusual enough to motivate the child strongly.
- Any time the child is aggressive, say "no hitting." At the end of the day or interval show the child the chart and say, "You didn't get a sticker this time because you hit."

At present, many experts believe that children *learn* aggression from parents, peers, or other models. Once learned, aggression may be reinforced with extra attention. Biological factors are also believed to play a role in the development of aggression, especially when the behavior is severe and highly disruptive.

Is professional help necessary?

Most children are only mildly aggressive. As they learn to put their feelings into words, they find more acceptable ways to deal with anger and frustration.

If your child's aggression seems excessive—creating problems at school as well as at home, for example—seek professional help from a social worker, child psychologist, or guidance clinic. Most treatment programs for children with behavior problems involve both parents and children.

AIDS

By the end of 1993, 5,234 pediatric cases of Acquired Immune Deficiency Syndrome (AIDS) had been reported to the Centers for Disease Control, and the CDC estimates that within the next few years, 10,000 to 20,000 children will have AIDS. AIDS is particularly devastating in children because of its rapid progression. The average age of diagnosis for a child is nine months, and 50 percent die within a year if untreated. Still, physicians are identifying ways to lower the risk in children, and drugs used to slow the course of the disease in adults are proving increasingly effective in children, too.

What causes AIDS?

AIDS is caused by infection with the human immunodeficiency virus (HIV). Once in the body, HIV targets a type of white blood cell called T4 lymphocytes and injects its genetic material, instructing the T4 cell to become an HIV factory. The virus then reproduces itself until the T4 cell dies, spewing forth millions of new viruses as it does so. As the normally protective T4 cells are destroyed, the immune system is thrown off balance—deficient in vitally protective T4 cells while the other white blood cells (T8) responsible for suppressing the body's immune response remain intact. The imbalance between these white blood cell types impairs the immune system's ability to ward off and combat infections, and the symptoms of AIDS develop.

How could a child contract AIDS?

HIV enters the body through direct contact with certain body fluids, including blood, semen, vaginal secretions, and to a lesser extent, breast milk. For over 90 percent of pediatric AIDS patients, transmission of the virus is from an infected mother to the baby, either before or during birth. The mother may or may not have symptoms herself. A very few babies may contract the virus through mother's milk. Some cases are the result of sexual abuse.

Researchers are carefully exploring the way AIDS is passed from mother to child to identify intervention points. One study suggests that delivering HIV-positive women by cesarean section may prevent some cases of AIDS. Other studies have found that certain drugs given to HIV-positive pregnant women may block transmission to the fetus.

Before 1985, some cases of AIDS were contracted through blood transfusions. Since that time, very strict controls were begun on the supply of blood and blood products.

When should parents suspect their child has AIDS?

A child born to a mother who is HIV positive faces a 30 percent chance of becoming infected before or during birth. If a mother does not know her HIV status, signs to watch for in her child include unusual infections, recurring infections, and severe, long-lasting effects from infections that are routine in other children—particularly infections of the lungs (pneumonia) and skin. Thrush, a common fungal infection in which whitish particles grow in the mouth, occurs persistently and severely in children with AIDS, as does diarrhea caused by parasites.

Also watch for developmental delays. Infection of the brain with HIV can prevent a baby from sitting, crawling, standing, and walking when healthy children usually do. Verbal and motor skills are lost rather than gained. Newborns face a higher risk of meningitis, a serious infection of the lining of the brain.

When should medical attention be sought?

The possibility of AIDS should be raised when a parent has the disease or engages in high-risk behaviors such as IV drug use or unsafe sex practices. If you suspect your child is at risk or may have symptoms of AIDS, seek medical attention as soon as possible. Early intervention can slow the course of the disease.

RECOGNIZING AIDS

Indications of AIDS include:
- *Pneumocystis carinii* pneumonia (PCP).
- Frequent and severe infections.
- Frequent fevers and diarrhea.
- Poor growth and weight gain.
- Developmental regression.
- Swollen lymph glands, spleen, or salivary glands.

Children with AIDS require a great deal of loving care. They are likely to be in and out of the hospital, needing daily medication and frequent checkups. Friends and family members can be very helpful but are often frightened and concerned about the disease. There is no need to fear close contact with a child who has AIDS. The virus is not spread through hugging, sharing eating utensils, or other forms of casual contact. Special precautions are needed only when there may be contact with blood and other body fluids—for instance, if the child has a severe cut or nosebleed. In such circumstances, the caregiver should wear gloves while administering first aid and clean any spilled blood with a solution of equal parts bleach and water.

Children with HIV infection can attend school and day care and enjoy the whole range of normal childhood experiences. Often these children need extra health and developmental services because of their medical condition.

How can the doctor tell if my child has AIDS?

Accurate diagnosis is complicated in a child because for as long as the first 15 months of life, he will harbor antibodies to HIV made by the mother and passed on before birth. A diagnostic AIDS test based on detecting those antibodies may therefore be positive for the first year or so even though the baby may not actually be infected with HIV. If a child is found to have HIV antibodies, more definite tests to detect the virus itself or some of its components may be employed to determine whether the infant has become infected. Such tests may be positive within the first few weeks or months of life.

What treatments are available?

Doctors are armed with an ever-expanding arsenal of drugs to keep the infections of AIDS at bay. In the first months of life, antibiotic drugs may prevent *pneumocystis carinii* pneumonia (PCP)—an often-fatal AIDS-related infection—and other bacterial infections. Good nutrition and vaccines for the common childhood illnesses can prolong survival, and support from loved ones can greatly improve the quality of an affected child's life. Experimental vaccines, such as one under development for chicken pox, are being studied for children with AIDS, in whom such an illness may be quite severe. Repeated intravenous injections of gammaglobulin may be used to ward off infection.

Once symptoms arise drug treatment begins. AIDS treatments are evolving in the same direction as many cancer treatments, toward combinations of drugs that work against the virus and its effects in different ways. The Food and Drug Administration has approved the use of zidovudine (also known as azidothymidine, or AZT) and dideoxyinosine (ddI) in children. AZT and ddI interfere with HIV's ability to replicate within human cells. Researchers are also engineering dozens of immune system chemicals to fight HIV. The National Institutes of Health funds medical-center programs to which HIV-infected children may be referred for the most up-to-date investigations and treatment.

Allergic Rhinitis (Hay Fever)

Up to ten percent of children occasionally suffer the sneezing and runny nose caused by allergic reactions of the upper-respiratory tract—or, *allergic rhinitis.* The most well known of these reactions, hay fever, also causes a scratchy throat and itchy, watery eyes. Hay fever is triggered by ragweed and various pollens in the spring and fall. Other substances, however, can also lead to respiratory allergies in children. These include molds (which may cause symptoms in the early spring and late fall), animal dander (tiny flakes of skin from beneath the fur of household pets), and dust mites (microscopic bugs that grow in house dust).

Although respiratory allergies are generally considered seasonal illnesses, those that are triggered by dust and animal dander can occur year-round. In small children, these allergies are more common than hay fever, which rarely shows up before the age of six.

Children who are prone to allergic rhinitis also tend to develop symptoms when exposed to cigarette smoke, strong fumes, and, in some cases, cold air. The incidence of asthma,

All allergies, including allergic rhinitis, develop when the immune system becomes sensitized to a particular substance or allergen, such as pollen. After sensitization, the immune system produces antibodies to the substance. These antibodies are attached to the surfaces of white blood cells called lymphocytes. When lymphocytes are exposed to the allergen again, protein particles from the allergen bind to the antibodies and stimulate the release of histamine, which in turn produces allergy symptoms.

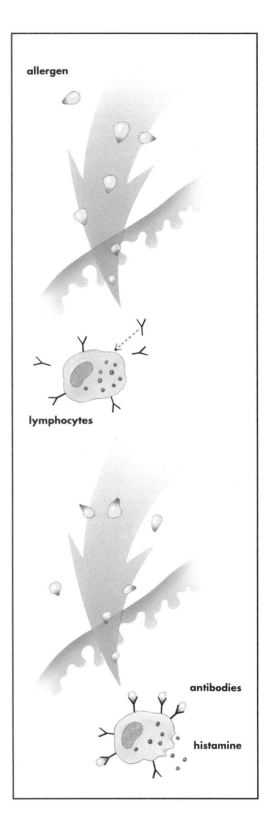

allergen

lymphocytes

antibodies

histamine

chronic sinusitis, and chronic middle-ear infections is particularly high in children with allergic rhinitis.

What causes allergic rhinitis?

The underlying mechanism is a *hypersensitivity* reaction to an inhaled foreign substance. Hypersensitivity develops when a child is exposed to an *antigen,* which is a protein that triggers immune-system production of a specific disease-fighting agent called an *antibody.* The immune-system response to the antigen triggers allergy symptoms.

The first exposure to an allergy-causing substance produces no reaction. Subsequently, however, the substance will lead to swelling of the tissues that line the nasal passages, watery eyes, and a profuse nasal discharge. The head may be stuffy, and the nose may be completely blocked.

When should I suspect that my child has allergic rhinitis?

Symptoms of allergic rhinitis are similar to those of a cold. As a result, it can sometimes be hard to tell the difference. Colds are more common in winter than in spring and fall, while the reverse is true of allergies. A cold usually lasts less than seven days and typically starts with a scratchy throat and watery nasal discharge, which rapidly becomes thicker and more opaque. Allergic rhinitis, by contrast, causes a watery discharge and almost constant sneezing. Not all allergic rhinitis patients, however, have sneezing symptoms. Children with allergic rhinitis usually exhibit persistent nose rubbing, because of the irritation or itch in the nose. Allergic rhinitis may be seasonal depending upon the allergen involved.

Is medical attention necessary?

Yes. Severe allergic rhinitis can be very uncomfortable and interfere with a child's normal functioning. Since prevention is often a simple matter of avoiding the substance that causes the reaction, it is worthwhile to find out what is causing the symptoms.

How can the pediatrician tell if my child has allergic rhinitis?

The pediatrician looks for physical signs that distinguish allergies from colds. Some children with severe allergies develop so-called *allergic shiners*—dark rings below the eyes. The nasal lining may appear puffy and bluish, and the tonsils and adenoids are often swollen. The

---

CARING FOR A CHILD WITH ALLERGIC RHINITIS

- Learn to recognize the signs of an allergy attack and, if possible, remove the trigger from the child's environment or remove the child from the environment.
- Do not allow smoking in your home, and sit in a nonsmoking area when you go out.
- Avoid giving the child over-the-counter nasal sprays, which can worsen symptoms.
- Use an air conditioner in the child's bedroom (or the entire house, if possible) when the pollen count is high if the child has hay fever.
- Keep the bedroom as dust-free as possible by eliminating heavy drapes, rugs, and knick-knacks and cleaning often.
- Ask about giving antihistamines at night only so that side effects such as drowsiness will not be disruptive.

pediatrician will also ask questions to determine whether symptoms follow an allergy pattern or a cold pattern. Finally, a sample of nasal secretions may be examined under a microscope to check for cells associated with allergic reactions.

What treatments are available?

Occasional bouts of allergic rhinitis can be treated with antihistamines. More severe allergies may require daily medication, at least during certain months. Corticosteroid nasal sprays can help children with debilitating seasonal allergy symptoms.

Children who have continuing problems despite these treatments may benefit from allergy shots (immunotherapy). Unfortunately, however, immunotherapy is expensive and time-consuming, and it does not produce immediate results.

Anal Fissures

An anal fissure is a small tear or cracklike sore in the mucous lining of the anus, the outlet through which fecal waste passes. Fissures are the most common cause of rectal bleeding in infants and older children. While parents may be alarmed to see a blood stain in their child's stool or diaper, there is usually no need for concern. Anal fissures can be treated successfully and seldom become chronic.

When should I suspect that my child has anal fissures?

If you see blood in your child's stools or diaper, anal fissures are a possible cause. Your child also may be constipated, refuse to defecate, or complain of pain when moving the bowels.

What causes anal fissures?

Anal fissures usually are caused by constipation. They develop when stools are dry and hardened and moving the bowels requires exertion. As the child strains, the anus stretches and the mucous lining cracks like a split lip. The passing stools irritate the wound and cause the surrounding muscles (the *sphincter muscles*) to go into spasm. Spasms are painful and can delay healing by leading to increased constipation.

How can the doctor tell if my child has anal fissures?

Your doctor can usually see the fissure by examining the exterior of the anus. In rare cases, a special viewing instrument called a *proctoscope* may be needed to inspect the inside of the anus and rectum.

Is medical attention necessary?

Yes. Although most anal fissures heal naturally or respond quickly to simple treatment, the pediatrician should be consulted. If constipation is the cause of the fissure, establishing a more regular bowel pattern should promote healing. Stool softeners, glycerin suppositories, or psyllium-containing powders will relieve constipation, but a change in diet may be necessary over the long term.

To speed the healing, the doctor may prescribe a hydrocortisone cream or ointment to the crack. Warm baths will soften the skin and may aid healing.

Anemia, Iron-Deficiency

Iron-deficiency anemia is a blood disorder caused by lack of iron, which is needed to produce the pigment *hemoglobin.* This pigment is the component of the red blood cells responsible for carrying oxygen throughout the body.

The most common kind of anemia in children is caused by iron-deficiency. Up to ten percent of young children in the United States are iron deficient, and the condition occurs most frequently between the ages of 6 and 24 months. Iron-deficiency anemia is usually simple to treat. Medication with iron supplements leads to a rapid and complete recovery. More importantly, however, most cases can be prevented with adequate nutrition.

When should I suspect that my child has iron-deficiency anemia?

Anemia develops so gradually that even the most conscientious parent can overlook the early signs. If your child seems pale, less alert, and more easily fatigued than other children, take a closer look. Check the color of the insides of the eyelids and lips, the nail beds, and the creases of the palm; in anemia, these areas are unnaturally pale. Finally, review your child's diet to make sure he is eating iron-rich foods or drinking an iron-fortified formula.

What causes iron-deficiency anemia?

Most cases of iron-deficiency anemia in early childhood can be traced to an iron-poor diet. The typical diet of a very young child—low in iron-rich foods like meat and vegetables and high in milk and cereals—cannot provide sufficient quantities of iron. Low birth weight babies are particularly susceptible because they have less iron stores to begin with and experience rapid growth spurts. Also common is bleeding from the bowel due to early introduction of whole cow's milk into the diet. The amount of blood lost may be too small to see, but over time it may lead to significant iron loss and anemia.

Is medical attention necessary?

Yes. A child with iron deficiency should be treated by a physician. Don't attempt to medicate your child with iron if you suspect anemia. Excess consumption of iron can be more harmful than iron deficiency. Also, the same symptoms can signal other, more serious problems that require different treatment.

How can the doctor tell if my child has iron-deficiency anemia?

Your pediatrician uses various laboratory tests to diagnose iron-deficiency anemia and—equally important—identify the cause of the deficiency. Most likely, insufficient iron in the diet or blood loss will be the culprit. When the cause is unclear, however, your doctor will want to perform more tests to rule out other problems such as an ongoing blood loss.

What treatments are available?

The doctor will probably prescribe daily iron supplements, usually taken in a liquid form with meals. (Although iron absorption is better if the medication is given between meals, it can cause stomach upset.) A complete recovery can be expected within two to four weeks. Iron therapy should continue for another six months, however, to replenish your child's iron stores.

IRON-RICH FOODS	
VERY GOOD	**GOOD**
Liver	Avocado
Beef	Blueberries
Beans	Poultry
Prune Juice	Peas
	Iron-fortified formulas, cereals, and breads
	Whole-grain cereals and breads
	Green leafy vegetables
	Potatoes with skin
	Dried apricots and raisins

Finally, getting on track with a healthy diet is a critical part of maintaining your youngster's health. The best management of iron-deficiency anemia is prevention.

Preventing iron-deficiency anemia

Breast-fed babies should be given iron supplement drops to prevent anemia. After the age of six months commercial infant formulas already are supplemented with iron, bottle-fed babies do not need these supplements. Since whole milk can cause the milk intolerance that leads to anemia, do not give it to a baby under one year of age.

After one year of age, if your toddler would rather fill up on milk than eat iron-rich solid foods, begin to limit the volume of milk to encourage a more varied diet.

Fussy eaters can be nudged along with a little imagination. Add an extra egg yolk to pancake batter. Add extra red meat or green vegetables in a favorite soup or stew. Offer special "treats" of little boxes of raisins or dried apricots.

Cooking in cast iron pots, especially foods such as tomato sauce, can add significant amounts of iron to your child's diet.

Offer your child plenty of citrus juices and fruits (vitamin C increases absorption of iron, while milk decreases absorption).

Getting Help

CALL YOUR DOCTOR IF YOUR CHILD:
- Is pale, listless or irritable.
- Tires easily.
- Seems more susceptible to infections.
- Has decreased appetite.
- Develops a craving for ice cubes, dirt, clay, or other nonfoods.

Anemia, Sickle-Cell

Sickle-cell anemia is an inherited blood disorder that occurs almost exclusively in blacks. It is caused by an abnormality in the pigment *hemoglobin,* the oxygen-carrying component of the red blood cells. The defective hemoglobin—called *hemoglobin S*—causes the red blood cells to become rigid and "sickle-" shaped rather than flexible and round. These deformed cells are brittle and easily destroyed, leading to the symptoms of sickle-cell disease.

When should I suspect that my child has sickle-cell anemia?

All black infants should be screened for sickle-cell anemia at birth. This is particularly important if there is any history of the disease in the family. A definitive diagnosis can be made with simple blood tests.

What causes sickle-cell anemia?

Sickle-cell disorders are passed genetically from parent to child. If both parents have a gene for hemoglobin S, their child has a 25 percent chance of inheriting both genes and getting sickle-cell anemia. If only one gene is inherited, half of the child's hemoglobin will be normal and will prevent the disease from developing. These children have *sickle-cell trait* and are usually healthy; however, they can pass on the abnormal gene to their children. One in 12 blacks are healthy carriers of the sickle-cell gene.

How does sickle-cell anemia develop?

Although the abnormal hemoglobin can be detected at birth, symptoms of sickle-cell anemia generally do not appear until the infant is about six months old. These symptoms include delayed growth and development and anemia, which causes fatigue, pallor, and increased susceptibility to infection. The first noticeable sign of the disease may be a painful attack known as a sickle-cell *crisis.* Such an episode often follows an infection or injury and affects various parts of the body, particularly the abdomen, long bones, joints, and chest. Vision problems can occur when the retina is affected. The severity and frequency of crises can vary tremendously.

What causes a sickle-cell crisis?

The body manufactures red blood cells continually. Healthy red blood cells are disk shaped and flexible, so they can circulate freely through the capillaries and other small blood

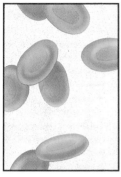

normal red blood cells   sickled red blood cells

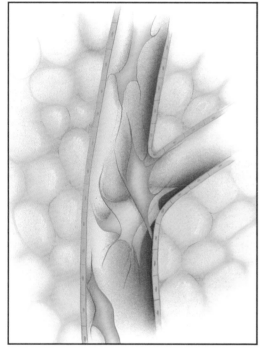

Sickle-cell anemia is an inherited blood disorder in which red blood cells are misshapen due to an abnormal type of hemoglobin—the oxygen-carrying molecule in blood.

vessels. After about 120 days, they are destroyed and replaced with new ones. In sickle-cell anemia, the red blood cells have a shortened life span of only two weeks or so.

The result is a low red blood cell count and chronic anemia. Moreover, in contrast to normal red blood cells, the rigid sickle cells cannot pass easily through tiny blood vessels. Impaired circulation leads to slower oxygen transport, which worsens sickling. This cycle can eventually interrupt blood flow to the tissues and organs, causing pain. This is a sickle-cell crisis.

What treatments are available?

There is no cure for sickle-cell anemia, but with your doctor's help, you can ease the discomfort of most crises and help prevent others. Moderate crises can be managed with medication to relieve pain and prevent dehydration. During more severe crises, oxygen may be given if your child's blood does not have enough. A blood transfusion before any

COPING WITH SICKLE-CELL ANEMIA

- Make sure your child receives all appropriate vaccines to prevent infections (including pneumococcal vaccine).
- Watch for infections and administer antibiotics promptly as prescribed by your doctor.
- Talk to your doctor about treating your child with antibiotics in advance (PROPHY-LACTICALLY) to prevent serious infections.
- Give the child daily oral supplements of folic acid because the disease increases the body's need for this vitamin.
- Take appropriate precautions when traveling in airplanes or to high altitudes (see "The dangers of high-altitude travel") on page 20.

medical or dental surgery can provide your child with healthy red blood cells, thus avoiding the crisis that might normally follow.

Black parents should make sure their infants are screened at birth. Early identification and treatment can minimize potential complications. Antisickle drugs are being tested, but at present, genetic testing and counseling are the only means of preventing sickle-cell anemia from being passed to a new generation.

The dangers of high-altitude travel

If your child has sickle-cell anemia, she will have to be cautious about high altitudes and air travel throughout life. The body normally compensates for reduced oxygen due to high altitudes and changes in air pressure in airplanes by increasing the amount of circulating red blood cells and hemoglobin. However, in a child with sickle-cell anemia, this could lead to an increase in abnormal hemoglobin and precipitate a sickle-cell crisis.

The child will probably be advised to avoid traveling to places more than 6,000 feet above sea level and to be cautious when flying. Stick to commercial airlines that have pressurized cabins and an emergency supply of oxygen aboard. Some people with sickle-cell anemia require oxygen support during any flight.

Appendicitis

The appendix is a small, worm-shaped offshoot of the large intestine that has no known function. Appendicitis develops when the appendix—for reasons that are still unclear—becomes inflamed. The great danger of appendicitis is that the organ can fill with pus and eventually burst, spreading bacteria throughout the abdominal cavity and causing a dangerous condition called *peritonitis*. To prevent this complication, an infected appendix should be removed surgically.

Appendicitis affects approximately one in 500 children under the age of 14 each year in the United States. It is rare in children under two, but at that age the consequences can be more serious.

When should I suspect that my child has appendicitis?

Appendicitis in a child may be difficult to diagnose because there are so many reasons for abdominal pain, and young children often cannot communicate just how bad the pain is. Appendicitis should be suspected if the pain begins as a dull or vague discomfort near the navel and then sharpens and localizes as it moves toward the lower right section of the abdomen, the site of the inflamed appendix. Within a few hours, the intensifying pain becomes constant and the lower abdomen becomes extremely sensitive to the touch.

Getting Help

CALL YOUR DOCTOR IF YOUR CHILD:

- Has sickle-cell anemia and develops signs or symptoms of infection.
- Has sickle-cell anemia and is experiencing vision problems.
- Has sickle-cell anemia and is suffering from a painful crisis.

Symptoms of appendicitis do not follow any set pattern, however. The precise location of the appendix varies from person to person and so will the focus on the pain. Frequently, the pain will be felt in the side, back, or anywhere in the lower abdomen.

Is medical attention necessary?

Yes. Appendicitis is a medical emergency. Untreated appendicitis can lead to a perforated appendix, which is a serious, life-threatening condition. If your child has vomiting, abdominal pain, and tenderness suggesting appendicitis, call your doctor immediately. If the pain is severe, go straight to the emergency room. Do not give your child anything to eat or drink or administer laxatives or pain killers.

Getting Help

CALL YOUR DOCTOR IF YOUR CHILD:

- Has abdominal pain that begins intermittently, then intensifies and becomes constant.
- Cannot move without pain.
- Cries out in pain when the tender area is touched.
- Feels sharp pain when coughing or sneezing.
- Has a fever, but no throat or ear pain.
- Lies with the right leg bent in or will not put any weight on the right leg.
- Has some of the above symptoms along with nausea, diarrhea, or constipation.

What treatment is available?

The only treatment is surgery to remove the appendix (an *appendectomy*). If there is time, your doctor will usually try to confirm the diagnosis first with a series of tests such as blood studies and abdominal ultrasound. On occasion, however, surgery must be performed immediately on the basis of symptoms alone.

An uncomplicated appendectomy is a simple, safe procedure requiring a hospital stay of no longer than three to five days. A course of antibiotics may be prescribed to eliminate any infection, and your child will be back to normal in two or three weeks. Surgeons are currently developing a method of performing appendectomies using a lighted magnifying instrument (a laparoscope) and surgical instruments inserted into the abdomen through a small incision.

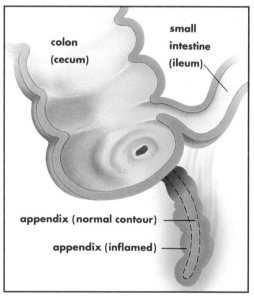

The appendix is located on the lower right side of the colon, near the juncture of the small and large intestines.

Arthritis, Juvenile Rheumatoid (JRA)

Juvenile rheumatoid arthritis (JRA) is the most common type of childhood arthritis. The illness commonly strikes children between the ages of two and four years. For unknown reasons, JRA is more common in girls than in boys.

Although its main manifestations are joint swelling, pain, and stiffness, JRA can affect other organ systems, including the lungs and heart, and it typically produces wide-ranging symptoms such as fever, fatigue, and loss of appetite. The most severe forms of the disease can cause permanent joint damage.

JRA occurs in three distinct subtypes that follow different courses over the first six months of illness. All the subtypes have the characteristic pattern in which symptoms periodically flare up and subside over several months or even years. (There are exceptions to this pattern. Some children have continuous, low-grade symptoms for a long period; others have one episode and then go into permanent remission.) By late adolescence or early childhood, 75 percent of JRA patients are in permanent remission.

What causes JRA?

Many experts believe that the underlying mechanism is an *automimmune* reaction, which occurs when the immune system mistakenly attacks normal body tissue. In this case, the joints are the primary targets, but other tissues can be involved as well.

When should I suspect JRA?

Symptoms that resemble an infection usually develop first. Fever (which can climb to 103 degrees Fahrenheit or higher, especially at night), a red rash on the chest and thighs, and swollen lymph nodes are common. Signs of joint involvement, such as stiffness (especially in the morning), limping, and pain, also typically develop. One or more joints may be red, swollen, and warm to the touch.

Is medical attention necessary?

Yes. To confirm the presence of JRA, your pediatrician will take the child's complete med-

---

TYPES OF JRA

The three main forms of JRA are:

- **SYSTEMIC-ONSET JRA,** characterized by intermittent high fever, inflammation of numerous joints, and a rash. Other organs are typically involved as well.
- **POLYARTICULAR-ONSET JRA,** defined by inflammation and pain in five or more small and large joints in a symmetrical pattern (on both sides).
- **PAUCIARTICULAR-ONSET JRA,** characterized by asymmetrical pain (occurring on only one side of the body) and inflammation in four or fewer joints, usually in a knee, ankle, or hip. It also causes fatigue, slow weight gain, and eye inflammation.

---

ical history, perform a physical examination, and draw blood for a series of tests. It is important to rule out infectious forms of arthritis such as **Lyme disease** (see entry), which can be cured with antibiotic therapy. If a diagnosis of JRA seems likely, the child may be referred to a pediatric rheumatologist for further testing, such as X rays and a sampling of fluid from the affected joints.

What treatments are available?

Based on the type and severity of the child's illness, the doctor may prescribe one or more of the following treatments:

- **ASPIRIN** reduces inflammation and controls fever and pain. High doses are given several times a day. Close monitoring is required to observe possible side effects and toxicity. No medication other than aspirin may be needed, at least on a long-term basis.

- **OTHER DRUGS THAT ARE SIMILAR TO ASPIRIN.** If symptoms persist or aspirin toxicity develops, a switch from aspirin to such alternatives as ibuprofen or naproxen may be needed.

- **STEROID INJECTIONS INTO THE JOINTS** eliminate pain without the dangers of injected or oral corticosteroids. This technique is suggested if only one or two joints are affected and aspirin or aspirinlike drugs are inadequate.

- **ORAL OR INJECTED STEROIDS IMMUNO- SUPPRESIVE** drugs (similar to drugs given to prevent rejection of transplanted organs) are reserved for the most severe cases of JRA.

- **MORE POWERFUL ANTIRHEUMATIC DRUGS** such as gold salts are used during bad flare-ups or when aspirin and similar drugs are inadequate.

Can complications occur?

Yes, but if the child is monitored closely, they can usually be managed. Children with JRA are susceptible to stomach pain, inflammation of the membrane surrounding the heart (*pericarditis*), inflammation of the membrane covering the lungs (*pleuritis*), and inflammation of the colored part of the eye (*uveitis*). JRA can also lead to anemia.

Other treatments

Physical and occupational therapy may be needed to maintain or increase the mobility of arthritic joints and promote independence in eating, dressing, and similar activities. In addition, rest is an important component of JRA management.

Persuading the child to stick to a reasonable schedule of exercise and rest may be a challenge. Parents can offer special rewards for younger children who comply without a fuss. Older children can be told the benefits of following the schedule—namely, more energy and better functioning.

Informal physical activity is just as important as prescribed physical therapy. Children should play as normally as possible and participate in sports such as swimming and bicycling.

Like any other chronic illness, JRA places emotional demands on both the child and the family. Ask your pediatrician for a referral to a family therapist or social worker with experience helping children who have chronic and potentially disabling conditions.

Asthma

Between five to ten percent of children in the United States suffer from asthma, a respiratory disorder that causes episodes of wheezing, coughing, and breathlessness. In most cases, the symptoms are mild, but some children with asthma have severe, frequent attacks. For these children—the majority of whom develop asthma before age three—the condition may lead to numerous emergency-room visits and hospitalizations. Even for children with severe symptoms, however, asthma can be controlled.

What happens during an asthma attack?

People with asthma have overly reactive bronchial tubes. The bronchial tubes are the airways in the respiratory tract, branching off the two mainstream *bronchi,* which are the large airways at the bottom of the windpipe. The bronchi carry air by way of smaller branches called *bronchioles* to the *alveoli,* tiny sacs in which the blood exchanges carbon dioxide (a waste product of cellular activity) for oxygen.

When a person with asthma comes into contact with an irritant (such as cigarette smoke), allergen (such as dust, mold, or pol-

---

COMMON ASTHMA TRIGGERS

- Dust.
- Animal dander (particularly from cats and dogs).
- Goose down and feathers.
- Smoke.
- Pollen.
- Cold air.
- Exercise.
- Colds.
- Strong odors.
- Car exhaust and other air pollutants.
- Sudden weather changes.

---

len), or some other trigger, the muscles that encircle the bronchial tubes go into spasms and the lining of the tubes becomes inflamed, leading to increased secretion of mucus. As a result, the bronchial tubes become narrower, causing tightness in the chest, cough, a hunger for air, wheezing, and an increase in respiratory and heart rate.

Early signs include slight coughing and a high-pitched wheezing sound when the child exhales. Mild attacks may not get much worse than this. In more severe cases, respiration becomes rapid, the skin pales, and the chest pulls inward with every breath. The child may vomit. As the attack worsens, the wheezing may become louder, although in very severe cases, little or no wheezing is heard because the breathing tubes are so narrow.

What causes asthma?

Two-thirds of childhood asthma cases stem from allergic responses to dust, animal dander, or plant pollens. Less frequently foods, drugs, or chemicals may cause wheezing. Children with this type of asthma often have other allergies such as eczema and hay fever. Their siblings and parents tend to have allergic sensitivities as well. The other third occur in response to an upper-respiratory infection (a cold or bronchitis), exercise, cold air, irritants such as smoke, or emotional upsets. Many children with asthma are sensitive to both types of triggers.

Following exposure to an irritant or allergen, the bronchial tubes may remain hypersensitive for weeks or months. Because of this reactivity, asthma attacks may occur without direct contact with a trigger.

When should I suspect that my child has asthma?

If your child has any type of allergy, it's a good idea to watch out for asthma. Likewise, children who tend to develop dry, hacking nighttime coughs and wheezing when they have colds or after they exercise may have mild cases of asthma.

You will know when your child has an acute asthma attack. In addition to wheezing, coughing, and shortness of breath, the child may become anxious and agitated. At the opposite extreme, children suffering severe asthma attacks often become abnormally lethargic.

What treatments are available?

A number of medications—all of which work by dilating the tightened bronchial tubes—are available to treat acute asthma attacks and prevent their recurrence. (See "Asthma medications" on page 27.) Depending on the child's age, the severity of the symptoms, and the circumstances (treating an acute attack or preventing recurrences), the medication can be injected, inhaled, or taken orally.

If the child has asthma only as an occasional complication of a cold (once or twice a winter), medication may be taken as needed at the

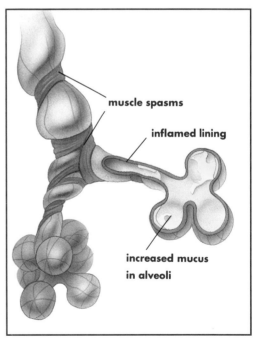

muscle spasms

inflamed lining

increased mucus in alveoli

A bronchiole during an asthma attack.

- Administer medication in the exact dose and at the exact time prescribed by the doctor.
- Avoid substances that trigger attacks.
- Consider allergy shots (immunotherapy) if your child is allergic to substances such as household dust and avoidance measures do not reduce the attacks.
- If cold air, exercise, or respiratory infections trigger asthma in your child, ask your pediatrician about administering preventive medication on an as-needed basis—for example, before going out on the coldest days, before gym class, or at the first signs of a developing cold.
- Smoking parents should stop.

first signs of a cold. Children who have asthma attacks regularly need daily medication to prevent recurrences and control symptoms. Likewise, children with severe, recurrent asthma often need medication regimens that combine different classes of drugs.

For children with allergy-related asthma, identifying and avoiding allergens is a key to successful prevention. Your pediatrician may recommend skin tests, in which tiny amounts of common allergens are scratched onto the surface of the skin to identify the ones that provoke reactions. After allergens have been identified, the doctor will advise you on allergy proofing your house. In addition, some children undergo immunotherapy (allergy shots), a process in which allergens are injected beneath the skin to dampen the abnormal immune-system response. Your child may need to have these injections on a weekly basis for a year or more.

Coping with asthma

Parents of children with asthma may become overprotective. Once you've nursed your child through one or two severe asthma attacks, you'll probably go to almost any lengths to avoid a recurrence—even if it means discouraging certain normal childhood activities. Being too protective, however, can set the stage for power struggles that go much deeper than the illness itself. Sometimes, children with asthma use the threat of an attack to get their way. They may also needlessly avoid exercise and other healthy activities.

To prevent these problems, keep your child's life as normal as possible. Stick to rules of acceptable behavior, particularly regarding bedtimes, meals, and other routines. If daily medication is necessary, it should become as automatic a part of the day as brushing teeth and putting on socks. At around age five, many children can assume some of the responsibility for taking their medication on schedule.

When attacks occur, stay calm and act fast. Remember that asthma is, by definition, reversible, and that very few attacks are severe enough to warrant hospitalization. Moreover, your own distress can heighten your child's anxiety, which may worsen the symptoms.

Using an inhaler or nebulizer

Most children with chronic asthma learn to take their medicine by inhaling it. Inhaled medications work faster than those taken by mouth. Also, because the drug goes directly to the lungs, a much smaller dose is needed, causing fewer side effects. Until about age four, most children use nebulizers, which infuse tiny droplets of medication into air from an air source (such as a portable compressor) attached to a mask that fits over the mouth and nose.

Older children can learn to use an inhaler, with which they self-administer a metered dose of medication in mist form. In this way, they may take cromolyn (which prevents attacks but does not relieve them) according to a schedule and terbutaline or a similar preparation at the onset of symptoms. Some corticosteroid drugs are also available in inhalers. Inhaled cortico steroids are used often for moderate or severe asthma.

Getting Help

CALL YOUR DOCTOR IF:
- Wheezing or difficult breathing fails to subside after medication is administered.
- Vomiting prevents the child from retaining the full dose of medication.
- You can see the child's chest moving in with every breath.
- Wheezing becomes inaudible but breathing remains difficult.
- The child's skin looks dusky and her lips and fingernails are blue.
- The child becomes uncharacteristically agitated or lethargic.

ASTHMA MEDICATIONS

Pediatricians prescribe four main types of asthma medications. Which drug is appropriate depends on the severity of the symptoms and the pattern in which they occur.

TYPE OF DRUG	EXAMPLES	HOW IT WORKS	AVAILABLE AS
Beta adrenergic agonist	albuterol, terbutaline metaproterenol	Dilates bronchial tubes, decreases airway irritability	Liquid, tablet, mist for inhalation
Methylxanthine	aminophylline, theophylline	Dilates bronchial tubes, decreases airway irritability	Liquid, tablet, timed-release capsule, intravenous solution.
Cromolyn sodium	cromolyn, nedocromil	Decreases airway irritability; prevents attacks	Mist for inhalation
Corticosteroid	hydrocortisone prednisone, beclomethasone	Decreases airway obstruction, reduces inflammation	Liquid, tablet, intravenous solution, mist for inhalation

Attention-Deficit Hyperactivity Disorder

Attention-deficit hyperactivity disorder, or ADHD, is the official name of a disorder sometimes loosely referred to as "hyperactivity" in a child. ADHD is associated with limited attention span, excessive and uncontrolled physical activity, and poor impulse control.

ADHD affects far more boys than girls, and it can become apparent by age four or five. A typical boy with this disorder may seem like a whirlwind of unstoppable energy, careening from one activity or game to the next. In gatherings of children or adults, he may become wild and unmanageable.

Children with ADHD find it nearly impossible to sit still or engage in a quiet activity for more than a few minutes. As a result, they almost always have problems at school.

ADHD needs to be treated. In addition to frustrating parents and teachers, ADHD may cause a child to place himself or others in danger. What's more, a child with ADHD may develop low self-esteem, as his inappropriate behavior sets him apart from other children. In some cases, especially in girls, ADHD does not include hyperactivity. Sometimes stimulant therapy works in these situations.

What causes ADHD?

The exact cause is still unknown, but recent research points strongly to a biological basis for the disorder.

When should I suspect ADHD?

Refer to "Recognizing attention-deficit hyperactivity disorder" on this page. Remember that high energy, impulsiveness, and inattentiveness are normal characterics in childhood, and all children will display some, or even all, of these symptoms from time to time. A definite pattern of symptoms must be evident for a diagnosis of ADHD.

RECOGNIZING ATTENTION-DEFICIT HYPERACTIVITY DISORDER

According to the American Psychiatric Association, your child may have ADHD if he shows at least eight of these behaviors for at least six months before the age of seven:

- Frequent fidgeting or squirming when seated.
- Difficulty remaining seated when required to sit.
- Easy distractibility by noises, sights, and other stimuli.
- Difficulty taking turns.
- Difficulty following through on instructions.
- Tendency to blurt out answers before a question is completed.
- Difficulty sustaining attention in play and work.
- Frequent shifting of activities without completing any task.
- Difficulty playing quietly.
- Excessive talking.
- Frequent interruptions or intrusions on others.
- Inattention to what others are saying.
- Tendency to lose things.
- Tendency to engage in dangerous activities.

(Source: DSM III)

- Provide a structured and predictable environment.
- Avoid overly stimulating places such as malls and grocery stores.
- Do not expect the child to concentrate on a task for extended periods. If he can focus on an activity for three minutes, set a modest goal of concentrating for five minutes, not ten or 20.
- Help the child reach this concentration goal by setting a timer for the desired time. When your child can remain with the same play activity for five minutes without getting distracted, reward him with praise and positive physical contact.
- Set up these trial periods several times a day. As the child is able to accomplish the goal, make the time longer.
- When the child engages in unwanted behavior, redirect him; suggest another, less disruptive activity, and if necessary, guide him into the alternate activity.

Getting Help

- Children with ADHD are at risk for other behavioral problems, learning disabilities, low self-esteem, and relationship problems. For this reason it is imperative that ADHD children get help.

How can the pediatrician tell if my child has ADHD?

Generally, parents or nursery school teachers notice the possible problem and mention it to the pediatrician. The doctor may administer tests to eliminate the possibility of certain neurological or physical disorders. If ADHD seems likely, it is useful to have the child evaluated by a team of child development specialists to determine if there are associated problems. A member of the team may observe the child at home and at school, and have parents and teachers answer a questionnaire about the child's behavior. Overall, the team looks for specific behaviors such as lack of concentration, distraction, daydreaming, impulsivity, or out of control behavior.

What treatments are available?

Children with the disorder are often treated with a drug of the stimulant class. In adults, such drugs can cause agitation and nervousness, but they can have the opposite effect on children with ADHD and increase their ability to concentrate. In some children, these drugs have side effects, including appetite suppression, sleeplessness and, rarely, delayed growth. For this reason, children must be evaluated carefully before receiving drug treatment. Close medical monitoring is also important while the child is on medication.

Counseling may help the child deal with the social adjustment problems and low self-esteem that frequently accompany the disorder. A child with ADHD may also benefit from a behavior modification program. This means a system of rewards and punishments that the child can depend upon to be enforced. To be most effective, the program should be set up in conjunction with the child's teacher, to ensure that rules are consistent at home and school.

Coping with ADHD

There is no known way to prevent ADHD. However, identifying and treating the problem as soon as possible will help control the symptoms and make life easier.

Autism

Autism is a serious, chronic developmental disorder, involving impairment of language development, social functioning, and play. Some autistic children are moderately to severely retarded but some are not. Children with autism have difficulty giving and receiving affection and responding appropriately to social cues. They tend to establish rigid routines in their daily activities and become upset whenever anything unexpected happens.

The term pervasive developmental disorder, or PDD, is currently used to include autism and other related disorders. About five children in 10,000 are autistic, and approximately 14 to 20 per 10,000 have some form of PDD.

Some children with PDD have mild or severe learning disabilities. Most require special education, but with time and care, they can learn many skills. Children with all the features of autism inevitably require special attention. Appropriate early intervention can enable some children with autism to function in mainstream classrooms; a few may even go on to higher education.

When should I suspect that my child has autism?

Many children with PDD appear normal until about the age of 18 months to two years, although in retrospect parents often recall that even as an infant, the child was aloof and unresponsive. Sometimes a severe illness or other traumatic event triggers regression or disappearance of language in a child with autism.

As the baby grows into a toddler, parents begin to notice odd behavior. The child may hate any change in routine. If she expects orange juice, apple juice may cause a tantrum. Facial expressions may seem inappropriate to the situation. Children with autism may seem oblivious to people's voices, or may echo what others say but appear unable to formulate meaningful sentences.

As a preschooler, the autistic child often withdraws into an inner world, becoming absorbed in repetitive behaviors such as spinning a top, rocking, lining things up, or repeating memorized phrases. She may be obsessed with numbers or letters without any interest in their meaning. Autistic children usually display one or more stereotypical physical movements such as hand-flapping, toe-walking, or head banging.

What causes autism?

Autism was first identified in 1943, and until only a few decades ago the condition was blamed on parents—specifically a cold, unresponsive mother. Now, however, most experts believe the PDD is an organic disorder of the central nervous system. The condition affects four times more males than females. There is

If your child exhibits several of the following behaviors, arrange for an evaluation to determine if there is a developmental disorder:

- Shows little interest in people.
- Doesn't make eye contact.
- Resists cuddling with parents, and prefers to play alone.
- May appear to be deaf, or at other times, hypersensitive to noise.
- May not respond when spoken to.
- Makes no clear attempt to communicate, even with gestures.
- Limits language to *echolalia,* which is repetition of words, sounds, and phrases.
- Does not engage in play that mimics adult activities.
- Does not engage in imaginative play; instead of "driving" toy cars, may line them up or take them apart.
- Rarely interacts with peers cooperatively.

certainly some genetic component, but some cases may also be related to abnormalities in brain chemistry or prenatal exposure to rubella. Since there is no physiological test to diagnose PDD, developmental psychologists rely on behavioral testing. For this reason, diagnosis is sometimes inexact. Doctors rarely diagnose PDD confidently before the child is three years old.

The chances that a mentally retarded child will display autistic behavior increase with the severity of retardation and the extent of diffuse brain damage.

What can I do if my child shows autistic behavior?

If your child clearly exhibits a number of the behaviors associated with autism, it is important to consult your pediatrician and obtain an evaluation to determine whether the child's development is normal. Most large children's hospitals have developmental teams that can perform such an evaluation and advise you on possible therapies. Some public school districts provide free testing.

If a disability is diagnosed, early intervention can stimulate your child's development and help relieve family stress. Speech, play, and behavioral therapy may help, and new treatments continue to be explored.

Bed-Wetting (Enuresis)

Most children are successfully toilet trained between the ages of two and four, and nighttime bladder control follows some six to 12 months later. When children older than five continue to wet the bed, the condition is given a medical name—*nocturnal enuresis.* The problem is common, affecting up to 15 percent of children between the ages of five and 15. In the vast majority of cases, enuresis does not signal any underlying medical or emotional disorder; it is simply the result of the child's small bladder capacity and ability to sleep deeply. In nearly all cases, the condition is benign and outgrown by puberty.

What causes bed-wetting?

The reasons for bed-wetting are not completely understood, although the condition seems to run in families. In most cases, no cause is found. It can develop following successful toilet training and a long period of nighttime dryness. This acquired or *secondary enuresis* is sometimes the result of a stressful situation such as an illness, the birth of a new sibling or a divorce. More rarely, bed-wetting is caused by an underlying medical condition such as a urinary tract infection or diabetes mellitus. In these cases, however, impaired bladder control will usually be present during the day.

Is medical attention necessary?

Most cases resolve themselves without medical treatment. If the lag between daytime and nighttime control becomes prolonged, however, your doctor can advise a course of action to help your child cope with and curtail nighttime incontinence. If your child has secondary enuresis, your doctor will want to examine him to identify and treat any underlying conditions that may be causing the symptoms.

COPING WITH BED-WETTING

- Use water-proof pads under the sheets to facilitate changing the bed after accidents.
- Lay out an extra pair of pajamas and set of sheets so the youngster can deal with the problem without waking the household.
- Limit before-bedtime drinks.
- Make sure the child uses the toilet before going to bed.
- Wake the child to use the toilet just before your own bedtime.
- Set an alarm to wake the child at some point in the night to use the toilet.

What treatments are available?

Once a medical problem has been ruled out, commonsense measures can cut down on the number of bed-wetting episodes until the child outgrows the problem. The best approach is a low-key one. Praise and reward dry nights and maintain a calm, reassuring attitude about wet ones. Resist the urge to scold or return a younger child to diapers, as this will only reinforce feelings of low self-esteem.

A number of prescription drugs are available to provide temporary relief from enuresis. These drugs are usually prescribed for older children who are under a lot of stress or who don't want to be left out of sleep-over parties or overnight trips. A moisture-sensitive alarm connected to the bed can sometimes be used to teach a child to waken before he has passed urine rather than after the bed is wet. Check with your physician before using this method, however.

If you suspect that your child's bed-wetting could be a response to anxiety or another emotional disorder, your pediatrician may suggest consultation with a therapist.

Getting Help

CALL YOUR DOCTOR IF YOUR CHILD:

- ☐ Is still wetting the bed after the age of five.
- ☐ Begins to wet the bed again after a long period of dryness.
- ☐ Has bladder control difficulty during the day as well as at night.

Birth Injuries

Complications in the process of labor and delivery can result in a wide variety of problems in the newborn. These problems, known collectively as birth injuries, can be mild or severe. One major cause is oxygen deprivation, which commonly occurs when the umbilical cord is compressed or twisted in the birth process. The other main cause is mechanical trauma, which may occur when the baby assumes an unusual position at the time of birth (buttocks rather than head first, for example) or when the baby is too large to pass through the birth canal easily.

The incidence of birth injuries has declined in recent years because of advances in obstetrics. Many birth injuries, however, are unavoidable, even with the best medical care. The risk of birth injury is greatest in cases of prolonged or premature labor.

What types of injuries can be sustained during birth?

Injuries most commonly involve the skin, head, bones, nerves, and brain. Most skin injuries are minor, consisting of bruises, scrapes, petechiae (small, flat, purplish-red spots caused by bleeding under the skin), or lumps. In general, they disappear within a few days of birth.

Birth injuries involving the head include *caput succedaneum,* which is a swelling over much of the skull that usually subsides within a few days, and *cephalhematoma,* which is a distinct bump that increases in size within two days of birth and gradually disappears over a few weeks or months. In addition, some infants suffer burst blood vessels in the eyes

which may make the eyes extremely red but rarely causes any lasting damage.

The most common bone injury sustained in birth is fracture of the collar bone, which is always a risk when a large baby is delivered. An arm or leg may sometimes be fractured during birth as well. Less common are fractures of the spine or ribs, but skull fractures are quite rare because a baby's skull bones are not yet fused, allowing the head to mold itself to the shape of the birth canal.

CARING FOR AN INFANT WITH A BIRTH INJURY

- Protect bruises, scraped skin, or swelling from additional trauma until healing is complete.
- Be careful dressing and undressing a baby with a bone fracture. If the collar bone or an arm is broken, do not put the arm on the affected side through the sleeve.
- Support the fractured bone while carrying the infant. When you lift an infant with a broken collar bone, place your arm under the back and shoulders. **DO NOT** lift the baby under the arms.
- If temporary facial paralysis keeps one eye open, protect it from injury until it can close.
- If facial paralysis makes nursing difficult, feed the baby with a medicine dropper or a soft rubber nipple with a large hole.
- If one of the infant's arms is paralyzed, support it at shoulder level while you dress her. Move the arm gently, avoiding unnecessary stress.

Infants are occasionally born with temporary paralysis of a facial nerve, which gives the face a lopsided appearance, especially during crying. This problem usually passes within a few days of birth, although it may last up to six months. A nerve that supplies one of the arms may also be injured during birth, usually leading to temporary (but occasionally permanent) paralysis of the arm.

The most serious birth injuries are those that affect the brain. They are caused by oxygen deprivation or bleeding within the skull or brain. These injuries vary greatly in severity. They may lead to long-term seizure disorders or cause cerebral palsy or mental retardation, but on the other hand, they may have no lasting effects.

How can the pediatrician tell if my child has had a birth injury?

During labor, fetal monitoring may indicate oxygen deprivation, in which case the pediatrician will be on the lookout for resulting problems. Otherwise, the pediatrician will examine the child for signs of injury immediately after birth and at least once more before hospital discharge. If the baby was in a breech position (feet or buttocks first) or the labor was long and difficult, the doctor will be particularly alert to signs of birth injuries.

What treatments are available?

Minor birth injuries, including most fractures, require no treatment except for careful handling and close monitoring to make sure the injury resolves as it should. Infants who have suffered oxygen deprivation during birth may need breathing support (mechanical ventilation) for awhile. If a brain injury results in seizures, they can be treated and usually controlled with medication.

Birthmarks

Birthmarks are skin discolorations that are present at birth or appear shortly thereafter. They can develop anywhere on the skin, although some types tend to appear most frequently in particular areas. (Flat vascular malformations or port wine stains, for instance, commonly appear on the face.)

Most birthmarks are harmless, and only a small proportion pose significant cosmetic problems. Furthermore, the most common types of birthmarks are temporary, disappearing before the child reaches school age.

In a few rare cases, a birthmark may suggest the presence of a serious underlying disorder or pose an increased risk of skin cancer. Pediatricians examine babies carefully to identify such birthmarks, many of which can be safely removed.

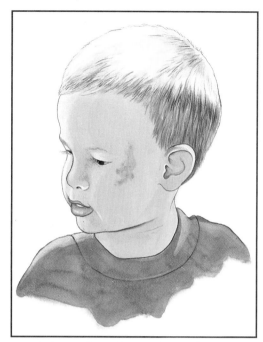

A typical strawberry hemangioma. These birthmarks usually disappear by late childhood.

How do birthmarks develop?

Different types develop in different ways. Some are the result of excess pigment cells in a small area, while others develop when tiny blood vessels overgrow or expand in the skin.

Is medical attention necessary?

A birthmark that is quite large, ulcerated, or located in an area where it interferes with functions such as eating does require medical attention. The rare types of birth marks associated with skin cancer should also be evaluated with special care.

At or soon after birth, the pediatrician will take note of ordinary types of birthmarks, and, if they are large, measure them. In later visits, he will check the birthmarks to see if they are regressing naturally or changing in any unusual ways. If a birthmark is disfiguring or potentially dangerous, the pediatrician may refer you to a dermatologist or plastic surgeon to have it treated or removed.

Getting Help

CALL YOUR DOCTOR IF:

- ☐ A birthmark changes in size, color, or shape.
- ☐ A birthmark bleeds or itches.
- ☐ A birthmark becomes sore or tender.
- ☐ Any new molelike growths appear, especially if they are irregularly shaped, discolored, or large.

- **CAFE-AU-LAIT SPOTS.** These are small, sharply defined areas of light to dark brown color. They are more common in dark-skinned infants, occurring in 12 percent of black newborns. Numerous café-au-lait spots, may indicate the presence of a rare inherited disease called neurofibromatosis.
- **MOLES.** Moles, also known as **PIGMENTED NEVI,** are rarely present at birth, developing instead throughout childhood and adolescence. Moles in newborns are typically somewhat larger than in adults, and they have the potential to become cancerous, so removal is usually recommended.

   Some infants are born with extremely large moles that may cover large segments of the body. Besides being disfiguring, these moles have a high potential to become cancerous, and they should always be removed.
- **MONGOLIAN SPOTS.** These are large, flat, bluish or black patches that as many as 90 percent of black and other dark-skinned infants are born with. They usually are located at the base of the spine or on the buttocks. They are entirely benign and usually disappear without treatment by late childhood.
- **PORT WINE STAINS.** Port wine stains are flat, red or purple discolorations caused by overgrowth of tiny blood vessels in the skin. They are present at birth, usually appearing on the face or limbs, and they grow along with the child rather than fading. Prominent or disfiguring port wine stains can be removed with laser treatment.
- **SALMON PATCHES.** Also known as **STORK BITES** and **ANGEL KISSES,** these deep pink patches are the most common birthmarks, appearing in about 40 percent of all newborns. Salmon patches are most often found on the nape of the neck, the middle of the forehead, and the eyelids. They usually fade and disappear before the first birthday.
- **STRAWBERRY HEMANGIOMAS.** These raised, bumpy spots appear on a baby's skin in the first two to five weeks of life. They may start out pale, then turn red or purple and grow larger, especially in the first six months. Strawberry hemangiomas are most commonly found on the head, neck, or shoulders. In contrast to port wine stains (flat hemangiomas), almost all shrink over the first two or three years and disappear by late childhood.

What treatments are available?

The rare birthmarks that require treatment can sometimes simply be cut out of the skin in a minor surgical procedure. Lasers have been developed that can remove certain red and brown birthmarks.

Blocked Tear Duct (Lacrimal or Nasolacrimal Duct Obstruction)

Crying is a natural part of infancy and childhood. In addition to expressing emotions, tears lubricate the eyes and keep them free from dust and other foreign particles. Since the *lacrimal system,* which produces tears, is not fully developed at birth, it usually takes several weeks before healthy babies produce enough tears to flow out of the eyes.

Tears are formed by the *lacrimal gland,* located in the outer portion of the upper lids. The tears flow down and across the eyes and are collected in small channels located at the inner corner of the eyelid, where upper and lower lids meet. Through these channels, the tears enter a sac (the *lacrimal sac*) from which they flow through a thin canal (the *lacrimal duct*) into the nose.

Blocked tear ducts are fairly common in newborns and young babies; they affect as many as six percent of all healthy infants born. The good news is that, properly treated, 90 percent of all cases resolve without surgical treatment by the time babies are 12 to 18 months old.

When should I suspect that my baby has a blocked tear duct?

You may notice that one or both of the baby's eyes appear excessively teary over the course of several days. There may be a mucuslike discharge, swelling, and/or redness. The baby may seem to be experiencing eye discomfort or pain, and may be difficult to console.

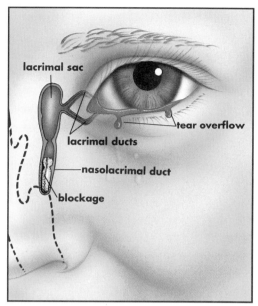

A blocked tear duct prevents tears from draining into the nasal passage.

What causes a blocked tear duct?

In newborns a blocked tear duct is usually due to a minor birth defect in which the membrane covering the tear duct at birth does not disappear. As a result, the duct opening is not formed. A cyst can also block a tear duct, as can an infection or trauma.

Is medical attention necessary?

It is important to consult your pediatrician promptly if you suspect the baby has a blocked tear duct. If left untreated, tears can accumulate in the lacrimal or tear sac, which can become infected by bacteria. The infection can spread into adjacent areas, such as the sinuses or adenoids. A physical examination of the child's eyes will be necessary to diagnose the problem and treat the underlying cause.

What treatments are available?

The pediatrician will probably show you how to massage the ducts to clear the obstruction.

Placing warm, moist compresses over the eyes may also be recommended. The pediatrician should show you how to clear the baby's eyes of secretions. If the tear-duct obstruction has caused an infection, antibiotic ointment or drops are usually prescribed.

In some cases, these treatments are inadequate, and an ophthalmologist should be consulted. As a last resort, surgery may be necessary to remove a cyst or open a blocked duct.

Coping with blocked tear ducts

Carefully follow your pediatrician's instructions for massaging the tear duct and clearing the baby's eyes. Always wash your hands before touching your child's eyelids, and rinse thoroughly, because traces of soap can increase irritation and tearing.

Getting Help

CALL YOUR DOCTOR IF:

■ Your baby has symptoms that suggest a blocked tear duct.

Boils

Boils, also known as *furuncles,* are bacterial skin infections that arise when a sebaceous (oil) gland is blocked or a hair becomes ingrown in its follicle—the channel along which it grows from its root to the surface of the skin. The boil may feel itchy or painful, and the child may be tired and feverish.

Boils begin as hard, painful red lumps; they grow bigger and more painful as white blood cells are drawn to the site to fight the infection. The white blood cells form a capsule or "head" around the infection, resulting in an abscess. This pus-filled head usually takes two to three days to burst or drain. By that time, the pain should be alleviated, and the boil should completely heal within another week.

Because infections spread easily from one hair follicle to another, boils sometimes appear in clusters called *carbuncles.* These clusters are more painful than single boils, and they tend to heal more slowly. If a child has been ill or has lowered resistance to infection for some other reason, boils are more likely to develop into carbuncles.

What causes boils?

Boils and carbuncles are caused by bacteria, many of which normally colonize on the surface of the skin. The strain of bacteria most commonly responsible is *Staphylococcus.* Because bacteria are everywhere in the environment, almost everyone may develop a boil at some point. However, boils and carbuncles are more likely to occur in conditions of poor hygiene or when illness lowers resistance to infection.

The bacteria in boils can sometimes spread from one child to another through ordinary rough and tumble play.

Coping with boils

Clean the skin around a boil with alcohol to help prevent the infection from spreading. To reduce the chance of irritating a boil, cover it with an adhesive dressing made of clean, dry gauze.

Never squeeze a boil; you may spread the infection by pushing the pus downward. Apply warm, moist compresses to the boil to encourage earlier drainage. Antiseptics and ointments are of little value. Follow the pediatrician's directions for home care.

Is medical attention necessary?

Yes, usually. Since boils will make children very uncomfortable, and since effective therapy is available a doctor should be consulted.

What treatments are available?

The pediatrician may prescribe a course of antibiotics to eliminate the boil or carbuncle. Follow her orders about the timing and size of antibiotic doses, and continue the medication for as many days as the doctor has prescribed, even if the symptoms have disappeared.

A pediatrician may also lance a boil (cut it open to drain the pus). Incision and drainage usually bring complete healing. If a child suffers from recurrent boils, a sample of the pus may be taken to determine the underlying cause of the infection. It may also be appropriate to do tests for some underlying cause, such as diabetes or an immune deficiency.

Getting Help

CALL YOUR DOCTOR IF YOUR CHILD:

- Has swollen and tender glands in the same area as the boil.
- Has red streaks under the skin radiating out from the boil.
- Has a boil in an awkward place—near the eyes, mouth, ear, under the armpit, or in the diaper area of a baby.
- Has a boil that has not come to a head in five days.

PREVENTING BOILS

The bacteria that cause boils are present throughout the environment, so prevention is often difficult. Helpful measures include:

- Encouraging frequent hand washing.
- Making sure a child bathes regularly.
- Cautioning a child not to touch another child's boil.
- Covering a boil with an adhesive dressing to prevent spreading the causative bacteria.

Bone Cancer

Until recently bone cancer was a devastating malignancy that rarely responded to treatment. Today, however, the combination of anticancer drugs, radiation therapy, and surgery has boosted the five-year survival rate to 80 percent. The most common forms of bone cancer in children are osteosarcoma and Ewing's sarcoma. Osteosarcoma affects about five children in a million each year and is more common in whites than in blacks. Ewing's sarcoma occurs less frequently and is hardly ever seen in blacks. Bone cancer is most likely to occur during adolescence—particularly in boys as they undergo the adolescent growth spurt. With early detection, the odds of a child surviving bone cancer are good.

When should I suspect a child has bone cancer?

The first signs of bone cancer are persistent bone pain and swelling at the site of the tumor. At first, the parent may assume that the pain is due to a bump or bruise, but it lasts beyond the few days usually required for healing. Closer examination of the area may reveal a tender lump. After several weeks, the child begins to limit motion of the affected limb, and gait and coordination may change. Eventually, bone fractures may occur.

How does bone cancer develop?

Bone cancer most often develops in the bones of the arm or the leg (particularly the femur), but it may also occur in the knee, shoulder, or hip, or in several bones at once. Bone cancer commonly progresses to the lungs, but it does not produce symptoms there for some time. The bones are also common sites for the spread of other tumors. When a lump or growth is found in a bone, it may be the first sign of cancer elsewhere in the body.

How can a doctor tell if a child has bone cancer?

Bone tumors usually can be detected on an X-ray examination. Many bone tumors are benign, however, so the doctor may order a biopsy, in which a small sample of bone tissue is removed for laboratory examination, to confirm the diagnosis. Other diagnostic measures include other radiologic studies, such as bone scans and CT (computed tomography) scans to assess the size of the tumor and to determine if the cancer has spread.

What treatments are available?

Osteosarcoma is treated by surgical removal of the cancerous bone tissue and usually requires amputation of the affected limb. If the bone tumor is localized, however, sometimes the limb can be saved by removing only the cancerous portion of the bone and reconstructing the arm or the leg with a bone graft or bone transplant. After surgery, treatment with anti-cancer drugs (chemotherapy) is given for many months to destroy any cancer cells that may have migrated to other parts of the body.

Ewing's sarcoma does not require surgical removal of the tumor. Instead, these tumors are treated with intensive irradiation of the involved bone (radiotherapy) followed by an extensive course of chemotherapy.

Getting Help

CALL YOUR DOCTOR IF YOUR CHILD:
- Has persistent bone pain with no sign of a bruise.
- Has a lump, redness, or swelling at the site of bone pain.
- Gradually begins to limp or limit the motion of an arm or leg.

Bow Legs and Knock Knees

Many children develop temporary bow legs or knock knees at some point in their growth and development. When the conditions are extreme or persist longer than usual, however, they may indicate the presence of structural abnormalities or disease.

From birth until about 12 to 18 months of

age, infants' legs are to some degree bowed, that is, they curve outward at the knee level in a shape resembling a bow, a condition known as *genu varus*. Toddlers are usually bowlegged when they begin to walk, but their legs straighten out toward the middle of the second year of life, when the lower back and leg muscles are well developed. During the third year of life, the legs often develop a curve in the opposite direction, resulting in knock knees, or *genu valgus*. The child's knees touch—or knock—when standing with feet apart. Knock knees, seldom severe, gradually diminish with age and usually disappear by the time the child enters school or soon thereafter. The condition tends to be more pronounced in overweight children.

What causes bow legs and knock knees?

A few rare disorders can cause the legs to bow. In one of these disorders (Blount's disease), the shinbone, for unknown reasons, fails to develop normally and becomes deformed. In another—rickets—bones and cartilage fail to develop properly because of a deficiency of calcium or phosphate, usually resulting from abnormal kidney function or a severe lack of vitamin D (see entry on **rickets**).

Severe knock knees can also result from injury, infection, structural abnormalities, or, rarely, a tumor. These causes are most likely if only one leg is affected.

Is medical attention necessary?

Not usually. Tests are necessary only if the problem is extreme or persistent, or if it affects only one leg. In such cases, bone abnormalities will be diagnosed on the basis of X rays.

What treatments are available?

If bow legs or knock knees are associated with disease, treating the underlying cause is the main priority. Treatment depends upon the underlying disorder, but it may include wearing supportive shoes or long leg braces. If severe bow legs or knock knees persist beyond the age of four years, surgery may be required. If no disease is involved, surgical treatment of knock knees is usually postponed until the child is seven or eight years old.

Getting Help

CONSULT YOUR PEDIATRICIAN IF:

- Bow legs persist in a child older than two years.
- Knock knees persist beyond seven years of age.
- Only one leg is bowed or turned inward in a child of any age.
- Bowing or knocking increases as the child grows older.

Breath Holding

During a temper tantrum or a bout of excessive crying, some children develop the habit of holding their breath until they turn red or even blue in the face. In rare cases, a child may faint momentarily or begin to twitch convulsively. As frightening as these episodes are for parents, breath holding is not dangerous or harmful. Occasional temper tantrums, possibly involving breath holding, are normal in toddlers. They should diminish in frequency and intensity after the age of four.

What cause breath holding?

No one knows exactly. Some children may be temperamentally predisposed to it. It is normal for toddlers to test limits and challenge rules as they move from total dependence on their parents to gradual independence. Breath holding, like temper tantrums, may be how a child expresses anger, frustration, or anxiety while making this vital transition.

Is medical attention necessary?

Call your pediatrician the first time breath holding causes your child to faint during a temper tantrum. This is especially important if the child falls. The doctor may want to examine him to rule out more serious underlying reasons for the loss of consciousness. In rare cases, when the pediatrician feels the behavior indicates an emotional disturbance, you may be referred to a mental health professional.

Coping with breath holding

The child will outgrow the habit of breath holding eventually. In the meantime, there are some measures you can take to minimize breath-holding attacks (see "Preventing breath holding" on this page). Be firm, gentle, and downplay the episode. Too much attention or caving in to demands could lead to more breath holding by teaching the toddler to use the attacks to manipulate others.

PREVENTING BREATH HOLDING

The best way to prevent breath holding is to maintain a consistent overall plan of discipline and respond in a calm, low-key manner each time an episode occurs.

- Stay calm during your child's temper tantrum.
- Try to distract the child. Offer a favorite toy, point out a passing airplane, or use a similar diversionary tactic.
- Make sure the child does not become overly tired or overstimulated.
- Avoid situations that may make the child unnecessarily frustrated or anxious.
- Make sure the child has a nap or quiet time every day.
- Set moderate limits for the child and stick to them.
- Make sure that any other adult caring for your child understands and follows the rules and limits you have set for your child in the same way you do.

Getting Help

CALL YOUR DOCTOR IF YOUR CHILD:
- Faints during a breath-holding attack.
- Twitches convulsively while breath holding.

Bronchiolitis

Bronchiolitis is inflammation of the bronchioles, which are small, thin-walled airways leading from the bronchi (which run from the windpipe to the lungs) to the *alveoli,* the air sacs of the lungs. The infection causes the bronchiole walls to swell, thicken, and fill with inflammatory cells, obstructing the passage of air and, in extreme cases, preventing the blood from picking up sufficient oxygen. Air becomes trapped in the alveoli, making it difficult for the child to breathe. Bronchiolitis is more serious than bronchitis, and it causes different symptoms. Since the infection extends deeper into the lung, it may resemble pneumonia (see entries on **bronchitis** and **pneumonia**).

The disorder usually occurs in the first two years of life, most commonly between two and ten months of age; it seldom strikes newborns. Most frequently, attacks occur during winter and spring, when viruses abound.

Most infants improve in three to four days with adequate supportive care, but a return to normal breathing may take two weeks. About one fifth of children develop persistent wheezing that lasts for several months. Children who had bronchiolitis in early childhood frequently develop asthma.

What causes bronchiolitis?
Bronchiolitis results from certain respiratory viral infections. An organism called *respiratory syncytial virus* is the most common cause.

When should I suspect bronchiolitis?
Bronchiolitis develops gradually, usually several days after exposure to someone with a respiratory infection. Call the doctor without delay if an illness that began as a common cold (nasal discharge, sneezing, diminished appetite, coughing, and low-grade fever) progresses to include symptoms of bronchiolitis, such as rapid, difficult, and noisy breathing; flaring nostrils; rapid heartbeat; and pale or bluish skin. All the infant's energies may be concentrated on breathing. Fever is present in 50 per-

cent of cases, but rarely rises above 101 degrees Fahrenheit.

Is medical attention necessary?
Yes. Babies with bronchiolitis may need special supportive care, such as supplemental oxygen and intravenous fluids, until the illness subsides.

What treatments are available?
Treatment focuses on insuring adequate breathing and preventing dehydration:

- Oxygen mist therapy and fluids may be provided.
- Drugs may be ordered to reduce fever.
- An antiviral drug, ribavirin, given through a special breathing apparatus, may be prescribed for severe bronchiolitis caused by the respiratory syncytial virus. Hospitalization is required.
- Antibiotics may be used in small, acutely ill infants to protect against secondary bacterial invasion.
- Corticosteroids may be given, in rare cases, to small infants with acute wheezing.

CARING FOR A CHILD WITH BRONCHIOLITIS

Infants with bronchiolitis usually start getting better within several days. The cough and other symptoms gradually disappear over a week or two. Generally, the disorder can be treated at home; however, hospitalization is necessary if the child's condition deteriorates.

Bronchitis

Bronchitis is a lower respiratory disease characterized by a deep, hacking (dry) cough that comes in sudden attacks. It results from inflammation of the *bronchial tubes,* the large airways that lead from the *trachea* (windpipe) to the lungs. The disease occurs in two forms: acute infectious bronchitis (usually viral) and allergic asthmatic bronchitis.

The disease is common in early childhood, particularly during the first four years of life; it afflicts boys more often than girls and occurs most frequently during the winter, the peak season for viral infections. In children, the trachea can be infected as well, a condition known as *tracheobronchitis;* if the *larynx* (voice box) also is inflamed, the disorder is called *laryngotracheobronchitis.*

The characteristic cough is the most troubling symptom of bronchitis. It worsens during sleep, waking the child frequently. In addition, the child may develop a wheeze (a whistling or sighing sound) with each breath as air passes through the narrowed bronchi over accumulated mucus.

What causes bronchitis?

In the past, bronchitis was often associated with measles and whooping cough (see entries on **measles** and **whooping cough**). Acute viral bronchitis develops when a virus causing an upper respiratory tract infection invades the bronchi, triggering inflammation and the secretion of excess mucus. Asthmatic bronchitis is triggered by exposure to a substance to which the child is allergic.

What happens during bronchitis?

A bout of bronchitis begins as an upper respiratory viral infection (a cold), with symptoms such as a running, stuffy nose and low fever. After that, a persistent hacking cough develops, lasting two to three days. The dry cough is succeeded by a loose cough that produces thick, yellow sputum.

Frequently, wheezing sounds develop when the child breathes, caused by the passage of air through mucus-clogged bronchi. Appetite loss and fatigue also are common, but they usually pass after two or three days. The cough itself should subside within seven to ten days.

The following supportive measures will speed the child's recovery from both types of bronchitis:

- Adequate rest.
- Adequate fluid intake to prevent thickened secretions from clogging the bronchi.
- Humidified air to ease the child's breathing and to loosen the secretions.
- Encouragement of the child's productive cough, which clears the airways by making the child spit up loosened mucus.
- Careful use of cough suppressants (so as not to completely suppress the necessary cough reflex) if unrelieved coughing prevents sleep and causes throat irritation.

same symptoms. The following characteristics suggest allergic bronchitis:

- The symptoms last longer than three or four weeks or recur frequently.
- There is a family history of allergic problems.
- The child has a history of wheezing, allergic rhinitis (inflammation of the mucus membrane of the nose) and allergic skin reactions.

What treatments are available?

For the most part, treatment is supportive, consisting mainly of rest and fluids. A cough suppressant may be prescribed, although it is

Is medical attention necessary?

Call your physician if the child develops sudden attacks of a persistent, hacking cough. Several different diseases (see entries on **bronchitis, bronchiolitis,** and **pneumonia**) can trigger such coughing spells. Bronchitis is the least severe of these disorders, and it usually has the mildest symptoms, but the doctor must rule out the others. By listening to the child's lungs with a stethoscope, the doctor will be able to detect the coarse wheezing sounds which are characteristic of bronchitis. A chest X-ray and sputum examination will facilitate the diagnosis.

After diagnosing bronchitis, the pediatrician will determine whether it is the viral or the allergic asthmatic form; they can have the

If the child is prone to bronchitis, the following measures will reduce the chance of recurrences:

- Avoid smoking at home. Infants exposed to cigarette smoke in the home are four times as likely to develop bronchitis as infants in a smoke-free environment.
- Wash your hands regularly and encourage frequent hand washing in the child to prevent the spread of viruses that cause bronchitis.
- Protect the child from exposure to conditions that trigger an allergic reaction.
- Protect the child from other environmental triggers, such as air pollution and cold climates.

important for the child to do some coughing to clear the airways of mucus. The physician may prescribe antibiotics if he suspects a secondary bacterial infection. In the case of allergic bronchitis, the physician will treat the allergies directly.

Cataracts

Some babies are born with or acquire opaque areas in the lens, a normally transparent structure that helps the eye focus light and form images. These defects, known as *cataracts,* may affect either one eye (unilateral) or both eyes (bilateral). Detected early in infancy, most cataracts can be surgically corrected without lasting visual impairments. Screening for them is therefore routine during well-baby medical checkups. Although most children with cataracts are otherwise healthy, this condition may, in rare instances, signal a serious but treatable underlying disease.

What causes cataracts?

A wide array of conditions can precipitate cataracts, but generally they belong to either of two categories: congenital or acquired. Cataracts can be acquired as a result of an eye injury or as a side effect to treatment with certain drugs or radiation. Childhood diseases such as rheumatoid arthritis can also be associated with cataracts. Children who have these kinds of cataracts tend to have better long-term visual function than infants born with the defect.

Congenital cataracts, which emerge before the first birthday, often run in families. Certain other hereditary visual disorders such as glaucoma (in which abnormal pressure builds up in the eye) can give rise to cataracts.

Inherited metabolic diseases also may promote cataract formation. In addition to diabetes, inborn deficiencies of enzymes needed to

CARING FOR A CHILD WITH CATARACTS

Parents' compliance with doctors' instructions often makes a substantial difference in the long-term status of a child's eyesight. Following surgery, the doctor may suggest that you:

- Place a patch over the child's stronger eye for increasing periods each day, according to the prescribed schedule. Continue this practice either until the physician terminates it or the child reaches five or six years of age.
- Get a prescription for extended- or daily-wear contact lenses for each eye previously affected. Growth of the eyes and rehabilitation of sight may necessitate frequent changes in the focusing power of these lenses.

break down the sugar found in milk (lactose) can lead to accumulation of another sugar called galactitol, which clouds the lens. These metabolic deficiencies are very rare.

For reasons not as yet thoroughly understood, cataracts also are more likely in babies with Down's syndrome or other chromosomal disorders. Finally, premature infants—especially those exposed to either infections in the womb or serious injury during birth—seem to be more prone to cataract formation than full-term babies.

When should I suspect cataracts?

Precise recognition of cataracts is a matter best left in the hands of an experienced physician. One or both eyes may look cloudy, with the opacities taking the shape of oil droplets or snowflakes.

Other signs are more indirect. Cataracts cause blurred and double vision, which can make body movements clumsy and delay achievement of certain developmental milestones.

Is medical attention necessary?

Yes. Cataracts usually can be corrected, provided that they are detected and repaired early. Then, with the right corrective contact lenses and other optical therapies, the child should be able to see normally.

Left untreated, however, cataracts in both eyes can touch off squinting or jerky eye movements that rob the infant of the visual stimulation needed for normal development. Eyesight can become permanently damaged in such cases.

How can the pediatrician tell that my child has cataracts?

To screen for cataracts, physicians test a special visual reflex in the first six weeks of life. Using the hand-held instrument called an ophthalmoscope, they aim a gentle red light beam across the pupil of each eye and look for a special visual response. Absence of the so-called red-light reflex helps the physicians to diagnose cataracts. If cataracts are found, pediatricians usually refer the patient to an eye specialist (ophthalmologist) for further evaluation and treatment.

Children with metabolic or genetic disorders that make them more vulnerable to the development of cataracts should have regular eye checkups. Many pediatricians can perform such checkups in their offices.

What treatments are available?

Because most cataracts tend to progress and expand, surgical removal usually is recommended soon after they are detected. The present standard of care includes surgical correction of a unilateral cataract as early as one or two months of age. Current operative techniques usually are successful, producing little if any scarring and doing away with the need for second operations. No procedure is without side effects, however. For instance, one or two of every ten patients undergoing surgical repair of congenital cataracts go on to suffer glaucoma.

Postoperative therapy involves using extended- or daily-wear contact lenses or special glasses. If only one eye has cataracts, the better eye is covered (patched) for progressively longer periods each day. This measure is necessary to strengthen the affected eye and prevent further visual impairment.

Thanks to soft and gas-permeable lenses, contacts can be easily fitted, even to an infant's tiny eyes. In some cases, more conservative therapies may be appropriate. For some partial cataracts, eye drops that dilate the pupil, together with patching of the better eye, do the trick.

Canker Sores

Canker sores, which are known medically as *aphthous ulcers* or *aphthous stomatitis,* are shallow ulcers that develop inside the mouth, particularly in the lining of the cheeks and lips or on the gums, tongue, or palate. The sores are more common in adults than in children, although they may occur at any age. They can develop one at a time or in clusters, and while they are not serious, they can be uncomfortable.

How do canker sores develop?

Canker sores begin as stinging, red, inflamed spots inside the mouth. Over the next several days, they increase in size and turn into well-defined round or oval ulcers that are grayish-white or grayish-yellow in the middle and bright red around the edges. They cause a burning, stinging pain, which sometimes interferes with eating.

The sores usually disappear within seven to ten days, but they may persist for up to two weeks. When healed, they generally leave no scars. Unfortunately, however, canker sores tend to come back and nothing can be done to prevent their recurrence, which may take place at intervals of weeks or months.

What causes canker sores?

It was once believed that these sores were caused by the *herpes simplex* virus, the same virus that is responsible for cold sores around the mouth, but this has been disproven. The underlying cause is still unknown. Some physicians now suggest that the sores are triggered by an autoimmune mechanism, in which the body's immune system assaults the tissues lining the mouth by mistake. Other possible causes include local trauma, allergy, and stress. The sores also tend to appear more commonly in people with malabsorption disorders and nutritional deficiencies of iron or certain vitamins.

Is medical attention necessary?

Yes—at least at the initial outbreak. Although canker sores are harmless and do not require treatment, other types of mouth sores with similar appearances—including herpes and thrush (which is caused by a yeastlike fungus)—should be treated. A pediatrician should look at any type of mouth sore a child develops to determine the likely cause and recommend appropriate treatment if needed.

What treatments are available?

No treatment can effectively eliminate canker sores, but you can take measures to relieve the symptoms and speed healing. Pain from minor sores can be relieved by rinsing the mouth with a peroxide solution (ask your pediatrician for mixing directions) or lukewarm saltwater. The doctor may recommend application of a corticosteroid cream to soothe more severe sores. Even though the sores are not caused by bacteria, topical application of an antibiotic is sometimes effective against them, possibly because secondary bacterial infection sets in after the ulcers erupt.

Getting Help

CALL YOUR DOCTOR IF YOUR CHILD:
- ☐ Develops numerous, large, or painful mouth sores.
- ☐ Develops mouth sores that last more than two or three days and show no signs of healing.
- ☐ Has trouble eating because of mouth sores.

Cat-Scratch Fever

Cat-scratch fever is an infectious illness that can affect people of all ages but is most common in children between the ages of five and 14. This disease, which usually develops as a result of a cat scratch, can cause lymph-node swellings, low-grade fever and other troublesome symptoms but is not overly serious. The disease is usually self-limited, and resolves in two to three months.

What causes cat-scratch fever?

Cats themselves are not affected by the illness, but they serve as carriers capable of passing the illness to humans through scratches or bites. The actual organism that causes the fever is difficult to grow in the laboratory, but it is a bacterium. The specific bacterium has not been conclusively identified, but it may be one with the unusual name Rochalimea. The illness is sometimes associated with a new pet, often a kitten less than six months old. Several members of a household may be affected at the same time.

SYMPTOMS OF CAT-SCRATCH FEVER

- Swollen lymph nodes in the armpit, neck, groin, or elsewhere.
- Loss of appetite.
- Low-grade fever.
- General tiredness.
- Possible headache.
- Evidence of a cat scratch, which may be a reddened welt.

When should I suspect that my child has cat-scratch fever?

The most common symptom is a swollen lymph node, usually in the armpit or neck in an otherwise healthy child. Fever and other mild symptoms are present in 30 percent of cases. The child has usually had contact with a cat, although symptoms may begin after a scratch has healed.

Is medical attention necessary?

A doctor should probably investigate any persistent fever and lymph-node swelling. Blood tests as well as a tuberculin skin test may be ordered to rule out the presence of other disorders.

What treatments are available?

Sometimes an antibiotic (gentamycin) is prescribed to shorten the course of the illness. Generally, a period of rest is all that is needed. Keep the child home from school and in bed.

It's possible that the lymph nodes will abscess and ooze pus. If that happens, the doctor may determine that drainage or removal of the nodes is necessary. Lymph node removal also may be necessary for diagnostic purposes.

PREVENTING CAT-SCRATCH FEVER

Tell children to:
- Stay away from unknown animals.
- Inform you if they are bitten or scratched.
- Wash scratches or bites promptly with soap and water.

Getting Help

CALL YOUR DOCTOR IF YOUR CHILD:

☐ Develops signs and symptoms of cat-scratch fever. Although it is usually relatively harmless, it may lead (rarely) to complications of the central nervous system. Also, an illness that resembles cat-scratch fever might be another, more serious, animal-borne illness that has similar symptoms in its early stages.

Celiac Disease

Celiac disease is a disorder of the small intestine characterized by sensitivity to *gluten,* a protein found in wheat, rye, and other grains. When affected children eat gluten, their small intestine becomes damaged and cannot absorb nutrients properly.

Celiac disease is common in certain parts of Europe (especially Ireland). It occurs less frequently in the United States, affecting about one in 2,000 children in some areas. Over the past several years, the incidence of celiac disease has been on the decline.

In some patients, symptoms of celiac disease show up in late childhood or adolescence. In others, however, the problem appears in the first year of life, generally a couple of months after cereals are introduced.

What causes celiac disease?

A number of factors seem to be involved. First, a genetic abnormality probably makes certain

---

children prone to celiac disease. For the disease to develop, however, the child must be exposed to foods containing gluten.

When should I suspect that my child has celiac disease?

Babies and toddlers with celiac disease are irritable and they have poor appetites. They do not grow well and they develop chronic diarrhea with foul-smelling stools. The baby or child may have a bloated abdomen, shrunken buttocks, and weak legs. Other possible signs include mouth sores, a smooth tongue, excessive bruising, and swelling of the arms and legs. Symptoms vary greatly, however. Instead of having diarrhea, some children may become constipated. Vomiting also occurs in some children. On the other hand, some children show no symptoms except decreased weight and short stature.

Is medical attention necessary?

Yes. A number of conditions can cause symptoms similar to those of celiac disease, so a complete diagnostic workup is usually necessary. Cystic fibrosis may be confused with celiac disease.

How can the pediatrician tell if my child has celiac disease?

The evaluation begins with laboratory analysis of blood and stool samples. If the doctor suspects celiac disease, the child may be placed on a gluten-free diet to see if symptoms disappear. If they do, the next step is to reintroduce gluten and see if symptoms reappear.

To get a definite diagnosis, a small sample of tissue must be removed from the intestinal lining and examined microscopically. This

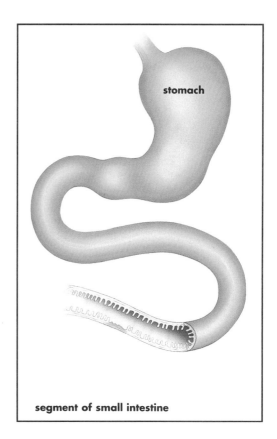

segment of small intestine

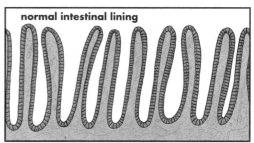

normal intestinal lining

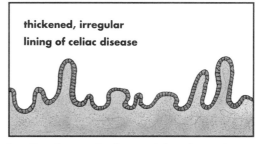

thickened, irregular lining of celiac disease

In celiac disease, foods containing gluten trigger development of irregularities in the lining of the small intestine.

- Consult a dietitian about designing a gluten-free diet for your child.
- If your child is in a play group, day-care center, or nursery school, you need to discuss her dietary restrictions with teachers and, possibly, supply your own food on certain days.
- Be casual and matter-of-fact about dietary restrictions; don't dwell on them, or they may become the focus of power struggles later on.

procedure can be performed using an *endoscope,* a thin, flexible tube inserted through the mouth and stomach to the upper part of the small intestine.

What treatments are available?

Treatment consists of totally excluding wheat and rye from the diet. Most patients can eat oats, at least in small amounts. When the disease is first diagnosed, the child may have nutritional deficiencies that need to be corrected with vitamins, minerals, or other supplements.

Getting Help

CALL YOUR DOCTOR IF YOUR CHILD:
- Has repeated bouts of diarrhea and vomiting.
- Fails to gain weight.
- Seems weak and listless.

Cerebral Palsy

Cerebral palsy is a term applied to several disorders caused by damage to the brain. Symptoms usually appear in the first year of life and include poor head control, feeding difficulties, and delays in motor development. As children get older, they have difficulty moving and controlling the arms, legs, and trunk, and they may be unable to stand or walk.

Depending on the type of cerebral palsy the child has, one or both sides of the body may be affected. The disease does not progress with age, but other factors, such as excess weight gain, may lead to increasing disability over time.

What causes cerebral palsy?

Cerebral palsy is often found in children who have suffered brain damage before, during, or immediately after birth. Not all children with cerebral palsy have such a history, though.

During birth, lack of oxygen and bleeding in the baby's brain may result in cerebral palsy. Head trauma and meningitis in the first days after birth are other potential causes. Premature babies are at a higher risk of developing cerebral palsy than babies born at full term.

When should I suspect that my child has cerebral palsy?

The disorder is sometimes difficult to detect before the baby is one year old, particularly if he was born prematurely. You should, however, suspect some kind of neurologic problem if your baby:

- Has difficulty sucking and feeding.
- Lies in an awkward position, especially with

one arm stretched out, the other arm above her head, and her neck turned toward the outstretched arm.

- Startles excessively.
- Shows a delay in reaching such developmental milestones as rolling over and pushing up on all fours. (See Chapters 1–3 for approximate ages at which such milestones are reached.)
- Prefers using one hand before the age of one year (suggesting weakness in the other).
- Crawls abnormally, using hands only or relying on one arm and one leg on the same side.
- Seems to be either excessively stiff or floppy.

How can the pediatrician tell if my child has cerebral palsy?

The diagnosis begins with a neurologic examination, which is usually supplemented by studies such as computed tomography (CT), which produces an image of the brain that may show abnormalities characteristic of cerebral palsy. In addition, doctors usually order a series of tests to exclude other possible causes.

What treatments are available?

Cerebral palsy cannot be cured, but it can be managed to prevent complications and maximize the child's independence.

The program of management involves specialists from several disciplines who work as a team. Specifics vary according to each child's needs, but most treatment programs include physical, occupational, and speech therapy.

Many children with cerebral palsy use mobility aids such as scooter boards, special strollers, and wheelchairs. These aids, as well as newly developed electronic devices that en-

hance disabled children's communication abilities, are often ordered through the clinic that coordinates all the child's care. About one-half of children with cerebral palsy have

---

PREVENTING CEREBRAL PALSY

Most factors that result in cerebral palsy are beyond the parents' control. You can, however:

- Consult a doctor before using medications during pregnancy.
- Take measures to prevent premature birth.

CARING FOR A CHILD WITH CEREBRAL PALSY

- Use feeding techniques that make it easier to suck, chew, or swallow food. For specific pointers, consult an occupational therapist.
- Feed the child plenty of fiber-rich foods to reduce constipation.
- Get involved in the child's speech therapy and physical therapy. Find out about exercises and techniques you can perform at home.
- If the child has speech or hearing difficulties, use alternative ways of communication, such as gestures, sign language, a communication board or book or an adapted typewriter or computer.
- Look into special government-mandated early intervention programs.

some degree of mental retardation, so the child may need to be in a special education program. Children with cerebral palsy may also require frequent medical attention for seizures, skeletal problems, and other complications.

Chicken pox

Chicken pox, also called *varicella,* is a highly contagious viral disease characterized by fever (usually mild) and a rash (sometimes severe) consisting of tiny blisters or vesicles. Caused by one of a group of organisms known as *herpes viruses,* it can occur at any age but is most common in childhood. In fact, most children have had chicken pox by the age of ten. After one attack, the child is usually immune for life. However, the virus that causes chicken pox remains dormant in the body. Later in life, it can be reactivated, causing a painful outbreak of *shingles,* or *herpes zoster.*

Chicken pox itself is usually mild, but it can become severe in newborns and children whose immune systems have been weakened by cancer, cancer treatments, AIDS, or immunosuppressive therapy to prevent rejection of transplanted organs. It can also cause severe complications, including pneumonia, in adults who escaped the infection during childhood. Epidemics of chicken pox occur in all seasons but are most common in winter and early spring.

How does chicken pox develop?

Chickenpox is caused by the *varicella zoster* virus, which spreads from one person to another through droplets carried by air. An infected child can transmit the virus for several days, starting about 24 hours before the rash appears and ending as soon as all the bumps have crusted over. The disease can also be passed from mother to fetus during pregnancy.

When should I suspect that my child has chicken pox?

Chances are you will know that your child has been exposed to chicken pox before he develops any symptoms. Most schools and day-care centers send home notices informing parents as soon as one or more children come down with the illness. Unfortunately, since the period of contagion usually begins before symptoms appear, there is really no way to avoid exposure during a community outbreak.

About two weeks after exposure to the chicken pox virus, the child may become cranky and develop a mild fever. Within a day or two, crops of tiny, red bumps will appear on the face, scalp, trunk, arms, and legs. The rash may cover the whole body or only a small area. Chicken pox lesions often develop on the mucous membranes of the mouth, anus, vagina, and urethra, which can cause greater discomfort.

What happens during chicken pox?

Within several hours of the first symptoms, the red spots progress to fluid-filled, teardrop-shaped blisters that are extremely itchy. The blisters begin to crust six to eight hours after they appear, but since new crops pop up over the next several days, it may take up to two weeks for all of them to break and form crusts. Most children recover completely within two weeks. The rash usually leaves no scars, unless the skin was badly scratched and infection set in. Occasionally, tiny, white spots are left behind when the crusts fall off the skin. In time, however, the skin returns to normal.

Is medical attention necessary?

If there is an identified outbreak in your community, the pediatrician may advise you not to bring your child to the office. Instead, he will give you telephone advice on how to relieve symptoms and recognize signs of complications. If you are not sure the illness is actually chicken pox, the doctor may need to examine the rash and make a definitive diagnosis.

What treatments are available?

In mild cases, no treatment is usually required beyond rest and controlling the symptoms.

CARING FOR A CHILD WITH CHICKEN POX

- To relieve itching, apply wet compresses or calamine lotion to the affected area. Colloidal oatmeal baths are also quite soothing.
- Keep the child's fingernails short and clean; you may have to put cotton mitts on infants.
- Change the child's clothing and bed linen daily.
- Bathe the child with soap and water at least once a day.

PREVENTING CHICKEN POX

There is no need to take drastic measures to prevent chicken pox in a healthy child; in fact, since the disease is much worse in older children and adults than in preschoolers, many parents feel that it is better to get it over with.

For certain people, however, chicken pox does constitute a serious threat. These groups include:

- Children with leukemia, immune deficiency, or another debilitating illness.
- Newborns whose mothers developed chicken pox around the time of delivery.
- Adults who have never had the disease.
- Pregnant women, particularly in the latest stages of pregnancy.

People in these groups should avoid children who are currently ill or have been in contact with other children who have chicken pox. If exposure occurs, the doctor may recommend a preventive injection prepared from the serum of people recovering from shingles. A chicken pox vaccine prepared from weakened, live varicella-zoster virus has recently been approved for immunization of children and will soon be included in the immunization schedules. It is expected that, as has been the case with measles, the incidence of chicken pox will decrease dramatically.

Occasionally, there is a need for antihistamines to reduce itching or for antibiotics to treat skin infection. When the disease is particularly severe or when it occurs in children with impaired immunity, the antiviral drug acyclovir may be given. When given early in the course of the illness, acyclovir may reduce the number of lesions and shorten the days of fever.

Circumcision

Circumcision is an elective surgical procedure usually performed on boys when they are infants, often within the first few days of birth. The procedure involves the removal of all or part of the foreskin, the piece of skin covering the tip of the penis. As a result of the procedure, the tip of the penis (called the *glans*) as well as the opening (called the *urethra*) are exposed.

Circumcision has been practiced for thousands of years as part of different religious and cultural traditions. Toward the end of the nineteenth century, however, American doctors began to advocate circumcision for *all* boys. This position grew from the belief (never scientifically proven) that the foreskin could easily harbor infection.

At present, most physicians take no strong stand for or against circumcision. While the procedure is still routinely performed in most hospital nurseries, the American Academy of Pediatrics advises against routine circumcision for all boys and suggests that parents need to make a personal decision after meeting with a physician to discuss the procedure's pros and cons (see page 57).

How is circumcision performed?

Circumcision is usually performed by a physician in a hospital about three days after birth. Virtually all hospitals with maternity departments provide the service. It can be done by an obstetrician, pediatrician, a family practitioner, or a specially trained rabbi. Some doctors choose not to do the procedure and will refer parents to a colleague.

The procedure, which takes about five minutes, should be performed only on healthy, stable infants. Sometimes families prefer to delay circumcision for a number of days for religious reasons.

For the procedure, the baby is placed on a plastic board lying on his back. His arms and legs are strapped down, his genitals are scrubbed, and his body is covered with paper drapes, leaving the physician access to the penis. The foreskin is pulled forward and placed in a special cutting instrument that quickly severs it from the glans. After the surgery, a light dressing may be placed on the penis. This dressing comes off the next time the baby urinates.

Because local anesthesia can cause complications in infant circumcisions, it is generally not used.

Pros and cons of circumcision

Pros

- Circumcised males face less risk of urinary tract infection during infancy.
- There may be less chance of cancer of the penis, a rare disease that occurs almost exclusively among uncircumcised adult males.
- Female sex partners of circumcised men may have less risk of developing cervical cancer than those of uncircumcised men.
- Many people believe that circumcision reduces susceptibility to sexually transmitted diseases, although there is no known evidence to support this belief.

Cons

- In rare cases, the incision results in severe bleeding or becomes infected.
- The procedure may be painful.
- Many people believe the foreskin serves a useful purpose in protecting the sensitive membrane of the glans.
- Some people believe that the removal of the foreskin decreases sexual pleasure in adult life.

CARING FOR A BABY AFTER CIRCUMCISION

- If possible, stay with the baby during the circumcision. If that is not possible, make sure the baby receives parental comfort right afterward.
- The penis should heal within ten days. During that time, the exposed glans at the tip may be somewhat red and sore, and there may be minimal bleeding and some yellow secretion around the incision, neither of which is a problem. Until healing has finished, place petroleum jelly on the glans at each diaper change. Keep diapers loose, and change them frequently. Try to keep the baby off his stomach. If the baby seems feverish or the glans develops painful blisters and sores, call your doctor.
- After a circumcision has healed, the penis requires no special care, although it's important to keep the area clean. (This also holds true for a child who has **NOT** been circumcised.) During an uncircumcised child's first few years, the foreskin will naturally separate from the glans. At that time, it will be possible to gently retract the foreskin while cleaning the area.

Cleft Lip and Palate

Cleft lip and palate are common facial malformations, appearing in about 5,000 infants born in the United States each year. Approximately half of these infants have both types of cleft, with the remaining cases divided evenly between cleft lip and cleft palate.

Cleft lip and palate can be quite disfigur-

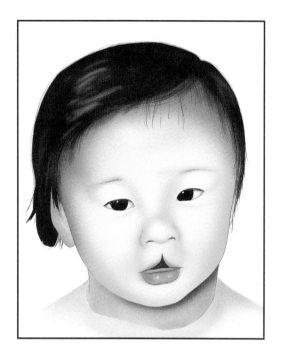

ing, in addition to creating a number of potentially serious difficulties with feeding, hearing, and speech. Fortunately, however, cleft lip and palate can be surgically repaired with excellent results, although the process is sometimes lengthy and complicated. Sophisticated therapeutic techniques also can help an affected child learn to eat and speak normally.

Most children's hospitals use a team approach in treating cleft lip and palate—that is, a primary pediatrician coordinates the work of several different specialists, including surgeons, dentists, speech and hearing therapists, and mental health professionals.

How do cleft lip and palate develop?

About the fourth week of gestation, the tissues of the face begin to form. During this time, the primary palate, which eventually forms the upper lip and gums, and the secondary palate, which eventually forms the roof and back of the mouth, start to grow.

During the fifth and sixth weeks of gestation, clefts are present in the primary palate on each side of the upper lip; these clefts run into the openings that will become the nostrils. The clefts normally fuse by the seventh week, creating the facial area between the nostrils and mouth. A cleft lip results when these clefts in the primary palate fail to fuse.

The cleft in the secondary palate, running from the back of the mouth to the bottom of the uvula, normally fuses between the tenth and twelfth weeks of fetal development. A cleft palate results when the secondary palate does not fuse.

Cleft lips and palates vary greatly in size, shape, and degree. A cleft lip may be confined to the upper lip, extend to the nostrils, or be

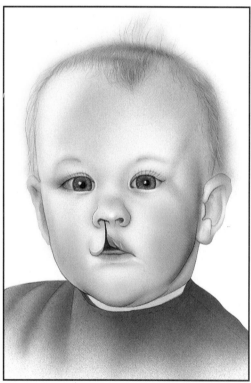

A cleft may be confined to the upper lip or extend to the palate.

complicated by defects in the palate. Cleft palates may involve both the hard and soft palates, the soft palate alone, or just the *uvula,* which is the rounded piece of tissue that hangs down at the back of the palate.

What causes cleft lip and palate?

In many cases, a tendency to develop a cleft lip or palate is inherited. For the malformation to occur, however, it is believed that unidentified environmental triggers must also be present. The genetic influence seems to operate more strongly in producing clefts of the lip than of the palate. Despite the evidence of genetic influence, though, eight out of ten cases of cleft lip and palate occur in children who do not have relatives with similar malformations.

In a small percentage of cases, clefts appear

CARING FOR A CHILD WITH CLEFT LIP AND PALATE

The day-to-day care of a child with a cleft lip and/or palate poses numerous challenges. They include:

- **FEEDING PROBLEMS.** The opening in the baby's mouth or lip prevents normal sucking. Specially designed nipples permit infants with cleft lip and palate to get adequate nutrition and develop the jaw muscles used in sucking. Custom-made prosthetic palates can also help babies nurse and take bottles until surgical repair is possible. Even with the help of these devices, though, feedings may take longer and require more patience on the part of the parent.
- **EAR INFECTIONS.** Children with cleft palates are particularly susceptible to infections of the middle ear. Repeated ear infections at an early age can lead to hearing loss, so careful monitoring and prompt treatment are imperative. During regularly scheduled checkups, the pediatrician will look for developing infections and prescribe antibiotic treatment at the first sign of trouble.
- **ABNORMAL TOOTH DEVELOPMENT.** A cleft involving the gums usually affects the growth and development of adult teeth. Some permanent teeth may be positioned incorrectly or simply fail to grow. Therefore, dental specialists are involved in caring for children with cleft lip and palate both before and after surgical correction. In many cases, dental plates are needed to replace missing teeth during childhood, and oral surgery and orthodontia are often necessary to reposition misaligned teeth.
- **SPEECH AND LANGUAGE DIFFICULTIES.** In normal speech, muscles in the soft palate allow the speaker to direct the passage of air through the mouth or the nasal cavity. A child with a cleft palate may be unable to close off the nasal cavity completely. When the child makes vowel sounds, air escapes through the nose, giving speech a nasal sound. The same loss of air can weaken a variety of consonant sounds.

Speech therapy can effectively counter these difficulties. The child may also be fitted with a prosthetic palate that will simplify word formation.

---

with other defects, all of which can be traced to a single gene. A hereditary disorder of the sort is referred to as a *cleft syndrome;* more than 300 such syndromes have been identified.

What treatments are available?

The ultimate treatment goal is to close lip and palate clefts through surgery, leaving as little scarring as possible. Several separate operations performed at different stages of development are often needed to meet this goal. Surgical repairs of the lip and nose are generally scheduled during the first two to ten weeks of life. A subsequent operation is sometimes necessary at four to five years to correct the shape of the nose and lip for medical as well as cosmetic reasons.

Repair of the palate is usually performed between six months and two years of age. The goal is to fuse the cleaved segments to allow normal development of the upper jaw, as well as to promote normal speech and breathing.

Clubfoot

Clubfoot is a general term for several congenital foot malformations involving bones, muscles, and tendons. The foot can be fixed in an abnormal position, flexed, extended, turned in, or turned out at the ankle, with toes lower or higher than the heel. Clubfoot may affect one or both feet and is twice as common in boys as in girls. Heredity is a factor in the development of the condition. Treatment begins shortly after birth and includes exercise, plaster casts, and/or splints to manipulate the foot into a normal position. In some infants, sur-

gical correction is required. With early treatment, children with clubfeet can grow up to walk and run normally.

What causes clubfoot?

The cause of clubfoot is unknown, but there are several theories. During fetal development, the foot passes through a number of stages in which it is flexed and turned outward until it assumes its normal position, which should happen by the seventh month. If this developmental process is interrupted, the foot may remain frozen in one of these primitive positions, probably for genetic reasons. Restricted movement in the womb may also contribute to the development of clubfoot. Some doctors theorize that both genetic and environmental forces play a role in the development of this malformation.

Many mothers feel guilty about giving birth to a baby with a clubfoot, but occurrence of this deformity is beyond the parents' control. Nothing they did or failed to do causes clubfoot, and no measures can be taken to prevent the disorder.

Is medical attention necessary?

Early treatment is critical, since rapid growth in infancy provides ample opportunities for remodeling the foot. In fact, the sooner treatment begins, the greater the chances that the child will eventually walk normally. Fortunately, clubfoot is usually apparent at birth, so treatment is often initiated within hours of the delivery. At this early stage, correction is much easier because the joints are very flexible and the infant's ligaments are particularly supple.

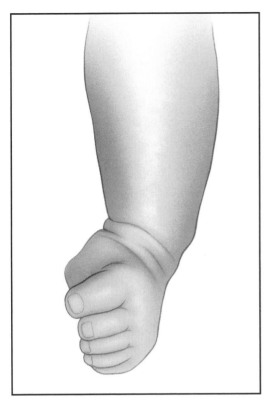

Clubfoot, an abnormal twisting of the foot, is present at birth.

What treatments are available?

In mild cases, treatment includes stretching exercises and special shoes or splints, but many babies require leg casts extending from feet to groin. The orthopedist manipulates the baby's feet into the closest possible approximation to a normal position and immobilizes them there with casts or adhesive taping. Manipulation and casting are repeated every few days for the first two weeks of the child's life and then at intervals of one to two months. When the deformity is fully corrected, the foot will be maintained in an overcorrected position for several weeks in a cast. Afterward, the baby may have to sleep for some time with the feet in a splint to prevent recurrence.

If manipulation does not correct the clubfoot, surgery is required, sometimes when the baby is only two to three months of age. It may involve releasing tight ligaments or lengthening tendons to place bones in a normal position. In infants and younger children, surgery is usually necessary only on soft tissues, not on bones. By the first year of life, a treated clubfoot may look almost normal, but because this disorder tends to recur, the child will require orthopedic care throughout childhood.

Cold Sores

Cold sores, also called fever blisters, are small blisters most commonly found around the lips or nose. They are symptoms of a viral infection known as *oral herpes.* The initial infection with herpes, *primary herpes,* is more severe than subsequent episodes, although in young children the first attack may be mild enough to pass unnoticed. Oral herpes is very contagious but poses no serious health threat. Most herpes sores clear up shortly with no specific treatment.

What causes cold sores?

The virus responsible for oral herpes in children is almost always *herpes simplex* type I, a very common virus in children and one that will affect most people at some time in their lives. It is transmitted by contact with another person's active infection, either directly by kissing or indirectly by sharing eating utensils or toys that come in contact with the mouth. It cannot be transmitted through the air or from a person whose infection is dormant.

When should I suspect my child has oral herpes?

If a child has recurrent cold sores, it is likely that he or she has oral herpes resulting from a previous—possibly unnoticed—primary infection with herpes simplex I. In some children, however, the primary herpes infection is more severe. Painful sores may develop around the lips and inside the mouth on the palate, interior cheeks, and gums, making it difficult for the child to eat or swallow. In some cases, a fever and flulike symptoms develop. After a day or so, the blisters break, but the accompa-

nying mouth ulcers may take several days to heal. Complete recovery from the accompanying symptoms of an initial attack can take two or three weeks.

After the symptoms of the primary outbreak have subsided, the virus retreats to nerves in the infected area and becomes dormant. In some children, the virus is reactivated from time to time by a stimulus such as illness, stress, or sunburn, causing a cluster of cold sores to appear on or around the lips or nose. These blisters cause little or no discomfort in young children. In a few days, they grow larger, burst, crust over, and disappear completely.

Is medical attention necessary?

It is a good idea to have your doctor confirm the diagnosis. This can be done easily with physical examination.

What treatments are available?

There is no cure for oral herpes. The cold sores will usually heal quickly on their own without specific treatment. If the child's primary infection is severe, the doctor may prescribe a medicated mouthwash to numb the pain and acetaminophen to relieve discomfort and treat the flulike symptoms. Cool compresses or ice can help alleviate pain. Over-the-counter preparations for cold sores should be used only on the advice of your doctor. Steroid-containing ointments can cause the infection to spread and should not be used. Finally, if the child's cold sores are persistent or frequent, your doctor may prescribe a medication called *acyclovir,* which works by inhibiting the virus's ability to duplicate.

Getting Help

CALL YOUR DOCTOR IF YOUR CHILD:
- Has frequently recurring or severe cold sores.
- Complains of eye pain or impaired vision or you see a white patch on the eye. Corneal ulcers caused by herpes simplex infection can be serious if not treated.

Colds

Babies, toddlers, and preschoolers are highly susceptible to colds. On average, a child may have three to eight colds a year. For unknown reasons, some children are more prone to getting colds than others. Among all children, however, the frequency of colds usually decreases with age. Children in day care tend to bring home more colds than those who are not cared for in group settings, but this early ex-posure to many cold viruses makes them less vulnerable once they reach school age.

What causes colds?

Colds are caused by viruses that are transmitted through droplets released into the air in sneezing or coughing. They can also be spread through touch. Cold viruses can live on objects such as toys, door knobs, and dishes for up to 72 hours. During this time, they pass from the surface of an infected object or the hand of an infected child to the hand of a healthy youngster. When the healthy child rubs his nose or eyes, the virus enters the body. Within two to four days, it can spread throughout the upper airways, causing a runny nose, a scratchy throat, sneezing, coughing, and burning eyes.

Cold symptoms usually last for three or four days, or until the inner lining of the nose sheds the virus. They may, however, persist for up to ten days. Occasionally a runny nose and cough may linger for weeks.

How can I tell colds from other illnesses?

The signs and symptoms of colds closely resemble those of many other disorders. Symptoms of influenza are similar but more severe.

PREVENTING COLDS

The best way to protect a child from catching more than his share of colds is to encourage frequent handwashing, discourage eye and nose rubbing, and regularly wipe down toys and surfaces with a disinfectant solution.

CARING FOR A CHILD WITH A COLD

- Since dry air can make the symptoms worse, maintain high humidity in the house or near the child's bed.
- Elevate the child's head by moving the head of the crib mattress up a notch or providing extra pillows. (Use pillows only for older children.)
- Do not give cough-suppressing medications unless the doctor prescribes them; coughing clears the airways and prevents further infection.
- Give acetaminophen (Tylenol, Tempra, Datril, Panadol, and other brands) if the child has an oral temperature over 101 degrees Fahrenheit.
- Never use decongestant nasal sprays for more than three or four days—after initial relief, they may have a rebound effect and cause worse congestion.

Allergies may also cause a runny nose, but they do not produce a fever and are often associated with constant and consistent bouts of sneezing. A nasal discharge may occur when a foreign body is lodged in the nose, but in these cases the discharge is likely to be bloody and foul-smelling. Bacterial infections such as strep throat tend to strike more suddenly and make children sicker than colds do.

Is medical attention necessary?

Most colds can be handled at home. Medical attention is necessary only if signs and symptoms of complications develop. Possible complications of colds include **middle ear infections, sinusitis, bronchitis,** and **pneumonia** (see separate references). Some chil-

dren with asthma tend to have attacks in conjunction with colds, which also may necessitate medical attention.

What treatments are available?

More than 100 different cold medications are on the market, but their effectiveness is limited and they may not be safe for children. Check with the doctor before giving a child any cold remedy. In some cases, he will recommend an expectorant (a cough medicine that loosens mucus in the chest) or a decongestant for use at bedtime. In general, though, the best bet is to tough it out, since the side effects of medications can be worse than the cold itself.

Getting Help

CALL YOUR DOCTOR IF:
- A cold lasts longer than three or four days.
- Your child complains of ear pain, which may suggest an ear infection.
- There is a change in the nature of the cough, which may suggest a more serious infection of the airways.
- There is a sudden elevation in the child's temperature.
- Breathing becomes abnormally shallow and rapid.

Colic

About one out of every five newborn babies suffer the frequent, prolonged crying bouts known as colic. Spells of colicky crying can occur at any time of day, but they are most common in the late afternoon and evening. The causes of this nerve-racking but fortunately harmless problem of infancy are poorly understood, but it's currently felt that immaturity of some part of the baby's system—possibly the digestive tract, possibly the nervous system—may be to blame.

How does colic develop?

The exact source of a colicky baby's distress remains a mystery. In any discussion of colic, however, it is important to emphasize that all babies cry, often for reasons parents cannot fathom. The baby may be fed, changed, rocked, sung to, and soothed in every imaginable way and still keep crying. The question, then, is when this normal crying signifies colic. By some definitions, true colic exists only when babies cry for three or more hours straight, every day (or almost every day) at about the same time of day—usually between 6 and 11 P.M. This pattern generally begins between the second and fourth weeks of life and lasts for three or four months.

When should I suspect that my infant has colic?

Babies with colic typically start crying suddenly and appear to be in pain. Their eyes are squeezed shut, the mouth is open, the fists are clenched, and the legs are drawn up to the abdomen or stretched out stiffly. Because these crying bouts typically end with the passage of

---

RECOGNIZING COLIC

An infant may have colic if:

- Crying lasts for several hours.
- Crying tends to occur at the same time daily, usually in the early evening.
- Crying is loud and persistent.
- Crying is accompanied by pulled up legs, shut eyes, clenched fists, and a pained expression.

---

rectal gas or bowel movements, it is assumed that the gastrointestinal tract is somehow involved. Colic is more common among firstborns and males, although no one knows why.

What causes colic?

The current favorite explanations for colic are an immature digestive tract, gas in the small intestine, or the infant's frustration at her inability to interact with the environment. Some doctors suspect that infants are most vulnerable at the end of the day because they can sense the household tension that normally begins to mount at that time.

Colic is usually not caused by an allergy to cow's milk or a component of formula. Often a colicky child has her food changed repeatedly, only to find one that seems to be tolerable at just about the time the persistent crying is normally outgrown. Also, contrary to popular belief, breast-fed babies develop colic as frequently as do bottle-fed children.

Is medical attention necessary?

Not for colic itself. You should, however, mention the baby's crying pattern to the pediatrician during a regular checkup so that she can rule out physical problems that could be responsible. Always consult a doctor if a crying session lasts more than four hours.

Once physical problems are ruled out, the pediatrician can offer reassurance that the baby is fine and support for the parents as they cope with the problem. Often, parents relax and cope more effectively as soon as they know that the baby is healthy and the symptoms never last more than three months.

Coping with colic

If picking up and carrying the baby seems to help, go right ahead and do it; you cannot spoil your infant. Other tips for dealing with colic and crying are given in Chapter 1. Birth to Three Months, Volume I, Part One, and in "Common Childhood Symptoms" Volume I, Part Three.

Colitis

Colitis is an inflammatory disease affecting the colon (large intestine), the lower portion of the digestive tract, which leads to the rectum. This inflammation can lead to formation of ulcers in the mucous membrane lining the colon, creating the potential for bleeding, intestinal perforation, and a life-threatening infection called *peritonitis*.

How does colitis develop?

In children, the most common cause of colitis is bacterial infection with organisms such as *Shigella*. Other types of colitis that may affect children are *ulcerative colitis* and Crohn's disease. These conditions develop for reasons that are not fully understood, and they may recur throughout life.

When should I suspect that my child has colitis?

The hallmark of colitis is loose bowel movements containing mucus, pus, or blood. Abdominal cramps usually accompany this symptom. The bowel movements come on with great urgency, and may occur several times a day. Other signs to look for are abdominal bloating and rumbling. In ulcerative colitis and Crohn's disease, weight loss and poor growth may occur over time. Nausea, vomiting, and fever are often present in a bacterial colitis.

The frequent diarrhea of colitis has secondary effects to watch out for. If the stool is very bloody, the child may suffer from blood loss or anemia. Dehydration may also develop.

Is medical attention necessary?

Yes. Blood in the stool is always a serious sign that should always be brought to a doctor's attention.

How can the doctor tell if my child has colitis?

The workup starts with a careful medical history and physical exam. A pediatric gastroenterologist, who specializes in digestive disorders among youngsters, may examine the colon and rectum with an instrument called a *colonoscope*. During colonoscopy, a small sample of tissue (a biopsy) may be removed from the lining of the colon and examined microscopically for changes that suggest colitis. A culture of the stool to search for bacteria or other pathogens that cause colitis will also be done.

What treatments are available?

Colitis resulting from bacterial infection (dysentery) will be treated with appropriate antibiotics. Ulcerative colitis, believed to be an auto-immune disease, is a chronic illness and will be treated differently from infectious colitis.

Mild ulcerative colitis or Crohn's disease, which consists of intermittent bouts of cramps, diarrhea, and possible weight loss, may be treated by the physician at home with rest and medication, which may include a sulfa drug (sulfasalazine), corticosteroids, or other anti-inflammatory drugs. The child should avoid milk and milk products and high-fiber foods, which can contribute to diarrhea. A hot water bottle may alleviate the cramps.

In moderate and severe ulcerative colitis or Crohn's disease, hospitalization is necessary. The child is lethargic, with weight loss and poor appetite. In the hospital, the child is fed intravenously and given appropriate drug treatment. In very rare cases, if bleeding persists, part of the colon may have to be removed.

Getting Help

CALL YOUR DOCTOR IF:
- Your child's bowel movement contains blood.
- Symptoms of diarrhea and cramps occur repeatedly.
- Your child is tired and is losing weight.

Communication Disorders, Developmental

For many children, the acquisition of speech is anything but a smooth, natural process. Words simply do not come easily to these children, and their social functioning and school success may suffer as a result.

A child who is able to speak but has trouble making himself understood (or understanding the speech of others) is said to have a *specific communication disorder*. These disorders are divided into three main subtypes depending on whether the main problem is with pronouncing words, formulating meaningful phrases, or understanding spoken language.

These three subtypes have many features in common. Although all become apparent early in life most children who have trouble forming words learn to speak by school age but a portion will be dyslexic or show more subtle inadequacies. They also affect males more often than females and tend to run in families. Finally, and not surprisingly, they all have a negative effect on school performance.

Delayed development in language and speech is the most common developmental disability in children, affecting approximately 10 percent of all children.

When should I suspect that my child has a communication disorder?

Children's acquisition of language should follow a fairly predictable pattern, although there is great room for variation, particularly in the ages at which children say their first words and sentences. In general, however, a child should follow the pattern summarized below.

- Says two or three words; makes animal sounds. Not easily understood by strangers.

AGE 2

- Uses phrases of two or three words.
- Uses "I," "me," and "you."
- About 50 percent intelligible.

AGE 3

- Says 4–5 word sentences.
- Knows about 900 words.
- About 75 percent intelligible.

AGE 4-5

- Can use past tense correctly; uses "yesterday"; uses complete sentences with adjectives, adverbs.
- Knows about 1,500–2,100 words.
- 100 percent intelligible.

AGE 5-6

- Understands "if," "because," and "why."
- Knows about 3,000 words.
- Makes most sounds correctly; may distort *s*, *z*, *sh*, *ch*, and *j*.

LONG-TERM OUTLOOK

Most children with developmental language disorders can express themselves verbally by school age, but residual problems often persist. Children with articulation problems commonly catch up by the fourth grade, usually with no residual problems.

Children who have more severe problems often have learning disabilities, expecially with reading, reading comprehenion, and spelling. Rarely, such expression and receptive language defects may persist into adulthood.

What causes communication disorders?

In the vast majority of cases, the cause is unknown. Most likely, however, subtle brain abnormalities, some of them genetic, interact with environmental influences (such as the amount of talking that goes on in the home) to produce communication disorders.

Is medical attention necessary?

Yes. If you suspect that your child is not developing normally, consult your pediatrician without delay. The doctor will examine your child and perform a series of tests designed to rule out such causes as hearing loss, mental retardation, autism, and disorders associated with structural brain lesions, such as cerebral palsy. Once these have been eliminated, the doctor will probably refer you to a speech and language pathologist or a psychologist trained to work with language disorders.

How can the doctor tell if my child has a communication disorder?

There are three methods available for assessing speech and language development. The first is direct observation of the child's language skills. The doctor or speech pathologist will interact directly with the child, talking, asking questions, or playing, depending on the child's age. Second, the doctor will question the parents. This involves taking a history of the child's use of language from about age one to the time of the consultation. Finally, speech pathologists use several different standardized tests for assessing language development in children. The choice of a specific test or tests is based on the age of the child and the type of impairment.

What treatments are available?

The treatment for any of the specific communication disorders is speech and language therapy by a certified speech pathologist. Sometimes educational and psychological problems accompany these disorders, so additional counseling may be needed as well.

CARING FOR A CHILD WITH A COMMUNICATION DISORDER

Parents play a key role in encouraging their children to expand their verbal capabilities. The following are some guidelines for helping:

- Provide listening opportunities. Speak to the child about on-going activities. Say "open" each time a door is opened. Repeat the word several times. Give the child the opportunity to speak or repeat what was just said.
- Choose a vocabulary that is useful, easy to pronounce, and understandable to the child.
- Encourage vocabulary building by prompting the child to say the word before fulfilling a request, for example, to say "drink" before getting a beverage.
- If the child says two words, answer with three or four word phrases.
- Always reinforce the child's attempt to communicate with verbal praise and affection. Give support, not criticism.
- Don't correct mistakes. Instead, repeat and expand. If the child says "pisketti," respond, "Yes, we're having spaghetti for dinner."
- Don't anticipate all the child's wants. Wait for the child to express them.

Conjunctivitis

Conjunctivitis, or inflammation of the membrane lining the eyelids and covering the eyeball, is the most common eye disease in children. Symptoms frequently begin in one eye but usually spread to both within a day or two. The eyes are red and the eyelids are often swollen. In addition, the eyes may develop an oozing discharge that blurs the vision and may glue the eyelids together, particularly during sleep. The eyes are often itchy and sensitive to light, but usually not painful.

What causes conjunctivitis?

Conjunctivitis is often caused by viral infections. Bacteria are another frequent cause. Allergies, injury, and contact with chemicals or noxious vapors can also produce the condition.

Babies may contract conjunctivitis during birth if the mother has a sexually transmitted disease such as chlamydia or gonorrhea. Newborn babies may also contract bacterial conjunctivitis. Birth-related eye injuries or

blocked tear ducts (see entry) can cause conjunctivitis as well.

When should I suspect that my child has conjunctivitis?

The symptoms of conjunctivitis tend to appear suddenly. Look for constant eye rubbing, watery red eyes, and sticky eyelids, particularly in the morning. Older children may say they feel a grain of dust or an eyelash in the eye.

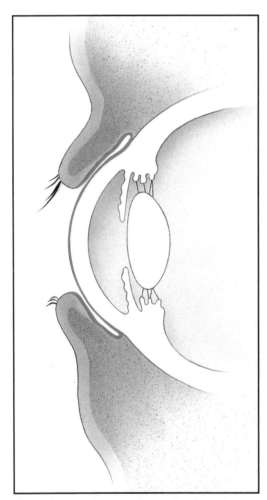

The conjunctiva is a membrane that lines the eyelids and covers the surface of the white of the eye.

Is medical attention necessary?

Although mild conjunctivitis may resolve without treatment, medical evaluation is needed to rule out potentially severe infections involving the cornea. If conjunctivitis is diagnosed and treated promptly, it usually clears without a trace in both newborn and older children.

What treatments are available?

Bacterial conjunctivitis is usually treated with local application of antibiotic drops or oint-

ADMINISTERING EYE MEDICATION

- Lay the child face-up on a flat surface.
- If necessary, get someone to help hold the child's head still.
- Ask the child to look up. To get an infant to look up, dangle a colorful object over the top of the head.
- Use one hand to pull the eyelid down.
- Rest the hand holding the dropper or tube on the child's forehead to reduce movement.
- Turn your wrist so that the dropper or tube is over the eye and release the prescribed amount of medicine into the space between the eyeball and eyelid.
- Instruct the child to keep her lids closed for a few seconds.
- Place eyedrops in the inner corner of an infant's eyes if they are tightly closed. The medicine will flow into the eye when the eyelids open.
- Wait until an extremely resistant baby goes to sleep to apply ointment. Pull down the lower lid and place the ointment on its inner surface.

- Apply cold compresses to reduce swelling.
- Avoid bright sunlight.
- Encourage careful handwashing to avoid the spread of infection.
- Keep the child from rubbing her eyes.

ment. Allergic conjunctivitis may be treated with antihistamine eye drops or ointment. Most viral conjunctivitis usually needs no treatment. If the eye infection is caused by the herpes virus, the cornea will also be involved. This rare condition requires therapy with the antiviral drug acyclovir.

If a newborn has conjunctivitis, the doctor will remove some cells from the lining of the eyelid and grow them in a culture medium to determine the exact cause, so that appropriate treatment can be prescribed.

Never use ointments containing corticosteroids against conjunctivitis without consulting a doctor. They may relieve symptoms dramatically when the condition is due to allergy, but in some bacterial and viral infections of the eye, they aggravate the disease and cause irreversible damage.

Getting Help

CALL YOUR DOCTOR IF:
- Your child has red, swollen, irritated eyes with a discharge.

Cradle Cap

Cradle cap is a form of seborrheic dermatitis in which crusty, yellowish scales accumulate on a baby's scalp. The condition is very common, affecting some 50 percent of newborns during the first few months of life. Although somewhat unsightly, cradle cap is harmless; it causes no discomfort or itching and rapidly disappears with proper scalp hygiene.

What causes cradle cap?

The cause is unknown but is probably linked to the oil-producing sebaceous glands, which are located primarily on the scalp, face, and genitals. During early infancy, these glands are very active and secrete excessive quantities of sebum, a mixture of cellular debris and fat. If the hair is infrequently shampooed, sebum accumulates on the scalp and causes cradle cap. Parents sometimes inadvertently set the stage for cradle cap by failing to wash their newborn's scalp thoroughly for fear of injuring the fontanelle, or soft spot. The skin covering the fontanelle is just as resilient as the rest of a baby's skin, however, and will not tear or puncture easily.

When should I suspect that my baby has cradle cap?

If you notice yellowish, greasy-looking, scaly patches on the baby's scalp, cradle cap is probably the cause. Occasionally, scaling can also be seen around the hairline, nose, ears, and eyelids.

The condition usually develops in the first few weeks of life and disappears after a few months, but—if the scalp is not kept thoroughly clean—it can continue to recur throughout the first year of life.

What treatments are available?

Removal of the crusts and regular, thorough cleansing of the scalp will eliminate cradle cap in virtually every case. To remove the scales more easily, massage mineral or olive oil onto the baby's scalp and allow it to soften the scales. Then use a wash cloth or soft toothbrush to gently scrape away the crust. Be sure to follow this procedure with a thorough washing—perhaps with a mild antidandruff shampoo—because leftover oil can aggravate cradle cap. A soft-bristled brush and a fine-toothed comb are helpful in removing the scales from the baby's hair. Repeat this process as often as necessary to remove the cradle cap completely.

Once the condition has cleared up, frequent, vigorous shampooing and daily brushing usually will keep cradle cap from recurring. If the condition persists, the doctor can prescribe a stronger shampoo or topical preparation.

Getting Help

CALL YOUR DOCTOR IF:

- ☐ Cradle cap does not respond to home treatment.
- ☐ The rash spreads to other parts of your baby's body.
- ☐ The rash is itchy or inflamed or shows signs of infection.

Croup

Croup is a general term that describes inflammation and narrowing of the upper parts of the air passages that lead into the lungs, interfering with breathing. Younger children are at greater risk because their airways are small and more pliable, and the slightest swelling can lead to obstruction of breathing. Crying or anxiety may further worsen the symptoms.

In children younger than three years, croup most commonly takes the form of *laryngotracheobronchitis,* an inflammation involving both the upper and lower respiratory tracts. This inflammation usually starts in the upper airways and descends to the lungs. In older children, only the voice box or the windpipe may be affected. In its most severe form, croup is a manifestation of epiglottitis, or inflammation of the tissue flap that closes off the windpipe (see entry on **epiglottitis**). Epiglottitis is a true medical emergency, since it completely blocks off the child's airways.

When should I suspect that my child has croup?

A mild infection of the upper airways is usually the first stage in all kinds of croup. Symptoms develop gradually, and there may be a mild or high fever. Children are restless and complain of pain during coughing. In spas-

---

SYMPTOMS OF CROUP

- Barking cough.
- Noisy breathing.
- Wheezing and hoarseness.
- Difficulty breathing.

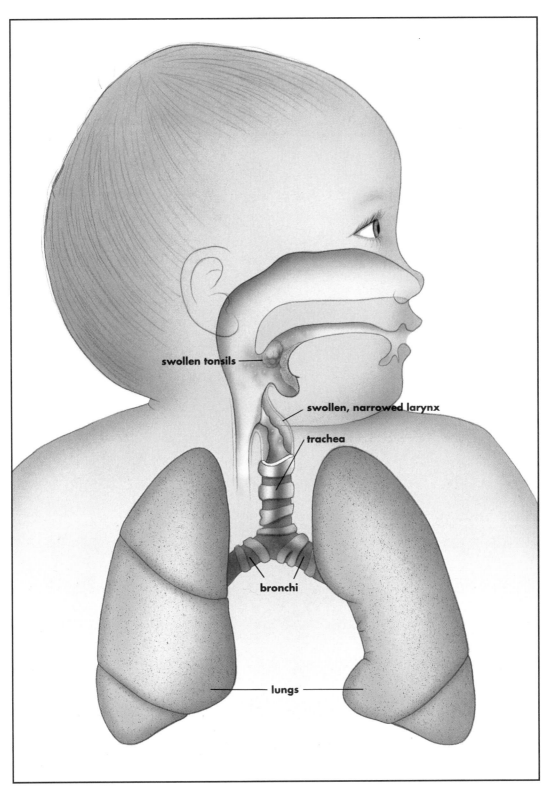

swollen tonsils

swollen, narrowed larynx

trachea

bronchi

lungs

Croup is a general term for inflammation of the
upper air passages. In small children, the lower
air passages leading to the lungs are often
affected as well.

modic croup, by contrast, there is no fever, and symptoms develop suddenly, usually at night. The child may wake up with breathing difficulty and have a sudden bout of coughing. Croup is more common in the winter months but can occur at any time during the year.

How does croup develop?

Croup usually is caused by viruses and less commonly caused by bacteria. Respiratory allergies may set the stage for the infection. The viruses that cause croup are as varied as those responsible for the common cold and influenza; therefore, one episode of croup does not give a child protection against another.

Is medical attention necessary?

Yes. Even though croup is usually mild and disappears rather quickly, may also indicate the presence of a very serious respiratory tract infection (see **epiglottitis**). The symptoms of croup are similar to those of bacterial epiglottitis which is a true medical emergency. If your child has a croupy (barking) cough, is unable to speak, is leaning forward, is pale, has noise coming through the windpipe on each breath, and/or is drooling, it is essential to call the doctor, who may advise coming in to the office or emergency room.

Symptoms of uncomplicated croup usually get worse at night and wane during the day, but they generally clear within three to seven days. If the disorder lasts longer, an underlying problem—a malformation of the airways, bacterial infection, or a foreign body lodged in the air passages—may be interfering with the healing process.

If croup persists or recurs frequently, the pediatrician should do a careful examination that may include taking X rays or using an endoscope—a tubelike instrument equipped with lenses and a light—to view the airways.

What treatments are available?

Children with croup may require oxygen and medications to help open the airways. Very rarely, children may need temporary placement of a breathing tube to bypass the obstruction. The tube usually is removed within a day or two. A breathing tube, along with antibiotic therapy, is necessary in cases of epiglottitis. Because croup is caused by a virus, it is not treated with antibiotics.

One traditional component of treatment is maintaining moisture in the atmosphere because inflammation and swelling cause the mucous lining of the airways to dry out, which creates further breathing difficulties.

Getting Help

CALL A DOCTOR IMMEDIATELY IF A CHILD DEVELOPS SYMPTOMS OF CROUP. TAKE THE CHILD TO THE HOSPITAL EMERGENCY ROOM IF SHE:

- Has rapid, difficult breathing.
- Turns pale or blue.
- Is sweating and anxious.
- Has rapid pulse and flaring nares.
- Is increasingly restless.
- Is leaning forword in an attempt to breathe.
- Is unable to speak.
- Is drooling.

Cystic Fibrosis

Cystic fibrosis is a chronic, inherited disease that affects the mucus-producing glands of the body and severely impairs the digestive and respiratory system. It affects approximately one in 2,000 white newborns, but is rare in black and Asian children. In recent years, early diagnosis and improved treatments have increased the life expectancy of children with cystic fibrosis. The course of the disease varies widely, with some children suffering chronic but manageable symptoms and others developing life-threatening complications.

In 1989, researchers isolated the abnormal gene responsible for cystic fibrosis.

What causes cystic fibrosis?

Cystic fibrosis is a genetic disorder. If both parents are carriers of the defective cystic fibrosis gene, their child has a 25 percent chance of inheriting both those genes and developing the disease. If only one abnormal gene is inherited (that is, from only one parent), the child will not have symptoms of the disease but will be capable of passing on the defective gene to the next generation. One in 40 whites are healthy carriers of the cystic fibrosis gene.

How does cystic fibrosis develop?

Most of the symptoms of cystic fibrosis are caused by a malfunction of the mucus-producing glands. Instead of producing thin, free-flowing secretions, the glands secrete thick, sticky mucus that blocks small passages in organs such as the pancreas and lungs, interfering with digestion and respiration and resulting in malnutrition, as well as frequent bouts of bronchitis, pneumonia, and other respiratory illnesses.

When should I suspect that my child has cystic fibrosis?

If you have a family history of cystic fibrosis, don't wait for signs or symptoms. Genetic testing is now available to identify carriers of the disease. However, in the absence of a family history and genetic testing, the diagnosis may be difficult. In a newborn, intestinal obstruction due to retained meconium (the substance that fills the large intestine before birth) is often the first sign of cystic fibrosis.

At first, a baby with cystic fibrosis may be small for his age and have a tendency to catch colds easily. In time, the baby will begin to lose weight despite a voracious appetite. Because the pancreas malfunctions, undigested food is excreted in large, foul-smelling, frothy stools.

Most children with cystic fibrosis develop respiratory symptoms before the age of one, leading eventually to frequent and severe bacterial respiratory infections like pneumonia and bronchitis.

What treatments are available?

Standard treatment includes preventive treatment with antibiotics (prophylaxis) to prevent lung infections, twice-daily "postural drainage" (pounding on the back and chest) to loosen and expel phlegm, and dietary supplements of pancreatic enzymes in powder or capsule form to assist fat digestion. Treatment methods are rapidly improving, and several new, still-experimental drugs show great promise. Combined heart and lung transplants have also greatly benefited some

patients. In addition, researchers are experimenting with gene therapy. Already, attempts to transfer a healthy copy of the cystic fibrosis gene to the lungs of mice have been successful. Experiments with gene therapy in humans should soon be underway.

Coping with cystic fibrosis

A diagnosis of cystic fibrosis can seem overwhelming to parents. Reaching out to others by joining a support group can help families deal with the stresses and demands of this disease. See the "Directory of Resources" at the end of this book for a listing of organizations.

Genetic counseling also will be helpful to parents of a child with cystic fibrosis who are considering another pregnancy.

Getting Help

CALL YOUR DOCTOR IF YOUR CHILD:
- ☐ Fails to grow and gain weight despite a healthy appetite.
- ☐ Passes pale-colored, abnormally large stools.
- ☐ Has a chronic cough or chronic diarrhea.
- ☐ Develops frequent, severe respiratory infections.
- ☐ Is tired and short of breath after minimal exertion.

Deafness

Partial or complete hearing loss can severely impede a child's development unless it is diagnosed early. Deafness deprives the child of vital information about the outside world and limits the child's ability to communicate with others. It also disrupts the ability to produce and understand speech. Children with a hearing loss that persists until the age of five years are unlikely to learn to speak clearly.

Young children with hearing problems are often mistakenly considered to be retarded. However, if partial or complete hearing loss is detected early, it should not prevent the child from developing perfectly normal intellectual skills or from having a happy, rewarding life.

When should I suspect that my child is partially or completely deaf?

Deafness often is overlooked for long periods of time, particularly in small babies. Deaf infants may have a normal cry at birth and start to babble at the same time as babies with intact hearing. However, while babbling normally increases with age and becomes more complex, in deaf babies it diminishes after approximately the seventh month. Hearing should certainly be tested in all children who fail to start talking by the age of 18 months. Deaf toddlers may have frequent temper tantrums caused by frustration at not understanding others or not being understood.

What causes deafness?

A baby may be born deaf when there is a family history of deafness or when the mother had rubella or syphilis during pregnancy or took medications that lead to hearing-related birth defects (such as antimalaria drugs). Deafness may be part of a syndrome or disorder present at birth, but sometimes it is the only abnormality and its cause is unknown. Premature infants have a higher risk of being deaf than infants born at full term. Another risk factor of deafness is brain trauma during delivery.

After birth, the most common cause of hearing loss is middle ear infection, particularly when it is chronic or recurrent. Other important causes of deafness are meningitis, measles, and mumps.

Is medical attention necessary?

Medical attention is a must because the doctor may be able to identify a reversible cause of deafness and prescribe treatment. It is also important to establish the kind of deafness that affects your child, which can only be done with special instruments.

How can the pediatrician tell if my child is partially or completely deaf?

Severe hearing loss is readily apparent. A baby who cannot hear at all will not turn her head toward a sound, and a child who cannot hear will not speak properly or respond to speech. Milder degrees of hearing loss often are detected in screening programs conducted by school health personnel.

What treatments are available?

If the cause of deafness cannot be eliminated and a hearing aid does not restore hearing to normal, the child will need special training in speaking, lip reading, and—if deafness is severe—sign language. If deafness is present from birth, treatment should begin before the age of six months. At the beginning, the training mainly takes place at home, but special schooling may be required later. It is also important that your child receive sufficient visual and other stimuli to compensate for her impairment.

CARING FOR A CHILD WITH HEARING LOSS

A child who is partially or completely deaf will require a great deal of attention on your part. Here are some of the things you can do to help your child develop normally.

- Encourage your child to use the voice and teach her that the voice is a means of communication.
- Use every alternative means of communication, such as pantomime and gesture.
- Learn sign language yourself so you can communicate with your child.
- Have your child watch your lips as you talk but do not exaggerate lip movements, because this only interferes with lip reading. Children may start to read lips when they are one year old.
- Encourage your child to read, and provide age-appropriate computer games if you have access to a computer.
- Avoid talking to your child with chewing gum or a pencil in your mouth and do not place your hands before your face.
- Provide warmth, comfort, and support as your child adjusts to living with a disability.
- Enroll your child in an early intervention project to ensure maximal learning opportunities.

Getting Help

CALL YOUR DOCTOR IF YOUR BABY:

- ☐ Does not startle when hearing a loud noise, such as clapping hands or a squeaking toy by the age of three months.
- ☐ Does not turn her eyes toward a familiar sound by the age of five months.
- ☐ Does not babble when talked to by the age of eight months.
- ☐ Cannot quickly localize the source of sound by the age of nine months.
- ☐ Does not recognize her name by the age of twelve months.
- ☐ Cannot say two or more meaningful words by the age of fifteen months.

Dehydration

Dehydration can develop when the body fails to replenish the water lost each day in urine, sweat, and feces. Although dehydration can result from inadequate intake of water, it is more commonly caused by abnormal water loss from the body, as in diarrhea or vomiting. Dehydration is a serious, even dangerous condition that requires a physician's immediate attention.

When should I suspect that my child is dehydrated?

If your child has been too ill to drink or has episodes of vomiting or diarrhea, be on the

Signs of significant dehydration include:

- Irritability
- Reduced skin elasticity
- Deep-set eyes
- Fewer tears
- Reduced urine output
- Dry lips and skin
- Increased pulse rate
- Depressed fontanelle (the soft spot in a baby's skull)
- Lethargy

lookout for signs of dehydration. If the child is mildly dehydrated, the only sign may be increased thirst. As dehydration progresses from moderate to severe, however, the number of symptoms will increase and become more severe.

What causes dehydration?

Common childhood illnesses like diarrhea and vomiting can cause your child's fluid supply to drop to abnormally low levels. Infants and young children are particularly susceptible to dehydration because they expel large amounts of water in the production of urine. Indeed, infants need to replenish nearly a quarter percent of their total body fluids each day, while adults must replace less than ten percent.

Is medical attention necessary?

Yes. The doctor may want to examine your child to determine the cause of the symptoms and to evaluate the degree of dehydration. Dehydration can seriously threaten a child's health by placing undue stress on the kidneys

and heart as they try to compensate for the fluid depletion. Prolonged and severe dehydration can lead to shock and even death.

How is dehydration treated?

The best treatment, of course, is prevention. Even if your child has no appetite when ill, encourage the intake of fluids. In cases of on-going diarrhea, the doctor may prescribe an electrolyte-containing fluid such as Pedialyte or a similar preparation for the child to drink. (Electrolytes are the salts that make up an essential component of body water.)

Most cases of dehydration can be treated at home with fluid supplementation. If the child is vomiting, too ill to drink, or unable to take in sufficient quantities of fluid to counteract the loss, intravenous fluid replacement may be required. This is known as parenteral fluid therapy and requires hospitalization. The nature of the child's illness and the severity of the dehydration will determine the course of parenteral therapy and the length of the hospital stay.

Getting Help

CALL YOUR DOCTOR IF YOUR CHILD:
- Shows signs of dehydration.
- Has severe diarrhea and episodes of vomiting for more than 24 hours.
- Has been too ill to drink for more than 24 hours.

Depression

Depression is a mood disturbance, characterized by feelings of sadness, worthlessness, loss, hopelessness, and a withdrawal from life and activity. Psychiatrists use the term *major depressive disorder* to distinguish serious depression from temporary and realistic feelings of sadness. Previously it was thought that clinical depression did not exist among young children, whose emotions are still forming—and who lack the vocabulary to describe the complex feelings they are experiencing. Currently, it is accepted that mood disorders such as depression do affect children, even very young ones. However, the condition occurs very rarely.

When should I suspect depression?

According to the diagnostic system of the American Psychiatric Association, [*Diagnostic and Statistical Manual of Mental Disorders* (third edition, revised)], if your child exhibits five or more of the following symptoms, she may be suffering from major depressive disorder. The symptoms should be present concurrently for at least two weeks, except for 3 and 9, which might not be apparent on a regular basis.

1. Sad or irritable mood.
2. Diminished interest or pleasure in activities.
3. Failure to make expected childhood weight gains.
4. Too little sleep, or too much sleep.
5. Agitated physical movements.
6. Fatigue or loss of energy.
7. Feelings of worthlessness or excessive guilt.
8. Lack of concentration.
9. Thoughts of death or suicide.

A troubled home environment can cause a parent to overlook signs of depression in a child. Sometimes a teacher, relative, or other care provider may alert a parent to certain behaviors in a child, such as "acting out" or learning problems, that are actually indications of depression.

School performance may suffer in a depressed child; in fact, depression is sometimes misdiagnosed as a learning disability. These learning problems usually correct themselves after the depression has been successfully treated.

If a child has recently experienced a serious trauma such as an illness or loss of a parent, depressive symptoms may be part of the normal recovery process. In such a case the symptoms are temporary, lasting up to six months, and a diagnosis of major depressive disorder is not applied.

What causes depression?

Numerous causes may underlie a child's severe depressive symptoms. Family dynamics can be a primary cause. For example, in a family where the father is too detached and removed from the child and the mother is overprotective to the point of stifling, the child could become depressed. A child who thinks of her parents as always being distant, angry, and critical, might also suffer from depression. So might a child whose sense of self becomes threatened due to intense pressure to conform to parents' expectations.

Some studies suggest that a tendency to be depressed can, in fact, be inherited, but there is no conclusive evidence to support this.

However, a severely depressed parent, unable to perform normal parenting tasks such as listening, stimulation, encouragement, or even preparing regular meals, can pass depression down to the child as surely as if the condition had been inherited.

Is medical attention necessary?

Yes. Depression is serious. If left untreated it can lead to future problems such as low self-esteem, inability to form relationships, and later in life, dependence on drugs and alcohol.

What treatments are available?

If a diagnosis of depressive disorder is confirmed, a mental health professional will develop a treatment plan. Professionals may differ dramatically in the treatments they prescribe. Some may advise a course of antidepressant medication, which seems to alleviate symptoms in children and can be stopped after the condition is stabilized. However, antidepressants have possible side effects, and some professionals oppose prescribing them for children.

Some professionals recommend psychotherapy, alone or in conjunction with drugs. The goals of therapy are to help the child confront anger that may underlie the depressive feelings, to build a stronger sense of self-worth, and to draw upon reserves of inner strength to combat depression now and in the future.

Coping with depression in a child

- If your child's verbal skills are strong enough, try to discuss what he or she is feeling. Ask about feeling sad, feeling empty, wanting to cry, or having bad feelings that won't go away. Give plenty of time for an-

Getting Help

Check with your pediatrician to make sure there is nothing physically wrong with your child. The next step is to consult a psychiatrist, psychologist, or other mental health professional. In making the diagnosis the therapist will take into account your child's moods, environment, family history, and patterns of behavior. She also may conduct diagnostic interviews with your child.

In children, the proper diagnosis of depression is extremely important. Any organic condition or stressful life situation that could mimic psychiatric symptoms must be ruled out. For example, a child might be suffering from child abuse, separation anxiety, or bereavement, any of which could produce the symptoms of depression.

swers, and don't pressure the child to respond. Pick a time when you both are relaxed and enjoying each other's company.

- When a preschool or younger child has difficulty expressing feelings, try to get a sense of what's wrong by observing facial expressions, body posture, tone of voice and level of activity. Offer support, affection, and time together to help alleviate the sad feelings.

Diabetes Mellitus (Insulin-Dependent Diabetes)

Diabetes mellitus is an impairment of the body's ability to metabolize glucose, the blood sugar which is the primary energy source for all body cells. The form of diabetes that usually afflicts children is known as *juvenile onset, Type I*, or *insulin-dependent diabetes.* It is most likely to develop between the ages of five and seven and during puberty.

How does insulin-dependent diabetes develop?

The basic defect in insulin-dependent diabetes is a malfunction of cells in the pancreas that produce the hormone insulin, which is required to convert glucose into energy. Insulin also controls the rate at which glucose is consumed by body cells.

In juvenile diabetes, the body's immune system, in a so-called autoimmune reaction, destroys the insulin-producing cells of the pancreas. Consequently, the blood retains abnormally high levels of glucose and the body cells have no energy source.

It is now thought that two factors must come into play in order for a child to develop diabetes. First, the child must have a genetic "predisposition" to diabetes. That means that somewhere in the child's genes there is a program for becoming diabetic. But that program does not get turned on unless there is a trigger—the second factor. The trigger may be a viral infection or some other stress to the system.

When should I suspect that my child has insulin-dependent diabetes?

Symptoms do not appear until most of the insulin-producing cells in the pancreas have been destroyed. Look for the following signs:

- Abnormal thirst
- Excessive urination
- Increased appetite
- Sudden weight loss
- Severe fatigue following light activity
- Irritability
- Nausea and vomiting

Is medical attention necessary?

Yes. Immediate diagnosis and treatment are essential. By the time nausea and vomiting appear, the child may already have dangerously high blood-glucose levels and severe acidosis due to the burning of fat by the body because glucose is not being utilized for energy.

If there is a family history of diabetes, a test for the antibodies that signal an autoimmune attack can identify a child at risk before symptoms appear; it may even be possible to predict when the disease will develop. A few hospitals have undertaken a new research program that treats at-risk children with immunosuppres-

sive drugs in the hopes of halting the autoimmune attack.

How can the pediatrician tell if my child has insulin-dependent diabetes?

Diagnosis requires only simple blood and urine tests. Most children who develop diabetes are hospitalized for a few days to regulate their insulin and diet and to learn about the disease. The length of the initial hospitalization will depend on the child's age, the availability of self-care training in your community, and the degree of glucose elevation.

What treatments are available?

Insulin therapy, in the form of daily injections, is the basic treatment. During the first week of insulin therapy, your physician will carefully monitor the child's response to determine the optimal daily dosage. Blood-glucose monitoring and daily injections of insulin will be necessary throughout the child's life. Even young children can learn to measure their own blood-glucose levels.

You should contact your doctor if your child develops any other illness. Even a cold or flu can mandate changes in the youngster's insulin dosage.

Maintaining safe blood sugar levels

A central goal of diabetes management is prevention of high blood-glucose levels. An acutely high glucose level carries the risk of a diabetic coma. In addition, a chronically elevated glucose level (even if only slightly elevated) seems to contribute to the evolution of complications such as eye and kidney damage and high blood pressure.

CARING FOR A CHILD WITH INSULIN-DEPENDENT DIABETES

The key to caring for a child with diabetes is to maintain a stable balance of insulin, diet, and activity to normalize glucose levels. Components of a management plan include:

- Daily insulin therapy, usually given in one or two injections (depending on individual needs).
- A diet low in sugar and fat and high in complex carbohydrates and fiber to help control blood sugar and cholesterol levels.
- Regularly scheduled meals to regulate blood sugar levels; stable dietary intake is crucial to the safety and effectiveness of the prescribed insulin dosage.
- Regular exercise to allow a minimum dosage of injected insulin.
- Checking blood sugar levels several times a day using a simple finger-stick device.

Conversely, low blood sugar is just as dangerous. If the child exercises strenuously and does not compensate by taking less insulin or eating extra carbohydrates or sugar, the glucose-insulin balance will be thrown off, producing a condition called *insulin shock,* which, untreated, can result in a potentially fatal coma. Treatment for low blood sugar is simple: Have the child consume sugar in a rapidly digestible form, such as orange juice, a hard candy, or a sugar cube. Be alert for the symptoms of low blood glucose, which include:

- Tingling throughout the body
- A cold or clammy feeling

Diabetes Mellitus (Insulin-Dependent Diabetes)

- Pallor
- Sweating
- Faintness
- Apprehension
- Headache
- Hunger
- Drowsiness
- Abdominal pain
- Mental confusion
- Mood changes (such as irritability)
- Rapid heartbeat
- Seizures
- Trembling

Caring for a child with diabetes

Learning the basic techniques to manage juvenile diabetes is only the first step in the child's therapy. It is also essential to accept the disease and the necessary adjustments in daily routine. Special clinics, clubs, and/or camps for children with diabetes offer children the opportunity to learn the elements of self-care among their peers. They also provide a source of emotional support to help children confront and surmount the emotional issues associated with the disease.

Diaper Rash

A newborn's sensitive skin is a poor defense against wet, soiled diapers, so most babies will probably have a diaper rash at some point. The good news is that diaper rashes are rarely serious and respond readily to home treatment.

When should I suspect that my baby has a diaper rash?

It's not hard to recognize a diaper rash. Inflamed red areas appear on the baby's skin in the region usually covered by a diaper—the lower abdomen, genitals, buttocks, and the folds of the thighs. The rash can be either dry or moist and sometimes look pimply. Left untreated, diaper rashes can become infected by a fungus or bacteria and will require the attention of a physician. You should suspect yeast infection if tiny red spots develop and eventually meld into a solid red inflamed area. Be on the alert for yeast infections if the baby is taking antibiotics, which can promote the growth of yeast. A bacterial infection can cause pus-filled pimples or oozing yellow patches and may be accompanied by a fever.

What causes a diaper rash?

The culprit is usually moisture. Infants urinate many times a day and have frequent bowel

---

PREVENTING DIAPER RASH

- Change the baby's diaper frequently.
- Gently and thoroughly clean the diaper area as soon as possible after bowel movements.
- Make sure disposable diapers or plastic pants are loose enough to allow air to circulate in the diaper.
- Apply a layer of ointment to protect the baby's bottom from accumulated moisture in the diaper. If the baby's skin is dry, use a lubricating lotion like petroleum jelly; if the skin seems moist, use a drying lotion like zinc oxide or calamine lotion.
- When the baby is ready for solid foods, introduce only one new food at a time. It will then be easier to identify and withdraw the food if it causes an allergic reaction like a diaper rash.

movements. The moisture can chafe your baby's delicate skin, while chemical substances present in urine and feces cause further irritation. Less frequently, the rash is an allergic response to disposable diapers, detergent used to launder cloth diapers, or a new food in your baby's diet.

Is medical attention necessary?

It is usually not necessary to consult a pediatrician for a simple diaper rash. Keeping your baby clean and dry should prevent most diaper rashes. If the signs of infection develop, however, a doctor's attention is in order.

What treatments are available?

Simple home remedies will clear up most diaper rashes as soon as they appear. (See "Coping with diaper rash" on this page.) The general goal should be to reduce the amount of moisture in the diaper area as much as possible.

Coping with diaper rash

- Change the baby's diapers more frequently.
- Do not use over-the-counter lotions or ointments while the baby has a rash without the advice of your doctor.
- If you use cloth diapers, don't use plastic pants until the rash is cleared up.
- Whenever possible, speed healing by leaving the baby's diaper off and exposing the skin to air.
- If you suspect an allergy to disposable diapers or detergents, try switching brands.
- Avoid using talcum powder or cornstarch. Neither is considered particularly helpful, and talcum powder can harm the lungs if inhaled.

Getting Help

CALL YOUR DOCTOR IF:

- ☐ Treatment at home does not clear up the rash after three or four days.
- ☐ The rash worsens or shows signs of infection.
- ☐ The rash begins to spread to other parts of the body.
- ☐ You suspect the rash could be due to an allergy. The doctor can help you pinpoint the possible allergen.

Earwax Buildup and Removal

Earwax (cerumen) is a yellowish-brown substance, medically known as cerumen, that is manufactured by the glands in the outer ear canal. Along with the hair that lines the canal, cerumen acts as a protective filter for the ear, blocking dust and other unwanted particles from entering the ear and damaging the sensitive organ. The amount of earwax produced and its consistency varies from person to person.

In most children, earwax works its way out of the ear naturally and painlessly. Problems develop only when large amounts accumulate and harden in the exterior canal. This blockage can prevent the child from hearing well. The condition is more bothersome than harmful and is easily remedied by removing the earwax.

- Never clean the ears with a cotton swab. This only pushes the wax deeper into the ear canal.
- Never insert anything into a child's ear. Even the most harmless-seeming object, such as a twisted piece of paper, can scratch the ear canal or perforate the eardrum.
- If the child has an ear infection, do not try to remove earwax by any method without consulting your physician first.
- If the child is predisposed to earwax buildup, periodically use hydrogen peroxide drops or flush his ears regularly (about every two months or so) to prevent blockages from developing.

When should I suspect that my child has a buildup of earwax?

If the wax in the ear remains impacted for too long, the outer canal may become irritated, resulting in an earache. In infants and toddlers, tugging at the ear and crankiness or crying often means their ear is bothering them. In the absence of an earache, however, parents may not realize their young child has an accumulation of earwax until it is detected by a physician during a routine checkup or physical examination for another illness.

Older children may complain of stuffy ears, pain, or a ringing in the ears. If the blockage has occurred gradually, the child may be unaware of diminished hearing. Parents should be attentive to signs of hearing loss, such as increased television volume or frequent requests to repeat what you have said.

Is medical attention necessary?

If you suspect that your child has excessive earwax, it is helpful to see a doctor. Although you may be able to see some wax simply by looking into the ear, the hard, blockage-causing wax accumulates farther down the canal. The physician can use an instrument called an otoscope to look into the canal and see if a buildup is causing the child's symptoms. The physician can then flush the ear to remove the wax.

What treatments are available?

Earwax can usually be removed safely at home if your doctor recommends. Have your doctor or nurse demonstrate the use of eardrops and flushing techniques.

Use a clean eyedropper to place a few drops of hydrogen peroxide into the ear to soften the wax. After three or four days of this regimen, the wax should soften enough to be flushed out with water.

A rubber bulb syringe can be purchased at a drugstore for this procedure. Fill the syringe

Getting Help

CALL YOUR DOCTOR IF YOUR CHILD:

- Experiences pain when the ear is being flushed out with water. This might indicate an infection or, more rarely, a punctured eardrum.
- Continues to complain of discomfort after irrigation or you suspect a hearing loss. If home treatment has proved ineffective, the doctor can remove the wax with a metal probe or suction device.

with warm, fresh water—not soapy water. Gently pull the ear up and back and squirt the water into the ear canal. Then tip the head to the side and allow the water and wax to drain out. The wax may come out in small pieces or a solid plug. You may need to repeat the process several times before the ear is clean.

Commercially prepared removal drops are also available and, depending on the hardness of the trapped wax, may be effective in removing the wax without irrigation.

Eczema

Eczema, or dermatitis, is a broad term used to describe dry, itchy inflammation of the skin occurring most commonly among children under the age of two. The two primary types of eczema are *atopic dermatitis* and *contact dermatitis*. The underlying cause of atopic dermatitis is dry, highly sensitive skin, but certain allergies—most commonly to foods, pollens, or house dust—are known to precipitate and aggravate the rash. Contact dermatitis, on the other hand, is an acquired allergy or irritation that develops only after a susceptible person has repeated contact with a specific substance such as poison ivy, strong soap, or other chemicals. Many cases of infantile eczema disappear by the age of three. About half of affected children, however, go on to develop asthma (see entries on **allergic rhinitis** or **hay fever**).

What causes eczema?

The causes are not completely understood, but the condition seems to run in families with a history of allergies and occur most often in children who have sensitive skin. Scratching aggravates the condition, often leading to broken skin and bacterial infection. Eczema can also be aggravated by heat, humidity, abrasion, and soaps, or psychological stress.

When should I suspect that my child has eczema?

The first signs usually develop by the age of three months. Red, scaly, sometimes oozing patches typically appear on the baby's cheeks, followed by inflammation of the scalp, arms, and legs. In toddlers and older children, the patches are drier, and they occur mainly on the neck, wrists, and ankles, and in the creases of the elbows and the knees. In severe cases, the affected skin becomes thick and leathery. Eczema rashes are extremely itchy, and they tend to make children cranky and irritable.

Contact dermatitis also causes an itchy rash, sometimes accompanied by blistering. But unlike atopic dermatitis, contact dermatitis develops only where the allergen has touched the child's body. Common contact allergens include **poison ivy, sumac,** and **oak** (see entry), as well as nickel, glues and dyes used in leather products and clothing, cosmetics, strong soaps, and certain fabrics and medications.

Is medical attention necessary?

Yes. The physician can prescribe treatment to help control the rashes. The child also may be referred to a dermatologist or an allergist for a series of tests to identify the offending allergens.

How can the pediatrician tell if my child has eczema?

The rash is usually easy to recognize. If an allergy is involved, however, it may be necessary to perform skin or blood tests to identify exact causes.

What treatments are available?

The most effective way to prevent and minimize flare-ups is to keep the child's skin moisturized, treat inflammation, and identify and remove irritating substances from the child's environment (see "Coping with eczema" on this page). The doctor can prescribe a cortisone-containing cream to relieve itching and inflammation. Once the rash is under control, treatment usually is switched to nonmedicated moisturizers to soothe the child's skin. The pediatrician also may prescribe an antihistamine to control itching. If the skin is broken and infected, a course of antibiotics may be necessary.

Coping with eczema

Eczema is essentially harmless, but it can make a child miserable. The following guidelines can help parents stop the itch-scratch-itch cycle.

- Keep fingernails and toenails short and clean to minimize scratching. If scratching is severe, wrap the baby's hands in soft cotton gloves or socks and pin them to the shirt cuffs.
- Bathe the child in lukewarm water only a few times a week, using a mild, moisturizing bath and nonsoap cleanser.
- Use skin moisturizers frequently.
- Dress the child in soft, all-cotton fabrics. Avoid wool and rough materials.

To prevent scratching of eczema or other rashes, place soft cotton mittens or socks on the baby's hands.

- Avoid hairy, furry stuffed animals and dolls.
- Launder clothes in mild detergent and rinse well.
- Avoid extremes of temperatures and excessive perspiration.
- Make sure your child gets enough rest.
- Try to identify irritating substances and eliminate them from the child's diet and environment.

Getting Help

CALL YOUR DOCTOR IF:

- ☐ There are indications of infection, such as oozing blisters, yellow crusts, severe inflammation, or fever.
- ☐ Your child comes into close contact with someone who has active cold sores, caused by a herpes infection. This can lead to possibly serious complications.

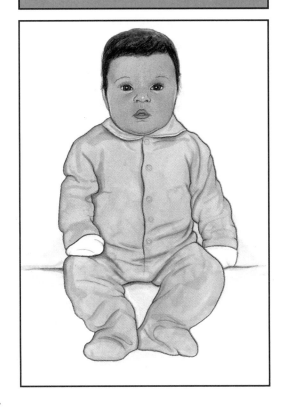

Encephalitis

Many viral infections can lead to encephalitis, or inflammation of the brain, a condition marked by fever, headache, nausea, drowsiness, speech and hearing impairment, and (in some cases) seizures and coma. The condition, while frightening, is usually not contagious, and most children who develop it survive without brain damage.

How does encephalitis develop?

Depending on its cause, encephalitis can occur as an isolated case, a localized outbreak, or an epidemic. Most often, encephalitis is a complication of a common viral infection, such as chicken pox, Coxsackie virus (which causes a severe sore throat), hepatitis, influenza, herpes, or Epstein-Barr. In the days before vaccines, encephalitis might follow a bout with measles, the mumps, polio, or rubella. Dozens of other viruses carried by mosquitos or ticks can also cause encephalitis.

When should I suspect that my child has encephalitis?

Those at highest risk for developing encephalitis are infants recovering from viral illnesses. Although some of the symptoms of encephalitis are common to many illnesses, others strongly suggest encephalitis. One such symptom is intense pain occurring when the child bends the neck forward to touch the chin to the chest. A stiff neck, back, arm, or leg also may suggest the condition. In general, however, encephalitis is a possibility any time a child suffers an apparent relapse in the final stages of recovery from a viral illness. Another clue is the speed with which symptoms develop—they may come on quite suddenly and worsen rapidly.

Is medical attention necessary?

Absolutely. If a child develops a constellation of symptoms suggesting brain inflammation, particularly after a viral illness, he should be taken to a hospital emergency room immediately.

How can the pediatrician tell if my child has encephalitis?

A child suspected of having encephalitis will be hospitalized for diagnostic tests and care. A lumbar puncture (also called a spinal tap) is performed to detect white blood cells in the cerebrospinal fluid, a sign of infection. An electroencephalogram (EEG) charts brain waves and may show a slowing of brain activity that accompanies encephalitis, and a computed tomographic scan (CT scan) can show the characteristic brain swelling. Blood tests can sometimes identify the cause of the infection.

What treatments are available?

Hospital care is mostly supportive—letting the infection run its course while keeping the child as comfortable as possible. Medications are determined by which organism is behind the infection. Antiviral drugs such as amantadine are sometimes administered; if the cause is a herpes virus, the drug acyclovir may be used. Doctors may also administer cortisone to lessen inflammation and anticonvulsants to fight seizures.

What are the chances of complete recovery?

The likelihood of complications depends upon the cause of the encephalitis. Fortunately, the more common causes have very low complication rates, and are hardly ever fatal. A few types, however, are quite dangerous. In Eastern equine encephalitis, an infection that also affects horses and is transmitted by mosquitoes, the death rate is 60 percent, and survivors are virtually always left with neurologic problems. Herpes encephalitis has a death rate of 25 percent.

Recuperation takes about two to three weeks after the child is released from the hospital. Continued bed rest is essential, along with good nutrition. If any muscles are stiff or weak, daily exercise or physical therapy may be necessary for a short while. Home care is simply a matter of regaining strength. When the child is eating and feeling well and is alert and strong, he can return to preschool or school.

Getting Help

CALL YOUR DOCTOR IF YOUR CHILD:
- ◼ Develops a headache accompanied by fever, pain when the neck is stretched, and sensitivity to bright light.
- ◼ Develops neurological symptoms (double vision, unequal pupil size, hearing impairment, personality changes) that increase in severity over several hours.

Epiglottitis

Epiglottitis is a medical emergency caused by inflammation and swelling of the epiglottis, the flap of membrane-covered cartilage lying behind the tongue that keeps food and drink from entering the windpipe. It is almost always caused by *Hemophilus influenzae* bacteria, type B. Epiglottitis develops suddenly, blocking the entrance to the windpipe; swelling also may affect the surrounding tissues of the throat, further obstructing air passage. Total obstruction can develop very rapidly, so emergency medical care is imperative.

Epiglottitis is most common in children three to seven years of age, but it also occurs in infants and adults. The greatest danger is to young children, whose air passages are narrow and therefore easily obstructed.

When should I suspect epiglottitis?

Symptoms of epiglottitis develop quickly in a previously healthy child or after a minor upper respiratory tract infection: They include:

- Sore throat and high fever (up to 105F) which appear suddenly.
- Painful swallowing and drooling.
- Irritability, agitation, and fear.
- A muffled voice that becomes scratchy or rasping as the condition worsens. The child may be completely unable to speak.
- Labored and rapid breathing, often noisy.
- Skin pallor or blueness.
- Characteristic posture: sitting up, leaning forward, mouth open, tongue protruding, and neck extended forward—a position that facilitates breathing.

- Rapid and shallow breathing as obstruction increases.
- Rapid heartbeat.

Is medical attention necessary?

Absolutely. A child with epiglottitis should be taken to an emergency room immediately. When en route to the hospital, follow these instructions:

- **DO NOT** inspect the child's throat by suppressing the child's tongue (with a spoon or another instrument). Doing so may completely block breathing.
- **DO NOT** allow the child to eat or drink.
- **DO NOT** force the child to lie down. Maintain the child's sitting position, holding him in your lap.
- Stay with and soothe the child in the emergency room while general anesthesia or other procedures are instituted.

What treatments are available?

In the hospital, an emergency X ray of the neck will be done to visualize the characteristic swelling of the epiglottis. Oxygen may be delivered via an oxygen mask. More commonly, a tube attached to a ventilator may be inserted through the child's nose into the windpipe to ensure an open airway. Once breathing is stabilized, the doctor will place the child on antibiotic therapy, (usually intravenous) to treat the underlying infection. In rare cases, a tracheostomy (an opening is made in the neck to insert a breathing tube directly into the windpipe) may be needed. Ventilation support may be withdrawn within eight to 12 hours, but in some cases is needed for several days.

PREVENTING EPIGLOTTITIS

Most cases of epiglottitis can be prevented with the HiB vaccine, which is currently given at two, four, six, and 12 to 15 months of age. (For more information, see **immunization**.)

Epilepsy/Seizure Disorder

Epilepsy, the most common neurological disorder affecting children, may be characterized by sudden, recurrent episodes of uncontrolled motor activity and, in some cases, impaired consciousness (seizures). Any condition that triggers disruptive electrical discharges in the brain can produce epilepsy. Although the underlying abnormality may not be correctable, seizures themselves can usually be controlled through drug therapy. There are a number of relatively benign genetic epilepsies of childhood, some but not all of which may be outgrown.

What causes epilepsy?

Seizures may develop as a result of a head injury, brain infection, brain tumor, drug or alcohol withdrawal or intoxication, stroke, birth trauma, or metabolic imbalance. In most cases, the underlying cause of a child's epilepsy is never discovered.

What happens during an epileptic seizure?

Epileptic seizures fall into two broad categories: generalized and partial. Generalized seizures, which involve the whole brain, fall into several subtypes. The least dramatic of these are *absence seizures* (also known as *petit mal* seizures), which consist of brief episodes of altered awareness during which the child may appear to be daydreaming. During an absence seizure, all motor activity stops, and the child stares blankly or blinks rhythmically and does not respond when touched or called by name. Absence seizures may last five to ten seconds and recur many times a day.

At the other extreme are *generalized tonic-clonic seizures* (also known as *grand mal* seizures) during which the child abruptly ceases activity, falls, and loses consciousness. During the initial phase of the seizure, lasting only a few seconds, the muscles stiffen. In the subsequent phase, the muscles undergo rhythmic, alternating contractions and partial relaxations, causing uncontrollable jerking motions (tonic-clonic seizures). Breathing may become irregular. After the seizure, which usually ends in less than five minutes, muscles relax, and the child may be confused and sleepy.

Partial seizures are categorized as simple or complex. A simple partial seizure may involve abnormal twitching, tingling, and sensory hallucinations. Consciousness is preserved and the child can often recount details of the seizures, which generally last several minutes. Complex partial seizures have a variety of manifestations, including staring, complex involuntary movements and hallucinations. They may involve a loss of consciousness.

When should I suspect that my child has had a seizure?

Tonic-clonic seizures are impossible to miss. Some of the more subtle types of seizures, however, may occur several times before parents or teachers recognize them. If the child occasionally seems unaware of his surroundings or experiences involuntary muscle contractions in one area of the body, he may have a seizure disorder.

It is important to note that the seizures some children have in association with fever do not constitute epilepsy. In addition, febrile seizures in early childhood are not usually associated with the later development of epilepsy.

Is medical attention necessary?

Yes. Any time you know or suspect that your child may have had a seizure, you should consult with a physician.

How can the pediatrician tell if my child has epilepsy?

After an initial seizure, the pediatrician (or pediatric neurologist) may order several tests, the most important of which is an electroencephalogram (EEG), a painless test that records the brain's electrical activity. It is often necessary to perform several EEG's in different circumstances (while the child is sleeping and while the child is looking at flashing lights, for example) to identify the type of seizure disorder present.

What treatments are available?

In the majority of cases, children's seizures can be satisfactorily controlled or reduced in frequency with drug therapy. The success of the therapy depends chiefly on the severity of the seizure disorder, as well as on the child's compliance in taking his medication, and on careful monitoring of blood levels by the physician.

One or more of about six different agents, called antiepileptic drugs, are generally prescribed for the treatment of epilepsy in children. Each of the drugs is useful in specific types of seizure disorders, and each has different dosage requirements and side effects that the physician takes into consideration before deciding which one to prescribe. In many cases, finding the proper medication and correct dosage level takes some time. Recent developments in specific types of brain surgery for intractable seizures offer new hope for very severe cases of epilepsy.

Erythema Infectiosum (Fifth Disease)

Around the turn of the century, doctors began numbering contagious diseases that produce somewhat similar rashes. Over time, most of these numbers fell out of use, replaced by more popular names such as measles (known in the numbering system as first disease), scarlet fever (second disease), and rubella (third disease). The only one of these illnesses to which the number stuck, in fact, was erythema infectiosum, which sometimes still goes by the name *fifth disease*. Erythema infectiosum is a mild childhood infection—so mild, in fact, that a child can have it without the parents' even noticing. Its hallmarks include a fine, pink rash covering the trunk and limbs and bright, red patches on the cheeks.

What causes fifth disease?

A highly contagious microorganism called *parvovirus B19* has been identified as the source of fifth disease. Symptoms appear between four and 14 days after a child contracts the virus. The illness often occurs in epidemics during late winter and spring. During an epidemic, as many as half of the children in a school may contract erythema infectiosum.

When should I suspect that my child has fifth disease?

Red cheeks—sometimes referred to as slapped cheeks because they look like they've recently received a sharp smack—are the most obvious sign. The patches of red, which are usually in the center of both cheeks, are slightly raised and warm to the touch.

A slightly raised, lacy, pink rash develops within a few days after the rash appears on the cheeks. It starts on the arms, then spreads to the thighs and lower legs, involving mainly exposed areas of skin. The trunk (chest, back, and abdomen) is less often affected.

PREVENTING FIFTH DISEASE

There is no way to keep a child from contracting E.I. once she has been exposed to the virus. The period of contagion is unknown, but probably prolonged. You theoretically can prevent your child from spreading the disease, however, by keeping her away from other people until both the rash and fever have disappeared. Isolation from other children is generally ineffective and unnecessary, however, because the disease is so mild and causes no complications.

Children rarely feel very ill with fifth disease. Even when the rash is present, the child may have a normal temperature and experience only minor discomfort. On the other hand, symptoms can include headache, sore throat, fatigue, mild fever, itching, and pink eyes. In rare cases, a child may feel achy in the knees and wrists.

Is medical attention necessary?

Usually it isn't. There is no specific medical treatment for fifth disease. Within five to ten days, the entire rash should fade, first from the face, then from the arms, trunk, and legs.

In some cases, days or weeks later, the rash will reappear for a short time, especially after

CARING FOR A CHILD WITH FIFTH DISEASE

- If the child has a fever, treat it with the appropriate dose of acetaminophen (Tylenol, Panadol, Tempra, Datril, and other brands) depending on the child's weight and height.
- If a stuffy nose interferes with sleeping and eating, ask your pediatrician whether the child can use an over-the-counter decongestant.
- Encourage the child to drink plenty of fluids.
- Dress the child in loose, comfortable clothing.
- Keep the child from coming in close contact with any pregnant women. Although most people have probably had fifth disease by the time they reach adulthood, a few are not immune to the virus. If a pregnant woman does contract the virus—particularly in the first trimester—it can be harmful to the fetus.

sun exposure, exercise, bathing, or being outside in the cold. This brief recurrence causes little or no discomfort.

External Ear Infections

Infections of the external ear (*otitis externa*) are characterized by redness, burning, itching, and aching in the ear canal. Sometimes the fleshy part of the outer ear (the pinna) is also involved. Otitis externa is often referred to as swimmer's ear, especially when it is a result of a fungal infection.

What causes external ear infections?

External ear infections may be caused by many different microorganisms—bacteria, fungi, yeasts, viruses, or parasites. Chances of infection taking hold are greatest if the ear is irritated and the protective, waxy lining of the ear canal is removed—a common occurrence among children who spend long periods swimming or playing in the bathtub. A break in the skin of the ear canal, caused by an insect bite or foreign object, can also set the stage for infection to develop. Allergic reactions to hair-care products sometimes inflame the ear canal and lead to infection as well.

When should I suspect that my child has an external ear infection?

Children with external ear infections may complain of itching, burning, and pain in the ear. The ear canal may look red and moist, and the entire ear may be tender to the touch.

Is medical attention necessary?

Yes. External ear infections may spread to the middle ear. They also cause intense discomfort, which easily can be relieved with proper treatment.

How can the pediatrician tell if my child has an external ear infection?

The doctor usually can identify such an infection by examining the ear with an *otoscope* (a lighted, hand-held viewing instrument). If standard treatment fails to clear the infection

---

CARING FOR A CHILD WITH AN EXTERNAL EAR INFECTION

- Administer acetaminophen (Tylenol, Panadol, Datril, and other brands) in appropriate doses for the child's age and weight to relieve pain.
- Keep the ear dry until the infection is cleared up. Avoid swimming, and cover the ear during showers and baths.

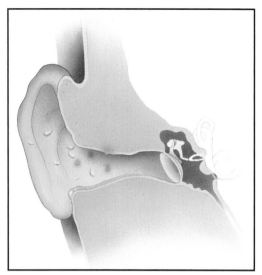

In an external ear infection, the ear canal becomes red, swollen, and moist. Pain and itching are common.

up within two days, material is scraped from the ear canal and sent to a laboratory for a culture test to determine what organism is involved.

What treatments are available?

Initial treatment consists of applying an antibiotic cream or antibiotic drops. In some cases, the doctor leaves a strip of gauze soaked in an antibiotic solution in the ear canal for about two days. If the infection seems to be caused by fungus, antifungal drops or ointment will be used.

Administering ear drops

- Have the child lie face up on a flat surface and turn the head to the side opposite the affected ear.
- Pull the fleshy part of the ear (the pinna) down and back to straighten the ear canal in a child under age three. Pull the pinna up and back in children over three.
- Hold the medication dropper in the other hand, resting the forearm, if necessary, on the head to prevent movement.
- Put the tip of the dropper in the ear and release the prescribed number of drops.
- Have the child remain lying down in the same position to allow the drops to pass down the ear canal.
- Apply slight pressure to the area just in front of the ear canal (between the jawline and the ear) to push the drops downward.

PREVENTING EXTERNAL EAR INFECTIONS

If your child has a tendency to develop frequent external ear infections, you can take the following preventive measures:

- Keep the child's ears dry.
- Do not let the child stay in the water more than one hour.
- After swimming, have the child shake her head to remove excess water. Dry the *external* part of the ear with the corner of a towel.
- **NEVER** attempt to clean a child's ears with cotton swabs, hair pins, or other long objects. Such objects can injure the skin of the ear canal, remove the oil that protects the canal, and puncture the ear drum.

Fetal Alcohol Syndrome (FAS)

The term fetal alcohol syndrome (FAS) refers to a cluster of physical, mental, and behavioral abnormalities associated with prenatal exposure of the fetus to alcohol, which occurs when a pregnant woman drinks heavily. Babies with FAS display distinctive physical characteristics, including a short, upturned nose that has a flat or sunken bridge, small eye sockets, an abnormally small head, and a thin upper lip. They also may show signs of developmental deficiencies such as abnormally low birth weight and slowed growth after birth, as well as central nervous system symptoms such as hyperactivity, mental retardation, and poor motor coordination. The severity and type of abnormalities depend on the amount of alcohol consumed and the fetus's stage of development during heaviest consumption. Children born to mothers who are alcoholics are particularly subject to FAS.

Fetal alcohol effects (FAE) are a less severe form of FAS. Children with FAE may have low birthweights, some physical malformations, and behavioral and learning problems.

Fetal alcohol syndrome is one of the three most widely known causes of birth defects and mental retardation. It affects one in 750 babies born—or 5,000 children each year. Fetal alcohol effects are believed to occur in many more infants. Some estimates indicate evidence of FAE in one out of every 300 to 400 births and perhaps up to 35,000 children a year. Drinking alcohol during pregnancy is *the* primary preventable cause of birth defects in this country. It is estimated that ten to 15 percent of children with mild mental retardation also have FAS or FAE.

How does FAS develop?

Alcohol is a depressant. Since it crosses the placenta from mother to fetus, it depresses the fetus's central nervous system, affecting growth and development. Alcohol is normally metabolized in the liver and eliminated through the digestive system; however, in a developing fetus, the liver is not fully formed, and alcohol may remain in the fetus long after the mother's liver has eliminated it from her body. If the mother consumes alcohol during critical developmental stages, the chances of birth defects are increased.

It is not known precisely how much alcohol a mother must consume for her baby to develop FAS or FAE, but it seems that there is a relationship between the amount of alcohol consumed and the severity of the birth defects. The timing of the drinking is also crucial. Drinking during the early months of pregnancy may be particularly dangerous since that is when brain development takes place.

Alcohol consumed in large quantities anytime during pregnancy may lead to FAS. Daily alcohol consumption is not necessary for FAS to develop; one or two episodes of binge drinking may, in some cases, interfere with fetal development.

Even moderate alcohol consumption during pregnancy may cause fetal alcohol effects. Some studies indicate that as little as one or two drinks each day may increase risk of miscarriage, stillbirth, or birth defects. Although an occasional drink during pregnancy is not likely to cause birth defects, many physicians and other experts (including the Surgeon General and the National Council on Alcoholism) advise pregnant women to abstain from drinking altogether. Since the fetus seems most susceptible to the effects of alcohol during the first trimester, some physicians advise women not to drink while trying to conceive.

What treatments are available?

Children with FAS often require extra medical care, special education, and assistance in daily living. They may have trouble forming lasting

---

DRINKING DURING BREAST FEEDING

Breast feeding folklore has long held that drinking a beer or a glass of wine before nursing enhances the let-down reflex, which makes milk flow into the breasts. Unfortunately, recent evidence suggests that this practice may have the unintended result of delivering a healthy dose of alcohol right to the baby. In addition, heavy drinking may reduce the amount of milk available to an infant. Although an occasional drink (one to three a week) will probably do no harm, the current recommendations by groups like the National Council on Alcoholism advise nursing mothers to continue to abstain from alcohol.

---

relationships with others and may not be able to participate actively in family or community life.

Careful attention to the needs of children with FAS can improve their life chances. It is critical that their parents or foster adoptive parents respond to their developmental and behavioral needs with direct and prompt intervention.

Getting Help

CALL YOUR DOCTOR IF:
☐ You are pregnant or are contemplating pregnancy and you have questions or concerns about your alcohol consumption.

Food Allergies

All allergies, whether caused by food, inhaled substances, or substances that come in contact with the skin, are the result of an immune-system reaction similar to an attack against a bacterium or virus. About 90 percent of children's food allergies are triggered by milk, eggs, peanuts, wheat, or soy products. Other common food allergy triggers are nuts, fish, and shellfish. Less than five percent of infants and children have food allergies. Allergy to eggs or milk is often outgrown by the third year of life.

What happens during an allergic reaction to food?

Food may trigger classic allergic responses such as hives (large, itchy, red bumps on the skin), rashes, and respiratory problems. In the worst cases, they may cause severe swelling in the throat and a rapid drop in blood pressure, a pattern known as anaphylaxis. Some people with food allergies develop mainly gastrointestinal symptoms, which may include nausea, vomiting, diarrhea, gas, and bloating.

Sometimes, a more mild reaction known as food intolerance is mistaken for a food allergy. A food intolerance produces digestive symptoms similar to those caused by some food allergies, but intolerance is a result of direct effects of food components, rather than an immune system response. The most common food intolerance is lactose intolerance, an inborn inability to digest the sugar in milk. Another recently recognized food intolerance is to a sweet substance called sorbitol that is abundant in pear, cherry, and prune juices and some candies. Sorbitol intolerance can cause chronic diarrhea, gas, and abdominal pain, particularly in children who drink several cups of juice a day.

What causes food allergies?

In an allergy, a substance perceived as a threat (usually a specific antigen found in a particular food) binds to the *IgE* type of antibody (a protein produced by the white blood cells). IgE in turn binds to cells called *mast cells.* The clinging IgE complex causes the mast cells to release several chemicals called histamines. (These are the chemicals that antihistamine drugs fight.) Histamine exerts powerful effects on the body. When it penetrates the skin, fiery red welts rise up. Elsewhere, histamine stuffs up noses and bring tears to the eyes. In rare cases, histamine release can cause anaphylactic shock.

CARING FOR THE CHILD WITH FOOD ALLERGIES

- Be certain to alert the day care provider or preschool teacher of the child's allergy.
- Teach the child which foods to avoid.
- Be sure that the child knows never to eat food from someone else's lunch box.
- Consider having the child wear a medical necklace or bracelet warning of the allergy, especially if there is a history of severe symptoms.
- Ask your doctor if any over-the-counter medications can be used to deal with symptoms.
- If the child's allergic response is mild, check with your doctor about a trial of the offending food every six months or so.
- If the child's reactions are life-threatening, ask about having an epinephrine (Adrenalin) injector at home.

Is medical attention necessary?

Yes, particularly if a child has a severe reaction to a food. Reactions with widespread redness of the skin, hives, wheezing, hoarseness, low blood pressure, or severe vomiting or diarrhea may be quite dangerous. If there is any doubt at all about which is the offending food, the pediatrician may refer you for evaluation by an allergist who may do limited skin testing to help identify which foods in a meal caused the symptoms. Sometimes the suspect food needs to be fed in the office to confirm sensitivity. Feeding of suspect foods at home is to be avoided because of the possibility of provoking a severe reaction.

What treatments are available?

The primary treatment for food allergies is simply to avoid the responsible foods, but this can be difficult, particularly if you eat in restaurants or purchase packaged food.

Parents of children who have had severe reactions (anaphylactic shock) should ask the pediatrician about injection devices for epinephrine (Adrenalin). This is the first-line drug for such reactions. Children with severe reactions should also have a Medic-Alert® tag to identify their problem in the absence of parents. Children who only have very mild reactions may benefit from oral antihistamines when they are accidently exposed to the food.

Getting Help

CALL YOUR DOCTOR IF:

◼ Your child tends to develop specific symptoms with an hour of eating certain foods.

Flatfoot

Flatfoot is the absence of an arch in the foot. All babies are born with flat feet, but normal arches usually develop around the age of two-and-a-half years.

A flat foot often looks normal when no weight is placed on it, but the arch disappears when weight bearing is applied. Therefore, many parents of children with flat feet become concerned only when they see the unusual width of their toddler's wet footprints. They fear that flatfoot will lead to future disability.

Fortunately, such worry is usually unnecessary.

To maintain balance when learning to stand or walk, babies hold their feet wide apart in a position that distributes body weight over the entire foot, including the arch, so they appear to be flatfooted. However, as a child grows and becomes more stable, she usually brings her feet closer together, shifting the weight toward the center of the foot. In some children, this transition does not occur because of the true anatomical abnormality of flatfoot.

When should I suspect that my child has flatfoot?

Conduct a quick test: try to place a finger under the child's arch while she is standing; if the finger does not fit, the arch is too low. If more than one finger can fit under the arch, it is probably too high. (If the arch is exaggerated and the tips of the toes are turned under, the deformity is referred to as **clubfoot;** see separate entry.)

Some infants give the false appearance of flatfoot because of a fatty pad below the arch. If they stand on tiptoe a normal-looking arch usually becomes apparent.

Is medical attention necessary?

If the child still has flatfoot beyond two-and-a-half years of age, he may try to compensate for the strain the foot abnormality places on the ligaments and muscles. As a result, the child may develop aching feet and legs, muscle cramps in the calves at night, and **toeing in** (see separate entry) to avoid strain. In addition, the child may become easily fatigued and avoid strenuous activity.

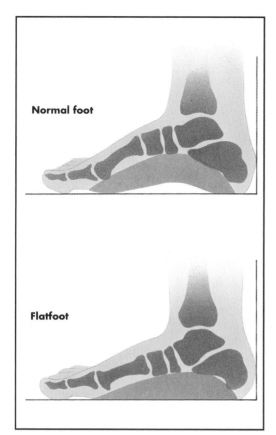

Flatfoot is the absence of an arch in the foot.

Special care is necessary only if the child has an abnormal gait or foot pain. Here are some recommendations:

- Avoid shoes with strong foot support (such as high-top or rigid boots), which may prevent the arch from forming normally.
- Ask the pediatrician about shoe inserts or another device to alleviate foot strain.
- Ask the pediatrician about foot exercises. Opinions vary as to whether such exercises can strengthen the arch. Some physicians recommend having the child walk on tiptoe five to ten minutes a day or pick up marbles with the toes.

What causes flatfoot?

Flatfoot sometimes runs in the family, in which case it is caused by hereditary looseness or weakness of the ligaments and muscles that support the foot. Young children with flatfoot often have other lax joints, including the knees, elbows, wrists, and thumbs. They may, for instance, be able to bend the thumb against the surface of the forearm.)

What treatments are available?

Flatfoot requires treatment only if it causes discomfort to the child. Simple measures will usually relieve symptoms, although they may be needed for several years (until the muscles and ligaments mature and properly support the foot) or, in some cases, for life. These measures include:

- A felt, rubber, or leather pad placed under the inner sole of the shoe.
- Corrective shoes with arched metal prostheses or special heel wedges called *Thomas heel.*

In rare cases in which the foot is too rigid rather than too lax, and has a bony abnormality in place of the arch, flatfoot may require more aggressive treatment.

Food Poisoning

Food poisoning, a type of gastroenteritis (digestive tract inflammation) caused by eating contaminated food, results in severe abdominal cramps, repeated vomiting, diarrhea, and muscle weakness. These symptoms develop suddenly between three and 24 hours after the food is consumed.

Some types of food poisoning are quite dangerous, especially to infants and small children. Fortunately, proper handling and storage of food can usually prevent the problem.

How does food poisoning develop?

Food poisoning is generally caused by bacteria allowed to multiply in improperly refrigerated or stored food. Some microbes, such as *Staphylococcus,* release toxins that inflame the stomach, causing nausea and vomiting. *Salmonella* bacteria (commonly found in raw eggs and shellfish and responsible for many cases of food poisoning) act directly on the intestinal lining, causing painful cramping. Shigella, another food-borne microbe, is responsible for severe diarrhea (dysentery).

In babies, food poisoning is often caused by E. coli bacteria, which are passed from contaminated fluids in bottles. Botulism, a potentially deadly form of food poisoning that ultimately leads to paralysis, is caused by a toxin produced by the bacterium *Clostridium botulinum* in cans that have not been sealed properly.

Another form of botulism known as infant botulism is caused by bacterial spores sometimes found in honey. If the baby eats infected honey, the organism may produce toxin in the digestive tract. This type of botulism produces constipation, hunger, thirst, listlessness, loss of muscle tone, and inability to suck in children under a year of age. In severe cases, the respiratory muscles of the chest become paralyzed, requiring artificial respiration until recovery.

When should I suspect that my child has food poisoning?

It can be hard to distinguish food poisoning from **viral gastroenteritis** (see entry). The symptoms of food poisoning may come on more suddenly, however, and other members of the household (or classmates) who ate the same food also will be affected.

Is medical attention necessary?

Yes. The younger the child, the greater the risks of complications such as dehydration. Call your pediatrician if your infant has vomiting and diarrhea. A baby who has been vomiting and had diarrhea for six hours or longer should be taken to an emergency room. With

---

PREVENTING FOOD POISONING

- Discard all food that has been improperly prepared or stored, even if it does not look or smell bad.
- Don't assume that a thorough reheating will kill all bacteria in improperly stored food. Staphylococcus bacteria, for example, release a toxin that is resistant to heat.
- Refrigerate leftovers before they cool down. If food is cooled or reheated slowly, salmonella can reproduce.
- Hot mayonnaise is a notorious breeding ground for bacteria. It's best to leave mayonnaise-based salads out of the picnic basket on hot summer days.
- Leave foods that could spoil out of your child's lunch box.
- Never give honey to an infant under a year old.

For one- to six-year-olds:

- Be certain that a child recovering from food poisoning gets plenty of rest.
- Follow the doctor's instructions for replacing fluids lost through diarrhea and vomiting. Many doctors recommend solutions such as Pedialyte.
- Withhold food until the doctor instructs you to resume feedings.
- Reintroduce other fluids gradually, starting with clear soup, tea, gelatin, and flat soda. Avoid milk for a while.
- Proceed to rice cereal and potatoes after a day or two of the clear diet.
- Let the child resume a normal diet in about three days.

For infants:

- Continue breast feeding (if you normally do so), but cut out formula feedings and solid feedings for as long as the doctor recommends. Infants are more likely than older children to need hospitalization and intravenous feedings.

an older child, you can wait a little longer to see if symptoms abate, but if they do not improve within 24 hours, see a doctor.

What treatments are available?

Hospitalization may be necessary to administer intravenous fluids until the body has rid itself of the poison. Both forms of botulism can be treated by administration of an antitoxin that neutralizes the bacterial toxin responsible for the symptoms.

Genetic Disorders

More than 5,000 different genetic disorders have been identified in humans. Some, such as cystic fibrosis and muscular dystrophy, are so serious that people who risk passing them to the next generation may choose not to have children. Others, such as color blindness, are completely benign. In between are a wide range of conditions, the precise causes of which scientists are now beginning to unravel.

What causes genetic disorders?

A genetic disorder is caused by a mutation, or change, in a gene. A gene is a sequence of building blocks of deoxyribonucleic acid (DNA) that instructs a cell to manufacture a particular protein. Genes are arranged on 23 pairs of chromosomes located in the cell's nucleus.

How do genetic disorders develop?

The symptoms of some genetic diseases are caused by an abnormal or absent protein, which in turn is caused by a defect in the gene that tells the cells to produce that protein. The genetic mutations that give rise to genetic disorders may be passed from one generation to another or arise spontaneously in the reproductive cells (sperm and egg) that unite at conception to form a new individual. When the mutation occurs spontaneously, the affected child is the first in the family to have the condition.

Genetic diseases are transmitted in three main patterns—dominant, recessive, and sex-linked. Both parents must carry and pass on the same defective gene to transmit a recessive disorder to their children. Only one parent must carry a defective gene for a dominant disorder to be transmitted. Sex-linked disorders are passed from mother to son on the X chromosome, one of the two chromosomes that determines gender. Geneticists estimate that all people have at least seven or more recessive mutant genes, but the chance of two unrelated people having the same mutant gene is very low.

Another type of condition involving heredity occurs when a child receives an abnormal number of chromosomes. Down syndrome, for example, arises when an embryo's cells contain one extra chromosome. These conditions, however, are not passed through the generations in predictable patterns. Instead, they are the result of accidental errors in chromosome distribution occurring at conception.

One final type of genetic disorder is caused by an inherited predisposition which, when combined with a particular environmental trigger, produces symptoms. Many common diseases, such as diabetes and heart disease, are believed to have this type of genetic component.

When should I suspect that my child has a genetic disorder?

Possible symptoms of genetic disorders are extremely wide ranging. Rather than worrying about these disorders after children are born, parents should review their family medical histories—on both sides—before having children. Do your aunts, uncles, and siblings (and their children) have any particular disorders in common? If so, find out everything you can about the disorder, and mention it to your physician when you start planning your own family.

Is medical attention necessary?

Yes. If there is an identified genetic disorder in your family or your partner's, ask your doctor for a referral to a genetic counselor or medical geneticist. In recent years, scientists have developed tests to determine whether individuals carry specific disease genes that run in their families. Such tests can help prospective parents make their own choices about having children. Some common genetic diseases can also be detected prenatally in the fetus.

What treatments are available?

Unfortunately, there is currently no way to correct a defective gene. Improved therapies, however, are giving children with serious genetic disorders longer, more comfortable lives.

The outlook may improve even more in the next few decades. Researchers the world over are in the process of conducting a huge study, called the human genome project, in which all of the genes that make a human are undergoing systematic analysis. This project has already spawned numerous diagnostic tests and experimental treatments. Researchers are now working on ways to deliver healthy genes or proteins precisely where they are needed in the bodies of afflicted individuals.

Gonorrhea, Congenital

Of all venereal diseases for which statistics are kept in the United States, gonorrhea is the most common. It is caused by *Gonococcus* bacteria, and its symptoms range from a mild discharge to a widespread infection affecting the joints, the Fallopian tubes in women, the eyes, the throat, and other organs.

Gonorrhea is referred to as *congenital* when it is passed from an infected mother to her newborn baby. A baby with congenital gonorrhea may develop an infection in the eyes, throat, and anus. A newborn with a widespread congenital infection may also develop arthritis.

Eye infection (referred to as *gonococcal ophthalmia*) can lead to blindness. At the turn of the last century, it accounted for almost one-fourth of cases of blindness in the United States. Since then its incidence has dropped sharply, because of widespread use of prophylactic treatment in the delivery room. All newborns receive an installation of silver nitrate or erythromycin eye drops to prevent gonococcal ophthalmia.

What causes congenital gonorrhea?

Gonorrhea is transmitted between adults through sexual activity. A baby born to a mother with gonorrhea can become infected while passing through the infected birth canal. Less commonly, the fetus may become infected while in the womb, if the membranes rupture; some newborns delivered by cesarean section after membrane rupture may develop gonococcal eye disease. When infection occurs in the womb, no preventive measures can be taken. A newborn baby may also become accidentally infected after birth through contact with an infected mother or another individual with gonorrhea.

When should I suspect that my child has congenital gonorrhea?

Obstetricians routinely test expectant mothers for a number of infections, including gonorrhea. If the mother is infected, she will be treated before giving birth.

If the infection is not detected in the mother, the baby may show symptoms of eye disease within three days after delivery. Look for a watery discharge that quickly thickens and may contain pus and blood; the discharge may cause the eyelashes to stick to one another. Usually, both eyes are affected. The baby's eyelids swell; sometimes the swelling spreads to the eye itself or the area around it. Ulcers may appear on the cornea. Early treatment is imperative to cure the disease promptly.

The bacteria may spread through the eye to other organs, causing widespread infection, arthritis, or even cardiac inflammation. Symptoms of gonococcal arthritis usually occur in the first one to four weeks after birth; they may include fever, rash, joint tenderness, and swelling.

Is medical attention necessary?

Call your pediatrician if the newborn develops any of the following signs:

- A discharge from the eyes.
- Swollen eyelids and sticky eyelashes.
- Swollen, warm, and tender joints.

What treatments are available?

As soon as the disease is diagnosed, the infant must be hospitalized. The child will receive injections of penicillin for seven to ten days. The joints of a newborn with gonococcal arthritis usually must be drained of fluids and pus. Eye infection requires frequent baths with a sterile saltwater solution to remove discharge. In addition, an antibiotic ointment may be applied. The eye disorder usually resolves within several days.

In the past 20 years, some strains of gonococcal bacteria have developed resistance to penicillin. If so, the disease will respond to other antibiotics.

Preventing congenital gonorrhea

The key to preventing congenital gonorrhea is to detect the disease in the expectant mother before it can pass to the baby. These techniques are used:

- Testing material from the cervix for gonococcal infection at the mother's first prenatal visit.
- Taking a second cervical culture later in the pregnancy, for women at high risk for gonorrhea.
- Taking oral and rectal cultures from infants born to a mother with untreated gonorrhea to check for the presence of infection.
- Administering Ceftriaxone to full-term infants born to a mother with gonorrhea.
- Treating the eyes of all newborn infants with antibiotic drops or a silver nitrate solution to prevent gonococcal ophthalmia.

Hair Pulling, Compulsive

Many children deliberately pull out bits of hair once in a while. Such behavior is similar to other self-soothing rituals such as stroking a lock of hair or a favorite stuffed animal. Occasionally, however, hair pulling turns into a compulsive habit. Children who fall into this habit can end up plucking out enough hair to leave bald spots on the scalp and in the eyebrows.

What causes compulsive hair pulling?

Causes vary from child to child, but compulsive hair pulling almost always is related to anxiety. Whether it's the result of family troubles, difficulties at preschool and play, or more deeply seated emotional conflicts, anxiety upsets a child's sense of well-being. Engaging in hair pulling helps some children cope with this discomfort.

When should I suspect that my child is pulling out hair compulsively?

Patchy bald spots in easy-to-reach areas of the scalp are often the first clue. You may also observe the child in the act of pulling out hair. If the child complains of stomachache, she may also be swallowing strands of scalp hair. Hair loss alone, however, does not necessarily signal hair-pulling behavior. Other scalp ailments also can cause patchy hair loss. (For instance, see entry on **ringworm.**)

Is medical attention necessary?

Yes; professional attention is usually needed to help compulsive hair pullers overcome their anxiety and find better ways to cope with stress. The first step is a visit to a pediatrician, who will examine the child and try to identify the stresses underlying the problem. Next, the doctor may refer the family to a child psychiatrist, psychologist, or some other trained counselor.

What treatments are available?

Mild cases may respond to simple behavioral intervention. Parents may, for example, be shown how to set up a system to reward the child for every day she does not engage in hair pulling. The pediatrician may also apply a coating substance (collodion) to the child's bald patches to stop further hair pulling.

Getting Help

CALL YOUR PEDIATRICIAN IF:

■ You see your child pulling hair from her scalp on a daily basis.
■ You notice bald patches on your child's scalp, particularly around the hairline.
■ Your child keeps pulling out her hair in spite of your attempts to discourage it.
■ Your child repeatedly swallows hair after pulling it out.

Some type of counseling is usually recommended to address underlying sources of anxiety. Such counseling generally involves the family and begins with an evaluation of the child's interactions with parents, teachers, siblings, and peers.

Head Banging

Babies use a number of techniques to calm or soothe themselves. Some suck a thumb, others stroke a blanket or rock themselves to and fro. Some may even bang their heads repeatedly against the sides of cribs and similar hard, immobile objects. Distressing as this habit may be, it serves the same purpose as thumb sucking and similar rituals, and most babies outgrow it before their fourth year. Anywhere from five to 15 percent of normal babies do it. For unknown reasons, three-fourths of all head bangers are boys. Many babies combine head banging with rhythmic rocking. Although these activities may look strange, they are generally harmless and, in most cases, safe to ignore.

How does head banging develop?

Head banging usually appears during the first year of life. At some point in the process of learning about themselves, babies may discover that the combination of motion and other sensations associated with head banging is pleasurable or soothing. As a result, they may bang their heads to calm themselves during stressful times. Overstimulation seems to trigger head banging in some babies, although in some situations babies may bang their heads as a type of stimulation. Head banging often shows up for the first time during periods when mobility is restrained, such as during an illness or following an injury.

What causes head banging?

Although there are many theories, no one knows the real cause. Head banging is found among all sorts of children, those who are physically and emotionally fine as well as youngsters with developmental disabilities and sensory impairments. One thing that babies who bang their heads share is a need for repetitive activity, often in preparation for sleep.

Is medical attention necessary?

Usually it isn't, although you may want to mention head banging to your pediatrician during a well-baby visit to find out his or her opinions about the behavior. Unless it is excessive, most doctors advise parents against trying to stop their child's head banging. If there is any risk of injury, measures such as padding the sides of the crib may be recommended.

The pediatrician may ask about the baby's daily routines to identify any unrecognized sources of stress that could contribute to the behavior. He or she also may suggest certain types of parent-baby play designed to promote the baby's optimal development, thus reducing the need for frequent, prolonged head banging. Finally, if the baby persists in head banging after the age of three, a visit to a child psychologist may be in order.

What treatments are available?

Children with developmental disabilities who engage in severe head banging may need med-

ication to control the habit. Children sometimes wear helmets to prevent injuries as well.

Psychologists treating older children for excessive head banging begin by identifying and
trying to eliminate the sources of stress that
trigger the behavior. A behavioral program
that rewards avoidance of head banging may
also be instituted.

Getting Help

CALL YOUR DOCTOR IF YOUR BABY:

- Engages in long periods of head
  banging and seems uninterested in
  his surroundings.
- Can be soothed only by banging
  his head.
- Does not respond to your efforts
  to soothe him.

Head Lice

Head lice were nearly eradicated in the 1940s
through the use of strong pesticides like DDT.
Since pesticide use in people has been banned,
however, these annoying parasites have come
back with a vengeance. The good news about
head lice, however, is that they don't carry disease and that they are easily treated.

Lice are highly contagious; they can spread
between people who have never met via upholstered theater seats, department store
clothing, or coat checkrooms. In the presence
of a head louse, no child or adult is invulner-
able—no matter how scrupulous the family's
hygiene.

Although head lice can strike any one at any
age, they are most common among school
children because schools have communal coat
closets, where lice spread easily among closely
hung hats, scarves, and jackets. The practice of
sharing hair ornaments, common in school-
age girls, also promotes the spread of lice.

When should I suspect head lice?

Look for the following signs:

- Intense scalp itching, particularly behind
  the ears and along the hair line at the back of
  the neck; the itching results from a skin reaction to the saliva of the lice.
- Lice eggs (nits), which appear as tiny, silvery
  clumps virtually cemented to the hair shaft
  near the roots.

Is medical attention necessary?

Yes. If your child has head lice, you will probably be able to tell; the signs are hard to miss.
For treatment recommendations, though, it is
best to consult a physician.

What treatments are available?

Unfortunately, there is no single-step method
for curing lice infestation. You will have to follow each of these steps.

- Kill the adults with a lice-killing shampoo,
  applied vigorously. Dangerous kerosene
  shampoos, used in the past, have been replaced by *pyrethrin shampoos*, which are
  available without prescription. Pyrethrin is
  a natural pesticide that is deadly to lice but
  safe for people.
- Follow the antilice treatment with a regular
  shampoo.

To remove any surviving lice or nits (which can take as long as a month to hatch), observe the following procedures:

- Immediately sterilize all personal clothing, bed linens, and stuffed animals belonging to the infested child. Wash them in hot water (at least 130 degrees Fahrenheit), dry them in the sun or put them in a hot dryer for at least 20 minutes, or have them dry-cleaned.
- Vacuum all upholstered furniture thoroughly and treat with Lysol or lice spray. Do the same for rugs, and other objects that cannot be cleansed in the washing machine.
- Check all other family members for lice and nits; follow the same procedures on any other infested person.

- Teach your child not to share combs, brushes, hats, or other clothing.
- If your child's day-care center or preschool has only open coat closets, ask about the possibility of installing individual lockers or cubbies.

Getting Help

CALL YOUR DOCTOR IF:
- ☐ Scratching has caused open sores on the scalp.
- ☐ A child under two is affected.
- ☐ Itching is so unbearable that medication is necessary.
- ☐ You are not sure whether lice are the cause of the problem.

- Pick the nits with a fine-tooth comb, removing *every* egg bonded to the hair shaft. It may help to dip the comb in a solution of equal parts vinegar and water to loosen the nits. Start removing the nits while the hair is still wet. Part hair into four sections. Then pull up a one-inch tuft and comb it carefully from base to tip. Comb meticulously, frequently wiping nits from the comb with a tissue. Keep the hair wet during the process. The process can take an hour or longer if the child has long, thick hair, so provide some distraction—such as TV or a video game. A week to ten days later, repeat the entire process to catch any nits missed on the first round.
- If lice have settled on the eyelashes, apply petroleum jelly three or four times a day to banish them within a week.

Heart Defects, Congenital

In the first eight weeks after conception, the fetal heart changes from a kind of primitive, coiled tube into a complex, functioning organ. Many things can go wrong in this process. The partitions between the heart's chambers may fail to develop properly, leaving abnormal connections between the two sides of the heart, or the valves connecting the chambers may be displaced, narrowed, or completely closed. Blood-vessel abnormalities may occur as well. Finally, the baby's heart and circulatory system may fail to make the necessary adaptations to life outside the womb.

Malformations such as these are known as *congenital heart defects,* and they occur in about eight of every one thousand babies born. Over 35 specific congenital heart defects have been identified; for descriptions of the most common defects, see the accompanying chart. Some of these abnormalities may not be noticed until late infancy or even early childhood.

What causes congenital heart defects?

In 90 percent of cases, no cause can yet be identified. Heredity plays a role; a child whose parent (especially the mother) has a congenital heart defect stands a slightly increased chance of a cardiac abnormality. Certain congenital heart defects tend to occur as part of well-identified chromosomal abnormalities such as Down syndrome. A small percentage of cases stem from infections such as *rubella* (German measles) the mother contracted during pregnancy. The mother's use of alcohol during pregnancy also is associated with congenital heart defects, as is the use of medications to control epilepsy. These defects also occur in greater than expected numbers among babies whose mothers have diabetes or are over 40.

The vast majority of congenital heart defects are thought to stem from a combination of genetic and environmental factors.

When should I suspect that my baby has a congenital heart defect?

In about one-third of cases, a heart defect is apparent to the pediatrician and newborn-care nurses in the hospital shortly after birth. Some cases are identified by a fetal electrocardiogram as early as the fourth month of pregnancy. Such babies may have bluish skin caused by oxygen deprivation, abnormal heart sounds, or congestive heart failure, a condition caused by the heart's inability to pump enough blood to meet the body's needs.

After the baby is home from the hospital, feeding problems, fatigue, irritability, and poor weight gain become apparent. In toddlers, poor appetite, short stature, lower weight, decreased energy, and frequent respiratory infections are common.

DIAGNOSING HEART DEFECTS

A technique called *two-dimensional echo cardiography* is used to diagnose most heart defects. This test, which is similar to ultrasound, produces a cross-sectional image of the heart, and provides information about the pattern and rate of blood flow within the heart. In some instances, echocardiography has been used successfully to diagnose fetal heart defects before birth.

Doctors in a few medical centers are also experimenting with magnetic resonance imaging (MRI)—a technique that converts radio waves from chemicals in the body into computer generated images of tissues—to evaluate some types of heart defects.

In complex cases, cardiac catheterization is necessary. After contrast dyes are injected into the heart's circulation through a catheter, the cardiologist takes still and moving X-ray pictures of blood as it passes through the heart. Such information is often essential for planning corrective surgery.

How can the pediatrician tell whether my child has a heart defect?

During regular checkups, the pediatrician looks for signs that suggest heart defects. If anything suggests heart disease, a visit with a pediatric heart specialist (cardiologist) is in order. Often, a heart murmur (see page 116) is the finding that leads to a consultation.

What treatments are available?

The treatment depends on the type of defect. A small hole in the wall between the heart's lower chambers (known medically as a *ventricular septal defect* or *VSD*) may close by itself without treatment. A slightly narrowed heart valve may cause no symptoms except a heart murmur and thus require no treatment.

More severe defects (such as a large ventricular septal defect) are usually corrected with surgery. The operation may be postponed until the second or third month of life—or, in some cases, even later.

The majority of complicated heart defects require open-heart surgery. Fortunately, most of these operations have a high success rate, often bringing immediate and dramatic improvements in the child's condition. In addition, new surgical procedures that do not require opening the heart are currently being developed.

Medication may be needed until the child undergoes surgery. Children with heart defects are at high risk of developing endocarditis (an infection of the heart lining), so they need antibiotics before having dental work or any type of operation. Even after corrective surgery, preventive use of antibiotics is still advisable.

COMMON CONGENITAL HEART DEFECTS	
TYPE	DESCRIPTION
Ventricular septal defect	Abnormal opening between the two lower chambers
Patent ductus arteriosus	The passage through which blood bypasses the lungs during fetal development fails to close after birth
Persistent truncus arteriosus	Coronary, pulmonary and systemic arteries all arise from a single artery at the base of the heart.
Pulmonary stenosis	Narrowing of the opening of the artery that carries blood from the heart to the lungs
Atrial septal defect	Abnormal opening between the two upper chambers
Coarctation of the aorta	Narrowing of the aorta, the large vessel that carries blood from the heart to the body
Aortic stenosis	Narrowing of the valve between the lower left heart chamber and the aorta
Tetralogy of Fallot	Four associated defects: a ventricular septal defect; pulmonary stenosis; displaced aorta; and enlargement of the lower right chamber
Transposition of the great arteries	Displacement of the aorta and pulmonary arteries so that each originates on the wrong side of the heart

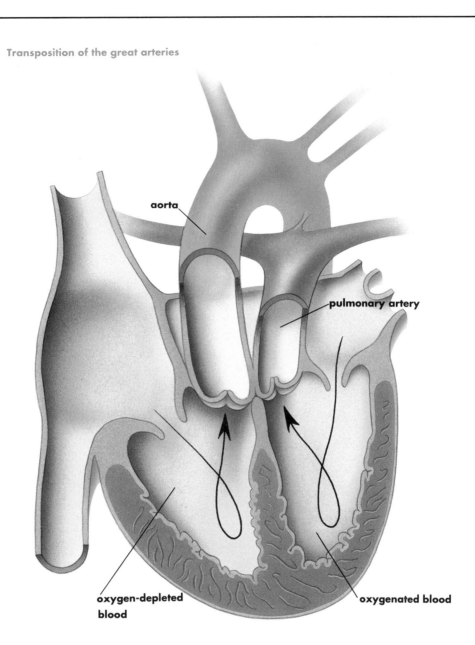

aorta

pulmonary artery

oxygen-depleted
blood

oxygenated blood

The aorta and pulmonary artery are reversed,
so that oxygenated blood is continuously
recirculated to the lungs and oxygen-depleted
blood is continuously recirculated to the body.

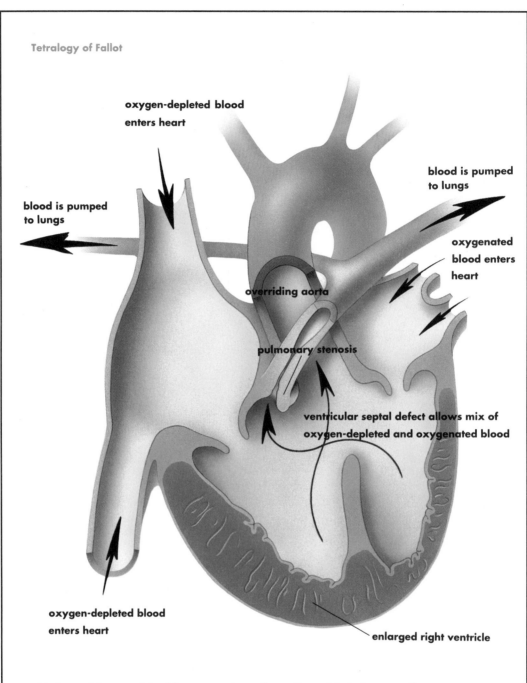

Tetralogy of Fallot

oxygen-depleted blood
enters heart

blood is pumped
to lungs

blood is pumped
to lungs

oxygenated
blood enters
heart

overriding aorta

pulmonary stenosis

ventricular septal defect allows mix of
oxygen-depleted and oxygenated blood

oxygen-depleted blood
enters heart

enlarged right ventricle

This heart defect consists of four separate malformations: A hole between the
right and left ventricles (ventricular septal defect); narrowing of the artery between
the right ventricle and the lungs (pulmonary stenosis); an enlarged right ventricle;
and location of the aorta directly over the ventricular septal defect (overriding aorta).

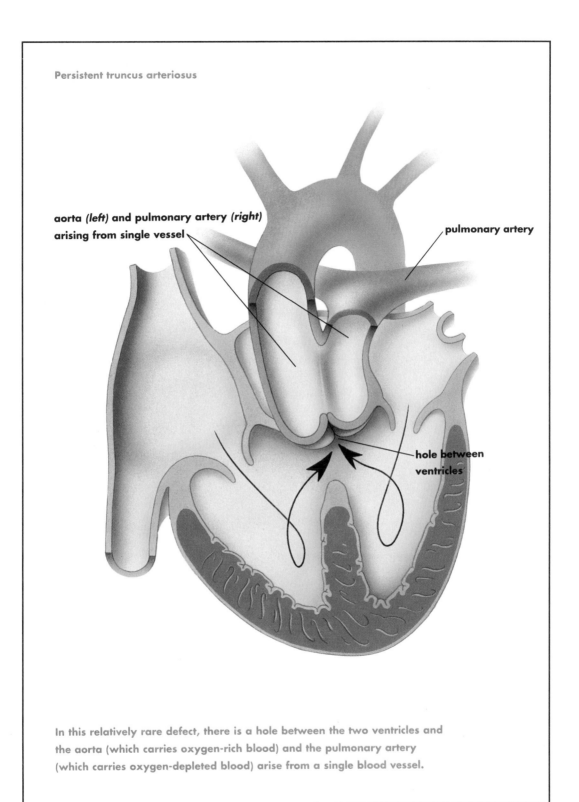

aorta *(left)* and pulmonary artery *(right)* arising from single vessel

pulmonary artery

hole between ventricles

In this relatively rare defect, there is a hole between the two ventricles and the aorta (which carries oxygen-rich blood) and the pulmonary artery (which carries oxygen-depleted blood) arise from a single blood vessel.

Heart Murmurs

A heart murmur is an abnormal heart sound detected when a doctor listens to the heart through a stethoscope. Some heart murmurs are signs of heart defects such as a hole between two chambers of the heart or a malformed heart valve. In children, however, the vast majority of heart murmurs arise from no known cause—and, fortunately, have no medical significance. These benign murmurs are known as *innocent murmurs,* and doctors estimate that up to 70 percent of active, healthy children develop them at some time. Furthermore, long-term studies of people who had such murmurs during childhood indicate that they are not associated with an increased risk of adult heart disease or any other lasting complications.

The vast majority of murmurs detected in childhood disappear by the time the child is ten to 14 years old. In about ten percent of cases, an innocent murmur persists into adulthood. Even in an adult, however, such a murmur does not indicate serious disease.

When should I suspect that my child has a heart murmur?

Heart murmurs are usually detected when a doctor examines the child with a stethoscope. Pediatricians often discover them during routine school screenings or in presport or precamp examinations.

Because newborns have rapid heart rates, their heart murmurs are harder to detect. To hear all the heart sounds, the pediatrician listens from several angles, including the armpit and the back.

What causes heart murmurs?

Innocent heart murmurs arise as part of the normal functioning of the heart. They may, for example, be due to vibrations of the heart muscle.

Murmurs also may be organic, arising from a variety of abnormalities in the heart's structure. For example, they may be present if a valve does not open properly or, conversely, if a valve leaks.

Is medical attention necessary?

Your pediatrician will determine if the murmur is innocent or requires further evaluation. Innocent murmurs require no medical attention. If the pediatrician determines that the murmur may signal a more complicated condition, the child will be referred to a pediatric cardiologist or a pediatrician experienced in heart disease for an examination. In fact, murmurs are by far the most common reason children are referred to cardiologists for evaluation.

How can the pediatrician tell if my child has a serious heart murmur?

By listening to the heart with a stethoscope, an experienced pediatric cardiologist can usually tell whether the murmur signals the presence of a defect. The doctor may also feel the child's chest and abdomen, tap on the chest, and take the child's pulse. To support the diagnosis, imaging studies of the child's heart may be needed, particularly echocardiography, which is a kind of ultrasound.

When does a child with a heart murmur require treatment?

Although the majority of murmurs turn out to be innocent, sometimes they do signal the presence of heart disease. In such cases, treatment depends on the underlying problem. If the structural deformity is severe, surgery may be required.

In some cases, no treatment is necessary, but certain precautions must be taken. For example, a murmur may signal that the child's heart contains a structural defect that is not dangerous in itself but makes the heart more prone to infection than a totally normal heart. Children with these types of defects may need to take special measures—such as taking antibiotics before dental work—to prevent such infection.

Hemophilia

Hemophilia is a blood-clotting disorder that affects one in 10,000 boys; it is rare in girls. The disease is usually hereditary, passed to sons by symptom-free mothers who carry a defect that interferes with manufacture of a protein necessary for blood clotting. As many as one-third of boys born with hemophilia have no family history of the disease. Their illness is termed spontaneous.

Thanks to medical advances over the past 15 years, boys with hemophilia are now able to attend school and engage in physical activities, although some limitations are necessary in the most severe cases.

How does hemophilia develop?

The genetic defect in hemophilia causes deficiency of a clotting factor, which is a blood component essential for coagulation. Boys with abnormally low levels of clotting factors have trouble recovering from wounds, and they may develop internal bleeding.

The severity of the disease depends on the degree of clotting factor deficiency. Children with mild hemophilia may have problems only after surgery or serious injury. Moderate disease may cause one or two bleeding episodes in a year. In severe hemophilia, however, the child may develop two or three bleeding episodes a week, many without any apparent precipitating injury.

Hemarthrosis, a common complication of hemophilia, occurs when blood oozes repeatedly into soft tissue, muscles, and joints (particularly the knees), causing pain and swelling and, in some cases, leading to deformity. For this reason, orthopedists (surgeons who specialize in the musculoskeletal system) often play a key role in managing hemophilia patients.

When should I suspect that my child has hemophilia?

A boy whose mother's family has a history of hemophilia can be given a blood clotting test at birth. If there is no family history, abnormal bleeding may become apparent when the child begins to walk. He may develop large bruises after minor injuries or bleed excessively (for hours or even days) from minor cuts. Bleeding after circumcision is a common presenting sign, as well as excessive bleeding after the loss of a tooth.

How can the pediatrician tell if my child has hemophilia?

Hemophilia is diagnosed by a blood test that measures clotting time and the amount of the different clotting factors present in the patient's blood.

RISKS OF CLOTTING FACTOR REPLACEMENT

- About ten percent of patients treated with clotting factor develop INHIBITORS, antibodies in the blood that can neutralize their coagulating effects. Although the presence of inhibitors makes treatment with clotting factor more difficult, it is still possible.
- In the past, clotting factor had to be extracted from large pools of donated blood. Because this blood was taken from so many donors, the risks of hepatitis B and/or AIDS transmission was enormous. Fortunately, newer manufacturing techniques and careful donor screening and testing of the blood have greatly reduced these risks.

What treatments are available?

Minor traumas often can be treated by applying cold compresses and pressure to the wound to induce clotting. More extreme bleeding episodes usually can be controlled with intravenous infusion of clotting factors. Hospitalization is sometimes necessary.

Clotting factor also can be used on a regular basis to prevent bleeding episodes. [If a child bleeds frequently, the physician may prescribe daily infusions. Infusions are scheduled before surgery or dental work.] Such infusions can be given at home after parents have learned the proper techniques.

Coping with hemophilia

Children with hemophilia used to live isolated, illness-oriented lives. Today's hemophilia therapies, however, are so advanced that the child can live a normal life if you take the following measures:

- Accident-proof your home as you would for any child.
- Guard against overprotectiveness. Too much emphasis on his illness and differences from other children can damage his self-esteem.
- As the child gets older, send him to regular school and allow him to play with friends.
- Encourage activities with a low risk of injury, such as swimming and hiking. Discourage contact sports.
- Have the child wear a Medic Alert medallion to notify others of his condition in case of emergency.

PREVENTING CHILDHOOD BLEEDING EPISODES

- Pad the child's crib and playpen to reduce the risk of trauma.
- Supervise the child carefully when he is learning to walk.
- Strictly avoid using aspirin or other drugs that reduce blood coagulation.
- Make sure the child is immunized against hepatitis B. Under current recommendations, all newborns receive this immunization within the first few days after birth.
- Teach the child proper tooth-brushing techniques early. Beginning at age two, take him for twice-yearly visits to a dentist familiar with hemophilia. These precautions will minimize the need for dental surgery.

Hemophilus Influenzae Type B Infections

Hemophilus influenzae organisms, the most common of which is type b (HiB), are among the many strains of bacteria that can grow in the respiratory tract without causing problems. Sometimes, however, they spread beyond control in the throat or middle ear or gain access to the bloodstream and other parts of the body, causing severe illnesses.

Why should parents be concerned about HiB?

HiB causes severe infections including epiglottitis (inflammation of the tissue flap that keeps food out of the windpipe) and meningitis, which can lead to permanent neurological problems, including deafness and mental retardation. Because HiB infections are so serious, a vaccine has been developed to prevent

HiB disease. Since the introduction of the vaccine, there have been many fewer cases of HiB infection.

How do HiB infections develop?

It depends on the site of the infection. Hemophilus bacteria can be responsible for middle ear infections, severe skin infections (known as *cellulitis*), bone infections (known as *osteomyelitis*), and joint infections (known as *septic arthritis*). HiB also can infiltrate the lungs, causing pneumonia, or the sinus cavities in the skull, causing sinusitis. The most feared HiB infections, however, are epiglottitis and meningitis.

In many cases, the mechanism by which HiB infection develops is poorly understood. Studies have shown that a high proportion of children harbor the bacteria in their throats at one time or another, so presence of the organism does not necessarily lead to illness.

Doctors believe HiB meningitis usually begins with an upper respiratory tract infection from which the bacteria enter the bloodstream and travel to the membranes surrounding the brain. This original infection, however, may not cause symptoms. Epiglottitis most commonly strikes children who show no other signs of infection, although in about one-fourth of cases there is a history of a preceding cold or sore throat. For unknown reasons, HiB epiglottitis rarely leads to meningitis or joint infection, even though the organisms are detectable in the bloodstream when the epiglottis is infected. More often, epiglottitis leads to HiB pneumonia or infection of the lymph nodes in the neck.

When should I suspect that my child has an HiB infection?

The symptoms vary according to the site of the infection, but fever, change in mood, and weakness are virtually always part of the picture. A child with meningitis may be irritable, vomit, and have a stiff neck. Infants with meningitis tend to be particularly irritable, especially in response to motion and other ordinarily soothing actions. Epiglottitis, which generally strikes children between the ages of three and seven, comes on suddenly and is marked by a severely high fever, inability to speak, drooling, and difficulty breathing and swallowing. Affected children commonly sit up and lean forward with their mouths open and tongue protruding. This is an emergency and the child should be taken to the hospital immediately. A middle ear infection caused by HiB has the same symptoms as other middle ear infections—pain, fever, and a feeling of fullness in the ear. HiB skin infections are most likely to appear on the face, causing pain, swelling, and red or purplish discoloration. Bone and joint infections, which typically affect the legs, cause fever, pain, and difficulty standing and walking. (For more in-

---

PREVENTING HIB INFECTIONS

- Make sure your child is fully immunized against HiB bacteria. Under current recommendations, one shot will not do it if the infant is less than 15 months of age. Your baby needs at least three or four injections to be protected completely.
- Regularly clean and disinfect toys shared by large groups of children.

---

formation on these conditions, see entries on **epiglottitis, meningitis, middle ear infections,** and **osteomyelitis.**)

Can my child be protected against HiB infections?

Yes. Immunization has been available since the mid-1980s. As of 1992, the American Academy of Pediatrics recommended use of one of two available vaccines that produce immunity in infants. (Earlier HiB vaccines were not effective in babies under 18 months of age—the age group in which the majority of serious infections occur.) One of the recommended vaccines, known as the *HbOC vaccine,* is given at ages two, four, and six months of age, followed by a final dose at 12 to 15 months. The other, known as the *PRP-OMP vaccine,* is given at two, four, and 12 to 15 months.

As with any immunizations, protection against HiB is greatly improved by vaccine, but not 100 percent guaranteed. Therefore, if your child has been immunized, but develops symptoms of cellulitis, meningitis, or epiglottitis, you should still seek prompt medical attention to obtain proper antibiotic treatment for the infection.

Getting Help

CALL YOUR DOCTOR IF YOUR CHILD:
- Has not been immunized against HiB.
- Has any signs and symptoms of infection, including fever, localized pain and swelling, or a stiff neck.

Hepatitis

Hepatitis is liver inflammation caused by a viral infection. The viruses responsible for the most common types of hepatitis (hepatitis A and hepatitis B) were identified some time ago. Other types of hepatitis (C, D, and E) have been identified recently. These types are uncommonly associated with disease in children.

Hepatitis A is a less serious disease than hepatitis B, which can become chronic and gradually lead to liver failure. Both infections, however, can follow a rapidly progressive course, destroying the liver and resulting in death.

In 1992, the American Academy of Pediatrics began recommending routine hepatitis B immunization for all children. The vaccine, which was formerly reserved for people in high-risk groups, is given in the first few days after birth, with boosters between one and two months of age and again between six and 18 months of age.

How does hepatitis develop?

The hepatitis A virus commonly passes from person to person when infected fecal material contaminates food or water. Careless diaper changing and lax hand washing practices promote the spread of the disease, as does poor public sanitation. Some outbreaks of hepatitis A have been traced to consumption of contaminated shellfish. Hepatitis B is passed in infected blood and (perhaps) other body fluids, which can enter the body through the mucous membranes of the mouth and genital tract, as well as through cuts, scrapes, blood transfusions, and use of contaminated needles.

Hepatitis B also can be passed from an infected mother to her baby during birth or gestation.

Both viruses have a fairly long incubation period—about 25 days for hepatitis A and three months for hepatitis B. During this period, an infected person can spread the virus even though symptoms are not yet present. In addition, some people with hepatitis B infection become chronic carriers of the virus. Although they recover from the initial illness, they continue to pass the disease to others.

When should I suspect that my child has hepatitis?

In many cases, you will know if your child has been exposed to hepatitis. If someone in the child's day care or preschool comes down with hepatitis, the teacher or school nurse will inform you and let you know what symptoms to watch for.

The initial signs and symptoms of hepatitis A—chiefly, nausea and vomiting—can come on suddenly, while hepatitis B tends to develop more gradually. Fever may occur in both infections but is more common in hepatitis A. Hepatitis B, by contrast, often causes aching joints and widespread itching, symptoms not usually associated with hepatitis A. Tenderness in the area of the liver (the upper, right portion of the abdomen) is common in both hepatitis A and hepatitis B.

The hallmark of both infections is jaundice, a yellowing of the skin and whites of the eyes caused by the buildup of *bilirubin,* a pigment normally excreted by the liver. Jaundice typically develops at about the time symptoms begin to fade—about five to seven days after their onset. At about the time when jaundice develops, the stools become pale and the urine darkens.

Hepatitis A may not produce jaundice in small children, so it sometimes goes undiagnosed or is mistaken for viral gastroenteritis.

Is medical attention necessary?

Yes. Any time a child becomes jaundiced, a visit to the pediatrician is in order. Other symptoms of hepatitis also warrant medical investigation, especially if they last more than one or two days.

How can the pediatrician tell if my child has hepatitis?

If the usual signs and symptoms are present, the doctor may order a blood test to measure antibodies to the virus. Tests of liver function, also performed on a blood sample, also may be needed.

What treatments are available?

Rest, fluids, and an easily tolerated diet are the only treatments for hepatitis. If a child is se-

---

PREVENTING HEPATITIS

- Wash all fruits and vegetables thoroughly before eating them.
- Always wash hands after changing diapers or using the bathroom.
- Always wash hands before handling food.
- Children should get a shot of gamma globulin (protective antibodies) if exposed to hepatitis.
- Have all children and other family members immunized against hepatitis B.
- Avoid raw shellfish.

---

verely dehydrated, he might be admitted to the hospital for administration of intravenous fluids. In most cases, complete recovery takes about a month, although some children have mild relapses a few months later.

Hernia, Diaphragmatic

Diaphragmatic hernia is a congenital malformation found in approximately one in 2,000 infants. It occurs when the diaphragm (the muscular wall separating the chest and abdomen) fails to develop normally during gestation, leaving a hole (usually on the left side) through which some of the intestines and other abdominal organs enter the chest. In severe cases, the stomach and intestines (and rarely the spleen, liver, and kidneys) displace the heart and lungs.

The disorder is life-threatening when severe, but about 50 percent of babies with diaphragmatic hernia survive with surgery. Occasionally, small, symptom-free hernias can remain undetected throughout the person's life or only appear when an X ray is taken for an unrelated condition.

What happens in diaphragmatic hernia?

During gestation, the abdominal organs of a fetus with diaphragmatic hernia are pushed up through the hole in the diaphragm. They may compress the lungs, preventing their complete development in about 40 percent of these cases. Some children with diaphragmatic hernias are also born with heart defects. After birth, the babies may have difficulty breathing and will be cyanotic, or blue.

What causes a diaphragmatic hernia?

A diaphragmatic hernia results when the muscles and connective tissues of the diaphragm do not fuse properly during fetal development, leaving an opening. The cause of the abnormality is unknown.

How can the pediatrician tell if my infant has diaphragmatic hernia?

Diaphragmatic hernia may be diagnosed before birth by means of ultrasound examination. In most cases, the diagnosis is made at birth, but if the baby is not in immediate distress, diagnosis may escape detection for several days. The newborn infant may have labored breathing, shortness of breath, blue skin, a sunken or hollowed abdomen (because the abdominal organs are in the chest cavity), and signs of intestinal obstruction, including vomiting, severe colicky pain, discomfort after eating, and constipation.

An X ray revealing the displacement of the abdominal organs into the chest will confirm the diagnosis.

What treatments are available?

If the diagnosis is established prenatally, surgery may be scheduled within the first few hours after the baby is born. A few hospitals are experimenting with techniques to correct diaphragmatic hernias before birth, but these procedures have not been perfected.

Children born with severe diaphragmatic hernia often require emergency resuscitation. If so, the immediate concern is to maintain regular breathing and to remove air and fluids trapped in the compressed lungs. With breathing stabilized, surgery is required to return displaced organs to the abdomen and close the hole in the diaphragm.

Mechanical ventilation is usually needed for several days or months after the surgery, before the underdeveloped lungs can begin to function on their own. A technique called extracorporeal membrane oxygenation (ECMO) is available in some hospitals to treat babies who have undergone surgery for a particularly severe diaphragmatic hernia or in some circumstances to improve ventilatory dynamics before operative repair is undertaken. In ECMO, the baby's blood is temporarily circulated outside the body through a machine for oxygenation for as long as three weeks if necessary.

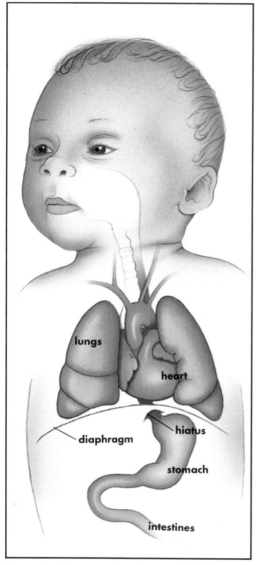 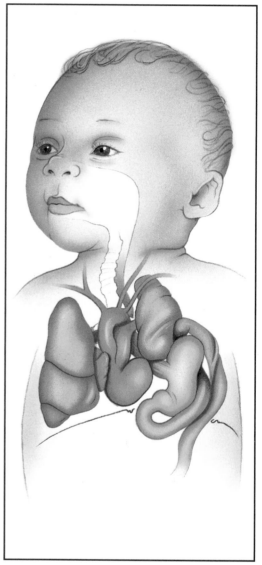

Normally, the stomach and intestines are held in the abdominal cavity by the diaphragm, a muscle that separates the chest and abdomen (left). In a diaphragmatic hernia (right), the diaphragm contains a hole through which abdominal organs move up into the chest, crowding the heart and lungs.

Hernia, Inguinal

An inguinal hernia is a protrusion of a portion of the small intestine into the groin through an opening in the membrane enclosing the abdominal cavity. This intestinal protrusion causes a prominent, nontender bulge.

Inguinal hernias are common in infancy and childhood; about one out of every 20 children—mainly boys—develop them. A hernia usually develops on only one side of the groin, although hernias, which appear on both sides, occur in about 20 percent of babies afflicted with a hernia.

Inguinal hernias pose no threat to health unless the protruding intestine becomes trapped in the abdominal opening. Such a hernia is described as incarcerated, entrapped, or strangulated. The entrapment will cut off the blood supply to the bulging piece of intestine, causing gangrene if the condition goes unrecognized and unrelieved.

What causes an inguinal hernia?

An inguinal hernia occurs when the peritoneum (the membrane that lines the abdominal cavity) fails to close fully during fetal development. In the fetus, the peritoneum has two projecting sacs running into the groin, one down each side, via a short passageway between the abdomen and the groin. In boys, these projections extend into the scrotum; in girls, they extend into the labia majora.

Before birth, the projections separate from the peritoneum, which then closes to form an intact membrane around the abdominal organs. The pouches dissolve in girls; in boys, they form the protective sacs that house the testicles.

In many otherwise healthy babies, the peritoneum fails to close at the point where the projecting sacs were attached. The intestine pokes through the opening, causing the characteristic hernial bulge. Sometimes, the peritoneal opening is very small, allowing only abdominal fluid to pass through; the bulge it forms is known as a **hydrocele** (see entry).

When should I suspect that my child has an inguinal hernia?

A swelling or puffy area in the baby's groin indicates a hernia. The bulge may be visible all the time, or it may appear only when the infant cries or has a bowel movement. In an older child, a hernia may appear only after vigorous activity or coughing.

In an uncomplicated hernia (one that is not trapped) the bulge is soft and can be gently pushed back into place; this type of hernia rarely causes discomfort or pain. An incarcerated, or trapped hernia feels harder to the touch, and it is likely to be quite tender.

Is medical attention necessary?

Yes. Call your pediatrician if you note the following symptoms:

- A swelling or bulge on either side of the child's groin.
- Pain or discomfort in the groin.

How can the pediatrician tell if my child has an inguinal hernia?

The physician can detect a hernia by visual inspection and physical examination. If a suspected hernia is not visible, the doctor may have to induce its appearance by pressing on the abdomen (which will make a baby cry and push the hernia out) or having an older child bear down on the abdominal muscles while standing.

What treatments are available?

Surgical repair of the abdominal wall is always required for an inguinal hernia. An incarcerated hernia requires immediate surgery. If an uncomplicated hernia is diagnosed in an infant, surgery usually is scheduled as soon as the infant is strong enough and healthy enough. Older children have more leeway; surgery usually is scheduled sometime within a month or two after the hernia is detected.

The surgical procedure to repair an inguinal hernia is relatively simple. The surgeon makes a small incision in the groin and pushes the intestine back into place in the abdomen. He or she then sews up the opening in the ab-

dominal wall and closes the incision. The operation takes less than an hour, and usually is performed on an out-patient basis.

Hernia, Umbilical

An umbilical hernia is a bulge in the navel caused by protrusion of the infant's small intestines through a hole or weakness in the abdominal wall at the point where the umbilical cord was attached during pregnancy. The bulge is usually smaller than one inch; longer protrusions are unusual. Small umbilical hernias may bulge out only when the baby is straining, crying, or coughing. Most hernias are soft to the touch and can be pushed back into place with gentle pressure.

Umbilical hernias are especially common in low-birth-weight babies and black babies. They occur more often in girls than boys. Umbilical hernias and **inguinal hernias** (see entry) are the most common hernias in infants.

With rare exceptions, umbilical hernias are neither painful nor dangerous. In less than one percent of umbilical hernias, however, the hernia becomes entrapped (or incarcerated), potentially cutting off the blood supply to the herniated intestine. An interrupted blood supply may make the intestine decay and become infected, a condition known as gangrene. The intestine can also become perforated by the constriction. An entrapped umbilical hernia is a medical emergency.

What causes an umbilical hernia?

The umbilical cord connects the fetus to the placenta, passing through an opening in the abdominal wall of the fetus and providing es-

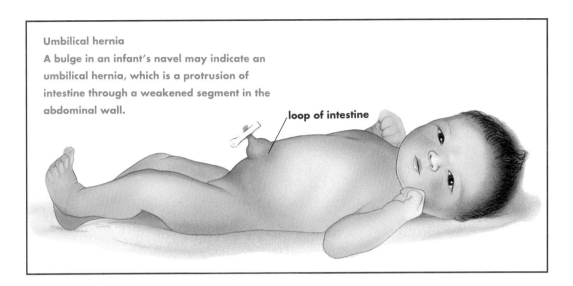

Umbilical hernia

A bulge in an infant's navel may indicate an umbilical hernia, which is a protrusion of intestine through a weakened segment in the abdominal wall.

loop of intestine

sential nutrients to the fetus. After birth, the umbilical cord is cut and tied to form the navel, and the opening in the muscles of the abdominal wall closes. In children with umbilical hernias, the muscles in the abdominal wall do not close completely, leaving either an opening or a weakened area. The intestines can then push through, causing the hernia.

When should I suspect that my child has an umbilical hernia?

Any bulge protruding from the infant's navel may indicate an umbilical hernia. If the hernia is soft and can be pushed back into the abdominal cavity, there is no reason for worry. If the bulge is hard to the touch and cannot be pushed into place or if the herniated area is tender, the segment of intestine may be entrapped.

Is medical attention necessary?

Only if the hernia is entrapped, which is a very rare occurrence. Umbilical hernias are benign. The pediatrician should, however, check for any changes in the hernia and determine whether it is receding properly during regularly scheduled medical checkups.

Most umbilical hernias that appear before the infant is six months old will disappear by the age of one. At or soon after that age, the muscles of the abdominal wall are usually closed. Larger hernias may take as long as five or six years to recede.

What treatments are available?

In most cases, no treatment is needed. Surgery, which takes under an hour and rarely requires a hospital stay, may be recommended for hernias that enlarge or persist past the age of five or six. Immediate surgery is needed for entrapped umbilical hernias.

CARING FOR A CHILD WITH AN UMBILICAL HERNIA

Do not bind the child's navel in an attempt to push the protrusion back in. This outmoded practice does not help and may possibly be harmful.

Hiccups

Just about every child gets an occasional case of the hiccups—sudden attacks of involuntary gasping that last no more than a few minutes. Infants frequently get hiccups as well. Brief spells of hiccuping are absolutely normal, although they can be annoying.

How do hiccups develop?

The mechanics of hiccups are well known: They result from spasmodic contractions of the diaphragm (the muscle that separates the abdominal organs from the chest cavity) that draw air quickly through the lungs. The accompanying rapid closing of the vocal cords at the top of the larynx produces the characteristic "hic" sound. But what actually starts or causes an attack of normal hiccups is not known.

Is medical attention necessary?

Most of the time it isn't. If hiccups last longer than two hours and home remedies fail, however, it is a good idea to call your child's physician. If hiccuping becomes severe and uncontrollable (which can, rarely, happen), the physician will look for an underlying condition that might be irritating the nerves of the diaphragm; treating such a condition usually will put an end to the hiccups. Rare cases of frequent and prolonged hiccups have been associated with such underlying conditions as pleurisy, pneumonia, and disorders of the stomach and esophagus.

What treatments are available?

Most hiccups go away by themselves without treatment. If they last more than a few min-utes, there are plenty of home remedies to stop them:

- Have the child take small, slow sips from a glass of water.
- Give the child a teaspoon of sugar.
- Have the child breathe into a paper bag for half a minute.

High Blood Pressure

Blood pressure is the force exerted by the blood as it courses through the circulatory system. If this force is consistently too high, it can damage blood vessels in the brain, eye, heart, and kidneys and lead to a number of complications, including strokes and heart failure.

Most people think of high blood pressure as a disease of adulthood. It is true that *primary* or *essential hypertension*—the type that has no clear cause and produces no symptoms until it is advanced—is detected mainly in the adult years. Increasing evidence, however, shows that essential hypertension often develops in adolescence. Young children, too, can have essential hypertension, although it is more unusual.

Severe blood pressure elevations in infants and small children usually result from *secondary hypertension,* which in turn is caused by an underlying disorder such as heart or kidney disease.

How does high blood pressure develop?

Normal blood pressure rises and falls depending on activity, time of day, and several other factors. These variations occur within a normal range because of a complex system of chemical signals that regulate the pressure of the heart's contractions, the amount of blood in the circulation, and the amount of resistance or tension in blood vessels. High blood pressure can develop when an organ malformation or disease process such as kidney inflammation disrupts this system. Presumably, some similar disruption occurs in essential hypertension, but the exact nature of the problem is unknown.

When should I suspect that my child has high blood pressure?

In some cases of secondary hypertension, the underlying problem will produce noticeable signs and symptoms. These may include fatigue and difficulty breathing in the case of heart problems and swelling of the hands, feet, and face, along with decreased urination, in the case of kidney problems.

Most of the time, though, high blood pressure causes no symptoms, which is why regu-lar blood-pressure checks are so important. Starting at age three, children should have their blood pressure measured at every well-child checkup.

How can the pediatrician tell if my child has high blood pressure?

Doctors measure blood pressure with an inflatable cuff and meter called a *sphygmomanometer*. The cuff (which should be a special, small size for a child) momentarily constricts a large artery while the doctor checks the meter and listens to the sounds of blood flow with a stethoscope. The reading gives two measurements: *systolic* pressure, which is the pressure when the heart contracts and pushes out blood, and *diastolic* pressure, which is the pressure while the heart is resting. The reading is given as the systolic over the diastolic pressure—for example, 110 over 70.

High blood pressure is diagnosed on the basis of three separate readings taken at different times. If the average of these three readings is higher than that for 90 percent of children the same age, the child is considered to have hypertension.

Children's blood pressure increases steadily as they grow. In general, a three-year-old with a blood pressure in the vicinity of 98 over 64 (the 75th percentile) is considered in the normal range. Children who are large and heavy for their ages also have higher blood pressure than smaller children, a factor the doctor will take into account in making the diagnosis.

What treatments are available?

The doctor starts by doing blood and urine tests, as well as X rays of the kidneys, to look for an underlying problem that may be re-

---

PREVENTING HIGH BLOOD PRESSURE

- If your child is becoming overweight, consult a registered dietitian for tips on slowing weight gain. Obesity is a major contributor to high blood pressure in children and adults.
- Encourage your child to be physically active.
- If high blood pressure runs in your family, ask your pediatrician to suggest other preventive measures to protect your child. You might, for instance, try limiting the child's consumption of salt.

sponsible for the blood pressure elevation. If such a problem is found, treating it should control the blood pressure.

Treatment for mild essential blood pressure may involve increasing exercise and reducing salt in the diet. If these measures do not work, or if the blood pressure is quite elevated, the doctor may prescribe medication—most often, a *diuretic,* which increases excretion of urine.

Hip Dislocation, Congenital

Congenital hip dislocation is a joint disorder present at birth in which the ball-like tip of the thighbone does not properly fit into the hip socket, making the joint susceptible to dislocation.

In most cases, the disorder will be noted and treated in infancy. If left unattended for too long, however, it becomes harder to treat and can permanently affect the child's ability to walk. Congenital hip dislocation affects one out of every 250 newborns and is more common in girls than in boys.

When should I suspect that my child has congenital hip dislocation?

Your pediatrician will check for the disorder during routine physical examinations at birth and during the first year of life. If the dislocation is only partial at birth, the condition can go unrecognized. If so, as months go by, the hip joint will become increasingly unstable and limit the range of motion in the affected leg. You should suspect congenital hip dislo-

cation if your child is unstable when placing weight on the affected leg and if his pelvis tilts toward the stable side while walking.

What treatments are available?

Many newborns with hip dislocations begin to improve without treatment within weeks of diagnosis. If no improvement occurs, however, the physician may fit the child's thighs with a brace to force the displaced thigh bone into proper position in the hip socket. The brace will still allow the baby some movement. In newborns, this treatment usually corrects the disorder in six to eight weeks.

After six months of age, the child may be too large and strong to tolerate wearing a brace and may have to undergo traction (the use of weights, ropes, and pulleys to realign the joint bones) and spend several months in a cast. If the defect is left untreated for too long, surgery may be needed to restore the joint to its correct position, and the child may have permanent problems in walking.

Getting Help

CALL YOUR DOCTOR IF:

- You or your spouse have a family history of congenital hip dislocation. This will alert the doctor to examine the child at regular intervals for symptoms of the disorder.
- Your child stands or walks with an unstable gait and his pelvis tilts to one side.

Hodgkin's Disease

Hodgkin's disease is a type of lymphoma, or cancer of the lymph nodes, part of the immune system that helps the body fight infection. It rarely occurs in children under ten; the youngest Hodgkin's patient ever reported was three years old.

Hodgkin's disease has one of the best cure rates of any type of cancer. As in other cancers, however, successful treatment depends on early detection—which depends, in turn, on recognizing symptoms.

How does Hodgkin's disease develop?

The exact cause of Hodgkin's disease is unknown. Malignant cells of the lymphatic system reproduce and infiltrate large lymph glands in the neck, armpits, and groin, and also the spleen (an organ located high on the left side of the abdomen, just below the ribs.)

When should I suspect that my child has Hodgkin's disease?

A classic early sign of Hodgkin's disease is swollen lymph glands, usually in the groin or armpit. The glands typically do not hurt, but feel hard and rubbery. The spleen may become swollen, and the child may develop the yellowish eyes and skin of jaundice, which indicates that the liver is not functioning normally. Constant, widespread itching, intermittent fever, weight loss, and night sweats are also symptoms of Hodgkin's disease. More general symptoms include fever and malaise. In some cases, however, the only symptom is enlarged lymph nodes.

Getting Help

CALL YOUR DOCTOR IF:
Your child has any symptoms suggesting Hodgkin's disease. Look for:

- Swollen, rubbery, nontender lymph nodes
- Yellowish skin and eyes
- Night sweats
- Intermittent fever
- Slowed growth
- Fatigue
- Widespread itching

Is medical attention necessary?

Yes. The signs and symptoms mentioned above are associated with Hodgkin's disease as well as a number of potentially serious disorders. Therefore, a complete medical evaluation is essential.

How can the pediatrician tell if my child has Hodgkin's disease?

Several different tests may be needed. Among them are blood and bone marrow studies to determine which types of white blood cells are affected, an X ray of the affected lymph nodes and channels (called a lymphangiogram), and a biopsy of an enlarged lymph node.

If these tests point to Hodgkin's disease, then the child is usually admitted into the hospital for "staging," an operative procedure that takes several days. Tissue samples are taken from several lymph nodes, as well as from the liver, bone, and the spleen (which is often removed). By analyzing these samples, the physician can tell precisely which cell types are involved, and how far the condition has progressed.

What treatments are available?

A combination of radiation therapy and multidrug chemotherapy usually cures Hodgkin's disease. The five-year survival rate is 90 percent, and the ten-year rate is 80 percent.

Hydrocele

Swelling of the scrotum caused by excess fluid in the sheath that surrounds the testicles is known as hydrocele. Hydrocele causes no pain, and it usually resolves without treatment. Occasionally, however, the condition is a result of a minor (and correctable) anatomical defect that increases the risk of **inguinal hernias** (see entry) in male infants.

How does hydrocele develop?

Hydrocele develops when the body either produces too much or absorbs too little of the fluid that cushions and lubricates the testicles within the scrotum. In some cases, the excess fluid results from incomplete closure of the peritoneum—the membrane that lines the abdominal cavity—during fetal development. This minor defect is quite common since the scrotum is formed from a saclike extension of the peritoneum.

Hydroceles generally become noticeable a few weeks after birth and must be differentiated from inguinal, or groin hernias.

Is medical attention necessary?

Although hydroceles usually resolve on their own, a doctor should be consulted any time

parents suspect some abnormality in a baby's genitalia.

How can the pediatrician tell if my child has hydrocele?

Pediatricians diagnose hydroceles by shining a light through the scrotum. The light will show the fluid-filled areas, although the testicles themselves will be opaque.

What treatments are available?

If the hydrocele seems particularly large or unlikely to subside unassisted, your pediatrician will probably recommend surgery to drain the excess fluid and, if possible, repair the source of the excess fluid.

Getting Help

CALL YOUR DOCTOR IF:
- ▪ Your child has swollen testicles after the immediate newborn period.
- ▪ Your child's testicles change in size throughout the day.

Hydrocephalus

As part of every wellness visit during infancy, the pediatrician takes a few moments to measure your baby's head. Such measurements are needed to check for normal development of the brain and skull. A rapid increase in the size of a baby's skull over the first few weeks or months of life may indicate the presence of hydrocephalus, a potentially dangerous condition in which excess fluid accumulates in the area surrounding the brain and in the ventricles within the brain. Fortunately, hydrocephalus can be treated surgically. If the treatment is delayed, however, permanent neurological damage may result.

What causes hydrocephalus?

Hydrocephalus develops as a result of any disease or malformation affecting the flow of cerebrospinal fluid, which is produced in the ventricles and absorbed from the spaces surrounding the brain and spinal cord. When an illness or anatomical abnormality blocks the flow of cerebrospinal fluid or interferes with its absorption, the fluid builds up, creating pressure within the brain. In infants whose fontanels (soft spots between skull bones) are still open, the head may become enlarged. After the skull bones have fused, the excess fluid cannot expand them. Instead, pressure builds up within the skull, compressing the brain.

In many cases, hydrocephalus is present at birth, which suggests that a malformation within the brain or spinal column is the cause.

CARING FOR A CHILD WITH HYDROCEPHALUS

- Be alert to signs of increasing pressure within the skull. These signs may include abnormal feeding patterns, vomiting, erratic breathing rhythms, and rapid heartbeat.
- In patients who have been treated with a shunt, one must watch for signs of infection (redness and swelling) where the shunt enters the skin. These infections, which occur in one out of five children with shunts, can be treated with antibiotics.

Hydrocephalus is a common complication of a condition called *spina bifida,* in which part of the spinal cord protrudes through the backbone. In some cases, meningitis—an infection of the membranes surrounding the brain and spinal cord—causes hydrocephalus. Infections in the mother also can lead to hydrocephalus in the fetus. In older babies and children, head injuries sometimes cause hydrocephalus, particularly if there is bleeding within the skull. Growths within the skull sometimes produce hydrocephalus as well.

When should I suspect that my infant has hydrocephalus?

Look for a swelling in the fontanel on the top-center part of the head. Also check for unevenness in the shape of the head, particularly enlargement in the forehead and temples. An older child who develops hydrocephalus may initially suffer from nausea, vomiting, and severe headache, particularly on awakening. Pressure within the skull also can lead to listlessness and impaired speech and coordination.

Does hydrocephalus require medical attention?

Yes. Increased pressure within the skull is a medical emergency.

How can the pediatrician tell if my child has hydrocephalus?

If a newborn is at risk of hydrocephalus because of premature birth or some other condition, the pediatrician may take frequent measurements of the head to detect an abnormal growth rate. To determine the cause of hydrocephalus in an infant or confirm the

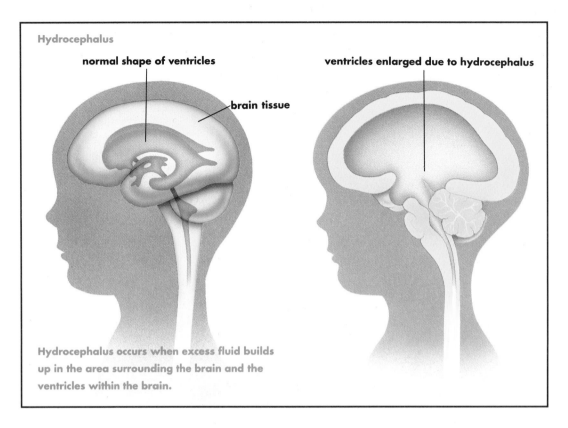

Hydrocephalus

normal shape of ventricles

ventricles enlarged due to hydrocephalus

brain tissue

Hydrocephalus occurs when excess fluid builds up in the area surrounding the brain and the ventricles within the brain.

presence of hydrocephalus in an older child, special X-ray studies that produce a three-dimensional image of the brain are necessary.

What treatments are available?

The standard treatment is the insertion of a narrow tube (a shunt) in one of the ventricles of the brain and diverting excess fluid to another body cavity, most often the abdomen. The tube is placed in the ventricle at the side of the head and tunneled under the skin along the side of the neck and chest to the upper abdomen. Often the shunt must stay in place indefinitely, being adjusted periodically to prevent blockage or accommodate growth.

If an anatomical problem underlies the hydrocephalus, it may be amenable to surgery.

Coping with hydrocephalus

- Even if the cause is never discovered, most children who receive prompt, appropriate care can develop normally—with mental capacity completely intact—and lead healthy lives.
- Relax the reins. Most children with shunts can participate with their peers in all activities except for contact sports.
- Seek support. Ask your pediatrician or hospital social worker to put you in touch with other parents whose children have similar problems. In many communities, support groups for parents with chronically ill children already exist.

female productive systems are present in the fetus. By eight weeks, the penis and urinary structures begin to form in the male fetus. The urethra develops as folds of tissue along the underside of the penis fuse together. Disruption of this fusion causes the urethral opening to form at an abnormal site.

What treatments are available?

Hypospadias can be corrected surgically with an operation that releases the bands of fibrous tissue and diverts the urinary flow to a newly created urethral opening in the normal position. Whether surgery is necessary depends on how severe the defect is and whether it interferes with urinary or potential sexual function. If surgery is needed, it should be performed before the baby is 18 months old. In some cases, only one operation is needed, but in others, the operations are done six months to a year apart. In the case of mild hypospadias, surgery is primarily done for cosmetic reasons. Although the surgery is complex, it requires only a short hospital stay. Infants with hypo-

Hypospadias

Hypospadias is a congenital defect of the penis. In this condition, the tube that passes urine from the bladder to the outside of the body (the urethra) opens on the underside of the penis or in the scrotum, instead of the end of the penis. In addition, bands of fibrous tissue on the underside of the penis often give it a sharp, downward curvature called *chordee*. Occasionally, boys with hypospadias also have other, less readily apparent, abnormalities of the urinary tract. To detect such abnormalities, the pediatrician may recommend an examination of the entire urinary system including the kidneys and bladder by means of special X-ray or imaging studies.

How does hypospadias develop?

Hypospadias is a developmental defect originating in the fetus. Until the sixth week of embryonic life, rudiments of both male and

RECOGNIZING HYPOSPADIAS

Hypospadias is usually recognized during the baby's first examination in the hospital nursery. Signs associated with the condition include:

- Downward curvature of the penis.
- A hood-like foreskin, rather than a foreskin that covers the glans completely.
- Undescended testicles. (This occurs in about 1 in 10 boys with hypospadias.)

spadias should not be circumcised because the foreskin may be useful in reconstructive surgery.

Children with hypospadias often have associated inguinal hernias. An inguinal hernia is visible as a bulge in the lower abdomen or scrotum.

Coping with hypospadias

- If possible, correct the abnormality before toilet training starts. A boy with hypospadias may develop psychological problems if he must sit down to urinate and others see that his penis is not normal.
- Obtain counseling for the child, if necessary, to help him handle insensitive remarks from others if surgery does not create a completely normal appearance.

Getting Help

CALL YOUR DOCTOR IF:
- There is any abnormality in the appearance of your baby's genitalia.

Imaginary Friends

Between the ages of two-and-a-half and six, children often create imaginary friends to play with. Although this development sometimes perplexes parents, it can be a positive sign that the child is devising creative ways to deal with being alone.

Why do children make up imaginary friends?

Imaginary friends help children deal with the normal anxieties of growing up. They often come into being at times of change or stress. For example, if a favorite friend moves away, the child may replace him with an imaginary friend. The birth of a new sibling may prompt a child to make up a playmate who isn't interested in the new baby. Likewise, the hospitalization of a parent, the death of a relative, or neglect on the part of a parent may cause a child to adopt an imaginary friend.

Imaginary friends also help children cope with being alone from time to time. For some children, they serve the same function as favorite toys and worn-out blankets. The "friend" or comfort object helps the child face the dark alone or deal with an unfamiliar situation.

What other purposes do imaginary friends serve?

Imaginary friends usually have names and well-developed personalities. Often, they are somewhat mischievous or naughty, allowing the child to express negative feelings and actions without having to take full ownership of them. For instance, an imaginary friend may strongly dislike certain foods, letting the child voice opinions about dinner without taking responsibility. Asked about a mess he made, a child may well blame the imaginary friend instead of confessing.

Responding to a child with an imaginary friend

By listening to the "conversations" your child has with an imaginary friend, you may be able to discern some of the child's fears and conflicts. For example, a child who talks often about a playmate who will never leave is probably afraid of abandonment. Talking about the issues and reassuring the child may help ease these fears.

Parents often wonder whether the child really believes the imaginary friend exists. Children may vigorously defend the existence of their imaginary friends, but they usually know that they are just pretend. In fact, your child's imaginary friend may quickly disappear in the presence of strangers or other children who might make fun of the fantasy.

There is no harm in playing along with your child's imagination. In fact, trying to convince your child that an imaginary friend doesn't exist may lead to unnecessary conflict. Most children will say good-bye to their imaginary friends as soon as they feel able to deal with their fears and negative feelings by themselves.

For more information on the emotional needs of preschoolers, see Chapters 6 and 7 of the development section of this book.

Immunization

Immunization is *the* most important preventive health measure parents can take for their children. Because of widespread immunization programs, illnesses like diphtheria, tetanus, and polio have all but disappeared. Even within the past few years, introduction of the HiB (*Hemophilus influenzae* type B) vaccine has reduced children's chances of developing HiB meningitis by 90 percent. All parents should be sure their children receive the full benefit of available immunizations.

What immunizations should my child receive?

Currently, the U.S. Public Health Service and American Academy of Pediatrics Committee on Infectious Diseases recommend the following schedule of immunizations. The combination vaccines are given together in one shot for convenience and to reduce discomfort for the child. As of this writing, varicella (chicken pox) vaccine was awaiting FDA approval for general use. By 1995, it should be included in the schedule of routine immunizations.

Hepatitis B

All infants born since the start of 1992 should receive three doses of hepatitis B vaccine—one at birth, one between one and two months of age, and one between six and 18 months. Children born before 1992 should receive the vaccine during their preteen years. (All adults, as well, should receive the hepatitis B vaccine.)

Diphtheria, tetanus, and pertussis (DTP)

These three immunizations are given in a combined injection. Shots are needed at two, four, six, and 15 to 18 months of age, with a final dose before starting school (at age four to six years). An adult booster should be given every ten years thereafter. This injection does not contain the pertussis component and has a reduced content of the diphtheria toxoid.

Oral polio vaccine

Oral polio vaccine (OPV) should be given at two, four, and six to 18 months, with a final dose before starting school. If the child or someone in the household has AIDS or another form of immune deficiency, or is receiving immune suppressive drugs (for cancer or organ transplantation, for example), an inactivated polio vaccine (IPV) is substituted.

Hemophilus influenzae type B

This vaccine protects against the bacterium responsible for most cases of meningitis and epiglottitis in small children. Two different HiB vaccines are effective in infants. One of them, the *HbOC vaccine*, is given at two, four, six, and 12 to 15 months of age. The other—*PRP-OMP vaccine*—is given at two and four months, with a final booster between 12 and 15 months of age. Either is safe and highly effective.

Measles, mumps, and rubella (MMR)

This combination vaccine is given at 12 to 15 months of age and generally not repeated until after school entry or age 11 or 12, to be certain immunity has been established successfully. If there have been measles outbreaks in your area, however, the first injection may be given as early as nine to 12 months of age, then repeated at 15–18 months.

How do immunizations work?

Immunizations protect the body against disease-causing agents by triggering the immune system (the body's built-in defense against disease) to produce antibodies, which attack and neutralize bacteria and viruses.

The only other way to develop antibodies is to catch the disease. Once children have had measles, for example, they won't get it again because, during the illness, the immune system manufactured antibodies against the measles virus. Immunizations work the same way, but they bypass the acute illness by using a form of the infectious agent that is too weak to cause illness but strong enough to make the immune system respond.

Why do children need immunizations?

There are several compelling reasons to immunize all healthy children. Most important is to protect the children themselves. Diphtheria, pertussis, tetanus, and polio are life-threatening conditions, as is *Hemophilus influenzae meningitis*. Though generally less serious, measles, mumps, and rubella also can make some children extremely sick and have long-lasting consequences.

In addition, widespread immunization of healthy children protects those who, because of illnesses such as cancer, cannot receive vaccines. While measles might cause a healthy child to remain home for a week or so, the same illness has a high likelihood of causing death in a child with a severely weakened immune system from AIDS, cancer, or cancer treatment.

By the same token, immunization of small children protects adolescents and adults who neither had the diseases nor received vaccines and thus are vulnerable. Many of these diseases can be particularly severe in adolescents and adults. Mumps, for instance, can in rare cases cause sterility in young men. Severe birth defects are common in infants of mothers who contract rubella (German measles) during pregnancy. Measles may cause serious pneumonia and hepatitis in adults.

What are the potential side effects of immunizations?

The side effects are usually quite mild, consisting of swelling and tenderness at the site of the injection. Low fevers and rashes sometimes develop after the MMR vaccine, due to the measles and rubella components. Mild fever occurs even less frequently following both the HbOC and PRP-OMP vaccinations against *Hemophilus influenzae*. Fever, irritability, and fatigue are common following DTP immunization, occurring in slightly more than half of the children. (See "The DTP controversy" on this page) for further discussion of this vaccine's side effects.) The oral polio vaccine has no reported side effects, but in extremely rare cases (1 in 700,000 first-time vaccine recipients), it has triggered full-blown cases of polio.

Are there any children who should not be immunized?

If a child has a high fever, immunization should be postponed until his temperature re-

THE DTP CONTROVERSY

The pertussis component of the DTP vaccine causes more side effects than any other routine immunization. In the 1980s, a handful of well-publicized cases in which children allegedly had severe reactions to this vaccine gave rise to a great deal of parental anxiety. It is important to put these events in context.

About one out of every 2,000 pertussis vaccine recipients have brief but disturbing reactions such as convulsions, prolonged and high-pitched crying, high fever, or a shocklike response. A much smaller number (approximately one out of every 100,000) may have a transient brain malfunction (*encephalopathy*), which can cause seizures, drowsiness, and disturbances in movement and speech.

While these side effects are a real cause for concern, they pale in comparison to the effects of the disease PERTUSSIS, or whooping cough. The illness mainly attacks infants and preschool children, causing uncontrollable coughing and gagging that often make it impossible to breathe. Pertussis can require weeks of hospitalization, and death—while unusual with modern medical care—does occur, particularly in infants.

Statistical studies of the disease have shown that unimmunized populations have ten times as many pertussis deaths as immunized populations. By contrast, not a single death has been conclusively linked to the pertussis vaccine.

turns to normal. A child with a mild illness and slight fever, however, can be immunized. Children with suppressed immune systems (due to chemotherapy, radiation, AIDS, or drugs given to protect transplanted organs) should receive the injected polio vaccine (IPV), which is made from killed virus, rather than the oral vaccine. The same precaution applies to children who live with immunosuppressed patients, who might catch the virus from a recently immunized child. Children with progressive neurological disorders or uncontrolled seizures should not receive the DTP vaccine, and any child who has had a prior, severe reaction to the pertussis component should receive only the DT in subsequent immunizations. Finally, children who are extremely allergic to eggs should be skin-tested before they receive the MMR, since portions of this vaccine are grown in cultures of chicken embryo cells.

Bad Memories

Before the advent of immunization, these diseases killed and disabled large numbers of children each year.

Diphtheria

This highly contagious bacterial infection is spread through airborne droplets expelled when an infected person coughs, sneezes, or breathes. When diphtheria-causing bacteria attack the respiratory tract, a gray membrane forms over the throat and nasal passages, and breathing may be obstructed. One strain of the causative bacteria produces a toxin that causes the neck to swell and leads to widespread organ damage.

Pertussis

This bacterial infection spreads rapidly through the same airborne route as diphtheria. The chief symptom is violent coughing brought on by eating, drinking, or exertion and occurring several times a day, so the child becomes exhausted. After the first several weeks, the frequency of coughing bouts diminishes, but they can recur for six months or longer. Infants may suffer nervous system damage, malnutrition, and poor growth. Unfortunately, this disease is on the rise, affecting older children who have lost immunity from early vaccines and infants who have not yet been vaccinated.

Polio

This viral infection has been almost abolished since the first vaccine was introduced in 1955. Most cases of polio are mild, similar to the flu and other viral illnesses, but a small number affect the central nervous system, leading to brain inflammation, paralysis, and even death,

---

CARING FOR A CHILD AFTER A VACCINE

Mild fever, achiness, crankiness, and pain at the injection site are common side effects of some vaccines, and they may appear immediately or a few days later. Ask your pediatrician for specific recommendations on how to soothe these discomforts. Generally, it is safe to give infants' or children's acetaminophen (Tylenol, Panadol, Tempra, and other brands) in age-appropriate doses to relieve fever. Some pediatricians even recommend administering these medications before the DTP vaccine if the child has had a previous reaction. Warm compresses can ease pain at the site of the injection.

Many children hate injections. Not only may some hurt, but they also make children feel uniquely powerless. Preschool children, who tend to worry about possible harm to their bodies, are particularly distressed by injections.

Parents can help by adopting a calm, matter-of-fact attitude. Since immunizations are usually given during routine well-child checkups, focus instead on other aspects of the visit such as the toys in the waiting room or the trinket the pediatrician will hand out at the end of the visit.

Extremely anxious children need more reassurance. Before this visit, they should be allowed to handle a syringe and practice giving shots to stuffed animals. A step-by-step explanation of what is going to happen is also helpful.

Most immunizations, with the exception of the MMR, are injected into the muscle rather than under the skin, so they are somewhat uncomfortable. Babies generally receive shots in the large muscle running down the backside of the thigh. After children start to walk, shots are given in the upper arm, but some large shots still need to be given in the thigh muscles or the buttocks.

Children handle shots better if a parent holds them and diverts their attention. For babies and toddlers, a brightly colored toy will do. Older children can recite a nursery rhyme, count, blow bubbles, or look out the window.

especially among infants under age one. Symptoms of paralytic polio include muscle weakness and spasms, pain, loss of certain reflexes, and retention of urine. Permanent paralysis occurs most often in the legs, although other parts of the body—including the muscles that control breathing—can be paralyzed as well.

Tetanus

This infection is caused by bacteria found in soil, dust, and the intestinal tracts of humans and animals. The bacteria typically enter the body through a wound such as a severe burn or puncture. When the bacteria multiply, they produce a substance that is toxic to the nervous system, causing muscle stiffness, which starts in the neck and jaw. In four out of every ten cases, tetanus is fatal.

Getting Help

CALL YOUR DOCTOR IF YOUR CHILD:

- Develops fever over 104 degrees Fahrenheit after an immunization.
- Cries more than three hours.
- Has convulsions.
- Becomes extremely listless or undergoes other changes in behavior.
- Loses muscle tone, breathes shallowly, and has a weak pulse.

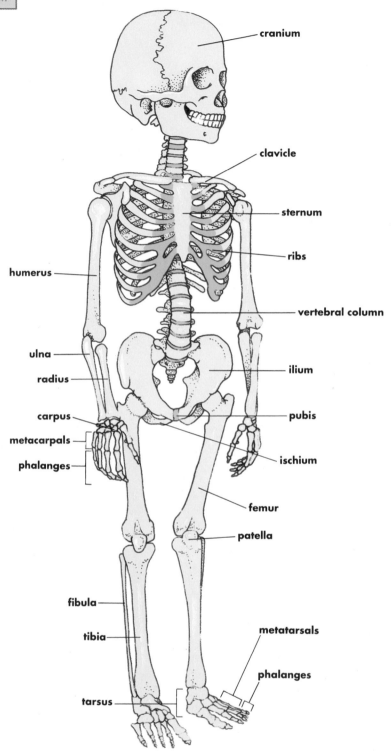

cranium

clavicle

sternum

ribs

humerus

vertebral column

ulna

radius

ilium

carpus

pubis

metacarpals

phalanges

ischium

femur

patella

fibula

metatarsals

tibia

phalanges

tarsus

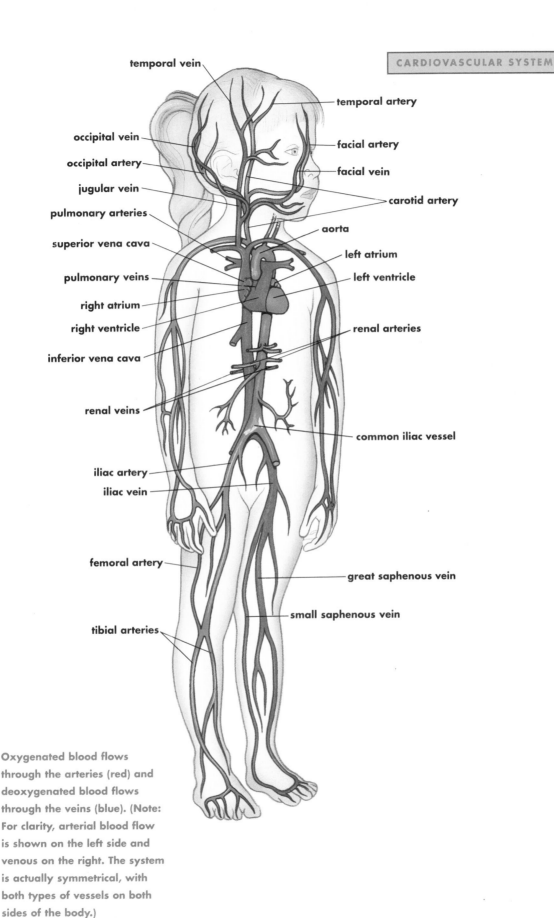

temporal vein

temporal artery

occipital vein

facial artery

occipital artery

facial vein

jugular vein

carotid artery

pulmonary arteries

aorta

superior vena cava

left atrium

pulmonary veins

left ventricle

right atrium

right ventricle

renal arteries

inferior vena cava

renal veins

common iliac vessel

iliac artery

iliac vein

femoral artery

great saphenous vein

small saphenous vein

tibial arteries

Oxygenated blood flows
through the arteries (red) and
deoxygenated blood flows
through the veins (blue). (Note:
For clarity, arterial blood flow
is shown on the left side and
venous on the right. The system
is actually symmetrical, with
both types of vessels on both
sides of the body.)

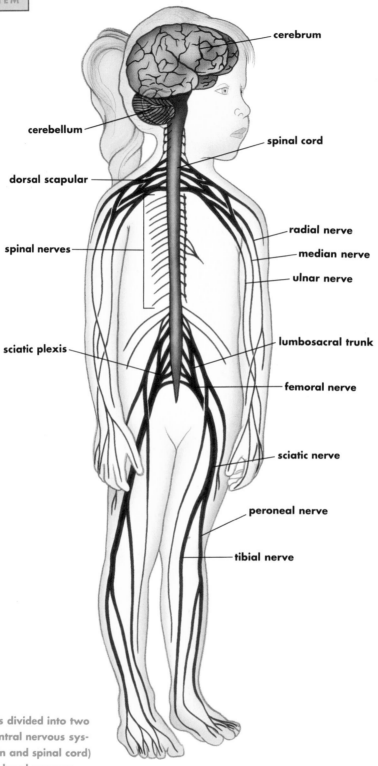

cerebrum

cerebellum

spinal cord

dorsal scapular

radial nerve

median nerve

ulnar nerve

spinal nerves

lumbosacral trunk

femoral nerve

sciatic plexis

sciatic nerve

peroneal nerve

tibial nerve

This system is divided into two parts: The central nervous system (the brain and spinal cord) and the peripheral nervous system (all over nerves). The peripheral nerves branch off of the spinal cord and carry messages between the brain and all parts of the body.

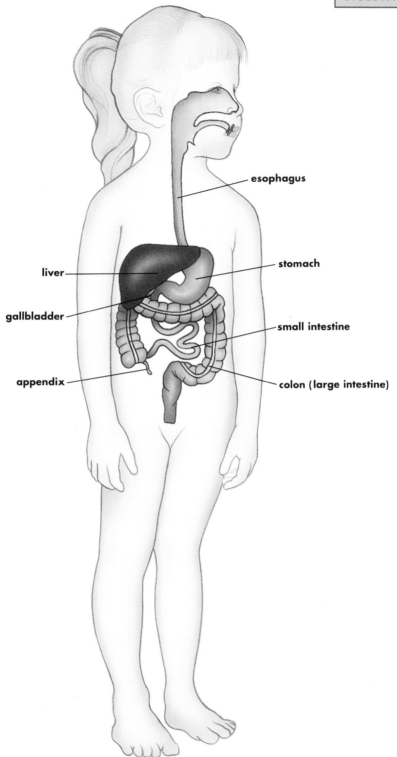

esophagus

liver

stomach

gallbladder

small intestine

appendix

colon (large intestine)

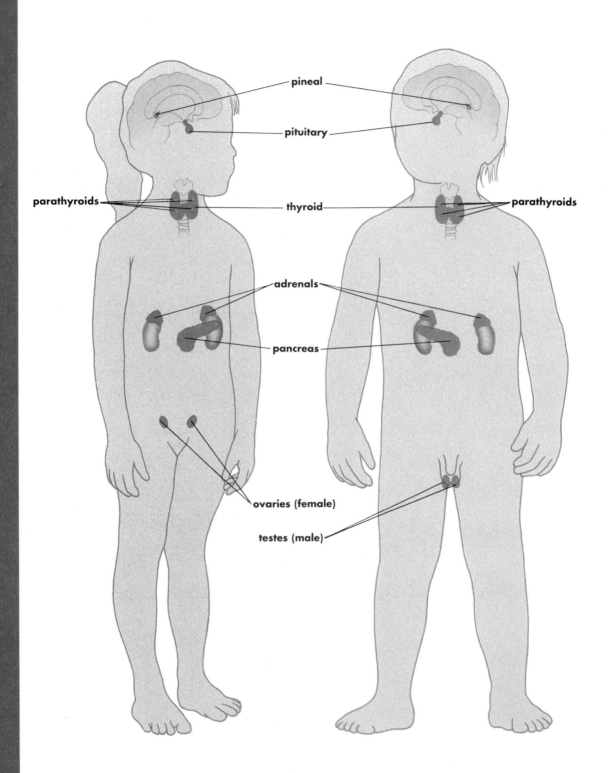

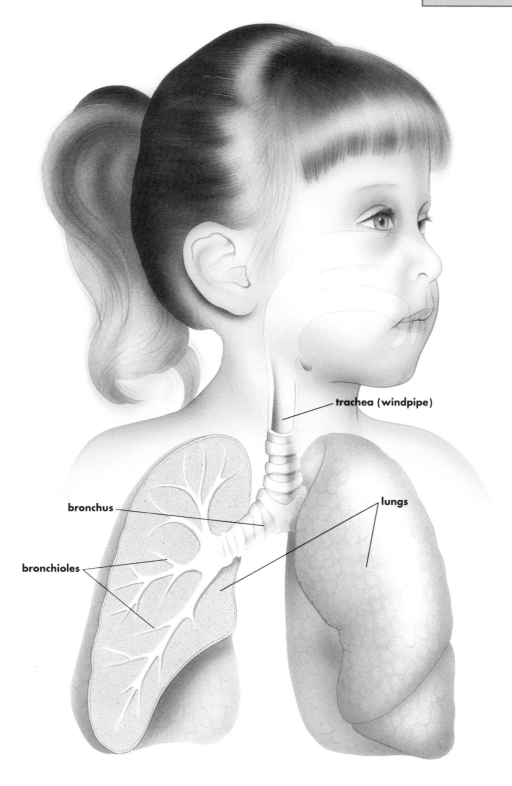

trachea (windpipe)

bronchus

lungs

bronchioles

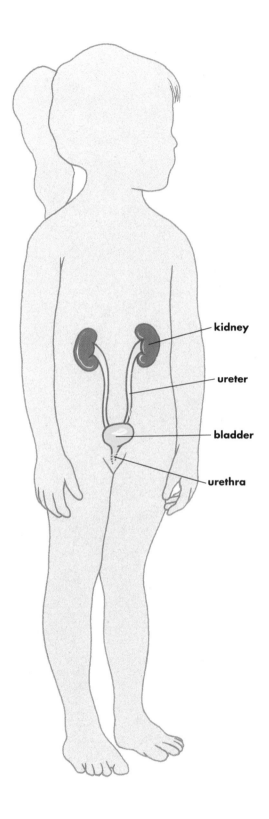

kidney

ureter

bladder

urethra

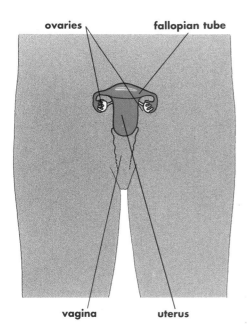

ovaries   **fallopian tube**

vagina   **uterus**

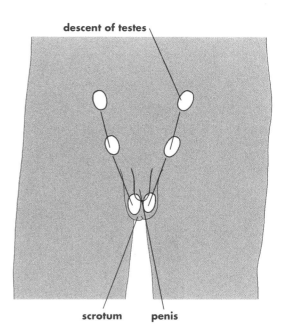

descent of testes

scrotum   **penis**

Prepubescent female *(left)* and male *(right)* reproductive systems

In males, the testes descend from the abdominal cavity to the scrotum during gestation.

GROWTH IN LENGTH OF BOYS

Boys: Birth to 36 months Physical Growth NCHS Percentiles

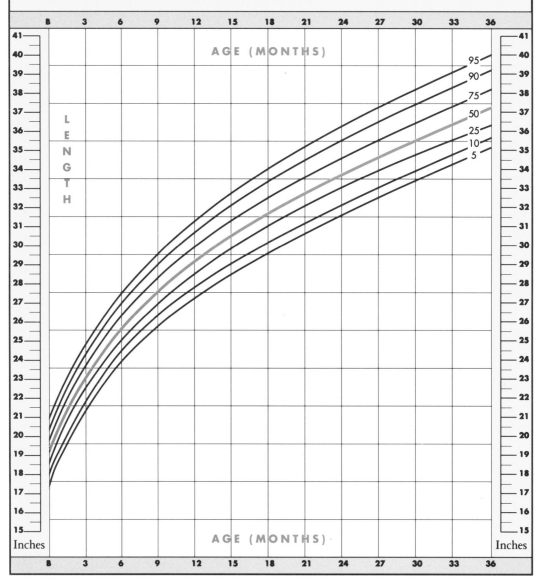

Adapted from: Hamil PVV, Drizd TA, Johnson CL, Reed RB, Roche AF, Moore WM: Physical growth: National Center for Health Statistics percentiles. AM J CLIN NUTR 32: 607-629, 1979. Data from the Fels Research Institute, Wright State University School of Medicine, Yellow Springs, Ohio ©1982 ROSS LABORATORIES.

ON THE FOLLOWING PAGES...

These charts, identical to the ones pediatricians use to plot infants' and children's growth, illustrate both the rapid rate of growth in the first twelve months of life and the wide range of normal heights and weights among children the same age. The curves reflect weight and height percentiles. A child who is in the 50th percentile for height falls right in the middle of all children of the same age in the sample, while one who is in the 75th percentile is taller than three-fourths of children in the sample. Pediatricians look for growth to follow a steady upward curve, with no abrupt shifts between percentiles. Whether a child is in the 10th or 90th percentile is generally unimportant, as long as his growth rate keeps him in about the same percentile from month to month in infancy and year to year in childhood.

GROWTH IN WEIGHT OF BOYS

Boys: Birth to 36 months Physical Growth NCHS Percentiles

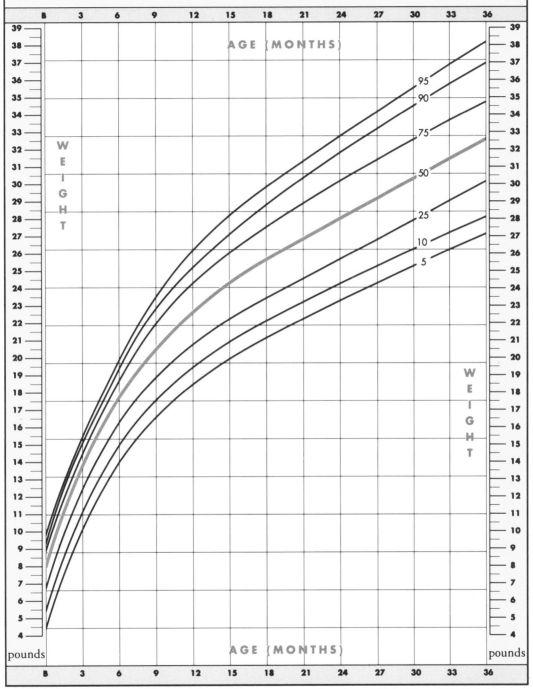

Adapted from: Hamil PVV, Drizd TA, Johnson CL, Reed RB, Roche AF, Moore WM: Physical growth: National Center for Health Statistics percentiles. AM J CLIN NUTR 32: 607-629, 1979. Data from the Fels Research Institute, Wright State University School of Medicine, Yellow Springs, Ohio ©1982 ROSS LABORATORIES.

GROWTH IN LENGTH OF GIRLS

Girls: Birth to 36 months Physical Growth NCHS Percentiles

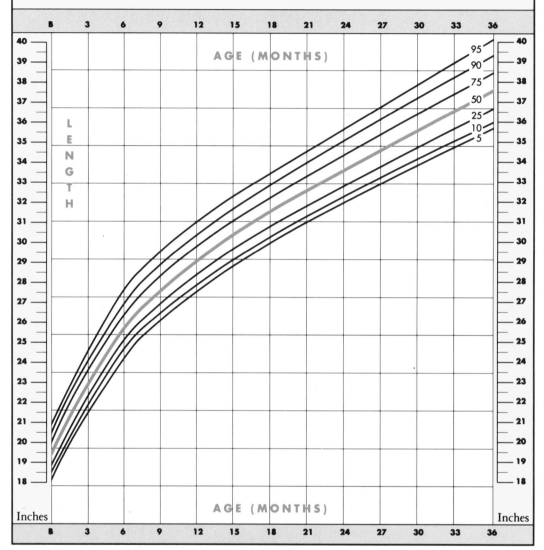

Adapted from: Hamil PVV, Drizd TA, Johnson CL, Reed RB, Roche AF, Moore WM: Physical growth: National Center for Health Statistics percentiles. AM J CLIN NUTR 32: 607-629, 1979. Data from the Fels Research Institute, Wright State University School of Medicine, Yellow Springs, Ohio ©1982 ROSS LABORATORIES.

GROWTH IN WEIGHT OF GIRLS

Girls: Birth to 36 months Physical Growth NCHS Percentiles

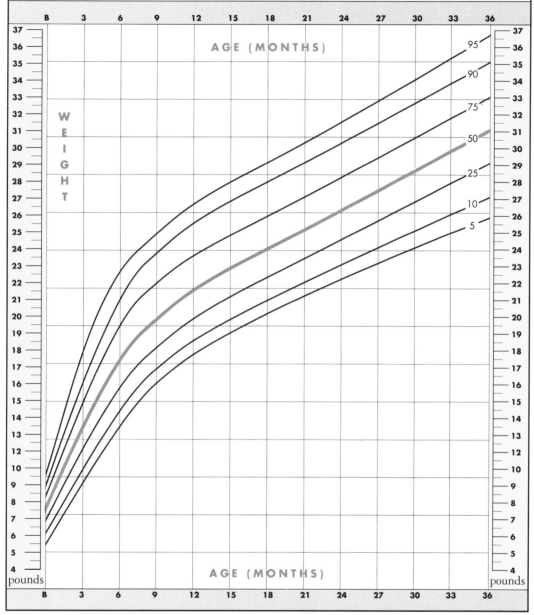

Adapted from: Hamil PVV, Drizd TA, Johnson CL, Reed RB, Roche AF, Moore WM: Physical growth: National Center for Health Statistics percentiles. AM J CLIN NUTR 32: 607-629, 1979. Data from the Fels Research Institute, Wright State University School of Medicine, Yellow Springs, Ohio ©1982 ROSS LABORATORIES.

Impetigo

Impetigo is a highly contagious bacterial skin infection that occasionally spreads among large numbers of children in day care, schools, and camps. It occurs most frequently in the summer months and in areas with a warm, humid climate.

The disease can develop in children of all ages. It begins with a rash of small, reddish blisters that rapidly increase in size. They soon rupture and leave a raw, moist surface with a yellowish discharge that forms a thick, honey-colored crust. The sores are commonly seen around the mouth and nose, but they can also develop on the scalp, arms, and legs. In some cases, individual sores fuse together to form a large, scablike crust. In one variety of impetigo, the broken blisters leave a raw, reddish spot covered by a shiny film instead of crusting over.

Apart from the rash there are usually no other symptoms, but in severe cases the affected skin may be swollen and tender to touch. Sometimes, there may be itching, a mild fever and swollen lymph glands.

PREVENTING IMPETIGO

- Seriously affected children should stay out of day care or preschool until two days after starting antibiotics.
- Keep the child's towels and washcloths separate from those of other family members, and launder them carefully after each use.
- If there is an outbreak of impetigo in the vicinity or in your household, apply an antibiotic cream to insect bites and wounds to prevent infection.

CARING FOR A CHILD WITH IMPETIGO

Whether the child receives antibiotics or not, the following measures will speed improvement.

- Trim the child's nails to prevent scratching.
- Give the child daily baths.
- Gently wash the affected skin with soap and water to remove the crust. Afterwards, dab the area dry.
- To make crust removal easier, apply wet compresses.
- Apply an antibiotic ointment or cream prescribed by the doctor.
- Give oral antibiotics as prescribed by the pediatrician.

How does impetigo develop?

The disease can be caused by two types of bacteria—*streptococci* and *staphylococci*. The infectious organisms can spread through direct contact or through contaminated objects such as sheets. The bacteria penetrate the skin through an opening—an insect bite, a cut, a wound, or an area already irritated by a condition such as eczema—and spread quickly to cause numerous sores.

When should I suspect that my child has impetigo?

Any time a child develops red sores that quickly crust over, he or she may have impetigo. Your suspicion should be particularly high if the child's siblings or classmates have similar sores.

Is medical attention necessary?

A doctor should examine sores that resemble impetigo since other conditions—paticularly **herpes** and **chickenpox** (see entries)—may look much the same. In addition, the doctor may scrape some material from the cells for laboratory examination—specifically, a culture to determine the type of bacteria involved.

In rare cases, streptococcal impetigo triggers a kidney disorder called **glomerulonephritis** (see entry). If streptococcus is identified in the sores, the physician may warn you to watch for signs and symptoms of this complication.

What treatments are available?

If the infection is mild and the affected area is small, treatment with antibiotic ointment may be adequate. However, many children need systemic antibiotics orally or by injection.

With proper treatment, impetigo improves within three to four days. Healing is complete in about ten days. If treatment is delayed, however, the infection takes longer to heal. Without treatment, it may persist for months and

leave scars or affect the color of the skin. It can also make the skin vulnerable to other infections, such as herpes.

Infectious Mononucleosis

Infectious mononucleosis is an acute viral infection. It has its peak incidence in adolescents between the ages of 15 and 17, but it commonly affects a much broader range of ages, including preschool and school-age children, although it is rare in children under age two. In adolescents, the incubation period after exposure is estimated as four to seven weeks; the period in younger children is unknown.

What causes infectious mononucleosis?

It is caused by the Epstein-Barr virus, which multiplies in the *lymphocytes,* white blood cells that normally play a key role in the immune system's defenses. The virus is transmitted through exchange of saliva.

By adulthood, most people have been exposed to the Epstein-Barr virus, but for unknown reasons, only a small percentage develop mononucleosis. Epstein-Barr virus is a type of herpes virus; other herpes viruses are responsible for chicken pox, cold sores, and genital herpes.

When should I suspect that my child has mononucleosis?

A child with infectious mononucleosis may develop flulike symptoms, including headache, sore throat, malaise, and fatigue, with or

---

Getting Help

CALL YOUR DOCTOR IF YOUR CHILD:
- Has sores with brownish crusts, particularly around the nose and mouth.
- Has raw, film-covered, red spots on the face or other areas of the body.

without fever. Two to five days later, the acute phase begins; it is characterized by fever and swollen lymph glands in the neck, under the arms, and in the groin. The tonsils may swell, making swallowing difficult and painful. In some cases, the tonsils become so enlarged that they obstruct breathing.

Is medical attention necessary?

Yes. It is vital for a doctor to diagnose mononucleosis so that the child will receive proper care.

How can the physician diagnose infectious mononucleosis?

Frequently the doctor can base the diagnosis on observation of a blood smear under the microscope: The presence of abnormal lymphocytes indicates mononucleosis. Further blood tests are performed, however, to confirm the diagnosis and to determine the extent of liver involvement.

Can complications result from infectious mononucleosis?

Yes. If the child develops jaundice (a yellowing of the skin), it may indicate mild liver damage, which occurs in about ten percent of cases. Enlargement of the spleen frequently accompanies mononucleosis, and rupture of the spleen is the most serious potential complication. Anemia may develop late in the disease.

What treatments are available?

No widely available drug is effective against mononucleosis. The standard treatment is usually rest to allow the immune system to recover. The physician will determine the

---

CARING FOR A CHILD WITH MONONUCLEOSIS

- Follow the physician's guidelines as to the amount of rest your child needs. Unfortunately, rest is one of the most difficult and frustrating treatments a normally energetic child has to tolerate. Your encouragement and support can go a long way toward making the recovery easier.
- Don't try to speed your child's recovery by encouraging activities too quickly; premature resumption of activities can cause a relapse.
- Swollen tonsils can make swallowing extremely painful, so a child with mononucleosis may have trouble taking in adequate fluids to prevent dehydration. High-calorie liquid supplements such as Ensure are appealing, and they have the added bonus of countering the weight loss that occurs as a natural part of the viral infection. Some experimentation will help you find fluids the child can tolerate best; fruit juices, broth, and pudding are favorites among many sick children.
- When the child's strength returns and the physician advises resumption of some elements of normal routine, it may be helpful to ease the child back to school by starting with half days.
- Contact sports should be avoided until all traces of the disease have disappeared and the spleen is back to normal size.

---

amount of rest required and the extent to which activities must be curtailed on the basis of the severity of the child's symptoms.

Tylenol may help reduce the pain of swollen glands and sore throat, and an anesthetic gargle may relieve throat pain and increase the child's tolerance for eating and drinking. In the presence of severe anemia or tonsils so swollen that they obstruct breathing, the doctor may prescribe a corticosteroid drug to alleviate these problems.

How long does mononucleosis last?

The course of mononucleosis varies among individuals. Frequently, the disease goes unrecognized in infants and young children. Some patients experience only a mild form of the disease and recover with moderate amounts of rest, while others require bed rest for several weeks due to continuing severe fatigue. Fever may last about two weeks. Almost everyone recovers within four to six weeks, but it can take months before the child feels completely back to normal. Sleepiness, low energy, and depression may persist for two or three additional months. Liver and spleen involvement may take three months to disappear.

Getting Help

CALL YOUR DOCTOR IF:
- Your child develops a high fever and severe sore throat after several days of fatigue and other vague symptoms.

Influenza (Flu)

Every winter brings the threat of an outbreak of influenza, a viral infection of the respiratory system that, during most outbreaks, strikes up to 20 percent of the population in an affected region. Babies and children of all ages are prone to influenza, but those who attend school, preschool, or day care are most likely to be exposed.

For most of the population, the flu is only a nuisance requiring bed rest and interfering briefly with normal activities. It can, however, be a dangerous illness for some people, including the very young.

What causes flu?

Influenza, or flu, is caused by several types of viruses that attack the upper and lower respiratory tracts—the nasal cavities, throat, windpipe, and lungs. The three main types of influenza virus are classified as types A, B, and C, but there are many variants within these types. Type C is usually mild, like a cold. One bout of this type of flu confers immunity for life. The viruses that cause types A and B, however, continuously undergo changes so that having suffered through one year's strain of flu gives no guarantee against catching the flu again.

How does flu spread?

Influenza viruses spread easily when an infected person sneezes or coughs. Hand and other bodily contact can also spread it. Some people who are infected—known as carriers—develop no flu symptoms, but they can spread the infection to others who may develop the illness.

Of the several forms of flu, influenza A is the most severe and can last the longest. It can start suddenly with a high fever, which begins to subside after about two days. Five days later, most other symptoms should be disappearing, although respiratory problems (runny nose, cough, and sputum production) may persist for seven to ten days. Influenza type B may not last as long or produce such severe symptoms.

When should I suspect that my child has flu?

The first warning may be news that the child's classmates have the flu. Symptoms of the flu sometimes come on suddenly. Look out for a runny nose, cough, headache, and sore throat, along with more generalized symptoms such as headache, chills, fever, appetite loss, muscle aches, and weakness. Some children with the flu also develop vomiting, diarrhea, or both.

Is medical attention necessary?

Yes. The pediatrician will want to monitor the child's illness because influenza can potentially cause several complications. The most common complication is a secondary bacterial infection of the sinuses, middle ear, or lungs. In rare cases, pneumonia develops as a complication of the flu.

How can the pediatrician tell if my child has flu?

If a child has flulike symptoms in the midst of a community-wide flu outbreak, the diagnosis is fairly straightforward. The pediatrician will, however, perform a physical examination and throat culture to check for strep throat, a bacterial infection that may have similar symptoms.

What treatments are available?

For uncomplicated influenza, treatment focuses on alleviating the symptoms. Bed rest is the most important measure. In addition, the

PREVENTING INFLUENZA

Flu viruses are so easily spread that standard preventive measures such as hand washing provide only slight protection. Because flu is dangerous for certain groups, vaccines are developed each year from a combination of the type A and B viruses causing the previous year's influenza outbreaks. If new viruses are similar to those of the previous year, these vaccines can be quite effective. Although not all children need the vaccine, your pediatrician will probably recommend it if your child has:

- Chronic heart or lung problems, including asthma.
- Diabetes, kidney disease, or a disorder associated with abnormal hemoglobin.
- A compromised immune system.

pediatrician may recommend acetaminophen to reduce fever and aches, as well as fluids to counter the dehydrating effects of fever and vomiting or diarrhea. If necessary, the pediatrician also will prescribe a cough suppressant. Although two antiviral drugs (amantadine and rimantadine) have been proven effective against the flu, both have significant side effects and both need to be started immediately after the onset of symptoms. Therefore, these drugs are rarely used, especially in children.

When the child's fever has gone down, bed rest is no longer necessary. Even so, most children will continue to tire easily for several more days. It is probably best to wait at least a week from the onset of symptoms before resuming full activity, including school or day care.

Intestinal Obstruction

Regurgitation, diarrhea, and constipation are fairly common in infants. When these problems occur with abnormal frequency, however, they may be signs of intestinal obstruction, a serious condition in which a blockage develops in the stomach, small intestine, or large intestine. Such an obstruction may be present at birth or develop later in infancy or during early childhood.

How does intestinal obstruction develop?

Intestinal obstruction can develop in several different ways. An infant may be born with a congenital intestinal malformation that causes narrowing or twisting of a section of the small or large bowel. **Pyloric stenosis** (see entry), in which the passage between the stomach and small intestine fails to open properly, is the most common intestinal obstruction in infants. Newborns with a condition called *Hirschsprung disease* typically develop obstruction of the large intestine because they lack certain nerves that control function of the large intestine. The result is a greatly enlarged colon and severe constipation. Affected infants may also get sudden high fever and rectal bleeding. About ten percent of babies born with cystic fibrosis have intestinal obstruction caused by retention of meconium, the greenish-black substance that fills the colon before birth.

In the first two years of life, one of the major causes of intestinal obstruction is *intussusception,* in which one portion of the intestines is pushed into another like a folding telescope. Another possible cause is an **inguinal hernia** (see entry), in which a segment of intestine protrudes through the abdominal lining into the groin.

Unless corrected, intestinal obstructions can severely compromise a baby's or child's nutrition and fluid balance. Ultimately, the area above the obstruction may rupture, allowing intestinal contents to spill into the abdominal cavity and resulting in **peritonitis** (see entry), a serious infection.

When should I suspect that my child has intestinal obstruction?

The pediatrician or hospital nursery staff will notice if the baby fails to pass meconium within 12 to 24 hours after birth. Failure to pass meconium strongly suggests the presence of an intestinal obstruction. Other symptoms in the newborn include vomiting and abdominal bloating.

In older children, the major symptom of intestinal obstruction is abdominal pain,

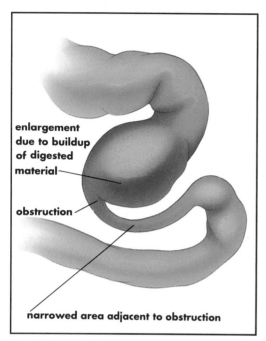

enlargement
due to buildup
of digested
material

obstruction

narrowed area adjacent to obstruction

A segment of small intestine containing an
obstruction.

which may be either sharp or dull. If the child
cannot yet talk, signs of abdominal pain may
include grimacing and pulling up the legs.
Other signs of intestinal obstruction in older
children include nausea, repeated vomiting,
abdominal bloating, and constipation.

Is medical attention necessary?

Yes. The signs and symptoms of intestinal obstruction warrant immediate medical care.

How can the pediatrician tell if my
child has an intestinal obstruction?

If the obstruction is caused by a hernia or pyloric stenosis, the pediatrician may be able to
make the diagnosis on the basis of a physical
and ultrasound examination. X rays of the intestinal tract, taken after the contrast material

barium is swallowed (or placed in the stomach
through a tube) or administered as an enema,
can help locate the site of the obstruction.

What treatments are available?

If the doctor suspects an intestinal obstruction, the child will be hospitalized and seen
immediately by a surgeon. In most cases, surgery is necessary to remove the obstruction,
although a twisted intestine occasionally returns to normal without surgery.

Getting Help

CALL YOUR DOCTOR IF YOUR CHILD:

■ Fails to pass meconium (greenish-
black fecal matter) within 12 to 24
hours after birth.

■ Is grimacing and pulling up the
legs, indicating abdominal pain, or
your child complains of stomach
pain, particularly in conjunction
with vomiting, abdominal bloating, and constipation.

*Jaundice, Physiologic
(Neonatal Hyperbilirubinemia)*

A yellowish discoloration of a normal newborn baby's skin is known as physiologic
jaundice or neonatal hyperbilirubinemia. (Bilirubin is the chemical in blood that causes
jaundice.) The condition is quite common
and usually harmless in healthy newborns,
most of whom are no longer jaundiced by the
end of the first week of life. In certain infants

(particularly premature ones), however, jaundice is a more serious symptom that requires close medical attention.

Infants of Asian descent, Native Americans, and Eskimos are more likely to develop hyperbilirubinemia—and to have extremely high levels of bilirubin—than Caucasian infants. The condition is less common in black infants than in whites or Asians.

What causes jaundice?

Jaundice is a sign that the baby's blood contains an excessive amount of *bilirubin,* a substance released when old red blood cells break down. Normally, bilirubin is removed from the blood stream, processed in the liver, and passed from the body in the feces as part of a fluid called bile. In newborns, however, this process tends to be inefficient, partly because the liver is immature and partly because a large number of red blood cells are broken down soon after birth. Most of the time, the situation corrects itself over the first several days of life. If the baby is premature, however, bilirubin levels may reach very high levels in the blood, creating a dangerous situation in which the substance may be deposited in the brain and cause permanent damage.

How does jaundice develop?

If a newborn baby's bilirubin level is higher than normal, the skin may take on a yellowish tinge. Jaundice usually appears first on the baby's face. It may then worsen, spreading to the chest, stomach, and legs. The pediatrician will note the condition and treat it (usually by exposing the baby to fluorescent light) if necessary.

For reasons that are still unclear, breast feeding sometimes triggers jaundice in newborns between two and four days after birth. This occurrence may be due in part to the limited amounts of fluid and calories babies get from nursing before the milk supply is established. It is more likely, though, that some component in breast milk interferes with the excretion of bilirubin.

Is medical attention necessary?

Bilirubin levels normally drop and jaundice disappears in the first week of life. If the bilirubin level is very high or does not drop on its own, however, the pediatrician will take steps to decrease it.

How can the pediatrician tell if my infant has jaundice?

Pediatricians examine all newborns every day until they are discharged from the hospital. The examination is carried out while the baby is undressed and in a well-lighted area, so skin discoloration will be obvious. To detect jaundice in black and other dark-skinned infants, pediatricians compress the skin slightly, which reveals underlying yellowness.

If a newborn is jaundiced, the pediatrician will generally recommend a laboratory test to determine the level of bilirubin in your baby's blood. This is probably the most common test performed on newborns. If the bilirubin level is excessively high and remains high over several successive tests, the pediatrician will recommend treatment.

If you are taking your baby home from the hospital within 24 hours of birth, your nurse or doctor may show you how to watch for the development of jaundice in your baby's skin and eyes.

What treatments are available?

The most common treatment is phototherapy, in which the infant is placed under bright, fluorescent lights, which convert bilirubin to a form that is easily excreted. Phototherapy, which usually lasts only a day or two, is indicated if jaundice is severe or does not subside on its own.

The doctor may also suggest that you halt breast feeding for 24 to 48 hours, another technique to help the baby's liver expel bilirubin. If very high levels of bilirubin develop, particularly in premature infants, an exchange transfusion may be needed to remove the bilirubin from the baby's blood. Finally, the pediatrician may take blood tests to monitor the baby's bilirubin level and to determine if the jaundice is a symptom of another underlying disorder.

Kawasaki Disease

This puzzling disease, first described in 1967 by a Japanese pediatrician, occurs mainly in children under age five and affects boys more often than girls. The disease causes a high fever, bloodshot eyes, swelling of the lymph glands in the neck, and a number of skin changes, the most striking of which are bright red lips and swelling, redness, and peeling skin on the palms and soles. In about one percent of cases, serious heart abnormalities develop.

For unknown reasons, Kawasaki disease is more than five times as common among children of Asian descent than among Caucasian children. In the United States, the incidence of the disease has increased steadily since 1974, when the first cases were reported.

What causes Kawasaki disease?

The cause is not known, although its symptom pattern and tendency to occur in clusters within communities suggests that it may be infectious. The fact that it involves several organ systems, however, indicates that it may, instead, be an autoimmune disease—that is, a disease that occurs when the immune system produces antibodies that attack the body's healthy tissues. Environmental factors also may play a role in its development.

What happens during Kawasaki disease?

The disease progresses through several stages. The young child or infant first experiences a high fever, irritability, eye redness, swelling of the hands, feet, and lymph nodes, and a rash. This phase, which lasts a week to ten days, gives way to a second phase in which fever subsides but other symptoms—frequently, arthritis and peeling skin on the hands and feet—appear. It is during this second phase—which lasts three to four weeks—that serious heart problems may develop. In the third phase, the child generally feels much better, but laboratory tests continue to show abnormalities in the blood, and heart problems may still develop. Complete recovery may take more than twelve weeks.

The most frightening cardiac complication of Kawasaki disease is the development of aneurysms (balloonlike swellings) in the walls of the coronary arteries. A coronary aneurysm can give rise to a blood clot, which in turn may block the artery and cause a heart attack.

How can the pediatrician tell if my child has Kawasaki disease?

Pediatricians base the diagnosis of Kawasaki disease on the presence of several of the disease's characteristic signs and symptoms. According to established guidelines, a child almost always has five out of six major signs and symptoms of Kawasaki disease (fever; conjunctivitis; redness and inflammation of the mouth and lips; redness, swelling, and/or peeling skin on the hands and feet; a rash, mainly on the trunk; and swollen lymph nodes in the region of the neck).

What treatments are available?

Kawasaki disease is treated with high dose intravenous gamma globulin therapy, which is usually administered in the hospital. Early treatment always reduces the possibility of coronary aneurysm formation. High doses of aspirin for several weeks are often given since some evidence shows that aspirin together with gamma globulin shortens the duration of the illness.

During the second phase of the disease, the doctor will monitor the child's heart function

---

Getting Help

CALL YOUR DOCTOR IF YOUR CHILD:

- Develops a sudden, high fever and any of the eye, mouth, or skin changes characteristic of Kawasaki disease.
- Is recovering from Kawasaki disease and develops chest pain, pallor, and difficulty breathing, which suggest serious heart problems.

---

with various tests, including an electrocardiogram and an echocardiogram. Both tests are painless. In addition, a chest X ray may be taken. Some or all of these tests may need to be repeated periodically for several months after recovery is complete.

Kidney Disease, Polycystic

This hereditary kidney disorder occurs in two main forms. The more common form, known as adult polycystic disease (APCD), usually develops in adulthood but may, in rare cases, manifest itself in infancy or childhood. Much less common is infantile polycystic disease (IPCD), wich is usually apparent soon after birth and is accompanied by liver abnormalities.

In both forms of the disease, the kidney is riddled with fluid-filled growths called cysts. These cysts, which usually appear in both kidneys, severely impair kidney functioning. In the infantile form of the disease, the kidneys may be either enlarged or underdeveloped.

Some infants also are born with a noninherited cystic kidney disorder called multicystic kidney of the newborn. This disorder, which usually affects only one kidney, occurs when the ureter (the tube to the bladder) develops abnormally, causing the kidney to degenerate into an irregular mass of cysts.

How does polycystic kidney disease develop?

APCD is inherited as a dominant trait, which means that 50 percent of the children of an affected parent will develop the disease. IPCD is inherited as a recessive trait, which means that both parents carry the disease gene—and the child must inherit both copies—to develop the disease. In this circumstance, 25 percent of children will develop this rare disease.

When should I suspect that my child has polycystic kidney disease?

Multicystic kidney of the newborn is usually discovered soon after birth, since the abnormal kidney can often be felt as a large mass in the abdomen. If the other types of polycystic disease do not become apparent during infancy, they may cause a number of symptoms later on, including enlargement of the liver and spleen, pain in the side and lower back, and frequent urinary tract infections. The kidneys may, in addition, become so large that they can be felt as hard masses on the sides of the trunk.

How can the pediatrician tell if my child has polycystic kidney disease?

The main diagnostic tools are ultrasound, computed tomography (CT) scanning, and conventional X rays.

What treatments are available?

Treatment options are limited. Because cysts recur, surgery to remove them is ineffective. Ultimately, polycystic kidney disease progresses to kidney failure, necessitating dialysis (filtering of the blood with an artificial kidney) or transplantation.

Getting Help

Since polycystic kidney disease is usually hereditary, couples with family histories of the disease should seek genetic counseling to determine whether they risk passing it to their children. For more information, see entry on genetic disorders.

Kidney Failure

When the kidneys fail—which can happen as a result of a number of different disorders, only some of which are primarily kidney diseases—waste products build up in the blood, causing serious complications. Acute kidney failure is the sudden loss of kidney function; chronic kidney failure develops gradually.

To function normally, the body really needs only one working kidney. As soon as the kidneys' filtering capacity falls much below 50 percent, however, problems begin to appear, worsening as filtering capacity drops. With special measures such as dietary restriction and medication, however, children can survive even after kidney function has fallen to five or ten percent of normal.

When should I suspect that my child has kidney failure?

Acute kidney failure is usually a complication of some other serious illness. Generally, parents first notice that the child stops urinating or urinates very infrequently. Other symptoms include body swelling, drowsiness, and irregular heartbeat.

The first signs of chronic kidney failure are usually loss of energy and easy fatigue. As the condition progresses, the child may lose appetite (particularly in the morning), pass less urine than usual, and drink more fluids. The child's skin also may grow pale and develop a sallow, muddy appearance. Other symptoms include headaches, muscle cramps, nausea, weight loss, puffy face, bone or joint pain, and bruised, dry, or itchy skin. Children with chronic kidney failure also experience slowed growth.

What causes kidney failure?

Acute kidney failure may occur as a complication of shock, dehydration from diarrhea, persistent vomiting, blood loss, burns, or trauma. Such failure is usually temporary and can be reversed by administration of fluids. Sometimes the problem originates when the kidney itself is damaged by disease or adverse reactions to some drugs.

Chronic kidney failure can be caused by chronic diseases of the kidneys, such as **nephritis** (see entry). It also may be due to chronic infection (pyelonephritis) often resulting from malformations of the kidneys and urinary tract. Kidney failure may be a complication of diabetes in older children and adolescents.

How is kidney failure treated?

Treatment of acute kidney failure depends on the underlying cause. If it is caused by dehydration, the child receives large amounts of fluids. In all other cases, however, fluids must be restricted in order to prevent blood pressure elevation. The child usually is given diuretics to remove excess fluids from the body. Children with acute kidney failure are treated in a hospital.

Treatment of chronic kidney failure consists of eliminating the underlying disease whenever possible and preventing further loss of function. Children with chronic kidney failure may require drugs to correct their metabolism and treat high blood pressure, and they generally need to follow dietary restrictions.

Children with limited kidney function may need *dialysis,* a procedure in which the blood is circulated through a machine or fluids are filtered through the peritoneal membranes of the abdominal cavity. Dialysis is sometimes used as a temporary measure in acute kidney failure, but it may be required on a regular, long-term basis if the child's kidneys are permanently damaged.

Children with chronic, progressive kidney failure may be good candidates for kidney transplantation, in which a healthy kidney from a deceased donor or living relative takes the place of the failing kidneys. Kidney transplants are among the most common and successful transplant operations.

PREVENTING KIDNEY FAILURE

The following are some precautions you can take to prevent kidney failure:

- Prevent dehydration. Be sure a child with diarrhea or vomiting gets enough fluids.
- Control high blood pressure and diabetes, which may damage the kidneys.
- If your child has chronic kidney failure, take precautions to avoid other diseases or infections that may further strain the kidneys.

Kidney Malformations, Congenital

The kidneys, a pair of organs located in the lower back, are composed of millions of tiny tubes called *nephrons*. As blood passes through the nephrons, vital substances are retained in the circulation while nitrogen-containing wastes, which form the urine, drip out into a central pooling area, the renal pelvis. From the renal pelvis, urine travels to the bladder, from which it is excreted.

Of all the organs in the body, the kidneys are the most vulnerable to congenital malformations. Fortunately, many of the more common congenital kidney problems cause no symptoms. They may, in fact, go completely unnoticed unless they are detected on X rays taken for some other reason.

TYPES OF KIDNEY MALFORMATIONS

- **ECTOPIC KIDNEY.** This malformation occurs when one kidney fails to rise to the midsection, remaining below the waist instead. Ectopic kidneys function normally despite their location.
- **KIDNEY MALROTATION.** A kidney that does not rotate properly during fetal development is malrotated. A malrotated kidney faces the wrong way, but it works.
- **RENAL AGENESIS.** This malformation occurs when a kidney fails to develop. However, as long as one healthy kidney remains, the absence of the other kidney poses no serious threat.
- **HYPOPLASTIC KIDNEY.** A hypoplastic kidney is small and underdeveloped. Since such a kidney may contain precancerous cells, its presence is a greater cause for concern.
- **SUPERNUMERARY KIDNEYS.** In this malformation, two normal kidneys drain into a duplicated or triplicated renal pelvis.
- **HORSESHOE KIDNEY.** In this malformation, the two kidneys are fused into one large, horseshoe-shaped organ. A horseshoe kidney lies low in the back because it is too large to rise.

How do kidney malformations develop?

Normally, the first tiny kidney tubules appear during the fourth week of prenatal development. By the eighth week, a complete (if small) rudimentary pair of kidneys is present, although not in the location where they should be at birth. Through the remainder of the prenatal period, the kidneys rise and rotate to take their eventual place in the lower back. Many kidney malformations develop at this latter stage, when one of the kidneys moves only part of the way into its normal position. More rarely, problems occur in the first eight weeks. In these cases, one kidney may be incompletely formed or improperly attached to the blood supply or ureters (the tubes that carry urine to the bladder).

When should I suspect that my child has a kidney malformation?

Most kidney malformations do not produce symptoms. Before birth, a kidney malformation in the fetus may cause an excessive or deficient amount of amniotic fluid (the liquid in which the fetus floats) in the uterus. If the obstetrician detects this problem, a fetal ultrasound may be ordered to check kidney structures.

Repeated urinary tract infections and urinary stones are also possible signs of kidney malformations. In addition, kidney malformations may occur in certain congenital syndromes (groups of symptoms and features that occur together) such as **fetal alcohol syndrome** (see entry).

Is medical attention necessary?

Since the kidneys are able to function normally in the majority of kidney malformations, special medical care may not be necessary. If a child has only one functioning kidney, however, special care should be taken to avoid urinary tract infections, since damage to the remaining kidney can lead to kidney failure.

Labial Adhesions

Irritations of the vulva—the external female genitalia—are common in infant and preschool girls. Wet and soiled diapers, detergent residues in diapers and underpants, and all kinds of soap (particularly bubble bath) can cause redness, itching, and inflammation in this sensitive area.

Labial adhesions are common in girls in the first few years of life but also occur in older children. The labia minora (the pinkish inner lips of the vulva) become fused together during the process of healing following vulvar irritation. The result looks like a malformation of the genitals: When the labia majora (the larger, outer lips of the vulva) are spread apart, a solid membrane is visible, completely covering the vaginal opening. There may be a small urinary opening at the upper end of the membrane, but the inner sides of the labia are not visible. It also may be possible to see a thin line running down the middle of the membrane where the edges of the labia met.

How do labial adhesions develop?

Irritation that may be minor enough to go unnoticed generally precedes the development of labial adhesions. As the irritation heals, new cells on the edges of both labia minora stick to each other as if they were part of the same structure. In a short time, the two labia are fused into a single membrane. The cause is unknown.

Once labial adhesions develop, urine buildup behind the membrane may lead to further irritation, creating a kind of vicious cycle in which inflammation never subsides completely and the labia remain fused.

When should I suspect that my daughter has labial adhesions?

A quick visual inspection of the vulva during a diaper change should alert you to the presence of labial adhesions. Pediatricians generally perform such examinations during routine checkups as well.

Most of the time, adhesions themselves produce no symptoms. In some cases, there may be discomfort and difficulty urinating. If the adhesions are causing soreness, the child may rub the vulva excessively.

How are labial adhesions treated?

No treatment is necessary unless the adhesions are associated with repeated urinary tract infections and pain on urination.

If the adhesions require treatment, the pediatrician will prescribe an estrogen cream to be applied to the labia. This treatment, which usually continues for about a month, resolves almost all adhesions, although continued application of petroleum jelly may be necessary to keep the labia from fusing again. It is not advisable to separate the labia forcefully or with surgery, since the trauma of these procedures often leads to further irritation and repeated formation of adhesions.

PREVENTING LABIAL ADHESIONS

- Clean the diaper area, including the labial minora, during each diaper change.
- Use a clean, wet washcloth and water rather than a commercial baby wipe to clean the diaper area.
- Launder cloth diapers and underpants in mild detergent.
- Avoid bubble baths and extremely soapy water.
- Treat diaper rash promptly. Let the baby go without diapers as much as possible.

Are girls with labial adhesions at risk of other genital or urinary-tract abnormalities?

Not at all. Unfortunately, though, many parents are so distressed by the abnormal appearance of labial adhesions that they insist on treatment. While the treatment is also harmless, all the fuss may place an undue focus for the child and her family on her genitalia.

Severe labial adhesions that obstruct the flow of urine can lead to urinary tract infections, which require antibiotic treatment. If the pediatrician diagnoses such an infection (see **urinary tract infections**) in a girl with labial adhesions, both conditions will probably be treated.

Getting Help

CALL YOUR DOCTOR IF:
- You notice anything unusual about your baby's genitals.
- Your baby cries when urinating.
- Your child complains of pain, burning, or itching in the genital area.

Lead Poisoning

Lead poisoning develops when people ingest or inhale lead, usually over a long period of time. Although people of all ages are susceptible to the problem, children are especially vulnerable to its long-term effects, particularly if they ingest lead during the first two years of life, when the nervous system is still developing. Children also absorb more of the lead they ingest than adults, a factor that compounds their risk of building up toxic levels of lead.

How does lead poisoning occur?

The main cause of lead poisoning in children is ingestion of contaminated paint chips and dust in old homes and apartments. It is estimated that as many as 60 percent of buildings in older cities such as New York, Philadelphia, and Boston may have lead paint on their inside walls. In crowded metropolitan areas, lead-containing car and truck emissions may also contribute to lead poisoning.

A fetus can develop lead poisoning if the mother was exposed to high levels of lead during pregnancy. In addition, some evidence indicates that women who were exposed to high levels of lead during their own childhoods can pass lead to their infants in breast milk.

Parents who work in environments with high lead levels may inadvertently expose their children to lead dust on their clothes and hair. Children living in homes near factories with lead-containing emissions also may be at risk.

Pottery glazes used to contain lead. The use of such materials is now illegal in the United States, but occasional cases of acute lead toxicity are reminders that antique, imported, and improperly produced eating vessels are a potential source of lead.

What happens when a child has lead poisoning?

Inhaled or ingested lead tends to build up in the body, particularly in the bones but also in other body tissues. As toxic levels of lead build up, a number of subtle abnormalities become evident.

PREVENTING LEAD POISONING

- If you live in an apartment or house that was built before World War II, use a home test or get a professional company to determine if there is lead paint in your home. If there is, it should be replaced (by removing the painted woodwork and replacing it with new), sealed off with a latex sealer, or removed (using special chemicals and safety gear). For more information on lead paint and old houses, send for the booklet "What You Should Know about Lead-Based Paint in Your Home," from the Consumer Product Safety Commission, Washington, DC 20207. (To expedite, write "Publication Request" on the envelope.)

- Remove all flaking or peeling paint from the areas where your child plays. Hallways, windows, and doors are most apt to be in bad repair because of the increased traffic in these areas.

- Use a high-power vacuum to free carpeting and floors from lead and other dust.

- Your young child should NOT be in the house during the de-leading process. This is a good time to visit friends or grandmother for a few days.

- If possible, use air conditioning instead of opening windows if you live near a highway or factory.

- Choose ceramic dinnerware and glassware made in the United States and certified lead-free by the manufacturer.

- Check with your local water authority and find out the level of lead in your drinking water. If the plumbing in your building is old, have an inspector determine the lead level of the water coming out of the faucet. If it is too high, switch to bottled water.

The U.S. Centers for Disease Control consider any lead level over ten as elevated and requiring monitoring. Treatment for lead poisoning is generally initiated at levels above 25. At this level, a child may appear listless and slow to react. Weight loss may occur, and frequent, minor illnesses are common. The child's IQ also may be compromised.

Children with extremely high levels of lead experience more dramatic symptoms. They commonly develop anemia, and their hands and feet may tingle and lose sensation. Children may also lose coordination and regress in development. Children with lead levels above 80 micrograms per deciliter of blood may suffer brain damage, persistent vomiting, and convulsions.

There is now evidence that even low levels of lead in the blood may cause subtle symptoms. Affected children may not grow as rapidly as their peers, and their IQs may not increase normally as they mature.

How can the pediatrician tell if my child has lead poisoning?

The pediatrician may notice subtle signs of chronic lead poisoning such as delayed development, poor coordination, and behavior disturbances. The diagnosis is made by measuring levels of lead in the blood. In areas where the risk is high, all children between ages one and five years may be periodically tested for lead poisoning.

What treatments are available?

First and foremost, the source of the lead must be identified and removed from the child's environment. Children with lead poisoning need to undergo chelation therapy, in which a drug that binds to lead is infused into the bloodstream. Once the chelating agent picks up the lead, it can be excreted. In severe cases, however, several chelation treatments may be necessary.

What are the long-term effects?

If high levels of lead are detected early enough, the child should recover completely. There is some evidence, however, that subtle neurological symptoms such as reduction in IQ may not be fully reversible.

Learning Disabilities

Learning disabilities, also known as *specific developmental disorders,* are conditions that may impair a child's ability to keep up with peers in reading, writing, speaking, physical coordination, and math skills. Such conditions do not result from lack of intelligence; an affected child may have average or above average intelligence. They result when a particular skill or ability fails to develop at the expected age. Learning disabilities differ from other developmental disorders in the limited range of their effects; unlike mentally retarded or autistic children, learning disabled children show impairment in only one or a few specific areas. For example, a child with a learning disability might be above average in math but way below in reading.

These problems commonly become apparent during the early school years. They affect from five to 20 percent of school-age children, most of them boys. Other conditions, such as attention-deficit hyperactivity disorder and depression, often accompany learning disabilities.

When should I suspect that my child has a learning disability?

Children with learning disabilities often have one or more of the following characteristics:

1. Problems in listening, speaking, reading, writing, spelling, or mathematics.
2. Short attention span.
3. Difficulty in following directions.
4. Distractibility.
5. Low frustration threshold.
6. Poor memory.
7. Poor coordination and clumsiness.
8. Organizational difficulties.

What causes learning disabilities?

Learning disabilities are believed to arise from abnormalities in the physiology of the brain. There is also some evidence of a genetic cause, since a child is more likely to develop learning disabilities if others in the family have them.

Rarely, learning disabilities are associated with problems during birth, particularly brain injury or exposure to infection. Higher rates of learning disabilities also correlate with low birth weight, as well as with maternal drug, alcohol, and tobacco use. Other possible causes such as dietary allergies and vitamin deficiencies have not been well substantiated.

Is medical attention necessary?

Yes. You should consult your child's doctor as soon as problems become apparent. Some symptoms may show up before school age, as in, for example, a toddler or preschooler with inadequate language skills. In many cases, the learning disability may not appear until first or second grade, or even later, when the child falls behind others in class. The earlier the problem is identified and diagnosed, the better.

How can the doctor tell if my child has learning disabilities?

The doctor will conduct an initial interview with you, your child, and possibly your child's teacher. He will want to know about your family history, any possible problems during the pregnancy and delivery, and your child's medical history. An examination to rule out vision or hearing problems, other neurological disorders, or other conditions that might contribute to a learning problem should follow.

The doctor then may administer simple screening tests, which usually consist of a series of questions posed to the child and parents, possibly in addition to a few tasks for the child to perform. If these tests suggest the presence of a learning disability, the next step is usually referral to a specialist such as a child psychologist or developmental pediatrician, who can conduct more detailed tests to determine the specific type of disorder affecting your child.

What treatments are available?

Remedial education is the main tool in dealing with learning disabilities. This generally means giving special attention to compensate for the disorder through tutoring or scheduled visits to a school resource center. Schools are required by law to provide such attention to children diagnosed with learning disabilities.

Academic skills disorders

- Developmental reading disorder (also known as dyslexia). This disorder causes impairment in word recognition and reading comprehension skills.
- Developmental expressive writing disorder. This disorder results in difficulty spelling and expressing thoughts through words.
- Developmental arithmetic disorder. In this disorder, math skills are well below intellectual capacity or grade level.
- Nonverbal learning disability. This disorder is characterized by difficulty with visual spatial skills and often arithmetic, and personality traits such as depression and shyness.

Language and speech disorders

- Developmental articulation disorder. Children with this disorder substitute or omit speech sounds, giving the impression of baby talk but speak in full sentences.
- Developmental expressive language disorder. Children with this problem hear and comprehend normally but do not produce age-appropriate speech.
- Developmental receptive language disorder. This disorder is marked by failure to understand and produce language at an age-appropriate level.

Motor skills disorder

- This disorder (also called developmental coordination disorder) is characterized by difficulty performing everyday tasks that require physical coordination, such as handwriting.

Special education enables the child to stay in a regular classroom setting as much as possible, although in some severe cases, full-time special education may be needed.

The earlier treatment begins, the better; so preschool children with deficient language skills should receive help as soon as possible. Studies have shown that children whose problems are identified in preschool do better in school if they receive training in specific perceptual and language skills. The method is to build ability in tasks such as sorting, shape recognition, and speech awareness before starting school.

Children who have **attention-deficit hyperactivity disorder** (see entry) as well as learning disabilities may benefit from stimulant drugs, which increase their ability to concentrate on one thing at a time.

Counseling can help children with learning disabilities cope with stress, depression, or anxiety. Social-skills training can help children who are teased by their classmates.

Also, parents sometimes need help coping with their children's problems. Learning to understand and accept the child's learning disabilities often goes a long way toward improving the family atmosphere.

Coping with learning disabilities

Children with learning disabilities often have problems with self-esteem, social adjustment, and age-appropriate behavior at school and at home. They are also vulnerable to feelings of sadness or depression. Such children need a great deal of encouragement and require a lot of patience.

It is best to speak openly with your child.

Explain that everyone has strengths and weaknesses—someone who reads well, for example, may be unable to carry a tune. Help your child understand his pattern of learning, and teach him coping skills. For example, if the child cannot remember things, make lists or plan ahead.

Look for ways your child can succeed. Offer plenty of praise for things the child does well. All children have strengths and weaknesses. Children with learning disabilities need to be taught strategies to compensate for the weak areas.

Help your child develop social skills. Invite children over to play. Role-play or discuss social situations in private if you see your child responding to friends inappropriately.

Finally, it is vital to be an advocate for your child's education. Get a quality evaluation and the best treatment, and don't stop until you do. If severe reading problems are identified and addressed in the early grades, children may return to appropriate grade level within two years. If problems aren't identified and treated by fifth grade, few will catch up to grade level. There is no cure for learning dis-

abilities, but children who receive proper treatment, particularly in school, can learn to compensate for their problems, which need not result in insurmountable obstacles to higher education or rewarding career choices.

Leukemia

Leukemia, the most common form of childhood cancer, accounts for one-third of all cancers diagnosed in children each year. In leukemia—as in all cancers—one type of cell grows out of control. Since the cells involved in leukemia, white blood cells, are essential to the body's immune system, abnormalities in their growth severely lower the body's resistance to infection. Leukemia can occur at any time during childhood, but most cases develop between the ages of three and five.

Although any cancer diagnosis is serious, leukemia is now one of the most successfully treated forms of the disease. As with other types of cancer, chances of a cure are greatest when the disease is diagnosed and treated in its early stages. Thanks to great advances in the management of childhood leukemia over the past 25 years. The majority of affected children will achieve long-term remissions, with an increasing number apparently cured.

How does leukemia develop?

Blood is comprised of plasma (the liquid portion) and three kinds of cells: red cells, white cells, and clear cells (called *platelets*). White blood cells are fundamental in fighting infection.

PREVENTING LEARNING DISABILITIES

Because the exact cause of learning disabilities is unknown, no precise preventive measures can be identified. In general, though, good prenatal care may reduce the chance that a baby will eventually have learning problems. Do not use alcohol, tobacco, or drugs during pregnancy.

All blood cells originate in the bone marrow, the soft substance in the interior channel that runs through the long bones. Leukemia develops when some trigger—as yet unidentified—causes one or more white cells to mutate in its early development within the bone marrow. Once a mutated white cell develops, it proliferates rapidly and uncontrollably, overcrowding the bone marrow and preventing production of adequate amounts of normally functioning blood cells. Via the bloodstream, the abnormal cells spread throughout the body.

These abnormal white blood cells crowd out the normal blood cells in the marrow, leading to anemia and impaired blood clotting. In addition, the lack of normal white blood cells opens the door to severe infections.

The exact cause of leukemia is unknown. Children with certain genetic disorders (such as Down syndrome) seem to have an inborn predisposition to developing the disease. Since most children with these disorders do not develop leukemia, it seems likely that a second factor (such as exposure to some environmental toxin) is required to initiate the disease process.

When should I suspect that my child has leukemia?

Possible symptoms include:

- Fatigue, pallor, weakness, malaise, increased heart rate, and irritability.
- Frequent fever and infections (results of insufficient white blood cells).
- Increased bruising, nosebleeds, and gum bleeding (results of insufficient platelets).

- Limping (a result of bone soreness).
- Enlargement of the spleen, liver, lymph nodes, thymus gland, and kidneys (a direct result of proliferating white blood cells).

What are the different types of leukemia?

Leukemia is classified according to the speed at which it progesses (acute or chronic) and by the type of white blood cell it affects. Acute forms account for 97 percent of childhood leukemias. They are characterized by a quick onset and rapid progression; in as little as two months, abnormal white cells may have crowded out almost all normal blood cells. The less common chronic leukemias develop more slowly, over two years or more.

The most common leukemia affecting children is *acute lymphocytic leukemia (ALL)*, marked by abnormal proliferation of a type of white blood cell known as *lymphocytes.* This form affects about 80 to 85 percent of children with the disease. *Acute granulocytic leukemia* and *acute monocytic leukemia,* much less common, are often referred to collectively as *acute nonlymphocytic leukemia.*

What treatments are available?

The goal of leukemia therapy is to eliminate all the abnormal white blood cells, making way for new, healthy cells to develop, multiply, and resume normal functioning. Chemotherapy is usually the first choice. A number of different drug combinations have been developed to kill abnormal bone marrow cells; the physician's choice depends on which type of leukemia the child has.

During the initial phase of treatment, the

child also receives blood transfusions and antibiotics. Chemotherapy is usually continued until all detectable abnormal cells in the bone marrow have been destroyed, usually by four to six weeks. To maintain the remission, the child will receive a less intense course of chemotherapy at regular intervals, usually for two to three years.

A child whose leukemia has gone into remission (meaning that all detectable abnormal cells have disappeared) must be watched carefully for signs of relapse, particularly within the first year after the drugs are stopped.

Other treatments

Bone marrow transplants have become increasingly important in the therapy of childhood leukemia. This procedure, performed after intensive radiation or chemotherapy to destroy the unhealthy marrow, involves intravenous infusions of marrow cells from a donor who is immunologically compatible—ideally a sibling. Bone marrow transplantation usually is recommended for children with newly diagnosed ALL in remission and for children with ALL who have experienced one or more relapses.

Bone marrow transplantation is lengthy, risky, and expensive. Parents whose children are undergoing the treatment may need extra emotional support from their extended families, as well as from mental health professionals.

Coping with leukemia

The responsibility of caring for a child with leukemia can take a toll on parents. Here are some suggestions to help you cope:

- Arrange for help at home, including babysitters.
- Do not isolate yourself socially, but avoid people who are not supportive.
- Learn about community resources, such as a support group with other parents of children with cancer.
- If necessary, seek professional counseling.

Getting Help

CALL YOUR DOCTOR IF YOUR CHILD:

- ■ Develops any signs and symptoms of leukemia, which can appear quite suddenly; be particularly alert to unusual bruising, unexplained pain and limping, frequent nosebleeds, and bleeding gums.

Lupus

Systemic lupus erythematosus (known as lupus) is an inflammatory disease that affects organs throughout the body. Lupus is an autoimmune disease, triggered when the immune system produces abnormal antibodies that attack the connective tissue of the skin, joints, kidneys, lungs, heart, and central nervous system. Blood disorders also occur in most afflicted children.

About 15 percent of lupus cases occur in children, who often are affected more severely than adults. A syndrome similar to lupus often occurs in newborns whose mothers have lupus.

When should I suspect that my child has lupus?

The first symptoms of lupus are nonspecific. They include fever, fatigue, and weight loss lasting for several months. More specific symptoms then emerge. The most common of these are pain in the joints and a butterfly-shaped rash on the bridge of the nose and cheeks. Other symptoms include dry and brittle hair (sometimes hair loss); skin pallor or blueness; sensitivity to cold, especially in the hands and feet; and patches of reddish skin on the palms of the hands and the soles of the feet. In addition, the kidneys, heart, lungs, liver, or central nervous system may be involved.

How can the pediatrician tell if my child has lupus?

With the exception of the butterfly rash, all symptoms of lupus occur in several other disorders as well. Diagnosis therefore depends upon a characteristic spectrum of symptoms supported by blood tests that reveal the presence of abnormal antibodies.

What causes lupus?

Heredity seems to play an important role in its development. People with parents or siblings who have lupus are at somewhat greater risk than average. Although the exact cause has not been determined, lupus seems to result from a combination of genetic factors and environmental influences, such as infection.

What treatments are available?

Rarely, mild cases with few symptoms besides arthritis are treated with aspirin alone, although more powerful anti-inflammatory drugs, including corticosteroids, usually are required. Cyclophosphamide, an immunosuppressive drug, may be needed in cases of severe kidney disease.

Once it appears, lupus usually remains a lifelong affliction. With modern therapies, however, lupus can be managed successfully.

CARING FOR A CHILD WITH LUPUS

To help a child with lupus:

- Encourage adequate rest.
- Protect the child from emotional stress.
- Observe the dietary restrictions recommended by your doctor or nutritionist.
- Avoid sunlight if it increases symptoms.
- Avoid activities that trigger or aggravate symptoms.
- Use physical theapy to optimize muscle function.
- Make sure the child wears warm, layered clothing in the winter, avoids swimming in cold water, and avoids holding cold objects.

Getting Help

CALL YOUR DOCTOR IF YOUR CHILD:

- ☐ Complains of joint pain or develops a limp.
- ☐ Develops a rash on the cheeks and across the bridge of the nose.

Lyme Disease

Lyme disease is a relatively new infectious illness, first identified in the town of Old Lyme, Connecticut, in 1975. The disease is caused by a bacterium transmitted by the bite of infected ticks. Cases of Lyme disease have been reported throughout the continental United States, but infectious ticks seem to be most active in the Northeast, the upper Midwest, and the Pacific Northwest. In the Northeast and Midwest, the tick is carried by deers. In the West the tick is carried by a mouse. The tiny ticks' life cycle makes them most active—and likeliest to bite—in the spring and summer.

Lyme disease is progressive. If antibiotic therapy is given in the early stages, most people respond very well. Unfortunately, Lyme disease is often missed for weeks or months because it is not recognized. Response to treatment begun late may be minimal. Joint manifestations begin one week to two years after the intial illness, lasting for weeks to months and usually recurring for several years. Heart inflammation, meningitis, and facial palsy can also develop. Lethargy and fatigue may be constant and incapacitating. These late-stage complications are almost completely avoidable with early treatment.

When should I suspect Lyme disease?

Because deer ticks are so tiny, most people never notice being bitten. If you live in an area where infected ticks are active, be suspicious of any flulike illness that your child develops during the spring, summer, or early fall.

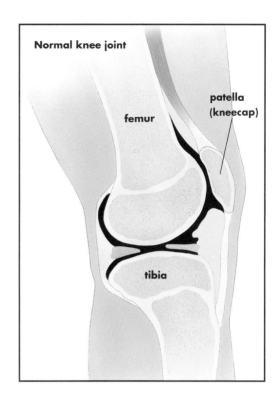

Normal knee joint

femur
patella (kneecap)
tibia

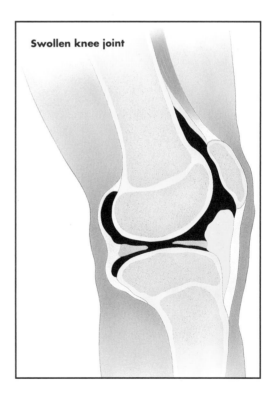

Swollen knee joint

Lyme disease can cause inflammation and swelling of the large joints, especially the knee.

The first sign of Lyme disease is often a distinctive, circular rash appearing from several days to two weeks after the tick bite. Beginning like a tiny red pimple, the rash expands to a red circle that may be clear in the center, resembling a bull's eye. Even without treatment, the rash will usually disappear within a few weeks. However, nearly half of all people with Lyme disease never develop the classic rash. Among those who do develop a rash, 50 percent go on to have small red blotches and circles in the thigh or groin within several days. Conjunctivitis may also appear.

The next early sign to watch for is a flulike illness, characterized by a headache, aching muscles, fever, chills, painful joints, a stiff neck, or a sore throat. Even without treatment, this illness will usually disappear within a week

CARING FOR A CHILD WITH LYME DISEASE

Beyond antibiotic therapy, no special home care is needed for children with Lyme disease. The following steps will aid in the child's recovery from flulike illness and fever:

- Keep the child at home (and, if necessary, in bed) until the fever passes.
- Give acetaminophen (Tylenol) to ease discomfort.
- Give the child extra fluids (juices and soups) to prevent dehydration.
- Encourage the child to resume as many activities as possible after the acute illness passes. Make sure he or she gets some exercise.

PREVENTING LYME DISEASE

Most people in an infested area cannot avoid all exposure to infected ticks. Follow these steps to reduce the risks:

- Teach the child to stick to paved sidewalks and roads instead of walking through leaves or brushing against shrubbery.
- Dress child in light-colored clothing so ticks will show up more easily.
- Spray clothing with a tick repellent containing the chemical *permethrin,* if it is available in your area.
- Apply repellents containing DEET *with great care* to exposed skin, except for the face and hands; follow package directions scrupulously.
- When the child comes indoors, first examine the clothing and then strip the child to check the entire body for ticks. Check the hair carefully.
- Similarly inspect and comb pets who go outdoors.
- If you find a tick attached to the child's skin, remove it immediately with pointed tweezers. (See "The Basics of First Aid" in Vol. I) Removing a tick before it has been attached for more than 24 hours greatly reduces the risk of infection. (Try to save the tick for the physician's examination; do not apply any fluids or chemicals to it.)
- Have your child bathe or shower daily, especially after picnics or romps in the woods.

to ten days, although the accompanying fatigue may persist for weeks or months.

If the disease escapes detection in these

early stages, many children go on to develop arthritis, abnormal heart rhythms, and nervous system problems.

How can the pediatrician tell if my child has Lyme disease?

Diagnosis of Lyme disease is difficult. Your doctor will order blood tests to look for antibodies to the causative bacteria, but such antibodies take time to develop, so they may not appear in the early stages of the illness. Therefore, the diagnosis is usually based on a careful history and examination of the child, the child's symptoms, and the activity of ticks in your area.

What treatments are available?

If Lyme disease is suspected, the doctor will prescribe an antibiotic—frequently, amoxicillin. The choice of antibiotic depends on the stage of the disease and the child's age and allergic history. When diagnosed early, Lyme disease usually is treated with oral medication alone. If the child has developed the more se-

---

Getting Help

CALL YOUR DOCTOR IF YOUR CHILD:

■ Develops a flulike illness in the spring or summer and you live in an area where Lyme disease is common.

■ Develops a red, circular rash that does not itch.

■ Complains of joint pain or begins to limp.

---

rious complications of later Lyme disease, she may need intravenous therapy and may require hospitalization.

Measles (Rubeola)

Until the mid-1970s, when measles immunization became routine, this viral infection was an extremely common childhood illness. Over the next ten to 15 years, outbreaks of measles became less common but occasionally occurred, mainly among schoolchildren and college students who had neither been immunized nor had the illness. In the late 1980s, however, there was an alarming resurgence of measles, particularly in certain urban areas, including Chicago, Dallas, Houston, Los Angeles, New York, Philadelphia, and San Diego. As a result, immunization efforts have been stepped up, and a decision was made to add a second immunization for school aged children. This has helped control the problem.

Why all the fuss about what used to be considered a routine illness? The fact is, measles is potentially dangerous—not just to tiny infants and chronically ill children, but to strong, healthy children, in whom the infection can lead to pneumonia, brain inflammation, and other complications. For that reason, immunization is absolutely essential. (For a rundown of the recommended immunization schedule for all infectious diseases, see **immunizations.**)

When should I suspect that my child has measles?

Measles outbreaks are most common in late winter and early spring. The primary characteristic of the disease is a red rash that begins behind the ears and around the hairline and spreads downward, eventually covering the body. Coldlike symptoms, including fever, nasal congestion, red eyes, and coughing, develop three to five days before the rash and last throughout the illness. A few days after the onset of these symptoms, tiny, white spots (called *Koplik's spots*) appear on the tongue and the lining of the mouth.

Once the red rash appears, the temperature can climb as high as 105 degrees Fahrenheit, and the child is likely to feel quite ill. Nausea, vomiting, and stomach pain may develop, particularly in small children. Because the disease commonly causes inflammation of the membrane covering the eye and inner eyelids (conjunctivitis), the child may be sensitive to light.

How does measles develop?

The virus (which is called *rubeola virus*) is highly contagious. It passes from person to person in moisture droplets expelled during coughing or sneezing. The infection takes hold in the respiratory tract, undergoing an incubation period of about ten days before spreading to the lymph nodes and bloodstream and causing symptoms. From start to finish, an uncomplicated bout of measles lasts about ten to 14 days, but the rash itself lasts only about six.

Is medical attention necessary?

Yes. It's important to know whether your child has measles or some other illness that causes a rash.

How can the pediatrician tell if my child has measles?

The pediatrician will examine the child carefully to look for typical rash Koplik's spots.

What treatments are available?

There is no specific treatment for measles, but the doctor may recommend measures such as giving the child acetaminophen to reduce fever and offering fluids every hour or so. Severe coughing, which commonly develops in the course of measles, may be relieved with a cool mist humidifier. If you use a humidifier, though, be sure to fill it with distilled water and clean it regularly.

Getting Help

CALL YOUR DOCTOR IF YOUR CHILD:

- Has not been immunized and is exposed to measles. If the vaccine is given promptly, it may prevent severe disease from developing. Alternatively, a gamma globulin injection—which is made up of antibodies from patients recovering from measles—may offer protection after exposure.
- Develops any unexplained high fever or rash.

Meningitis

Meningitis is an infection of the meninges, the layered membranes that support and protect the brain and spinal cord. The disease most commonly strikes infants and children between the ages of one month and five years, although it can affect people of any age. Children under age two are particularly susceptible, and boys are affected more often than girls. Meningitis is always a serious condition that warrants emergency medical care.

What causes meningitis?

A variety of microbes can cause meningitis. The most serious forms are caused by bacteria which spread through the blood to the meninges from infections elsewhere in the body, such as the lungs, the sinuses, or the throat.

Newborns sometimes develop meningitis as a result of infections their mothers contracted during the last week of pregnancy. Rupture of the fetal membranes more than 24 hours before birth also increases the risk of meningitis in a newborn, as does premature birth. Other factors associated with meningitis in children of all ages include severe burns, head injuries, and chronic illnesses such as sickle-cell anemia.

Viruses such as the Coxsackie virus and those responsible for chicken pox and mononucleosis also can cause meningitis. This type, known as *aseptic meningitis,* is generally less serious than the bacterial type.

When should I suspect that my child has meningitis?

Meningitis causes nonspecific symptoms in infants and toddlers. Often, parents will simply have a strong sense that all is not well, even though dramatic symptoms such as a high fever may not be present. Instead, the infant may be unwilling to nurse or take a bottle. Sucking may be feeble, and diarrhea and vomiting may occur. The baby may be listless, irritable, and the temperature may be elevated or abnormally low. Drowsiness, irregular breathing, and seizures also may occur. Another possible sign is bulging of the soft spot in the top center of the baby's head.

Symptoms in older children include irritability, agitation, and loss of appetite, followed by the abrupt onset of fever, chills, headache, nausea, and vomiting, sometimes along with confusion. This pattern is by no means uni-

---

PREVENTING MENINGITIS

Until the mid-1980s, *Hemophilus influenzae* type B was the bacterium responsible for most cases of meningitis in children, especially in the under-two age group. Widespread immunization against this organism has caused a sharp decline in the number of cases of meningitis. The American Academy of Pediatrics strongly urges that all children be immunized against this organism. (For more information, see separate entries on **immunizations** and **hemophilus influenzae type b (HiB) infections.**)

Vaccines against other organisms associated with meningitis also are available, although they are recommended mainly for children at high risk of infection due to chronic illness or suppressed immunity.

versal, though. Some children develop signs and symptoms more slowly, so the disease looks at first like a case of the flu. Children old enough to verbalize their symptoms may complain of back pain, neck stiffness, and sensitivity to light.

Is medical attention necessary?

Yes. It is extremely important to determine the cause of meningitis and start treatment as soon as possible.

How can the pediatrician tell if my child has meningitis?

If meningitis is a possible diagnosis, the pediatrician will perform a lumbar puncture (spinal tap), in which a sample of the fluid that surrounds the brain and spinal cord is withdrawn from the spinal column through a large needle. Laboratory tests of the spinal fluid determine whether meningitis is present and identify the responsible organism.

What treatments are available?

An infant or child with bacterial meningitis will be hospitalized and given intravenous antibiotics, along with medication to control fever and fluids to prevent dehydration. A child with bacterial meningitis is isolated from other patients. Nurses, doctors, and parents may have to wear protective gowns and gloves in the child's room. The child's close contacts will need to take antibiotics as a precaution against developing the disease or reinfecting the child.

In cases of aseptic meningitis, hospitalization and isolation may be necessary until bacterial meningitis is ruled out. Otherwise, treatment is focused on relieving discomfort and waiting for the infection to subside, which usually takes three to ten days.

What are possible complications of meningitis?

Infants and children with bacterial meningitis may develop hydrocephalus, brain abscess, and impaired hearing, vision, and poor muscle control. In addition, bacterial meningitis sometimes leaves a child with a long-term seizure disorder. Some evidence suggests that children who have had meningitis run an increased risk of developing behavior problems, learning disabilities, and attention-deficit disorder. In general, though, the outlook for children with meningitis has improved greatly in recent years, thanks to better antibiotics and more rapid diagnosis.

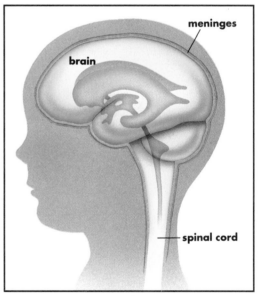

The meninges (colored red above) are actually three different membranes. They become inflamed in meningitis.

Mental Retardation

Mental retardation is a developmental disability that affects roughly three percent of the population. People with mental retardation function at below-average intellectual levels, as measured by IQ tests and other psychological assessment techniques.

Three-fourths of people with mental retardation are classified as "mildly retarded." These individuals, whose IQ test scores fall between 52 and 68 (compared to an average score of 100 in the general population), usually are able to live independently or semi-independently as adults, provided they have the right kind of training as children.

When should I suspect that my child is mentally retarded?

Children who are mentally retarded achieve several developmental milestones more slowly than their peers. Thus, they may not master such skills as sitting and walking (which usually occur in the first year of life) until well after their first or even second birthdays. Speech also develops quite slowly; severely retarded children may never learn to talk spontaneously.

Mental retardation usually becomes apparent during the first or second year of life. Although normal children develop at vastly different rates, a clear pattern of lags in several areas suggests a problem. (For summaries of important developmental milestones throughout the first two years, see Chapters 1–4.) Other disorders, including behavior problems, autism, and neurological problems, are often associated with retardation.

What causes mental retardation?

Most mental retardation is probably caused by a combination of genetic and environmental factors. About five percent of cases are genetic. Down syndrome, which occurs when a baby has one extra chromosome (one of the structures in the nuclei of all cells that hold and transmit genetic information), is the most common identified genetic cause. Almost as common, particularly among males, is fragile X syndrome, in which a segment of the X chromosome (one of the chromosomes that determines gender) is abnormal. Children with this syndrome vary in intelligence from the low end of the normal range to severely deficient. They have a number of distinctive physical characteristics such as a protruding tongue, stubby fingers, and eyelids that appear to slant upward. Children with Down syndrome also have a high frequency (30 to 40 percent) of congenital heart defects. The likelihood of having a baby with Down syndrome is greater among women over 35 than among younger women, and it increases with advancing maternal age.

Certain diseases or infections in the mother can also result in mental disabilities in the baby, as can maternal abuse of drugs or alcohol. Difficulties in the birth process (for example, premature birth, ·birth injuries, and temporary oxygen deprivation) sometimes result in mental retardation as well.

How can the doctor tell if my child is mentally retarded?

If you suspect that your child is significantly delayed, get testing as soon as you can. Your doctor can do an initial screening based on motor skills achievement and social responsiveness. If the doctor suspects a disability, he may refer you to a psychologist or other mental-health expert who can give your child a number of tests of intelligence and *adaptive behavior,* which comprises social and self-care skills, to determine the severity of the problem.

What treatments are available?

Children with mental retardation can receive help from an array of public, private, and non-profit agencies that specialize in developmental disabilities. Mental retardation is a lifelong condition for which there is no cure. However, retarded children are able to learn, and many can have happy and rewarding lives. Teaching should begin in infancy with early

intervention enrichment programs that focus on sensorimotor development.

All states are now required to have early intervention programs for developmentally disabled children beginning at birth, and the public schools must provide special education beginning at the age of three. These programs teach skills such as toilet training, self-feeding, dressing, and speech. As children move up through school, daily living skills, as well as reading and speech, are taught.

If other conditions coexist with retardation, these conditions also need treatment. A child with seizures needs medication, and a child with behavior problems may need counseling and behavior modification.

Coping with a mental disability

- A mentally disabled child needs the same love and support as any other child.
- Don't expect your child to keep up with peers, but don't set your expectations too low. Retarded children *can* learn.
- Become an advocate for your child. Find the best school setting and make sure it provides needed training. Explore and use any community services that could help your child, including schools, camps, and recreational and vocational programs.
- Don't be burdened by guilt or depression. If you feel stressed, frustrated, or unhappy, get help. Turn to parent groups for support. If your child needs constant care, there are community based respite programs to help you. Organizations that may be of help are listed in the Resource Directory section at the end of this book.

LONG-TERM OUTLOOK

Most people with mental retardation can live rewarding and productive lives. With the necessary skills for taking care of themselves and relating to others, mildly retarded people can hold jobs and live on their own. Moderately retarded and some severely retarded people can learn to work in certain settings geared toward their abilities and live in group homes or similar residences. There they can learn to do some things for themselves, such as dressing and preparing simple meals. They can often go out alone, shop, and attend recreational activities. Most important, they can make and maintain friendships. Severely retarded people will always need full-time care but even they can continue to learn as long as someone will teach them.

Middle Ear Infections

Earaches are very common in early childhood. By age three, two-thirds of children have had an ear infection, and half of that group get them repeatedly.

In infants and preschoolers, the middle ear, which lies between the eardrum and the tiny bones of the inner ear, is most prone to infection (*otitis media*).

When should I suspect that my child has an ear infection?

Middle ear infections typically develop when a child has already been suffering from a cold for a few days. The symptoms often come on suddenly, with an abrupt spike in fever that coincides with the development of severe ear pain. The symptoms may be more subtle, though; some children simply become fussy or listless, stop eating, and develop a slight (if any) fever.

Children too young to complain of pain often pull or scratch at their ears. In some cases, vomiting and diarrhea occur. Severe infections may rupture the ear drum and cause a discharge of pus or clear fluid from the ear canal.

If your child has had one or more ear infections, be alert for recurrences, especially during cold, flu, and allergy seasons. Children who had their first bout of otitis media as babies are more likely to suffer repeated middle ear infections throughout early childhood.

What happens during an ear infection?

Organisms from the nose and throat—most commonly, strains of bacteria such as *Streptococcus pneumoniae H. Influenzae*, Group A streptococci, or *Moraxella catarrhalis*—begin to multiply in the middle ear. The membrane that lines the cavity becomes inflamed and exudes fluid, causing pain, hearing loss, and other symptoms.

Why do children get ear infections?

The air pressure in the middle ear should be equal to that outside it. The *eustachian tubes,* which connect the middle ear to the back of the throat, expand and contract to maintain this equilibrium. The adjustments aren't always automatic, though, which is why abrupt changes in altitude (taking off in an airplane or going up in an elevator, for instance) can cause a temporary feeling of fullness or obstruction in the ear.

During a cold, the entire upper-respiratory system becomes swollen and filled with fluid, disrupting the function of the eustachian tubes. In small children, who may have short, narrow tubes, complete blockage sometimes occurs, trapping fluid and germs from the nose and throat in the middle ear. Too-wide eustachian tubes also can cause problems, since they may allow bacteria-laden nose and throat secretions to enter the middle ear. Either way, the stage is set for a middle ear infection, known medically as *otitis media.*

Is medical attention necessary?

Yes. The bacteria may spread to the inner ear causing hearing loss or the mastoid bone (the bone just behind the ear), possibly leading to meningitis or other serious complications.

In most cases, the pediatrician can diagnose otitis media by looking into the child's ear with an *otoscope* (a hand-held viewing device). A test called *tympanometry,* which measures air pressure in the middle ear, also may be per-

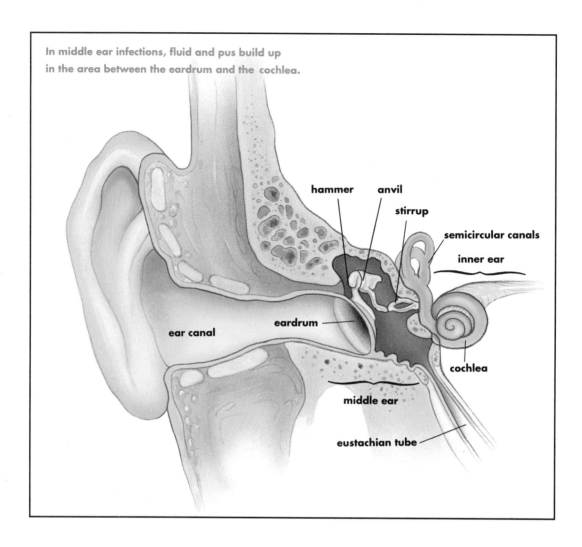

In middle ear infections, fluid and pus build up in the area between the eardrum and the cochlea.

hammer

anvil

stirrup

semicircular canals

inner ear

ear canal

eardrum

cochlea

middle ear

eustachian tube

formed to check for accumulation of fluid or pus. Usually a course of appropriate antibiotics will clear the infection. If the symptoms persist after three days of treatment, however, the doctor may want to try another antibiotic. At this stage, some pediatricians puncture the eardrum with a needle, which relieves symptoms by allowing fluid to drain from the middle ear and permits the doctor to identify the responsible bacteria.

Many children continue to have fluid in the middle ear for several weeks following a middle ear infection. If the fluid causes no symptoms, further treatment is usually unnecessary, although some doctors prescribe a second course of antibiotics. Children who have had repeated, severe ear infections should have their hearing checked regularly, since the condition can interfere with early speech and language development.

Other treatments

In about ten percent of cases, the ear retains fluid for three months or longer. When this

- Give children's acetaminophen (Tylenol, Panadol, Tempra, Datril, and other brands) to reduce fever and pain.
- For immediate pain relief, hold a hot water bottle or a towel-wrapped heating pad over the affected ear. To avoid burns, however, NEVER leave your child alone with a heating pad or hot water bottle.
- Offer plenty of cool liquids.
- If antibiotics give your child loose stools, call your doctor for recommendations on diet modification.
- Follow your doctor's orders about the timing and size of antibiotic doses, and continue the medication for as many days as the doctor has prescribed, even if the symptoms have disappeared.
- If your child's eardrum has ruptured or been surgically opened, protect the ear from water until complete healing has occurred.
- Keep your child at home as long as fever and pain persist. Once symptoms have resolved, children on antibiotics can safely return to day care or nursery school.
- If a child has repeated or prolonged ear infections, she should undergo a hearing test. Hearing impairment can interfere with speech and language development.

happens, the pediatrician may refer you to an ear, nose, and throat specialist. In selected cases, these specialists recommend *myringotomy:* insertion of tiny tubes into the eardrum.

Several recent studies have cast doubt on the long-term effectiveness of tube insertion; as a result, fewer pediatricians recommend it today. Instead, children with recurrent ear infections (generally defined as three infections within six months) usually are tried on long-term antibiotic therapy.

Coping with ear infections

If your child is among those who have recurrent middle ear infections, the frequent sick days and late night awakenings are bound to take a toll on you. Fortunately, even children who suffer bout after bout of otitis media rarely experience complications, thanks to the efficacy of modern antibiotics. Remember, too, that ear infections are most common in the toddler and preschool years; by the time your child reaches the age of six, the problem should be largely a thing of the past.

Preventing ear infections

There are no sure-fire methods to prevent children from getting otitis media. It may help, however, to:

- Encourage frequent hand washing.
- Teach children to cover their mouths and noses when sneezing and coughing.
- Discourage sharing of eating utensils and mouthing of toys.
- Keep play rooms well ventilated.
- Protect children from cigarette smoke; second-hand smoke increases the risk of chronic otitis media.

Getting Help

CALL YOUR DOCTOR IF:
- ☐ Your baby or child has any signs or symptoms of an ear infection.
- ☐ Ear infection symptoms persist after three days of treatment.

Molluscum Contagiosum

Molluscum contagiosum is a common, unsightly skin infection that usually develops in the trunk, face, and around the eyes. The lesions resemble warts or pimples, but are usually flesh-colored or white, and they range in size from about one-tenth of an inch to almost half an inch in diameter, although an occasional lesion is as large as one inch across. The lesions may be widely distributed or clustered.

As its name implies, molluscum contagiosum is contagious. A child might pick up the infection at a swimming pool or other public bathing area or simply through close contact with an infected playmate. There is no hard and fast information about the incubation period of molluscum contagiosum, but estimates range from two weeks to six months.

This infection is not particularly dangerous or painful.

What causes molluscum contagiosum?

The lesions are a result of an infection by a pox virus, which spreads not only from person to person, but also from one part of the body to another. For this reason, care must be taken that the lesions are not picked or squeezed, which can release the virus and allow it to spread. Because the incubation period remains unclear, it is usually difficult to determine exactly when or how a child was exposed to the infection.

When should I suspect my child has molluscum contagiosum?

Molluscum are flesh-colored or pearly-white, round, dome-shaped bumps that have a dim-

PREVENTING MOLLUSCUM CONTAGIOSUM

There are no surefire ways of preventing molluscum contagiosum, since the responsible virus spreads quite easily. The following precautions may, however, be of some help.

- Avoid letting your child have direct skin contact with anyone who has a rash.
- Don't let your child share towels and other personal items with others.
- If another member of the family has molluscum contagiosum, avoid sharing towels and clean the bathtub thoroughly with disinfectant after the infected person has bathed.

ple in the middle. That dimple, and the white material inside the bump, is what differentiates molluscum from other skin lesions such as warts. Molluscum usually do not cause pain or itching. Although the common sites are the trunk and face, they can sometimes be found on the pelvis, lower abdomen, and inner thighs. If molluscum lesions develop around the eyes, the child may suffer chronic conjunctivitis (inflammation of the conjunctiva, which is the membrane that lines the eye) or inflammation of the eyelids.

Children with eczema or dermatitis may develop clusters of molluscum contagiosum lesions in the same area as the other skin problem, which may cause confusion. In fact, children with eczema are more prone to molluscum, and they may develop widespread lesions, especially if they have been mistakenly treated with topical steroids, which tend to make molluscum spread.

How long does molluscum contagiosum last?

A single molluscum lesion may last about two months, and the entire outbreak may subside spontaneously between several months and a year. Sometimes, the infection will spread to a different part of the body and subside in the original area of infection. In some cases, molluscum contagiosum may stay in a limited area of the body for a long time, if not treated.

Is medical attention necessary?

Yes, but only to rule out other skin problems that require different treatment. Molluscum contagiosum itself is generally harmless. Medical attention may also be warranted if a molluscum lesion gets sore and inflamed, which indicates a possible infection.

What treatments are available?

Treatment is not absolutely necessary, since the infection usually subsides spontaneously within a year. If the lesions are quite noticeable and persistent, however, the doctor may recommend removing them by freezing with liquid nitrogen. Alternatively, the doctor may apply a substance that causes blister formation, which also destroys the lesions.

Getting Help

CALL YOUR DOCTOR IF YOUR CHILD:

- Has any unexplained rash or growth on the skin.
- Has molluscum lesions around the eyes.

Motion Sickness

Motion sickness, an abnormal response to movement in a car, airplane, boat, or other conveyance, is quite common in otherwise healthy children. Swinging, being carried piggyback, or riding a roller coaster all can cause motion sickness. Some children also develop motion sickness in response to images that create the illusion of motion, such as films taken from the perspective of a boat passenger. Particularly sensitive children may develop symptoms after riding only a few blocks in the back seat of a car. Whatever its cause, a bout of motion sickness can last for several hours after the motion stops.

The tendency to develop motion sickness usually diminishes with age, but for some it may persist into adulthood. It tends to arise most commonly in stressful situations. During World War II, for example, ten percent of all pilot trainees became air sick during their first ten flights. Also, astronauts have developed motion sickness during weightlessness.

What causes motion sickness?

Symptoms of motion sickness are believed to originate in the vestibular apparatus, the part of the inner ear responsible for balance and spatial orientation. One theory holds that the disorder develops when the apparatus receives an overload of visual information during motion. As a result, it relays signals to the brain stem causing it to trigger vomiting and the other symptoms of motion sickness.

Specific factors that predispose some children or adults to motion sickness have not been identified. Researchers have failed to find any particular abnormality in the vestibular system that could explain the problem, nor have they discovered why some relatively mild types of motion, such as piggyback riding, produce motion sickness, while more vigorous motion, like horseback riding, does not.

When should I suspect that my child has motion sickness?

Look for signs of sleepiness and apathy, as well as pallor, headache, sweating, drooling, and vomiting. Older children may complain of headache and nausea. After a prolonged spell of motion sickness, a child may well be totally exhausted.

PREVENTING MOTION SICKNESS

- When traveling by car, place the child in a high seat that allows a view of the road.
- Focus the child's attention on a stationary object outside the car (the horizon, for example), or have the child look straight in front of the car.
- Before starting the trip, give the child a small, high-carbohydrate snack such as a bowl of cereal. An empty stomach increases the chance that symptoms will develop.
- Make sure the car is well ventilated.
- When boating, the child is less likely to develop seasickness if he or she stays above deck, where the horizon is visible.
- Dramamine, Bonamine, and other oral medications, as well as medicated patches worn behind the ear, can prevent motion sickness, but check with your doctor before you use them. Once symptoms develop, oral medications usually do not work.

CARING FOR A CHILD WITH MOTION SICKNESS

- If possible, stop the motion that produced the sickness. If that is impossible, follow the preventive measures outlined above, or have the child lie down, keeping the head perfectly still.
- For severe motion sickness, the physician may prescribe tranquilizers or antihistamines to relieve symptoms.

Getting Help

CALL YOUR DOCTOR IF:

- ☐ Symptoms of motion sickness persist longer than three or four hours after the motion has stopped.
- ☐ A child who usually is able to tolerate any kind of movement suddenly develops severe symptoms of motion sickness.

Mumps

Mumps, an acute, generalized viral disease, was formerly extremely common in childhood, but its incidence has been drastically reduced in the United States through routine vaccination, which is required for kindergarten entry in most states. Immunization with the MMR (mumps, measles, and rubella) vaccine protects 95 percent of children from infection with the *paramyxovirus,* which causes mumps. The remaining five percent fail to develop immunity to the virus. (For information on the recommended schedule of information, see entry on **immunizations.**)

How does mumps develop?

Mumps is a highly contagious disease, spread via droplets of saliva expelled into the air (by sneezing, coughing, talking, or breathing) or transmitted by direct contact (by kissing or sharing eating utensils with an infected person). The disease quickly spreads among non-immunized children, so if you enroll your infant in any group program before completing the immunization series, you will find that they require mumps vaccine for all children.

When should I suspect the mumps?

Some children with the mumps initially develop symptoms that resemble those of the flu. They include appetite loss, fatigue, headache, malaise, low to moderate fever, and muscular pain (particularly in the neck).

The day after the fever develops, classic symptoms involving the salivary glands will emerge. There may be marked discomfort chewing and swallowing, and a painful reaction to acidic foods and beverages such as lemonade, orange juice, and the vinegar in salad dressing. The following day, the parotid glands located on the cheeks below and in front of the ears and other salivary glands in the neck may swell on one or both sides. The child also may feel discomfort ranging from tenderness to severe pain.

What treatments are available?

No medication is effective in treating mumps. Keep the child at home until the disease has run its course.

Is medical attention necessary?

Usually not. The doctor can often diagnose mumps on the basis of a description of the symptoms. But in some cases, the mumps can cause serious symptoms that require a physician's attention. Call the doctor immediately if any of the following complications occur:

- Listlessness and lethargy.
- Tenderness and swelling in a boy's testicles.
- Severe vomiting, which may mean the infection may have spread to the pancreas.
- A stiff neck and severe headache, which may indicate the development of viral meningitis.
- A fever over 104 degrees Fahrenheit.

CARING FOR A CHILD WITH MUMPS

Observe the following procedures:

- Isolate the child from anyone else in the household who has not been immunized. The child is contagious until all neck swelling and other symptoms have disappeared.
- Administer acetaminophen to lower fever and reduce pain.
- Apply warm or cold compresses on the neck to ease discomfort.
- Maintain fluid intake and nutrition, despite the child's reluctance. Cold drinks and soft, bland foods (such as mashed potatoes, mashed banana, scrambled eggs, and puddings or jello) are tolerated most easily.

Muscular Dystrophy

The muscular dystrophies are a relatively rare group of progressive, genetic diseases that gradually destroy muscle tissue. The most common childhood forms are Duchenne muscular dystrophy and Becker muscular dystrophy; both affect about one in every 3,000 male babies born. Less common forms of muscular dystrophy can affect both boys and girls.

The muscular dystrophies are classified according to age at onset, rate of progression, heredity pattern, and muscle groups affected. Symptoms vary with the type. The major forms of muscular dystrophy gradually weaken the muscles that control walking, manual dexterity, and breathing. Other symptoms can include mental retardation and neurological and cardiac involvement.

When should I suspect my child has muscular dystrophy?

Notify your pediatrician if the child exhibits the following conditions, possibly indicating muscular dystrophy:

- The infant lacks muscle tone or exhibits abnormal muscle weakness or difficulty breathing.
- The motor milestones (such as walking and running) are severely delayed.
- The calf muscles are abnormally enlarged.

What causes muscular dystrophy?

The muscular dystrophies are caused by gene defects that cause the muscles to deteriorate. Researchers have found that Duchenne and Becker muscular dystrophies are caused by defects of a gene on the X chromosome that nor-mally triggers production of the muscle protein dystrophin. The specific causes have not yet been identified in the other forms of muscular dystrophy.

How can the pediatrician tell if my child has muscular dystrophy?

Unless there is a family history of the disease, the diagnostic process can be lengthy. The child may need various blood tests to measure enzymes released by muscle degeneration; tests of muscle function will be performed as well. A muscle biopsy, in which a small sample of muscle tissue is removed and examined microscopically, also may be performed.

What treatments are available?

Current research suggests that transferring healthy genes into affected muscle may be beneficial. Because such treatment is still highly experimental, though, most therapy is aimed at relieving the child's symptoms and preventing complications; at present, there is no cure. The main treatment for the early stages of muscular dystrophy is regular physical therapy with passive stretching of key muscles and joint movement to reduce painful muscle contracture and possibly prolong walking. If joints become contracted, orthopedic surgery can provide some relief and improvement in function. Leg braces are helpful in prolonging independent standing and walking when muscles of the hips and legs have deteriorated to the point where the child cannot stand alone.

A child who can no longer walk must be equipped with a properly fitted wheelchair. Daily postural drainage is important to keep the lungs clear of accumulated fluids. If scoliosis sets in, two measures may help: an external shell-like body jacket designed to fit snugly around the trunk and reduce further curvature, and surgery to fuse the lower spinal column and relieve the curvature.

Nearsightedness (Myopia)

Nearsightedness, which is inability to see distant objects clearly, is the most common vision problem of childhood. It rarely occurs in infants unless they were born prematurely. Around the age of two years, however, some children become nearsighted, and the number of children with the problem steadily increases throughout the school years, peaking in adolescence.

What causes nearsightedness?

Nearsightedness results from a *refractive error,* which is an error in the way the eye bends the entering light rays that the brain translates into visual images. In normal vision, light rays converge and focus precisely on the retina, the visual apparatus lining the back of the eyeball.

In nearsightedness, the eyeball is too long from front to back, so light rays converge somewhere in front of the retina. The result is blurring of objects that are more than a few feet away. The farther objects are, the more blurry they appear.

A tendency to be nearsighted runs in families, although many children with nearsighted parents have normal vision. It occurs with particular frequency in children with Down syndrome, affecting 30 to 35 percent.

When should I suspect that my child is nearsighted?

Nearsighted children believe that everyone sees things the way they do, so you should not wait for the child to complain about poor vision. Look for behavior such as frequent eye rubbing, sitting close to the television, holding the head at an unusual angle, squinting, and clumsiness. A small number of nearsighted children may complain of dizziness and headaches.

The problem may not become apparent until the child starts school, at which time the inability to see pictures or writing at the front of the classroom may impair performance. Teachers generally notice such problems before the child falls far behind. Many parents find out about their children's vision problems as a result of school vision screenings.

Nearsightedness and other vision problems are often detected in the course of routine pediatric visits. Doctors start checking babies' vision at about the sixth to eighth week of age, when the ability to focus first emerges. Although precise measurements are not possible at this age, the doctor will watch the baby's eyes move together and one at a time (with the

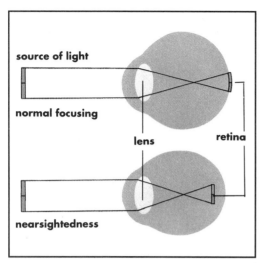

Nearsightedness occurs when the lens of the eye focuses light to a point too far in front of the retina.

other eye covered) while following an object. By age three, children can be screened with cards depicting familiar objects to determine a rough estimate of vision. Preschoolers and early school age children can be assessed using the Titmus test machine or letter E cards.

Is medical attention necessary?

Yes. Even the youngest nearsighted children need an assessment and, in most cases, glasses to correct the refractive error responsible for the problem.

What treatments are available?

The normal treatment for myopia is to wear corrective lenses (usually glasses), which should be prescribed by a pediatric ophthalmologist, a doctor who specializes in children's eye disorders. Pediatric ophthalmologists usually have a range of vision tests geared to the abilities of children, so they can measure the child's vision most accurately.

Since children's eyes grow and change rapidly during the first six or seven years of life, those who are nearsighted may need frequent vision rechecks (and, possibly, new glasses) approximately every six months. Because contact lenses require extra care, they are rarely prescribed for young children except in special circumstances.

Getting Help

CALL YOUR DOCTOR IF:

☐ Your child's school nurse or teacher thinks the child may have a vision problem.

☐ Your child acts like he or she may have trouble seeing.

Nephritis

Inflammation of the kidneys, known as nephritis, is a potentially dangerous condition that usually develops as a consequence of an infection elsewhere in the body. One type of kidney inflammation, known as *pyelonephritis,* is most often a result of direct bacterial invasion of the kidney via the lower urinary tract. Another type, known as *glomerulonephritis,* is often an indirect result of infection elsewhere in the body, although certain inherited disorders and immune system diseases also can trigger it.

All types of nephritis potentially can cause kidney failure, a breakdown in the kidney's ability to filter blood and regulate the normal balance of fluids. Instead of absorbing adequate amounts of proteins and other essential nutrients back into the body, failing kidneys lose these substances into the urine. Although most children recover from nephritis with no kidney damage, those who suffer kidney failure may require dialysis and transplantation.

How does nephritis develop?

In the course of a **urinary tract infection** (see entry), bacteria may travel up the ureters (the two tubes that connect the kidneys to the bladder) and multiply in the kidney, causing inflammation (pyelonephritis). Also, an infection or other disease process elsewhere in the body can result in the accumulation of antibodies and other proteins in the *glomeruli* (the kidney's filtering units). These substances lead to glomerular injury and inflammation (glomerulonephritis).

The most common form of glomerulonephritis develops after a strep infection and, in 90 percent of cases, resolves on its own. Other types of glomerulorephitis have a long, chronic, and often progressive course. On the other hand, pyelonephritis, which is caused by a bacterial infection is usually treated with antibiotics.

When should I suspect that my child has nephritis?

Bloody urine, which may appear pink, cola-colored, or cloudy, is the hallmark of nephritis, although the blood is not always visible to the naked eye. Most children with nephritis also feel quite ill. Their symptoms may include fever, poor appetite, nausea, weakness, and pain in the side.

Is medical attention necessary?

Yes. Since nephritis can lead to kidney failure and permanent kidney damage, a doctor's at-

---

POSSIBLE CAUSES OF NEPHRITIS

- Bacterial infection spread from the bladder.
- Antibody deposits resulting from a bacterial infection (or, more rarely, a viral infection) elsewhere in the body. Most cases of this type follow streptoccoccal throat or skin infections.
- Genetic disorders, particularly various types of hereditary nephritis. In one of the most common of these disorders (Alport's syndrome), hearing impairment usually accompanies chronic nephritis.
- Toxic reactions to certain drugs such as probenecid, which is given to boost the effect of antibiotics.
- Disorders such as lupus which are caused by a malfunction of the immune system in which antibodies attack the body's own tissues.

---

tention is essential. Possible complications requiring medical care include high blood pressure and fluid buildup. If these complications develop, hospitalization is usually necessary.

How can the pediatrician tell if my child has nephritis?

The pediatrician diagnoses nephritis on the basis of a physical examination and careful analysis of the urine. Blood tests are frequently performed as well to determine whether antibodies to certain bacteria (particularly one type of streptococcal bacteria) are elevated, indicating that the problem is a secondary effect of infection. In a few cases, the doctor may need to remove a small sample of kidney tissue (a biopsy) for laboratory examination.

What treatments are available?

Unless the child has an active infection, in which case antibiotics are administered, treatment usually consists of watching for complications and administering drugs to keep the body functioning smoothly until the kidney inflammation subsides. To decrease the swelling, the child's intake of fluids may have to be limited.

Nephrotic Syndrome

Nephrotic syndrome is a kidney disorder in which the tiny filtering units in the kidney (the *glomeruli*) are damaged. This impairs the kidneys' ability to filter and excrete waste products and water into the urine. Protein escapes into the urine instead of recirculating back into the bloodstream, causing a protein deficiency. Fluid is retained in the body's tissues because of the low blood protein. The urine volume is reduced and the body becomes swollen.

The cause of nephrotic syndrome is often obscure. If diagnosed and treated early, the disease usually resolves over time, although in rare cases it can become chronic.

When should I suspect my child has nephrotic syndrome?

The signs and symptoms of nephrotic syndrome develop gradually over a period of days or weeks. The first symptom may be weight gain, which a parent can easily misinterpret as a sign of normal growth. It is actually due to water retention, which soon causes puffiness around the eyes, followed by swelling of the face, abdomen, and ankles. (See "Recognizing nephrotic syndrome" on page 185 for a complete list of signs and symptoms.) Urine output decreases by as much as 80 percent; the urine looks dark and frothy. The child may be lethargic and have a poor appetite, but overall, may not seem very ill.

What causes nephrotic syndrome?

In most cases, the cause is unknown. The syndrome is frequently preceded by an illness such as an upper respiratory infection, but these in-

In rare cases, your doctor may recommend a renal biopsy, in which a small amount of tissue is extracted from the kidney through a needle and then examined in a laboratory.

What treatments are available?

The child will probably be hospitalized and placed on a diet high in protein and low in salt and fluids. Initially, high doses of steroids may be prescribed to lower the amount of protein in the urine and encourage remission of the syndrome. Steroids have significant side effects, though, and will be tapered off gradually. The bloating caused by fluid retention can be reduced with diuretic drugs. Your child may be given antibiotics to fight off any infections during this vulnerable period.

If caught early, the syndrome may be cured within weeks. However, relapses are common. In these cases, treatment must be resumed over the course of months or even years. In most children, continued treatment eventually eliminates the disease with no harmful effects.

fections are thought to trigger the syndrome, not cause it. In a few children, nephrotic syndrome may be due to drug reaction or to an underlying disease such as diabetes mellitis or lupus.

Is medical attention necessary?

Yes. A child with nephrotic syndrome is susceptible to a variety of serious infections, including pneumonia, peritonitis, and bloodstream infection. In rare cases, persistent nephrosis can lead to kidney failure.

How can the pediatrician tell if my child has nephrotic syndrome?

The physician will examine the child, take a medical history, and order blood and urine studies. If the child has nephrotic syndrome, the urine will contain high levels of protein, while the blood will show a protein deficiency.

Night Terrors

Night terrors are sleep disturbances in which a child, usually between the ages of three and eight, abruptly sits up in bed, screams, and cries inconsolably. Night terrors can be quite distressing to parents because the child is not only upset but also disoriented—so disoriented, in fact, that efforts at soothing are futile.

Night terrors are commonly mistaken for nightmares, but there are important differences. A child who wakes from a nightmare may be frightened, but he or she is rarely very disoriented. Some details of nightmares can be recalled, but night terrors are completely forgotten when the child wakes up. Finally, nightmares occur during the dream stage of sleep during the second half of the night, while night terrors seem to occur during the transition stage between the first, deep sleep of the night and the first period of dream sleep. Sleepwalking and sleeptalking also occur at this transition.

What happens during night terrors?

A child in the throes of a night terror may thrash around, moan, scream, and sob. The child does not recognize or acknowledge the parents, but their efforts at soothing—particularly touching and holding—may increase the agitation. The child's heart may pound, and breathing may be shallow. An episode may last anywhere from a few seconds to 20 or 30 minutes. Usually, the child simply grows quiet, lies down, and relaxes, never fully waking until morning.

What causes night terrors?

Night terrors are not responses to bad dreams or frightening thoughts. They seem, instead, to be caused by immaturity of some part of the central nervous system. Preschoolers are most likely to have night terrors, but babies under age two may also get them.

Is medical attention necessary?

You should see a physician if the child's sleep disturbances occur near morning, if the child wakes first and seems to know something is about to happen, or if the episode includes body jerking or stiffening. This type of behavior might indicate the presence of a seizure disorder rather than night terrors.

COPING WITH NIGHT TERRORS

- Do not try to wake a child during an episode of night terrors. Let the spell pass and ease the child back into a sleeping position when it is over.
- Try putting the child to bed earlier or providing a midday nap. Overtiredness may contribute to night terrors.

Non-Hodgkin's Lymphoma

A lymphoma is a cancer involving cells of the lymphatic system. **Hodgkin's disease** (see entry) is the most common lymphoma in the general population. Among children, however, several other types of lymphoma, classified together as non-Hodgkin's lymphoma, are more likely to occur. Unlike Hodgkin's disease, non-Hodgkin's lymphoma can run in families. Boys are affected more often than girls. Fortunately, this kind of lymphoma is highly treatable, and the cure rate is excellent, particularly if the illness is detected early.

When should I suspect that my child has non-Hodgkin's lymphoma?

Non-Hodgkin's lymphoma causes swollen and rubbery, yet painless, lymph nodes. A child with the disease will feel generally unwell, and jaundice (yellow skin and whites of the eyes) and anemia (caused by bleeding in the digestive tract) may develop. Weight loss is also common.

Is medical attention necessary?

Yes. A child with persistent swollen lymph nodes and other symptoms of lymphoma should have a thorough medical evaluation. The child may have to spend a few days in the hospital so that samples of the affected tissue can be removed and examined in a laboratory.

How can the pediatrician tell if my child has non-Hodgkin's lymphoma?

The key to accurate diagnosis (and effective treatment) is to identify the types of lymphocytes collecting in the lymph nodes and other tissues. If lymph-node biopsies suggest non-Hodgkin's lymphoma, a spinal tap and CT (computed tomography) scan may be done to see if the cancer has spread to the central nervous system.

What treatments are available?

A child with non-Hodgkin's lymphoma typically takes a combination of chemotherapeutic drugs (chemotherapy) for one to three years. The two-year survival rate is 70 percent. After two years in remission, relapse is very unlikely.

When non-Hodgkin's lymphoma is diagnosed at an early stage, when only cells in the small intestine are involved, treatment is successful 90 percent of the time.

Getting Help

CALL YOUR DOCTOR IF:

- ☐ Your child has several hard, rough, nontender lymph nodes.
- ☐ Your child seems generally ill, with poor appetite, listlessness, and pale or yellowish skin.

Obesity

Infants and young toddlers are expected to be somewhat pudgy. "Baby fat," in fact, is part of their appeal. In preschoolers, however, excess weight is the source of numerous problems, both emotional and physical.

Overweight children are often teased and left out of activities. As a result, they suffer low self-esteem, which makes fighting the problem even more difficult. Moreover, fat children run a high risk of becoming fat adults, putting them at long-term risk of such medical complications as high blood pressure, diabetes, and heart disease.

Formal definitions of childhood obesity vary, but in general, a child is considered obese if her weight is more than 20 percent above the average for children the same age, sex, and height.

What causes childhood obesity?

Obesity stems from a number of causes that all reinforce each other. Weight problems run in families; by one formulation, a child with one obese parent stands a 40 percent chance of becoming obese, and a child with two obese parents stands an 80 percent chance. Poor eating habits and distorted attitudes toward food also may increase the tendency to become overweight. Lack of physical activity is also an important contributor to obesity. Excessive television time and computer games are bad because they lead to lack of exercise and frequent snacking. Stress in the home may trigger overeating in some children. Harsh discipline, sibling rivalry, and strife between parents can lead to feelings of insecurity that some children assuage with excess food.

When should I suspect that my child is becoming obese?

You should be able to recognize a weight problem by comparing the child to her peers and checking the child's growth record. If weight is consistently in a much higher percentile than height, the child may be developing a problem.

Be careful not to mistake the normal roundness of infancy for a developing weight problem. If you have concerns, share them with your pediatrician.

Is medical attention necessary?

Yes. The doctor will ask questions about the family's and the child's eating and play habits. Most likely, the cause will be readily apparent: Too much food and too little exercise. The doctor may want to perform blood tests to rule

---

RECOGNIZING OBESITY

Your child may be developing a weight problem if she:

- Experiences a steady increase in weight *percentile* with each checkup.
- Eats large amounts of food or eats very frequently compared to age-mates.
- Tires easily during exercise.
- Uses food to soothe hurt feelings or cope with fears.

---

out hormonal disorders that can, in rare cases, trigger childhood obesity.

What treatments are available?

The doctor may refer you to a registered dietitian, who can help you modify your child's eating patterns to reduce overall calorie consumption. For children, the goal is not to lose weight, but rather to slow weight gain until vertical growth catches up.

Tips for slowing weight gain

If a child's weight falls outside the norm for her age—or if she is well above average in weight but barely average in height—the pediatrician may recommend some measures to slow the weight gain. These measures may include:

- Switching to skim milk (check with your doctor first if the child is under two).
- Avoiding fried foods.
- Limiting the use of butter and margarine.
- Avoiding processed baked goods such as cookies, cakes, and doughnuts.

- Avoiding snack foods such as chips.
- Limiting consumption of fruit juice to three or four ounces per day. If the child wants more, serve it diluted.
- Serving fresh fruit instead of juice, applesauce, or dried fruit.
- Presenting healthful foods in fun and attractive ways. For example, arrange a few raisins, a banana slice, and a peach slice into a face on a plate.
- Using less than a tablespoon of peanut butter per sandwich.
- Substituting low-fat cheeses such as part-skim mozzarella for American and cheddar cheese.
- Increasing the child's level of physical activity, particularly between the hours of three and six P.M., when most overeating takes place.
- Avoiding use of food as a reward or withholding of food as punishment.

> ### *Getting Help*
>
> **CALL YOUR DOCTOR IF:**
> - ◼ You have any concerns about your child's weight or any questions about your child's diet.

Oppositional Defiant Disorder

Most young children occasionally behave aggressively, refusing to comply with parent's orders, throwing tantrums, and hitting, kicking, or biting. When a child displays several of these behaviors consistently—day in and day out—over a period of six months or more, he or she may have a condition known as *oppositional defiant disorder*. This disorder normally appears during the grade school years, but it can begin as early as age three.

The behavior problems that mark oppositional defiant disorder usually occur at home, but also may appear at school. They may be a result of upsetting events in a child's life, or they may indicate a more serious behavior problem which will increase as the child gets older.

What causes oppositional defiant disorder?

Defiant behavior is part of a normal and crucial developmental stage, related to the child's attempt to establish self-determination and autonomy. A strong-willed child may run into problems if parents are overly controlling or exert authority arbitrarily. This may lead to a power struggle. The child's normal attempts at autonomy may develop into oppositional defiant disorder to guard against overdependence on the parents. Oppositional behavior can represent a misguided attempt to control the environment, not much different from infants' crying which brings their parents' response. As they grow up, most children learn socially appropriate ways to get what they want. Some, however, learn only inappropriate methods, becoming demanding, defiant, and difficult. Still other children may display oppositional behavior as a result of feelings of inadequacy stemming from a physical disability or mental retardation.

Oppositional defiant disorder occurs more frequently among children with neurological problems such as cerebral palsy or seizures, children from families where violence or abuse occurs, and children who receive inadequate supervision from their families.

When should I suspect oppositional defiant disorder?

Almost all children go through phases of ill temper and aggressive assertion of their independence. In fact, a classic example of normal oppositional behavior is the toddler period, during which children stretch their wings and express their growing autonomy from their parents. In oppositional defiant disorder, this expression becomes more intense and lasts longer. Oppositional behavior that occurs at normal developmental stages is of shorter duration and is similar to the behavior of other children the same age.

Is medical attention necessary?

Yes. A child with true oppositional defiant disorder usually becomes increasingly hard to manage at home and at school. In time, it interferes with the development of peer relationships, erodes school performance, and lowers the child's self-esteem. In the teen years it may evolve into a more serious behavioral disturbance such as a conduct disorder or drug or alcohol abuse.

What treatments are available?

Treatment usually consists of therapy with the child and the family. Your pediatrician will be able to refer you to a child psychologist or family therapist. Psychotherapy for children with the disorder focuses on resolving the conflicts related to developing independence and increasing the child's self-esteem. One effective

method has been cognitive therapy, which teaches children problem-solving skills and how to see situations from another person's perspective.

Parents also should receive counseling and training in order to change the way they manage the child. Parents can learn to reinforce (reward) positive social behaviors and decrease undesirable behaviors through time-out, removal of privileges, or other consequences.

POSSIBLE SIGNS OF OPPOSITIONAL DEFIANT DISORDER

A child with oppositional defiant behavior will exhibit at least five of these behaviors consistently over a period of at least six months:

- Frequent bad moods.
- Frequent arguments with parents and possibly teachers.
- Frequent disobedience and rule breaking.
- Frequent teasing and annoying others.
- Frequent blaming others for own problems and mistakes.
- Becoming easily annoyed by others, often peers and siblings.
- Frequently becoming angry, spiteful, and vindictive.
- Frequent swearing or use of obscenities.

SOURCE: DSM III.

Osteomyelitis

Osteomyelitis is a serious bone infection that occurs most often among children between the ages of five and nine, although it can develop in infants and adolescents. Without immediate and thorough treatment, the infection may damage the joints and the ends of the leg and arm bones, causing growth impairment and/or permanent disability. When the joint is infected by bacteria, the condition is called *pyogenic arthritis.*

When should I suspect that my child has osteomyelitis?

The first signs of osteomyelitis are complaints of pain with associated tenderness and an unwillingness to move the affected extremity. In many cases, the child develops a limp. In a baby, the first sign may be complete lack of movement in the affected limb. Fever, vomiting, swollen lymph glands, and other signs of illness also may appear. There may be local swelling and redness, and, if the joint is involved, a swollen knee, elbow, wrist, or ankle.

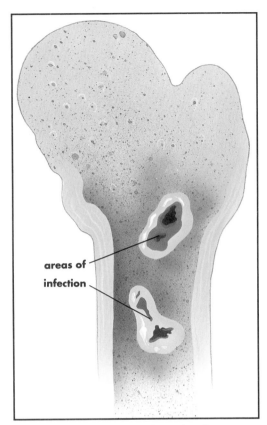

Osteomyelitis occurs when bacteria migrate through the bloodstream to bones—usually in a leg or an arm bone.

How does osteomyelitis develop?

Osteomyelitis usually develops when bacteria, sometimes from another infection such as a boil or an abscessed tooth, travel through the bloodstream to the bones. The infection usually settles in the matrix of a leg or arm bone, although it may develop in the feet, hands, pelvis, ribs, or vertebrae. In babies under a year old, osteomyelitis tends to occur in several sites at a time, whereas in older children, only one bone usually is affected.

Although the original source of the infection is often impossible to identify, children with certain conditions have an increased risk of developing osteomyelitis. These conditions include infected burns, cat or dog bites, impetigo (a skin infection), and chicken pox lesions that have been scratched open and become infected. Some children with underlying conditions such as sickle-cell disease or immune deficiencies are more susceptible.

Osteomyelitis begins as a bacterial infection in the bone, which can progress to an abscess. Depending on the blood supply, the abscess may remain in the central portion of the bone or spread to the growing end of the bone and invade the joint, causing arthritis. This complication is more likely to occur in the first year of life because the communicating networks of blood vessels nourish both the growth centers and the ends of the bones. In older children, these networks are separated, so arthritis occurs less frequently, or may occur independent of osteomyelitis. As delicate cartilage is destroyed by the infection, dislocations and fractures can occur, leading to deformity and altered growth. Strangely enough, and for reasons that are not well understood, osteomyelitis sometimes stimulates faster bone growth.

Is medical attention necessary?

Yes. A doctor should examine any child who has unexplained arm or leg pain, accompanied by fever, particularly if the limb is swollen and difficult to move.

How can the doctor tell if my child has osteomyelitis?

To reach a diagnosis, the doctor will examine the limb and take a blood sample to see if white blood cells are elevated (indicating infection) and to determine whether bacteria from the blood can be cultured in the laboratory. An important test is needle aspiration (withdrawal) of fluid from the affected bone or joint. By examining the fluid, the doctor can often determine the specific bacterium responsible and choose the best antibiotic with which to initiate treatment. To keep the pain of this test to a minimum, the child may be given an analgesic and local anesthetic at the site of the aspiration.

Other possible tests include an X ray (which may not show bone changes until the infection has been present over a week) and a

---

PREVENTING OSTEOMYELITIS

Fortunately, osteomyelitis is unusual in industrialized countries where children's health status is generally good. You can protect your child even more by getting prompt treatment for impetigo, boils, ear infections, and other potential sources of bacteria, especially staph organisms, that can enter the bloodstream and travel to the bone or joint. If your child is taking antibiotics for any kind of infection, make sure to complete the entire course, even if symptoms have gone away.

Hemophilus influenzae type B bacteria are responsible for some cases of pyogenic arthritis in infants and toddlers. Immunization against this type of bacteria is available and recommended by the American Academy of Pediatrics starting at two months of age. If you're not sure whether your child has been immunized, ask your pediatrician.

---

bone scan, in which a contrast material is injected to highlight bone destruction, and may show the infection location much earlier than a conventional X ray.

How is osteomyelitis treated?

If a child has signs and symptoms of osteomyelitis, intravenous antibiotic treatment starts immediately while the doctor awaits definitive test results. High dosages are administered for three to six weeks, until symptoms diminish and X rays demonstrate healing. A hospital stay is usually necessary, although the length will depend on the child's age and overall condition.

If antibiotics fail to bring improvement, or

---

if pus is removed from a bone or joint during needle aspiration, the abscess may need to be drained surgically.

Phenylketonuria (PKU)

Phenylketonuria (PKU) is a dangerous but treatable hereditary condition affecting one out of 10,000 children. Until recent decades, children with PKU always suffered brain damage and mental retardation. Now, however, the disease usually is detected and treated by means of a special diet before such damage can occur.

All infants born in the United States routinely undergo blood tests to diagnose PKU. If the test shows phenylketonuria, treatment is initiated immediately, in most cases preventing the serious, permanent effects of the disease.

The newest concern regarding PKU is the prevention of complications in the children of women who have been treated for the condition.

What causes PKU?

PKU results from an excess of an amino acid called *phenylalanine*, which is essential to the body's normal growth and development. Too much phenylalanine, however, damages the central nervous system.

Phenylalanine is present in high-protein foods. After the body has absorbed enough for its needs, an enzyme normally converts some phenylalanine to tyrosine, another essential amino acid; in PKU, however, that vital enzyme is absent or insufficient, so conversion to tyrosine does not take place. Instead, unused phenylalanine builds up in the bloodstream. The danger is greatest during the first year of life, when the brain is still developing. However, even if PKU develops later (which may happen if the child abandons the special diet), brain damage will occur.

PKU is a genetic disorder with a recessive inheritance pattern. If both parents are carriers (they have the gene, but not the disease), each baby has a 25 percent chance of inheriting the disease, a 50 percent chance of being a carrier, and a 25 percent chance of freedom from the defective gene. Prospective parents who already have a child with PKU or who have any reason to suspect that they are PKU carriers should consider genetic counseling.

How does PKU develop?

A child with untreated PKU will develop the following manifestations:

- Musty odor of urine and sweat
- Failure to produce the pigment melanin, resulting in light-colored hair, skin, and eyes (This sign is not always present.)
- An eczemalike rash
- Seizures
- Behavioral problems, including hyperactivity or excessive aggressiveness
- Abnormally small head after age six months
- Uncontrollable twitching
- Vomiting
- Decreased growth rate
- Brain damage and progressive mental retardation (symptoms may not appear for a few months)

What treatments are available?

Immediately upon diagnosis of PKU, a strict diet plan must be initiated and maintained indefinitely. The child must avoid foods high in phenylalanine (even a small excess can be damaging) but take in enough for normal development; balancing the level and assuring the child's compliance are the most difficult aspects of the diet. In the first few years of life, frequent visits to the doctor or a metabolic clinic are necessary. Periodic testing will be scheduled to monitor the child's phenylalanine level.

Up to age six months, infants with PKU are given formula low in phenylalanine. Limited amounts of breast feeding also may be incorporated into the infant's diet. The baby can start eating solid foods at the usual time, but the diet must exclude certain high-protein foods, such as animal proteins (meat, fish, eggs, and dairy products); high-protein grain products; and nuts. Be sure the child (as well as all caregivers, teachers, and school health personnel) know what foods to avoid when he is outside the home. A registered dietician can help you follow the diet with as little disruption in normal family eating patterns as possible.

In the past, children were taken off the special PKU diet sometime between the ages of five and eight. However, recent studies suggest that abandoning the diet that early may lead to learning and behavioral problems. Consequently, many authorities now suggest that the diet be continued indefinitely.

PREVENTING COMPLICATIONS IN INFANTS OF MOTHERS WITH PKU

There is no way to prevent or cure PKU. Infants of mothers who have had the disease risk mental retardation even if they do not inherit the abnormal genes. This is because extremely high levels of phenylalanine, which may persist in adults with PKU, can reach the fetus and interfere with its development. To avoid this outcome, the mother must begin the restrictive PKU diet before conception and maintain it throughout pregnancy.

Be aware that a physical trauma or minor illness can elevate the amount of phenylalanine in the child's blood even with strict compliance with the dietary restrictions. In such circumstances, seek medical guidance immediately.

Pneumonia

Pneumonia is a serious inflammation of lung tissue caused by either a bacterial or a viral infection. Newborns sometimes acquire pneumonia from bacteria in the maternal genital tract. More frequently, however, viruses are to blame for pneumonia in infants and children between the ages of two months and five years. One such organism, known as *respiratory syncytial virus* (*RSV*), is particularly common in winter and early-spring epidemics. Influenza viruses are also an important cause of pneumonia in children, especially older ones. These infections generally occur during outbreaks of flu during the winter.

When should I suspect that my child has pneumonia?

The signs and symptoms of pneumonia can vary a great deal, depending on its cause, the child's age, and the immune system's ability to fend off the infection. While it is not always possible to distinguish between viral and bacterial pneumonia, each possesses certain fairly typical characteristics.

Viral pneumonia in infants or young children often develops gradually following low-grade fever, runny nose, and diminished appetite for one or two days. These symptoms may then give way to increasing fretfulness, vomiting, cough, and rapid breathing. The child also may develop a wheeze.

Infants between the ages of four weeks and three months may develop a syndrome of pneumonia without fever and a sharp "staccato" cough. This type of viral pneumonia also has a gradual onset but shows no preference for any given season.

Bacterial pneumonia typically begins more suddenly than the viral variety. The cough may bring up sputum, and there may be chest pain and high fever. In some cases, however, the only symptoms are fever and rapid breathing.

How can the pediatrician tell if my child has pneumonia?

The doctor can determine whether pneumonia is a likely diagnosis by considering the child's age, the season, and the severity of symptoms. The physician recognizes pneumonia from symptoms and from the physical exam during which the pediatrician listening to the chest sounds with a stethoscope (*auscultation*), and by chest X rays. Tests of blood or sputum also may also be ordered, in order to identify the causative organism underlying pneumonia.

What treatments are available?

Bacterial pneumonia is treated with antibiotics such as erythromycin and amoxicillin. In most cases, treatment of viral pneumonia consists mainly of supportive therapy, which is aimed at easing the discomfort brought on by the illness, rather than attacking its cause.

Even though antibiotics are not effective against pneumonia caused by viruses, your child may be given an antibiotic while there is still uncertainty about what is causing the pneumonia. Such therapy does no harm to children with viral pneumonia. A child with chronic lung disease or congenital heart disease may be given specific antiviral agents for pneumonia caused by respiratory syncitial virus or influenza A.

Most older children with pneumonia can be treated successfully at home. A newborn with pneumonia generally needs to be hospi-

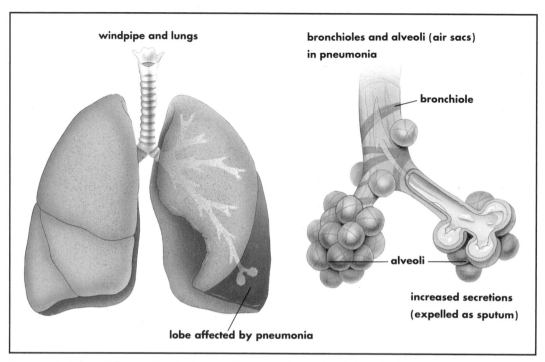

windpipe and lungs

bronchioles and alveoli (air sacs)
in pneumonia

bronchiole

alveoli

increased secretions
(expelled as sputum)

lobe affected by pneumonia

Pneumonia is lung inflammation that may affect an entire section (lobe) of a lung or occur in patches, most often in the lower part of the lung.

CARING FOR A CHILD WITH PNEUMONIA

- Maintain adequate fluid intake to prevent dehydration, a common complication of pneumonia's fever, hyperventilation, and loss of appetite.
- Maintain a humid environment in the child's bedroom to reduce the thickness of mucous secretions and prevent dehydration.
- Notify the pediatrician if the child is having trouble breathing.
- Make certain that all antibiotics or other prescribed drugs are taken at the proper time. Unless the pediatrician gives the go-ahead, don't discontinue the medicines—even if your child seems all better.

talized for observation and care if there are difficulties in breathing or eating, or if dehydration occurs. Once pneumonia has been resolved, a return visit to the doctor's office for a repeat physical examination and chest X ray is usually necessary to make certain that the chest is clear.

Getting Help

CALL YOUR DOCTOR IF:
- ❑ Your child develops any of the symptoms of pneumonia.
- ❑ Your child has high fever, cough, respiratory difficulty, decreased appetite.

Pneumothorax

Pneumothorax, also called an air leak or collapsed lung, is a fairly rare occurrence in children. A pneumothorax develops when air leaks from the lung and enters the pleural cavity, which is the area of the chest adjacent to the lungs. Once trapped, the air cannot escape, and the pressure it creates can collapse the adjacent lung and cause serious breathing difficulties. The severity of a pneumothorax depends upon the extent of the lung collapse and the degree of preexisting lung disease.

Newborns are most commonly (and dangerously) affected by this condition, but it also occurs in older children and adults. Emergency care is essential in afflicted babies; however, most recover completely.

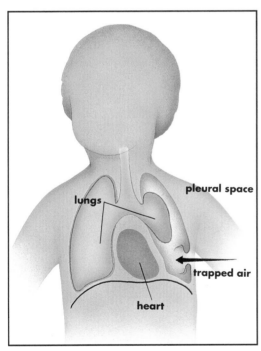

A pneumothorax occurs when air enters the space in the chest adjacent to the lungs.

What causes pneumothorax?

The exact cause of pneumothorax is not always clear. Most commonly pneumothorax results from increased pressure within the lung secondary to air trapping. Older children (especially males) may develop a spontaneous pneumothorax, which is simply a pneumothorax with unknown cause. The tendency to develop this kind of pneumothorax seems to run in families.

Pneumothorax may be caused by physical trauma, such as a penetrating injury to the chest. An inhaled foreign object also can trigger pneumothorax. It also may develop as a complication of a respiratory disease such as **pneumonia** (see entry), **cystic fibrosis** (see entry), or a lung abscess.

When should I suspect that my child has pneumothorax?

The main clue is the sudden development of rapid, shallow breathing. The child may be in pain, and breathing sometimes becomes difficult. Restlessness and irritability are also common. These signs are particularly important if the child already has a respiratory disease.

PREVENTING PNEUMOTHORAX

There is no known prevention for pneumothorax. In the case of infants, the best protection is competent emergency treatment if any respiratory problem arises. In older children, especially those who have had respiratory diseases, be alert to the signs and symptoms of this complication and get prompt medical care if they develop.

Is medical attention necessary?

Yes. A child with pneumothorax risks oxygen deprivation because of loss of lung function.

How can the pediatrician tell if my child has pneumothorax?

If a newborn shows signs of pneumothorax, the hospital staff may confirm the diagnosis by shining a bright light on the child's chest; the chest area into which air has leaked may become highly translucent. Chest X rays provide definitive diagnosis.

What treatments are available?

Treatment varies with the extent of the pneumothorax and the severity of the underlying disease. A small pneumothorax (affecting less than five percent of the lung) in an otherwise healthy child can resolve on its own within a week. Spontaneous pneumothorax usually only requires observation.

However, recurrent pneumothorax or any lung collapse affecting more than five percent of the lung may require surgical intervention to release the trapped air. This usually involves inserting a tube into the pleural area to allow trapped air to escape.

Poison Ivy, Oak, and Sumac

The rash caused by contact with the poison ivy, oak, and sumac plants is perhaps the most common form of allergic contact dermatitis. Almost everyone whose skin brushes up against these plants may experience an allergic reaction consisting of redness, small bumps, and intense itching. In severe cases, large blisters may develop and the rash may cover substantial areas of skin.

Because children spend long hours outdoors and love to examine flowers and plants (even uncultivated ones), they are highly vulnerable to these allergies.

How does poison ivy develop?

A child will not develop an allergy to poison ivy until he has touched the plant at least once or twice before. Subsequent skin contact with the plant triggers these antibodies, causing certain skin cells to release the chemical *histamine,* which is responsible for much of the swelling, itching, and blister formation.

The allergy-causing substance in poison ivy, oak, and sumac is an oily resin called *urushiol.* All parts of the plants contain this resin. Urushiol can get on clothing, pets, and (especially) hands and be easily spread from one part of the body to another, which is why poison ivy rashes are usually widespread.

The allergic reaction may begin as soon as urushiol touches the skin, but the full-blown rash usually takes about two days to appear. At that time, areas that came in direct contact with the plant or its resin turn red and very itchy. A few days after the first appearance of the rash, blisters appear. When these blisters break, yellowish crusts form. Itching typically subsides within about two weeks.

Although poison ivy is a potent allergy trigger, direct contact is required for the rash to develop; a child cannot get it simply from being near the plant.

When should I suspect that my child has poison ivy, oak, or sumac?

Any time a child develops a localized, moist, itchy rash a few days after playing outdoors, you should suspect poison ivy.

Is medical attention necessary?

Only if large blisters develop over extensive areas, or if the rash is near the eyes. A rash that starts out resembling poison ivy but spreads over most of the body or fails to improve after a week or so also should be checked out by a doctor. In addition, medical attention is necessary if a baby under one year of age gets a rash that resembles poison ivy.

How can the pediatrician tell if my child has poison ivy?

A careful examination of the rash is usually all that is needed. If there is any uncertainty, the doctor may refer the child to a dermatologist.

What treatments are available?

Mild cases can be managed with over-the-counter and home remedies such as cool compresses and calamine lotion. In more severe cases, the pediatrician may prescribe a cream or gel containing a corticosteroid, which reduces inflammation and itching. Antihistamines also may be recommended to reduce itching, particularly if it disturbs the child's sleep. Oral or injected corticosteroids are used only in the most severe cases.

PREVENTING POISON IVY, OAK, AND SUMAC

- Avoid poison ivy, oak, and sumac plants, and teach your children to do the same. Poison ivy may be a low bush or vine, and its pointed leaves grow in clusters of three. It can be found practically anywhere east of the Rocky Mountains. Poison oak also grows in three-leaf clusters, but the leaves are more rounded than those of poison ivy. The poison oak plant is most common in the Western states. Poison sumac bushes have pointed leaves that grow in fronds. These plants grow mainly in the damp areas of the Southeast.
- Have children wear long pants and sleeves when they walk in wooded areas with thick underbrush.
- Do not allow children to play in ungroomed areas at the edges of lawns and parks.
- Do not let pets roam freely, particularly if there are wooded areas in your neighborhood.
- Run cold water over skin that has come in contact with poison ivy, oak, or sumac. Flush the skin for several minutes to neutralize the urushiol, but do not scrub or use soap.
- Remove clothing that has touched poison ivy, oak, or sumac plants, and immediately wash it in hot water.

Precocious Puberty

When a young child begins to undergo the physical changes that normally occur in the early teens, the condition is known as precocious puberty. Although rates of sexual maturation differ from person to person, it is generally agreed that puberty beginning before age eight in girls and age nine-and-a-half in boys is abnormal. In most cases of precocious puberty, an underlying cause can be found and treated. Girls are five to seven times as likely to develop precocious puberty as boys.

When should I suspect that my child is developing precocious puberty?

The most telling signs are development of what are known as *secondary sex characteristics*—breasts, pubic hair, and menstruation in girls, and pubic hair, enlarged penis and testicles, facial hair, and vocal deepening in boys. In addition, children undergoing precocious puberty enter a period of rapid growth and weight gain similar to that of normal adolescence, when the bones harden and mature. The difference, though, is that these children have not completed the growth of their early years, and when their bones harden, growth stops.

How does precocious puberty develop?

The changes of puberty are triggered by the pituitary, a pea-sized gland near the base of the brain, and the nearby hypothalamus. Often, precocious puberty results from a problem in these two powerful glands, which are somehow turned on ahead of schedule. As a result,
affected children have elevated levels of sex hormones.

No cause can be found for many cases of precocious puberty. Sometimes, precocious puberty in either sex is due to a hormone-secreting tumor in the pituitary or hypothalamus.

Precocious puberty also may accompany chromosomal disorders, including Down syndrome or untreated hypothroidism (an underactive thyroid gland).

A form of precocious puberty called *medicational precocity* results from accidental exposure to estrogen in drugs or food. Medicational precocity consists mainly of breast development, which can occur in both girls and boys who have taken estrogen.

Children can be exposed to estrogen by ingesting birth control pills or estrogen-replacement medication. In addition, some nonprescription creams advertised as bust developers contain enough estrogen to affect a child who comes into repeated contact with them.

On a few occasions, estrogen given to livestock also has caused breast development in children. Several occurrences of abnormal breast development among children in Puerto Rico a few years ago were linked to chickens fed estrogen.

Is medical attention necessary?

Yes. Any girl who shows signs of sexual maturation before age eight (and any boy who begins to mature before age nine-and-a-half) should definitely see a doctor. Slightly older children entering puberty also could benefit from a doctor's attention, if only for reassurance.

Unless premature puberty is halted, growth of the long bones will cease too soon, resulting in short stature. One-third of children who enter puberty precociously are under five feet tall as adults.

How can the doctor tell if a child is developing precocious puberty?

A doctor can usually observe precocious puberty on physical examination. The parents may be questioned to rule out problems that may mimic precocious puberty—for example, a recurrent vaginal infection that causes menstrual-like bleeding. Possible sources of medicational precocity also may be uncovered in such an interview.

Blood and urine tests are performed to detect elevated levels of sex hormones. X rays, particularly of the wrist and arm, can show whether the bones are hardening. Both these changes indicate that the problem involves the pituitary, hypothalamus, or both. Special imaging tests (CT or MRI scans) are performed to detect tumors in the pituitary, hypothalamus, liver, ovary, or testes. These scans should be repeated periodically, because pituitary and hypothalamic tumors grow slowly and may not be detectable until a year or two after precocious puberty appears.

What treatments are available?

Surgery and radiation are the main treatments employed against tumors that trigger precocious puberty. In addition, powerful new drugs called *LHRH analogs* can reverse the signs of precocious puberty. These drugs reduce the secretion of sex hormones as soon as two weeks after treatment begins, and symptoms begin to disappear soon afterward.

Getting Help

CALL YOUR DOCTOR IF YOUR CHILD:
- Shows any signs of early sexual maturation.
- Seems to be growing and gaining weight too quickly.

Prematurity

About nine percent of infants are born prematurely, or before the 37th week of gestation. While some of these babies are mature enough to survive without difficulty outside the womb, many need special care (which is usually given in a neonatal intensive care unit, or NICU) for at least their first few weeks.

Because they are not fully developed, premature babies frequently have problems with breathing, feeding, maintaining body temperature, and fighting off infection. The smaller the baby is, the more serious these problems are likely to be. Babies who weigh less than 1,500 grams (three pounds and five ounces) at birth are most likely to develop complications of prematurity, but any infant weighing under 2,500 grams (five-and-a-half pounds) needs special attention. Because size is such an important factor in newborns' health, pediatricians are alert to potential problems in any low-birthweight infant (defined as one weighing under five-and-a-half pounds), whether the baby is born early or at term. With the care currently available, most premature babies do quite well.

What causes prematurity?

In most cases, the direct cause of premature birth is unknown, but a number of factors are associated with it. Among them are premature rupture of the membranes (i.e., the mother's water breaks early), premature separation of the placenta (the mass of tissue that nourishes the fetus) from the womb's wall, and maternal infections, particularly of the uterus or urinary tract. Women carrying multiple fetuses have an increased chance of giving birth early, as do women under 17 or over 34 years of age. For unknown reasons, black women are twice as likely as white women to have low-birthweight babies.

Problems in the fetus, such as organ malformations, are also associated with premature birth. In addition, premature labor occurs more frequently in women who have gained weight poorly during pregnancy or suffered severe nausea and vomiting. While most causes of low birth weight and prematurity are unknown, it is very clear that smoking, alcohol and drug use, and poor nutrition in the mother significantly increase the risk of low birth weight and preterm birth. Pregnant women should do everything possible to avoid these risk factors.

Because prematurity is associated with complicated pregnancies and unhealthful habits, mothers of premature infants have a tendency to blame themselves for going into labor early. Actually, preterm labor seems to result from a combination of factors, the strongest of which are probably beyond the mother's control. Many women who have excellent health habits and trouble-free pregnancies still give birth prematurely.

How are premature babies different from term babies?

They are smaller, of course, with less body fat (one of the reasons it's harder for them to stay warm) and thin, shiny, almost transparent skin that is often covered with fine hair. Premature infants have soft skull bones that have not been rounded out by the full pregnancy process. Their heads appear a bit flattened, a problem that resolves itself in time but can still be distressing to parents.

They behave differently as well. While term newborns lie with their arms and legs flexed and have some control over their movements, premature babies keep their limbs extended and relaxed. Premature babies also have poorly developed grasp, suck, and gag reflexes. As a result, they often have trouble feeding.

The immaturity of premature babies' organ systems puts them at risk of serious complications. Some of these complications occur by themselves, but many are the result of some other problem. Many premature babies suffer from apnea, a periodic halt in breathing that seems to result from immaturity of the nerve pathways that control respiration. Incomplete development of the lungs leads to a complication called respiratory distress syndrome, which may require use of a mechanical ventilator and special medications to help the lungs work better. Immaturity of the immune system leaves premature infants vulnerable to many types of infection. In addition, premature babies sometimes develop neurologic conditions such as cerebral palsy or bleeding in the area between the brain and skull, and some have permanently impaired vision due to a condition called retinopathy of prematurity. Because premature infants' livers are not fully developed, they often cannot handle the breakdown products of blood and become jaundiced (or hyperbilirubinemic). They may need treatment with phototherapy (lights) or exchange transfusions.

What types of care do premature babies need?

Premature babies need constant monitoring of breathing, heart function, and body temperature with the special equipment available in NICUs. Many need extra oxygen or breathing assistance from mechanical ventilators.

They also may need tube feeding, since their energy requirements are high but they can take in little if any food by mouth. Those who can suck need lots of encouragement and frequent, small feedings. Premature babies can be fed either breast milk or formula. Since babies have more trouble nursing than drinking from a bottle, mothers who want to breast feed usually express milk for bottle feedings until the baby gains some strength and coordination.

NICU nurses make frequent checks of each baby's appearance and monitoring equipment. They also listen to the heart, check blood pressure, look for changes in the baby's color, and measure nutrient intake and stool and urine output.

Most premature infants lie in incubators, which are clear, plastic boxes with portholes in the sides for reaching in and handling the baby. Incubators are artificially heated to protect the premature infant from losing body heat; some types of incubators automatically adjust their temperatures in response to changes in the baby's temperature.

Several recent studies have suggested that the round-the-clock noise, lights, and activity in NICUs may not be good for premature babies. As a result, many hospitals now lower the lights, cover the cribs or incubators with blankets, and maintain a quiet environment with as little disruption as possible during the night. Others keep the lights on but cover the infants' eyes with pads to simulate darkness at night, and still others allow the babies complete rest for several periods each day. In addition, nurses, doctors, and parents handle premature babies slowly and deliberately, since they are extremely sensitive to abrupt motion and other intense stimuli.

Researchers also have found that premature infants respond well to skin-to-skin contact. In some hospitals, parents are encouraged to massage their premature infants gently in the course of routine care, such as feeding, and a few hospitals are experimenting with a technique called kangaroo care, in which one parent holds the baby against his or her chest inside a pouchlike garment.

What are the long-term effects of prematurity?

For the first two or three years of life, most children who were born prematurely remain small for their ages, even though their growth rates are normal. While a few children born prematurely may have permanent problems such as cerebral palsy and impairments in hearing and vision, the majority have no serious difficulties. The smaller and more premature a baby is, the greater are the chances of long-term effects.

Coping with prematurity

Parents of premature infants face tremendous stress, especially if the baby has medical complications or spends a prolonged period in an NICU. Although NICU staffs try to involve the parents in as much of their baby's care as possible, it can be daunting for parents to assume total responsibility when their baby is ready to go home. The normal anxiety of new parenthood is compounded when parents must care for an extremely small, fragile infant who may have continuing medical problems. Here are some tips that may help.

- Even if your baby needs ongoing medical care, try to see yourself as a "regular" parent, especially after the baby comes home. Don't let clinical matters distract you from the joy of nurturing the new baby.

- Most premature infants are highly sensitive to stimulation; they turn away, become fretful, or doze off after a brief period of handling. A slow, gentle approach will work best during feedings and other periods of interaction.

- Remember that premature infants' behavior matches their gestational age more closely than their calendar age. A baby born a month early, for example, may not do the things a full-term two-month-old does (such as smiling and head turning) until the third month of life.

Getting Help

■ Parents of premature infants usually learn special techniques for caring for their babies before they take them home from the hospital. They often need help, however, in coping with the fear and guilt having a premature baby can arouse. Many find it helpful to discuss these issues in support groups for parents of premature infants. Most communities now have early intervention programs to help parents foster the development of premature babies. Ask your hospital social services department for a referral to such an early intervention program.

Prickly Heat

Prickly heat, also known as heat rash and miliaria, is a common problem among children who are still in diapers. Prickly heat is a skin irritation resulting from too much heat and moisture. It usually develops in hot, humid, summer months, but also can occur in colder temperatures—when a child is overdressed, for example. Prickly heat is rarely serious and usually responds readily to appropriate treatment.

When should I suspect that my baby has prickly heat?

Prickly heat produces an itchy, red rash, accompanied by small bumps or tiny fluid-filled blisters. It generally occurs in the creases or skin folds of the upper neck and back, armpits, and diaper area. One type—*miliaria crystallina*—mainly affects newborns and does not cause inflammation. Another type, *miliaria rubra*, occurs in older infants and children and is inflamed due to leakage of sweat beneath the skin. A third type, *miliaria pustulosa*, occurs when the blocked sweat ducts become infected.

What causes prickly heat?

Prickly heat is due to retention of sweat in the pores.

Is medical attention necessary?

It is rarely necessary to consult a pediatrician about prickly heat. However, if you take appropriate measures and the rash has not cleared up after three or four days, or has spread or worsened, a visit to the doctor is in order.

The pediatrician can check to see if the child is suffering from another condition—such as measles or chicken pox—which produce rashes associated with other symptoms. The child also may be experiencing an allergic reaction to a new food, detergent, or skin product.

Getting Help

CALL YOUR DOCTOR IF:
- The rash does not respond to appropriate measures, gets worse, or spreads.
- The child exhibits other symptoms with the rash, such as a fever and irritability.

PREVENTING PRICKLY HEAT

The best way to prevent prickly heat is to keep your baby or young child clean, dry, and comfortable.

- In hot and humid weather, try to keep the child in the shade, and avoid taking him or her out during the hottest periods.
- Give frequent, lukewarm baths in hot weather but be sure to dry the child's skin thoroughly afterwards.
- During cold weather, avoid overdressing the child. When you come inside, remove unnecessary layers of heavy clothing.
- Use clothing made of cotton or other breathable fabrics.
- Avoid greasy ointments and lotions, which hold moisture in.

Profanity

At around age four to five, most children will go through a phase of using swear words, obscenities or rude language. They may, for example, call people names like "stupid," use bathroom words like "poo-poo" or actually say four-letter words. Children are frequently unaware of the meaning of these new words they are trying out, but they quickly learn, from the reactions of adults and older children, that the words are powerful.

This behavior usually passes quickly in an environment where the words do not acquire the power to shock or gain attention. Parents dealing with this phase should try to remember not to react too strongly to the use of these words.

What causes young children to use obscenities?

Young children acquire "gutter" language in much the same way they acquire other language skills, by imitation, and this behavior is a normal part of a child's development. They may say "bad" words to be funny or to insult others. When a young child's wishes are thwarted, he or she may express anger by calling the parent "bad" names or saying something aggressive like "I'm going to kill you." School-age children may also pick up and use unacceptable language for its shock value.

What should I do if my child begins using obscene or otherwise objectionable language?

The best thing for a parent to do when this imitative language begins is to ignore it. Acting shocked, disturbed, or anxious only encourages the behavior by giving the child a delightful sense of power over you. In most cases, ignoring is all that is necessary to eliminate the behavior.

If the behavior persists, let your child know when he or she has used an inappropriate word. Help the child to explore other ways of expressing feelings, such as saying "I'm mad because you won't buy me candy."

Be a good role model for your child. Because children imitate their parents, it is best to avoid cursing, name-calling, and applying negative labels such as "brat" or "jerk" to your child or others.

Discuss the meaning of "bad" words and how they can be painful to others. Praise your child for expressing feelings appropriately.

If the above interventions do not succeed in eliminating the behavior, apply negative consequences. You might require a one-minute time-out (that is, a minute of isolation in a quiet place with no distractions) each time the child swears, or reduce privileges such as television time. Do not use extreme punishments such as washing the child's mouth out with soap, which is unnecessarily humiliating as well as dangerous, since it could damage the mouth or throat.

HOW TO DEAL WITH A CHILD USING PROFANITY

- Don't overreact. Ignore the behavior.
- Don't act shocked, surprised, or agitated.
- Calmly and firmly remind the child that others don't like swearing or profanity.
- Try offering substitute words like "shucks," or encourage the child to make up his or her own innocuous or funny "curse words."
- Reinforce the child's good behaviors with praise.
- Don't allow adults to swear or use profanity in the home.
- Help the child to discover new ways of expressing feelings.
- Apply negative consequences only after trying all other responses.

Progressive Neurologic Deterioration

Several severe but fortunately rare nervous system disorders first appear in infancy and early childhood. In these disorders an on-going problem permanently damages nerve cells and worsens over time. In many cases, early death is the outcome; in others, the child lives longer, but with progressive disability.

The nervous system, which controls our senses and coordinates all of our activities, body functions, and thinking is divided into two parts. The brain and spinal cord make up the *central nervous system,* which issues directions for all body activities and processes information gathered from the body and the outer world. The *peripheral nervous system,* which is the network of nerves branching out to the muscles, sense organs, and internal organs, provides communication lines necessary for proper functioning of the five senses, voluntary motor activities (such as walking and throwing a ball), and involuntary processes (such as heartbeat, breathing, and digestion).

What causes progressive neurologic deterioration?

Inherited deficits in enzymes or other essential body substances are often at the root of the problem. Some of these metabolic abnormalities affect body systems on so many levels that they are called *protean diseases.* Other cases of progressive neurologic deterioration are brought about by infection, and the cause of still others remains to be discovered.

When should I suspect that my child has progressive neurologic deterioration?

Loss of skill or slowing of maturation in any area of development may suggest a progressive neurological disorder. The child may develop a severe seizure disorder or suffer from uncontrollable small jerking movements. Weakness, poor coordination, and movement disorders may occur. Changes in personality or loss of vision or hearing may occur as well.

The symptoms are complex and depend on the cause as well as on which nerve cells (neurons) are involved. When cells that control voluntary motion (called the *upper motor neurons*) are damaged, muscles may become spastic, movements stiff, and reflexes abnormal. Diminished muscle tone and selective muscle wasting may accompany deterioration of *lower motor neurons,* which transmit signals to and from the peripheral nervous system. For descriptions of some of these syndromes, see the chart on "Disorders causing progressive neurologic deterioration" on page 208.

How is progressive neurologic deterioration treated?

Treatment depends on the cause. In general, however, cures are rarely possible. In most cases, the focus is on providing physical, occupational, and behavioral therapies, orthopedic devices, and medications to control seizures.

DISORDERS CAUSING PROGRESSIVE NEUROLOGIC DETERIORATION

DISEASE	SYMPTOMS	AGE OF ONSET
Duchenne muscular dystrophy	Weakness beginning in the legs and progressing through shoulders and trunk; delayed walking.	Three to five years
Infantile spinal muscular atrophy type 1 (Werdnig-Hoffmann disease)	Inactivity; weak shoulders; feeble cry; knees flexed; does not learn to roll over or sit.	Birth to two months (genetic disease)
Infantile spinal muscular atrophy type 2	Weakness first in arms and legs, later more generalized; breastbone may be depressed; little movement during sleep or relaxation; may learn to stand if holding something.	Two to 12 months (genetic disease)
Infantile spinal muscular atrophy type 3	May start normally, learn to sit unassisted from 6–8 months; develop weak thighs and hips but may learn to walk; waddling gait; outward curve of lower spine, protruding abdomen; may need wheelchair by age ten or later.	During second year (genetic disease)
Juvenile spinal muscular atrophy (Kugelberg-Welander disease)	Slowly progressing weakness starting in shoulders, thighs, and hips; may develop abnormal gait and curve of lower spine; may continue to walk or use a wheelchair later in life. May live normal lifespan.	Two–17 years (genetic disease)
Rett syndrome	First appear normal, then rapid decline of useful hand movement and speech. Hands begin making repeated gestures such as wringing and tapping. Little eye contact; abnormal breathing; seizures; failure to grow; progressive immobility.	Girls only, six–18 months (may be genetic)
Adrenoleukodystrophy	Personality changes; problems with schoolwork; problems in movement; sometimes seizures; progressive slowing of physical and mental reactions; stiff, awkward movements; vision loss.	Boys only, three–16 years

* The first five diseases are forms of muscular dystrophy. For more information, see entry on **muscular dystrophy.**

Psoriasis

Psoriasis is a skin disease in which new skin cells are produced too fast, resulting in a rash and other symptoms. About two out of every 100 Americans have psoriasis; only about ten percent of cases occur in the first decade of life, and the condition is quite rare in infants.

Red areas of raised, scaly skin—most commonly on the elbows, knees, fronts of the legs, backs of the arms, genitalia, back and scalp— are hallmarks of the disease. The condition may cause no apparent discomfort, or the skin may be itchy and sore. While psoriasis is usually a persistent, chronic disease, its symptoms come and go over time. There is no cure for psoriasis, but there are a variety of treatments that can alleviate its sometimes severe discomfort.

When should I suspect that my child has psoriasis?

Psoriasis begins as red and sometimes itchy areas of raised skin (*plaques*) on the elbows, knees, backs of arms, or any area of the body mentioned above. The raised patches may become dry, white, and flaky, or they may become silver and scaly, although the moist environment of the diaper area sometimes keeps the scale from becoming prominent. About one-quarter to one-half of children who develop psoriasis also develop pitting and other changes of their fingernails. If psoriasis begins in infancy, it usually appears first in the diaper area.

What causes psoriasis?

The precise cause of psoriasis is unknown. However, it often runs in families, indicating a possible inherited predisposition. For example, children whose parents have psoriasis are three times more likely to develop psoriasis than the rest of the population. The disease is uncommon among people of African and Japanese descent, as well as among Native Americans.

Psoriasis in babies may be worsened by direct contact with an irritating physical, chemical, or biological substance. Psoriasis also may appear at a site of injury or surgical incision, and even in areas commonly bound by tight clothing.

Is medical attention necessary?

Yes; only a physician can diagnose psoriasis and prescribe appropriate treatment for it. If any diaper rash does not improve after three or four days of home treatment, consult your pediatrician. This also applies to any rash that spreads beyond the diaper area.

The doctor will examine the child to determine whether the rash is due to psoriasis or some other skin problem. If psoriasis is suspected, the pediatrician will probably refer parents to a dermatologist.

What treatments are available for psoriasis?

The type of psoriasis and its severity determine how aggressively a pediatrician or dermatologist treats the disease. If an irritating substance is causing the psoriasis, its removal may clear up the problem.

Initially, the doctor may recommend application of an over-the-counter moisturizing agent or emollient. Psoriasis makes the skin dry and flaky, and emollients such as petroleum jelly help the skin retain water.

Other possible treatments, such as exposure to sunlight or ultraviolet light and the use of over-the-counter topical cortisone creams, should be carried out only under close medical supervision. In some cases, psoriasis is treated with creams containing strong substances such as dithranol or tar; however, these creams should not be applied in the genital area, as they may burn or further irritate the delicate skin there.

Coping with psoriasis

While there is no certain way to prevent or treat psoriasis, good hygiene plays an important role in controlling the disease.

* Keep the child's skin, clothing, and bed linen clean.
* Change wet or soiled diapers frequently.
* Follow the doctor's instructions in applying any ointment or other treatments for psoriasis.
* Keep the child's fingernails clean and clipped short to minimize risk of a skin infection caused by scratching.
* Bathe the child frequently in lukewarm or cool water to alleviate itching and discomfort.

Getting Help

CALL YOUR PEDIATRICIAN IF:
- Your child develops symptoms characteristic of psoriasis.

Pyloric Stenosis

Virtually all newborn babies occasionally spit up partially digested milk or formula soon after feedings. A baby who, starting around the second to fourth week of life, begins to spit up with increasing force and frequency may have a malformation of the digestive tract known as pyloric stenosis. In this disorder, the muscle surrounding the opening between the stomach and duodenum (the first part of the small intestine) is abnormally thick, stiff, and narrow. As a result, food cannot pass into the duodenum and forceful regurgitation occurs. The vomiting eventually makes the baby weak, constipated, dehydrated, and malnourished.

Pyloric stenosis is fairly common, affecting about one out of every 250 babies. For unknown reasons, the condition affects four times as many boys (commonly the first-born male in a family) as girls and occurs in whites more often than in black, Hispanic, or Asian infants. Likewise, the cause is unknown, although genetics may play a role, since pyloric stenosis seems to run in some families.

When should I suspect that my baby has pyloric stenosis?

Forceful vomiting, known medically as *projectile vomiting*, is the hallmark of the condition, but it may not appear immediately. Instead, the early signs of pyloric stenosis may resemble normal (but unusually frequent) infantile burping and spitting up, with the stomach contents flowing out the nose as well as the mouth. Within several days, however, projectile vomiting develops, with powerful stomach contractions ejecting the vomit one to four feet from the baby's mouth. This development is understandably alarming, and it usually prompts the parents to call the pediatrician right away.

In most cases, the baby vomits soon after a meal. The vomiting associated with pyloric stenosis can, however, occur several hours after feeding. Although the milk is curdled from being in the stomach, it does not contain the greenish-yellow bile characteristic of more complete digestion. The vomit may also contain black or rust-tinged material, which is actually blood from the irritated stomach lining.

Despite their inability to keep milk down, babies with pyloric stenosis nurse and take bottles eagerly because they're hungry. After a few days of vomiting, however, their weight gain and output of urine and stool drop off, and they may become weak and listless. Fever may also develop.

How can the pediatrician tell if my baby has pyloric stenosis?

Your report about when the vomiting developed and how it occurs will make the pediatrician consider the possibility of pyloric stenosis. A physical examination can usually pin down the diagnosis. In many cases, the doctor can actually feel the thick, hardened muscle in the upper right side of the baby's abdomen and see the abnormal movements of the stomach muscles. Sometimes, the doctor or nurse watches the baby eat and observes subsequent vomiting.

If the diagnosis is unclear, an ultrasound examination of the abdomen may be needed. This test uses the echoes from high-frequency sound waves projected into the abdomen to obtain a video image of the pyloric muscle, stomach, and surrounding organs.

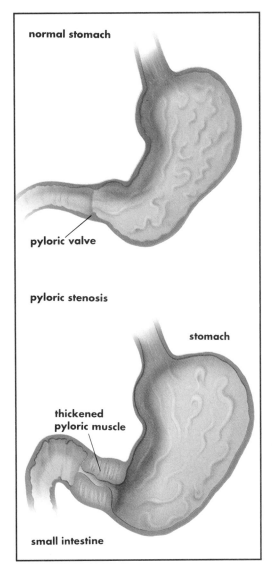

In pyloric stenosis, the pyloric muscle becomes very thick, blocking the passage between the stomach and small intestine.

What treatments are available?

The standard treatment is surgery to widen the thick muscle obstructing the stomach outlet. If the baby is not dehydrated, the operation may be done as soon as the condition is diagnosed. Many infants, however, need extra water and minerals delivered through an intravenous line for a few days before they can undergo surgery.

The operation is done under general anesthesia (so that the baby feels nothing) and lasts less than an hour. The surgeon reaches the stomach outlet through a cut in the upper right side of the baby's abdomen. The obstruc-

tion is removed by making a lengthwise cut through the tough and overgrown muscle fibers blocking the stomach outlet.

Reye's Syndrome

Reye's syndrome is a rare but serious condition affecting the brain and internal organs, especially the liver. First described 30 years ago, the syndrome became a topic of widespread concern in the United States in the mid-1970s, when an apparent increase in the number of cases took place. In the late 1970s, researchers discovered an association between aspirin use and Reye's syndrome. As a result of this finding, pediatricians now recommend acetaminophen for fever instead of aspirin. Since this change in practice, there has been a steady fall in the number of cases of Reye's syndrome. Its peak year (1979–1980), there were 555 cases. By 1989, there were 91 percent fewer cases among children under age five and 75 percent fewer among children over five.

How does Reye's syndrome develop?

The syndrome typically follows a viral illness such as influenza, chicken pox, or even a cold. In most cases, the child has taken aspirin to relieve the symptoms.

Symptoms of Reye's syndrome begin to develop three to five days after the child has recovered from the original illness. The first manifestations are irritability and lethargy, soon accompanied by severe vomiting. In many children, the syndrome does not progress beyond this stage. In others, however, confusion, seizures, and coma develop rapidly, sometimes in the course of a single day.

The symptoms are a result of swelling in the brain and damage to cells in many organs, including the liver (which loses normal tissue and becomes fatty) and the kidneys.

What causes Reye's syndrome?

The exact cause remains a mystery. Viral infections—not just flu and chicken pox, but also measles, mumps, and herpes—clearly play a role, but the virus is not the sole cause. Many experts believe that certain toxins (including aspirin) somehow interact with the vi-

---

PREVENTING REYE'S SYNDROME

- Do not use aspirin for chicken pox or any flulike illnesses.
- Aspirin should be reserved for special indications. Acetaminophen and ibuprofen are preferred medications for fever.

---

rus or by-products of the viral infection to trigger the syndrome.

When should I suspect that my child has Reye's syndrome?

Reye's syndrome is fortunately rare, so there really isn't much reason to suspect it every time your child vomits or acts cranky. On the other hand, you should never dismiss vomiting that doesn't let up for several hours. If vomiting develops soon after your child has gotten over chicken pox or the flu, the index of suspicion should be even higher. Severe vomiting in a child who has recently had a virus infection and taken aspirin is also cause for concern.

Is medical attention necessary?

Prompt medical attention and hospitalization are essential. The faster a child receives medical care, the greater the chance for complete recovery.

What treatments are available?

In mild cases, the only management necessary may be intravenous administration of fluids and glucose (a form of sugar) to replace what is lost through vomiting. In more severe cases, medication must be administered to reduce brain swelling. Doctors and nurses also need to monitor the child's breathing, intracranial pressure (pressure in the skull), and heart, liver, and kidney function to make sure the disease is not progressing. A spinal tap may be performed to rule out infections of the central nervous system (meningitis and encephalitis), which may cause symptoms similar to those of Reye's syndrome.

Rh Disease (Hemolytic Disease of the Newborn)

When foreign cells enter the body, an immune response is triggered, and the body produces antibodies targeted specifically against proteins on the foreign cells. Such a response can occur during pregnancy if a baby's fetal red blood cells carry a protein called Rh factor but the mother's cells do not. The result can be widespread destruction of the baby's red blood cells, a condition known as Rh disease or hemolytic disease of the newborn. Fortunately, steps can be taken to prevent this complication. Treatment is also available for the 5,000 cases that still occur in the United States each year.

How does Rh disease develop?

The presence or absence of Rh factor is designated by the + or − after your blood type. People who have A+, B+, AB+, or O+ blood have the Rh factor; those who have A−, B−, AB−, or O− blood do not.

Rh disease occurs when a mother, father, and child have incompatible Rh blood types—specifically, when the father and child have Rh+ blood (meaning they have the Rh protein) and the mother has Rh− blood (meaning she does not have the protein). When Rh+ fetal blood cells leak into an Rh− mother's bloodstream, the mother's immune system begins to manufacture antibodies that will recognize and destroy Rh+ cells.

Because it takes time to mount an antibody defense, the first Rh incompatible child is unaffected. If the fetus in a subsequent pregnancy is also Rh+, however, the mother's immune system will recognize the fetal blood as foreign and launch an antibody attack against it, causing Rh disease in the baby.

Newborns with Rh disease become severely jaundiced because of the buildup of bilirubin (the breakdown product of dead red blood cells). They also have swelling of the liver and spleen as a result of stepped-up production of new red blood cells. If the fetus or newborn does not receive a transfusion of Rh− blood, the heart and blood vessels collapse and generalized swelling sets in. Rh disease that progresses this far is called *hydrops fetalis*.

When should I suspect the possibility of Rh incompatibility?

Couples should make a point of knowing each other's blood types. If the woman is Rh− and

In the rare cases in which severe Rh disease does develop, the baby is given an immediate exchange transfusion of Rh− blood. This procedure removes accumulated bilirubin and provides the baby with red cells that will not be destroyed by the mother's antibody.

Your family is at risk of a child having Rh disease if:

- The father is Rh+.
- The mother is Rh−.
- The fetus is Rh+.
- The mother has previously been exposed to Rh+ blood and has not received RhoGam. Such exposure can occur from a prior pregnancy, a blood transfusion with Rh+ blood, a miscarriage, amniocentesis, or an ectopic pregnancy.

Rheumatic Fever

In children over the age of five, a bout of strep (streptococcus) throat may, in rare cases, lead to rheumatic fever. This illness results from the immune system's attempt to rid the body of harmful substances (toxins) produced by the strep bacterium. In the process, however, the antibodies also attack normal tissues in the joints, heart, skin, or nervous system.

Antibiotic treatment of strep infections in the United States and Europe has led to a steady decline in rheumatic fever in recent decades. Although it is rare, rheumatic fever still appears sporadically. Since the disease can damage the heart, every effort should be made to prevent it.

the man, Rh+, they should tell the obstetrician and pediatrician early in the pregnancy.

What treatments are available?

Obstetricians routinely determine blood type in pregnant women. If there is a possibility of Rh incompatibility with the baby, the woman is given an injection of a preparation called RhoGam during pregnancy and immediately after birth. RhoGam suppresses the antibody response in subsequent pregnancies.

Severe Rh incompatibility disease is now rare for several reasons, foremost of which is the availability of good prenatal and obstetrical care. In addition, only 15 percent of the population is Rh−, so the chances of Rh incompatibility are actually fairly low. Also, fetal blood enters the maternal bloodstream in only about 50 percent of pregnancies, so even if the fetus and mother are incompatible, an antibody reaction may not occur. Further, only

When should I suspect that my child has rheumatic fever?

Muscle or joint aches, as well as joint swelling and tenderness, are usually the first signs, developing three to eight weeks after a strep infection. This pain usually affects the hips, knees, shoulders, elbows, and wrists, and migrates from one area to another. Permanent joint damage does not occur. Occasionally, heart abnormalities develop without joint pain. In other cases, stomach pain, nosebleed, or weight loss are the initial signs.

What happens during rheumatic fever?

The bacterium responsible for strep throat—group A beta-hemolytic *Streptococcus*—produces a number of substances that can damage normal body tissues. This organism also contains a substance that resembles proteins found in the heart. As a result, antibodies produced to fend off strep also can target and injure the heart. A similar sort of immune-system cross reaction is probably also to blame for the other manifestations of rheumatic fever.

The syndrome can affect the central nervous system. Within two to six months after the initial strep throat, muscle weakness and poor coordination may develop, causing poor grasp, sloppy handwriting, and jerky movements. Odd facial expressions and rapid mood swings may also occur. This neurologic disorder is termed *Sydenham's chorea* or *St. Vitus dance*. Although distressing, this phase of the illness is almost always short lived, resolving without long-term consquences.

Rheumatic fever also may cause a rash composed of small red lesions with clear centers and wavy, well-defined borders. These lesions appear first on the trunk, followed by the arms and legs. Over bony regions such as the feet, hands, elbows, shoulder blades and spine, the skin may be marked by small, hard swellings (nodules) measuring about one-quarter or one-half inch wide.

How is the heart affected?

In some but not all cases of acute rheumatic fever, the heart valves may be inflamed and deformed. The mitral valve between the left collecting chamber (left atrium) and pumping chamber (left ventricle) is most commonly affected. The aortic valve may also be involved. Rarely the muscle (myocardium) of the heart and outside covering of the heart (pericardium) are also inflamed. In the most severe cases, heart failure may occur. It is important to know that the greatest incidence of severe heart disease occurs in children who have multiple attacks of rheumatic fever over months or years. That is why prevention of future repeated attacks by antibiotic prophylaxis is so vital (see treatment on page 217).

Is medical attention necessary?

Yes, absolutely. Even though rheumatic fever tends to run its course within two or three months after the initial strep infection, residual heart disease may remain. It may, in addition, evolve into permanent rheumatic heart disease. These difficulties are preventable if antibiotic therapy for strep infection is instituted promptly.

How can the pediatrician tell that my child has rheumatic fever?

The pediatrician looks for evidence of a recent strep infection by reviewing results of recent throat cultures and ordering laboratory tests for antibodies against strep toxins. Elevations in two or more of these antibodies point strongly to rheumatic fever. The pediatrician also evaluates the number and type of rheumatic fever symptoms.

What treatments are available?

Penicillin, administered either orally or by injection is highly effective in clearing the body of strep. Children allergic to penicillin can take erythromycin.

Antibiotic therapy orally on a daily basis or by injection monthly will be maintained for many years to prevent recurrences, which are most likely in the first three years. Penicillin or erythromycin usually is continued until the age of 18, or longer if the heart valves have sustained damage. This is referred to as antibiotic prophylaxis.

Bed rest, proper nutrition, and mild pain relievers are the mainstays of treatment in the acute stage of rheumatic fever. In some cases, corticosteroids are given to combat more-severe inflammations of the joints or heart. Depending on the severity of heart disease, cardiac medicines may be prescribed.

Rickets

Rickets is a bone disorder most commonly caused by a nutritional deficiency of vitamin D or an inherited inability to utilize vitamin D, which is essential for skeletal development. It also may be caused by very rare, inherited disorders of metabolism, certain types of liver and kidney disease, and diseases that interfere with the absorption of vitamin D. Since sunlight triggers the conversion of a substance in the skin to vitamin D, lack of sun exposure also can lead to vitamin D deficiency rickets. Premature infants, babies with dark skin, and breast-fed babies whose mothers are poorly nourished or unexposed to sunlight are at particular risk.

When should I suspect that my child has rickets?

Vitamin D deficiency rickets is most common in children between four months and two years of age. If other family members are affected, the inherited forms of the disease may be diagnosed in early infancy, since doctors will be alert to the possibility that it may develop. Otherwise, inherited rickets may not become apparent until the child starts to walk.

Symptoms of rickets include restlessness, irritability, trouble sleeping, pelvic pain, muscle weakness, and slowed development, such as difficulty in learning to crawl or walk. An infant with rickets may have extremely thin skull bones that get indented with slight pressure and spring back to normal when pressure is removed. Babies over six months old with rickets may have flattened, square skulls, and their fontanels (the soft spots on the head) may remain open longer than normal.

Affected children are prone to frequent bouts of diarrhea, bone fractures, or respiratory infections. Their teeth may come in late or have faulty enamel and decay early. The most noticeable sign of rickets, however, is bone deformity, which appears when the disease is advanced. Because the bones become soft, the legs may bow or turn inward. Curvature of the spine, enlargement of the ankles, knees, or wrists, and bending of the ends of the ribs (which causes the chest to thrust out) are other possible manifestations.

PREVENTING RICKETS

Rickets is rare in the United States because it is usually very easy to prevent. Virtually all cow's milk and all standard infant formulas are manufactured with added vitamin D. Vitamin D supplements are readily available for premature infants, vegetarians, and others who may not take in enough nutrients naturally. It often is recommended that nursing mothers who are vegetarians and have dark skin take these supplements. Foods that are high in vitamin D include:

- Vitamin D-fortified milk, margarine, and breakfast cereals.
- Liver, some fish, cod liver oil, egg yolks, and butter.
- In addition, some exposure to sunlight will help the body produce vitamin D, although precautions must be taken to avoid the pitfalls of overexposure.

What causes rickets?

As noted earlier, rickets results from deficiency or improper metabolism of vitamin D. If a child's diet is low in vitamin D—as may be the case with vegetarian diets that exclude milk—he may develop rickets.

Is medical attention necessary?

Yes. The diagnosis requires a careful checkup, and treatment should be prescribed by a physician.

How can the pediatrician tell if my child has rickets?

Diagnosis of rickets usually requires X rays, even if the pediatrician can spot the characteristic bone deformities of an advanced case. Blood tests usually are required as well.

What treatments are available?

Treatment primarily consists of giving the child vitamin D supplements in therapeutic amounts.

Getting Help

CALL YOUR DOCTOR IF YOUR CHILD DEVELOPS:

- Bowing of the legs or spine or any other bone deformity.
- Flattening of the top of the head.
- Enlargement of the joints such as the ankles, knees or wrists.
- Any fracture, especially one that seems to have occurred easily.
- Noticeable delays in development combined with poor sleeping habits and general irritability.

Ringworm

Ringworm is a general term used to describe a variety of fungal infections of the skin, scalp, and nails. (The name ringworm, which dates from the 15th century, is a misnomer; no worm is involved and the rash is not always circular.)

The fungi that cause ringworm can be found almost everywhere. Children can pick them up from pets, other humans, soil, and sand. Ringworm fungi flourish in moist environments. Thus, ringworm and other fungal infections are particularly common among children involved in sports, in which they tend to perspire heavily. By the same token, fungi thrive best in hot, humid summer weather.

Once ringworm sets in, it nourishes itself by absorbing the dead, protein-rich material called *keratin* that comprises the outer layer of skin. Although it is not dangerous, ringworm can make a child very uncomfortable by causing itchiness and sometimes painful fissures in the skin. Ringworm of the scalp is also often quite unsightly since it causes the loss of hair in patches.

What causes ringworm?

The infectious organisms that cause ringworm funguses are known as dermatophytes. The types that most commonly affect children are:

- *Tinea corporis* (the classic ringworm of body skin). This infection is marked by circular, scaly lesions with clear skin in the center. The lesions are most common on the arms or the trunk of the body, and they grow as the fungus depletes the nutrient supply on the skin surface within the circle. Tinea corporis occurs most frequently in young boys.
- *Tinea capitis* (scalp ringworm). This highly contagious infection spreads rapidly among school children, causing hair loss and scaling on the scalp. It is most common in young boys and rare after puberty.
- *Tinea unguim* (ringworm of the nails). This infection attacks toe nails and (less frequently) fingernails, causing unsightly nail

thickening, discoloration, and crumbling.

- *Tinea pedis* (athlete's foot) appears either as dry scaly patches or as wet, blistery lesions between the toes and on the sole of the foot. It is uncommon in young children.
- *Tinea cruris* (jock itch) affects the groin area with lesions of the scrotum and the upper, inner thighs. It is most common among pubescent males and adult men.

When should I suspect ringworm?

Ringworm does not always cause itching. Instead, look for a circular rash, hair loss, or scaly patches on the skin or scalp.

Is medical attention necessary?

Yes. You should consult your pediatrician when any new rash appears.

If the rash is a recurrence of an earlier fungal infection, treat it as initially instructed by the physician. If it does not respond to treatment in a week, contact the pediatrician and discontinue use of the topical agent.

How can the pediatrician recognize ringworm?

The doctor usually can diagnose ringworm by simple observation because of the characteristic appearance of the lesions. If there is any doubt, microscopic examination of scales or hairs may reveal the presence of the fungi or a culture can be obtained in the office.

What treatments are available?

Most fungal infections are easily treated with topical antifungal agents—creams for dry eruptions and powders for wet ones. Physicians often recommend one of three successful over-the-counter drugs called tolnaftate, clo-

trimazole, and miconazole. Most of these drugs work by interfering with the structure of the fungal membranes. Improvement begins quickly, but complete cure (even of simple ringworm) may take a month of therapy. If the lesion does not improve after a week, discontinue using the product and notify the physician.

Severe fungal infections may require a prescription topical medication or oral drugs. Oral medication is always necessary for ringworm of the scalp because the fungus can penetrate the hair follicles beneath the skin. Ring-worm of the nails also requires oral medication and may take months to resolve completely.

Rocky Mountain Spotted Fever (RMSF)

Rocky Mountain spotted fever (RMSF) is an acute, infectious disease transmitted by ticks. The distinguishing feature is a characteristic rash. With early treatment, most children recover fully and develop permanent immunity. Untreated, however, the disease can be severe. Early medical intervention is thus essential.

As the name implies, the disease causes a spotted rash and was first identified in the Rocky Mountain region. Now, more than half the annual cases occur in the Southeastern United States. Children from five to nine years of age are most frequently infected. Although the infected ticks are primarily encountered in the woods, they can also be found in suburban and occasionally urban areas. In almost half of reported cases, the tick bite was unnoticed.

What causes Rocky Mountain spotted fever?

RMSF is caused by *Rickettsia rickettsii,* a microorganism carried by rodents and other small mammals inhabiting infested areas. Ticks who feed on these animals acquire the microorganism and pass it along in their saliva. A child can pick up an infected tick directly when playing in a wooded, tick-infested area or indirectly from a pet who has picked one up.

When should I suspect that my child has Rocky Mountain spotted fever?

The initial symptoms mimic those of the flu. They appear about a week after the tick bite and may include muscle aches, headache, mild fever, chills, general malaise, appetite loss (sometimes with vomiting), and sensitivity to light. One to five days later, the characteristic

---

PREVENTING ROCKY MOUNTAIN SPOTTED FEVER

The only way to prevent RMSF is to prevent tick bites. The disease is prevalent in spring, summer, and fall, when ticks are active. During these times, take the following precautions:

- Avoid areas known to have high tick populations.
- If you live in or near a tick infested area, inspect outdoor pets every few days and promptly remove any ticks they may have picked up.
- Have your child shower or bathe at night after spending time outdoors.
- After children spend time in wooded areas, check them for ticks and teach them how to check themselves.
- When outside, wear heavy socks and long pants and use an effective tick repellent, preferably one containing DEET. Use DEET sparingly on children.
- Ticks rarely transmit the infection until they have fed for hours. Therefore, checking for (and removing) ticks after every outdoor play session is among the most effective preventive measures you can take.

rash appears, usually starting as a pale pink eruption around the wrists, ankles, hands, and feet. Within 24 hours, the rash spreads toward the center of the body, covering the face, neck, arms, legs, armpits, buttocks, trunk, palms of hands, and soles of feet. Unless the disease is treated, ulcers may form on the fingertips, nose, and earlobes around the fourth day after the rash appears. The discrete spots of the rash blend together and darken to resemble widespread bruising.

Is medical attention necessary?

Yes. Untreated, the infection can lead to serious complications involving the brain, heart, kidneys, and circulatory system.

How can the pediatrician tell if my child has Rocky Mountain spotted fever?

If a child who has had a tick bite or been in a tick-infested area develops flu symptoms and a characteristic rash, the pediatrician may order blood tests to check for evidence of the infection. Because ten percent of infected children do not develop the characteristic rash and many more recall no tick bite, the exact diagnosis can be elusive.

What treatments are available?

Until the diagnosis is confirmed and the child has begun to improve with therapy, hospitalization may be required. The mainstay of treatment is antibiotic therapy, usually with chloramphenicol and/or tetracycline, which may be delivered orally or intravenously for five days or until the child shows improvement and the fever lets up. Fluids and nutrients also may be delivered intravenously.

Roseola Infantum (Exanthem Subitum)

Roseola is a contagious disease, sometimes mistaken for measles, that most commonly occurs in children under the age of two. Although it can cause a high fever, roseola is usually harmless and short-lived.

What causes roseola infantum?

It is caused by a virus of the herpes family (human herpes virus 6 or HH 6) that was isolated in 1986. It is unclear how the virus is passed from person to person. Once a child is infected with the virus, roseola usually develops within seven to 14 days. After a child has had the disease once, it is impossible to catch it again.

What happens during roseola infantum?

Roseola begins as a fever which can range from 102 degrees to 105 degrees Fahrenheit and which usually lasts three to five days. The fever suddenly passes, and then a rash appears on the upper body.

When should I suspect that my child has roseola infantum?

The key to a diagnosis of roseola is the timing of the rash, which does not develop until the

PREVENTING ROSEOLA INFANTUM

Because most infants acquire the virus without any serious complications, it is fruitless to try to devise preventive measures as it circulates so widely among susceptible children.

- To treat fever and other discomfort, give the proper dose of acetaminophen (Tylenol, Datril, Panadol, Tempra, and others) according to the child's height and weight.
- Dress the child in lightweight, cool, comfortable clothing, especially when fever is present.
- If fever reaches more than 104 degrees, give the child a cool-water sponge bath.
- Whenever a child's fever rises quickly, there is a possibility that convulsions may occur. Be sure you know how to deal with them. (See "Convulsions and Seizures," in Volume I.)
- Encourage the child to take in more fluids. It is normal for the appetite to decrease.

Getting Help

CALL YOUR PEDIATRICIAN IF YOUR CHILD:

- ☐ Has a high fever that lasts more than three to four days.
- ☐ Has a convulsion.
- ☐ Develops symptoms besides fever, listlessness, and rash.

worst symptoms of illness—fever, loss of appetite, irritability, sleepiness, and swollen or droopy eyelids—have passed. The rash, which is spotty, pink, and slightly raised, begins on the trunk and eventually spreads to the upper arms and neck. It is brief in duration, sometimes lasting just a few hours, but nearly always disappears in one day.

Is medical attention necessary?

A physician can give advice on how to control the fever, usually with acetaminophen, but the disease must take its course. If the child develops additional symptoms or becomes more ill, a physician may order blood tests to rule out other conditions that cause fever in babies and toddlers. Roseola is one of the most common causes of a febrile seizure (a convulsion due to high fever) in the first years of life.

Rubella (German Measles, Three-Day Measles)

This viral disease is generally mild in small children. However, when it is acquired during pregnancy, rubella can be truly devastating. Rubella infection in a pregnant woman can cause a wide range of serious birth defects in up to 60 percent of infants exposed during the first month of gestation. Those defects may include heart and eye abnormalities, deafness, low birth weight, encephalitis (brain inflammation), and liver and kidney malfunction.

Fortunately, a rubella vaccine was licensed in 1969 and currently is given in conjunction with measles and mumps vaccines at age 15 months, followed in most areas by a booster at school entry. (For more information on this and other vaccines, see entry on **immunizations**). Thanks to rubella immunization, the number of cases of congenital rubella has fallen drastically in the past 20 years. Even so, small outbreaks of rubella occasionally occur, mainly among adults who neither had the disease nor received the immunization.

What causes rubella?

Rubella is caused by a virus known as *rubivirus*. It is passed from person to person when an infected individual expels fluid droplets in coughing or sneezing and a noninfected person inhales them. When a pregnant woman is infected with the virus, it passes to the fetus through the placenta. Fetal infection lasts throughout pregnancy. In fact, a baby with congenital rubella infection may still harbor the virus at the age of one year.

When should I suspect that my child has rubella?

Children's risk of catching rubella is fairly low. A child may develop the disease, however, if he is exposed to the virus before being immunized. Such exposure may occur from an infected child or adult, particularly if the family travels to an area where an outbreak is occurring.

The illness begins two to three weeks after exposure to the virus. In some cases, the rash (which consists of small, reddish bumps that start on the face and spread down to the trunk, arms, and legs) is the initial symptom, but in others, it is preceded by one to five days of mild fever, coughing, red eyes, and swollen glands. The rash itself lasts about three days, although it may disappear sooner.

Is medical attention necessary?

Yes. Any time a child develops a generalized rash, a doctor should be consulted.

How can the pediatrician tell if my child has rubella?

The main method of diagnosing rubella is by physical examination. It may be confirmed by measuring antibodies to the virus during the illness and after recovery. If the antibody levels go up dramatically between the two tests, rubella infection occurred.

What treatments are available?

Rest and acetaminophen (to reduce fever) are the only treatments needed. It is extremely important, however, for anyone with rubella infection to avoid contact with women who could be pregnant.

EXPOSURE DURING PREGNANCY

All women entering the childbearing years should be immunized against rubella. If a pregnant woman who has not been immunized is exposed to rubella, she should go to a doctor immediately to obtain an antibody test. When antibodies are present right after exposure, it means the woman is already immune to the virus and has no need to worry. If antibodies are not present, the woman should have a second test in about three weeks. Continued negative findings mean infection probably did not occur, but one further test, in three more weeks, is needed for absolute certainty. An antibody test that becomes strongly positive indicates that infection has taken place and the fetus is at high risk of having congenital rubella.

Scabies

Scabies is an intensely itchy skin condition caused by infestation with tiny, burrowing mites that lay their eggs within the outermost layer of the skin. Scabies infestations often look like brownish-gray, threadlike lines ending in black dots. These lines mark the path of the mite as it burrows under the skin. Itching usually develops a month or longer after the mite enters the skin. Small, red bumps erupt. Continued scratching can lead to a severe rash resembling eczema.

How does scabies develop?

Children can get scabies from skin-to-skin contact with someone who is already infested. Once the mite enters the skin, it deposits eggs and fecal material. As the eggs hatch and the mite population increases, itching develops gradually. This process may take four to six weeks. The picture may be complicated by a secondary infection, which occurs when bacteria enter skin broken by excessive scratching.

The symptoms of scabies infestation are often prompted by an allergic reaction, which develops when the immune system directs antibodies at the mites or their by-products. The fact that symptoms develop more quickly in second than in first infestations suggests that an allergic reaction is at work.

When should I suspect that my child has scabies?

Before age two, scabies infestation is most likely to affect the armpits, feet, and ankles. Older children more often develop lesions around the hands and wrists. Any time a child has an extremely itchy rash in these areas, sca-

bies is a possible explanation, particularly in a child who rarely develops skin irritations. If several members of a household develop similar symptoms, scabies or some similar skin infestation is a likely explanation.

Is medical attention necessary?

Yes. Scabies mimics many other skin irritations, particularly after being scratched for a few days, so the doctor should examine the rash and make a definite diagnosis. The doctor also will recognize the signs of a secondary bacterial infection, a common complication of scabies.

How can the pediatrician tell if my child has scabies?

Scabies is diagnosed by microscopic examination of cells from a suspicious-looking lesion. If a scabies infestation is present, mites, eggs, or feces will be visible.

What treatments are available?

Several creams and lotions are available to eliminate scabies mites. These preparations are typically applied to the entire skin surface

---

PREVENTING SCABIES

- Avoid close physical contact with anyone known to have scabies.
- Discourage children from sharing towels and clothing.
- Consider treatment for the whole household if one member has scabies.
- Use hot water to wash all clothes, towels, and bedding used by a child or adult with scabies.

---

from the neck down and left on for six to eight hours. In most cases, one treatment is sufficient to get rid of the infestation, but a second treatment is sometimes needed about two weeks after the first.

Because itching lasts for another two to three weeks after treatment, topical anti-itch medications are often prescribed as well. If there is a bacterial infection, antibiotics also are prescribed.

Scarlet Fever

This illness, characterized by high fever and a bright, red rash covering the entire body, occurs in conjunction some cases of streptococcal respiratory infection, or strep throat. In general, the widespread use of antibiotics to treat strep throat has made scarlet fever less common than it was in the past, but occasional outbreaks still occur.

Like strep throat, scarlet fever is most common among children over the age of three. It generally spreads in school and household settings.

What causes scarlet fever?

Scarlet fever is caused by a toxin that certain strains of streptococcal bacteria release when they infect the upper respiratory tract. It passes from person to person the same way strep throat does—through close contact between an infected and a noninfected person. When a child with the infection coughs or sneezes, bacteria-laden droplets are expelled. Children playing face to face, eating together, and sharing toys and eating utensils can easily pass strep infections back and forth.

When should I suspect that my child has scarlet fever?

The first symptoms, which may develop suddenly, include a high fever, headache, abdominal pain, nausea, and vomiting. Occasionally, abdominal pain and vomiting develop one or two days before the rash appears.

The rash, which consists of tiny, red bumps, begins on the trunk and spreads outward, covering the body in a matter of hours or days, giving the skin a rough sandpaper-like texture. Application of pressure makes the bumps disappear momentarily.

The rash generally spares the area around the mouth, although the lips (as well as the palms and soles) frequently turn bright red. The tongue, too, undergoes characteristic changes, turning white (with small flecks of red) early in the course of the illness, then becoming swollen and red (strawberry tongue). In addition, deep, red streaks may appear in creases formed by joints—in the armpits and elbow crooks, as well as in the groin and behind the knees. Evidence of strep throat (sore, swollen tonsils covered by whitish-yellow material) is usually part of the picture.

After three or four days, the rash fades and the skin begins to peel, particularly on the palms and soles. This peeling can last one to three weeks.

Is medical attention necessary?

Yes. It is important to get an accurate diagnosis of strep infections and scarlet fever, since many other conditions can cause similar symptoms. If a strep infection is present, antibiotic therapy is necessary to prevent complications such as rheumatic fever.

How can the pediatrician tell if my child has scarlet fever?

The pediatrician may suspect a strep infection if other cases of strep throat or scarlet fever recently have occurred in the community. To be sure of the diagnosis, she will take a throat culture. In this test, a cotton swab is rubbed against the back of the child's throat to remove secretions, which are then placed on growth medium and, after 24 hours, examined under a microscope for the presence of strep bacteria.

What treatments are available?

Penicillin is the drug of choice for children with scarlet fever. Once the bacteria are wiped out, the toxin that causes scarlet fever will be eliminated as well. Children who are allergic to penicillin may be given erythromycin instead. Treatment is continued for 10 to 14 days even if the symptoms disappear earlier.

Getting Help

CALL YOUR DOCTOR IF YOUR CHILD:

- Suddenly develops nausea, vomiting, and a red rash on the trunk.
- Complains of a sore throat after exposure to strep in school or day care.

School Avoidance

Almost every child experiences some fear and anxiety when starting day care, preschool or kindergarten. But for a small percentage of children, fear of attending school can become exaggerated and actually translated into physical illness. Some children develop stomachaches or headaches because they are so frightened of going to school. In the worst cases they actually refuse to go to school, causing a major struggle at home.

When should I suspect that my child has school avoidance?

Children rarely complain directly about fearing school. Instead, they develop various, nonspecific symptoms that keep them out of the classroom, such as abdominal pain, malaise, headaches, vomiting, and muscle aches.

One clue that such complaints are related to school avoidance is that the symptoms rarely occur during summer vacations or on weekends or holidays. The symptoms may become more obvious on Sunday nights or on school mornings, and be gone by the afternoon. Unlike a chronic class-cutter who prefers other activities to school, a child with school avoidance often wants to go to school but simply cannot face it. Another difference is that children who play hooky rarely stay home, while children with school avoidance do.

School avoidance occurs most frequently at three stages of life: at the start of school life, between the ages of 5 and 7; at the beginning of junior high, at age 11 or 12; and at around 14 years of age, when high school starts.

What causes school avoidance?

There are probably several causes; most likely, a unique combination of factors brings the problem on in each child. For some children, school avoidance is a form of exaggerated separation anxiety in which the child worries that some harm will befall the parent during the school day. In these cases, the parent may consciously or unconsciously encourage the child to stay home because of the parent's need for the child's continued attachment.

Some children may not like being compared in their abilities to other children. Attending school with peers may be challenging and threatening because they have not established a firm sense of self-worth and self-confidence. Still others may actually have reason to be afraid; they may be victimized by bullies or afforded no privacy in the bathroom or locker room.

Finally, an identifiable, traumatic event outside school precipitates a child's school avoidance in some cases. Potential triggers include the birth of a sibling or the absence of a parent or other significant family member.

What should I do if my child shows signs of school avoidance?

First, have the child checked by his pediatrician to make sure there is no underlying physical illness. Try to observe any pattern in the child's symptoms to help the doctor reach a diagnosis.

If the pediatrician finds no physical cause for your child's complaints and the evaluation suggests the presence of school avoidance, you may be referred to a mental-health professional such as a child psychiatrist or psychiatric social worker.

Is medical attention necessary?

Yes. School avoidance is unlikely to go away by itself unless there is a precipitating event at home or at school that somehow gets resolved. Fortunately, however, a brief, focused course

---

COPING WITH SCHOOL AVOIDANCE

Any parent who has dealt with the problem of school avoidance knows how painful it is to force a crying child onto a school bus or into a classroom. However, the number one concern should be to return the child to school as quickly as possible. Parents can help by:

- Making school attendance a nonnegotiable item. Staying home from school should not be an attractive option.
- Enlisting the help of school authorities in gradually returning the child to school.
- Examining their own needs in relation to the child, and seeking help if personal problems are identified.

---

of treatment usually gets the problem under control, particularly if the child is in the early elementary grades.

What is the treatment for school avoidance?

The exact form of treatment depends on the underlying problem. It is usually helpful if the whole family participates in the treatment plan. This may mean that the parents (and possibly the siblings) will receive counseling along with the child.

The approaches that have proved helpful in treating other kinds of phobias also have been successful for school avoidance. One of these, called *gradual desensitization,* involves slowly reintroducing the child to the school environment, starting with a few hours in a relatively nonthreatening part of the school (such as the nurse's or counselor's office) and gradually adding more time and moving closer to the classroom. Eventually, the child is eased back into the daily routine.

Scoliosis

Scoliosis is an abnormal curvature of the spine that causes pain and distorts the shape of the body. In a few rare cases, the constriction caused by the condition can impair the function of the lungs and heart.

Scoliosis usually becomes apparent during adolescence, but it sometimes develops earlier. Although the condition may correct itself as a child matures, careful monitoring and, in many cases, treatment, are necessary to avoid severe malformation. If detected early, scoliosis can be corrected without surgery in as much as 90 percent of cases.

What causes scoliosis?

Most cases of scoliosis are *idiopathic,* meaning the cause is unknown. Scoliosis is sometimes associated with disorders affecting the nerves and muscles, such as muscular dystrophy.

When should I suspect that my child has scoliosis?

The first indication may be difficulty getting clothes to fit properly. Hemlines don't seem to hang evenly, or one arm looks longer than the other. Most of the time, however, the condition is uncovered in a simple screening examination performed at school or in the pediatrician's office.

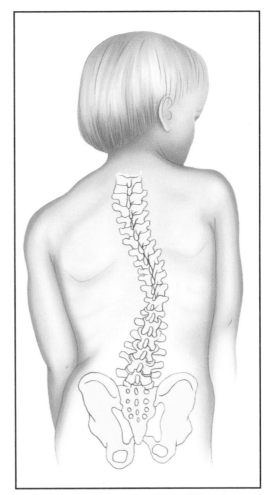

Scoliosis is an abnormal curving of the spine.

Is medical attention necessary?

Yes. Even though immediate treatment may not be necessary, it is a good idea for the child to undergo a thorough evaluation and periodic monitoring in case the condition worsens.

How can the pediatrician tell if my child has scoliosis?

The doctor examines the back while the child is standing and leaning over. If the ribs form a bump or the hips or shoulders appear uneven, the child probably has some degree of scoliosis. Further evaluation, usually by an orthopedic surgeon using X rays, is usually necessary to determine the extent and cause of the condition.

What treatments are available?

There are four main treatment options for scoliosis: Observation (for mild cases), electronic stimulation (in mild to moderate cases), bracing (in moderate to severe cases), and surgery (in severe cases).

The lightweight braces used to treat scoliosis do not hamper movement—in fact, children who wear them are encouraged to exercise. Braces can be worn for up to 24 hours a day, but some physicians prescribe part-time bracing for milder cases. On average, braces are needed for about three years, or until growth slows.

In electronic stimulation, electrical impulses are transmitted to the spinal muscles during sleep, causing contractions that pull the spine back in line.

Surgery is needed in only about one out of 100 cases, usually to correct curves of 40 degrees or more. The operation generally consists of implanting metal rods to fuse the spinal column.

If scoliosis develops between birth and age three, treatment is usually unnecessary. The type of scoliosis that develops between age three and adolescence is generally more severe; in these cases, braces are usually needed.

Getting Help

CALL YOUR DOCTOR IF:
- Your child frequently sits or stands in a way that seems to favor one side of the body.
- You notice any unevenness in the level of your child's shoulder blades or hipbones.

PREVENTING SCOLIOSIS

Even children who exercise regularly and maintain excellent posture can still develop scoliosis. Therefore, the best way to prevent damage from the condition is to detect and treat it early. Scoliosis usually can be detected in the course of a regular pediatric checkup or an in-school screening exam. Since scoliosis runs in families, parents with a family history of the condition should make a special effort to have their children checked.

Shingles

Shingles (herpes zoster) is a viral disease that develops when the chickenpox virus, which becomes dormant in certain nerves after causing acute illness, is somehow reactivated. The distinguishing feature of shingles is a painful rash that develops along the pathway of a nerve in which the virus has lain dormant.

Among people who have had chickenpox, only a small proportion ever develop shingles. The disease is relatively uncommon before age ten, but its incidence increases steadily with each decade of life. Fewer than one percent of people who develop shingles will have a relapse.

Several factors, including stress, injury, and weakening of the immune system, increase children's susceptibility to shingles.

Normally, shingles runs its course within a few weeks and causes no serious long-term complications. The symptoms are most severe in a child whose immune system is compromised.

When should I suspect that my child has shingles?

Shingles is very uncommon in healthy children; rashes are much more likely to be due to allergic reactions or skin irritation than to reactivation of the chickenpox virus at this age. However, you should suspect shingles if the rash was preceded by a flulike illness and pain along the nerve pathway. Look also for the distinguishing features of a shingles outbreak—namely, painful, blisterlike lesions appearing in a clear-cut line, on only one side of the body.

What happens during a shingles outbreak?

Flulike symptoms and pain often precede the outbreak by several days. The rash begins as red spots which quickly turn into blisters. Five to ten days later, the blisters fill with pus, dry up, and scab over. Fever, pain, and tenderness usually continue through this progression. Without treatment, new crops of blisters will appear for up to a week and the rash will persist for three to five weeks. The pain may last for months.

Is medical attention necessary?

Yes. Medication (see this page) can be given to reduce the severity of a shingles episode. A doctor also should perform a thorough workup to see if some underlying condition has made the child susceptible to shingles.

How can the pediatrician tell if my child has shingles?

Because the shingles rash has unique characteristics, the doctor will be able to identify it by sight.

What treatments are available?

Although there is no cure, the antiviral drug acyclovir by mouth or injection can shorten the outbreak and lessen its severity. Acetaminophen in appropriate doses for the child's age and weight may help reduce pain. Local applications of wet compresses or calamine lotion also can be helpful.

PREVENTING SHINGLES

Since a varicella vaccine has been developed and approved, its use in immunization schedules will reduce the incidence not only of chicken pox, but shingles as well.

Shyness

As many as 90 percent of adults admit to feeling inhibited in certain social situations. Nevertheless, parents find it painful to watch when shyness deprives their child of the pleasure of meeting new people and experiencing new situations and activities. Most toddlers and preschoolers will go through periods of shyness at one stage or another and eventually outgrow their shyness.

How can I tell whether my child is shy?

While there is no scientific definition of shyness in children, shy children react in the following characteristic ways when exposed to strangers and novel situations:

- They cling to their mother or another familiar person.
- Their speech and play are extremely restrained.
- They are frightened of new, noisy toys.
- They avoid dangerous activities.
- They are completely unaggressive.
- They avoid unfamiliar children.
- They may be unusually obedient to their parents.

What causes shyness?

No single cause of shyness has been identified. Some intriguing patterns, however, have emerged from long-range studies of how children's reactions to strangers and novel situations change over several years.

For example, beginning at a very early age, individual babies tend to respond characteristically to strange situations with either fearfulness or boldness. An estimated 20 percent of infants are born with what researchers call a *temperamental bias* toward shyness and timidity; their nervous systems seem to be more easily aroused than those of more uninhibited children. As further evidence of this nervous system excitability, many (but not all) children with shy temperaments were markedly irritable and had particularly erratic sleep patterns as infants.

Why do some children outgrow shyness while others remain shy? No one really knows.

No specific parenting style has been linked to shyness in children, but evidence suggests that certain environmental stress factors play a role. These can include prolonged hospitalization or chronic discord within the family (between siblings, between the parents, or between parent and child). Researchers suggest that if such chronic stressors are absent, a child with a temperamental bias toward shyness will probably become more outgoing as the years pass.

Is medical attention necessary?

Although shyness is a perfectly normal style of behavior that causes few serious problems for most children, it can, in some cases, indicate the need for help from a mental-health professional such as a child psychologist or psychiatrist. Consult with the pediatrician if your child's shyness severely limits participation in the usual activities of other children the same age. Also, a few sessions of counseling may be helpful if you have trouble dealing with your child's shyness.

What treatments are available?

Most of the time, no treatment is needed other than sensitivity and reassurance on the part of the parents. Some children develop transient shyness or social withdrawal in response to a stressful situation at home (such as the illness of a parent); in these cases, the child's shyness usually disappears within six months to a year after the problem has been resolved.

Some children become socially withdrawn because they have not learned the social skills necessary to make friends or interact with other children. Many will learn these skills when placed in less stressful situations, such as playing with a younger child or in a small group, where they feel safe enough to take on a more active social role.

Sibling Rivalry

Sibling rivalry is natural and, at least to some extent, inevitable in most families. In many ways, the lessons children learn from clashing with their siblings prepare them to be both cooperative and assertive outside the home. Sibling rivalry can become a problem, however, if parents expect their children to get along at all times or place undue blame for conflict on one child over the others.

What causes sibling rivalry?

Three basic drives—for attention, power, and possessions—promote sibling rivalry. Such rivalry may be particularly marked in children who are less than three years apart in age. Children spaced this closely are likely to compete aggressively for their parents' attention from the earliest days of the younger child's life. Upon the arrival of a new baby, first-born children may be particularly vulnerable to feelings of displacement and continue to act out the resulting anger for years to come.

Every group has its pecking order. Thus, it is natural for children to compete for dominance. Older children are bigger, of course, but younger siblings find their own ways to compete, perhaps by being smarter, more athletic, or more musical. Whatever a family's unique constellation, siblings almost always compare themselves and are quick to detect any discrepancies, real or imagined, in the treatment parents accord them. They also tend to belittle each other and tattle on each other for minor and major infractions of rules. Fights over possessions and territory are also quite common.

PREVENTING OR REDUCING SIBLING RIVALRY

- Involve your older children in the care of an infant, always under close supervision. You may, for instance, let a toddler take used diapers to a waste pail while praising her for being big and no longer needing diapers.
- Praise your older children often when visitors come to fuss over the baby. You might give a preschooler an inexpensive present whenever the baby receives one.
- Make the child feel important by asking her opinions about the new baby, such as, "What do you think we can do to stop her from crying?"
- Spend special time with the older child. Children are less likely to compete for their parents' attention if they feel individually loved and appreciated. If possible, try to spend some time every day alone with each child, doing something that child considers fun.
- Never appear to be amused or flattered by your children's competition for your attention.
- Make an effort not to show favoritism.
- Don't compare children. Although it's tempting to point out when one child is behaving well and the other isn't, the practice can damage the child's self-esteem. A child who is made to feel inferior will tend to get discouraged rather than try harder. In addition, comparisons promote rivalry and resentment.
- If the children fight, do not take sides. If you think punishment is called for, dole it out equally. Calling a time-out is a good way of putting an end to fighting. Place children in separate rooms or tell them to sit on separate chairs for several minutes to cool down.
- Praise siblings when they are playing cooperatively together.
- Reward sharing behavior. Praise the child if she shares a toy. If the child is unwilling to share, you may have to separate the children or remove the toy.
- Encourage individual interests.
- Don't use an older sibling as a baby-sitter for the younger one.
- Let each child develop her special talents.
- Ignore tattling. You might simply say, "If you can't get along, play separately for awhile."

Even with the best of planning, it is impossible to know in advance how your child will react to the birth of a brother or sister. A healthy adjustment is more likely, however, if you prepare the older child for the change. To this end, you should:

- Make the child feel included in the preparations for the new baby. Let her help set up the nursery, shop for baby items, and listen to the baby's heartbeat.
- Do not make promises that cannot be kept; for example, don't say that the child will soon have a new playmate.
- Move a toddler to a new bed or room in advance, so the change (if such a change is planned) is not associated with the new baby.
- Give the child the opportunity to get used to the caretaker who will look after her while the mother is away at the hospital.

Getting Help

CALL YOUR DOCTOR IF:

- You are unable to reduce sibling rivalry on your own using the methods above.
- Aggression between children becomes severe enough to cause injury.

On some level not far below the surface, most fights among siblings are really about competition for parental love and approval. Although sibling rivalry can never be eliminated, there are ways to encourage healthy and harmonious relationships among siblings and maintain a peaceful family atmosphere.

Sinusitis

Sinusitis is a bacterial infection of the bony cavities (sinuses) behind and around the nose, cheekbones, and brow. These cavities, which are lined with mucous membrane, serve to filter, warm, and moisturize inhaled air.

How does sinusitis develop?

The sinuses drain into the nasal passages through tiny ducts that easily can become blocked when the lining of the nose is inflamed in the course of a cold or similar illness. This blockage traps bacteria in the sinuses, leading to infection. Because upper respiratory illnesses occur so frequently among children, sinusitis is extremely common. According to one recent estimate, five to ten percent of all colds and viral sore throats are complicated by sinusitis. Contributing factors include malfunction of the tiny, hairlike projections (*cilia*) that propel secretions out of the sinuses, and abnormally thick sinus secretions. Sinusitis is common among children with cystic fibrosis, cleft palate, dental infections, or nasal polyps.

What causes sinusitis?

The most common cause is *Streptococcus pneumoniae,* the same bacteria responsible for the largest percentage of middle ear infections.

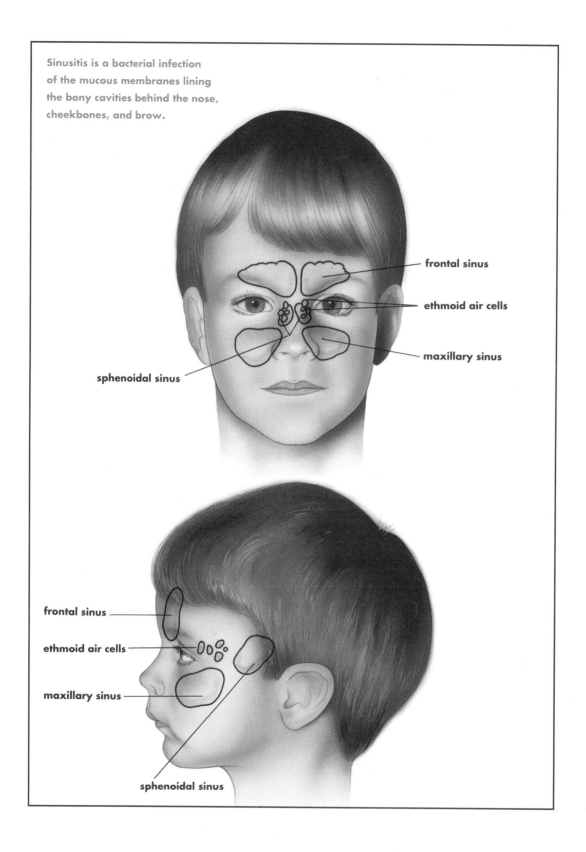

Sinusitis is a bacterial infection of the mucous membranes lining the bony cavities behind the nose, cheekbones, and brow.

frontal sinus

ethmoid air cells

maxillary sinus

sphenoidal sinus

frontal sinus

ethmoid air cells

maxillary sinus

sphenoidal sinus

Other bacteria (*Hemophilus influenzae* as well as group A *Streptococci* or *Staphylococci*) are also possible causes.

When should I suspect that my child has sinusitis?

Watch out for a severe cold or flu that fails to run its course within about ten days. Other common symptoms are a persistent daytime cough that worsens at night or on lying down. The nose may be stuffy or runny, occasionally producing pus, and the child may have foul-smelling breath. Fever may occur, although in many cases it is mild, and the child may complain of a headache. Occasionally, a child with sinusitis develops a high fever after a week or more of cold symptoms.

Is medical attention necessary?

Yes. Sinusitis is not only uncomfortable, but potentially dangerous, since it can lead to abscesses or bone infections.

How can the pediatrician tell if my child has sinusitis?

A lingering cold that doesn't seem to get better, along with other symptoms suggesting sinusitis, may prompt the pediatrician to make the diagnosis without further testing. To be absolutely sure, the pediatrician may take X rays of the child's face and skull.

What treatments are available?

Antibiotics (usually amoxicillin) are the mainstays of treatment. The doctor also may prescribe decongestant medication and recommend increased fluid intake to promote sinus drainage and relief of symptoms. If there is no response to a course of antibiotics and fe-

---

CARING FOR A CHILD WITH SINUSITIS

- Encourage rest and give plenty of fluids.
- Follow the doctor's instructions for taking antibiotics. Try not to miss any scheduled doses, and continue to give the medicine until the prescribed date (often for two or more weeks), no matter how well the child seems before that time.
- Apply hot packs to the head and face to relieve discomfort.

---

ver, facial pain, and headache persist, the sinuses may have to be drained by insertion of a needle through the nasal passages. (Most small children need a general anesthetic or a sedative for this procedure.) Material drained from the sinus then is cultured in the laboratory so that the causative organism can be identified.

Chronic, recurrent sinusitis may require surgery to enlarge the openings between the sinuses and the nose. This surgery is currently being performed with an endoscope (a tube-shaped instrument that combines microscopic viewing and surgical devices), so it is relatively minor and may not require a hospital stay.

Getting Help

CALL YOUR DOCTOR IF YOUR CHILD:

- Develops a high fever late in the course of a cold.
- Has cold symptoms that last longer than ten days without any sign of improvement.

Sleepwalking

About 15 percent of children between ages five and 12 experience one or more episodes of sleepwalking. This sleep disorder is a disruption of the normal sleep cycle, which consists of periods of deep, quiet sleep alternating with periods of more active sleep during which dreams occur. Sleepwalking episodes take place during the first sleep-stage transition of the night, which usually occurs between 90 minutes and two hours after sleep begins. Children generally wake partially and roll over, mumble, or smack their lips during this transition.

What happens during sleepwalking?

A sleepwalking episode typically begins when a sleeping child suddenly sits upright in bed, stands, and begins to walk aimlessly around the bedroom or house. A sleepwalking child's eyes are open but glassy and unfocused, and his movements are entirely without purpose. (Thus, a child who gets himself a snack in the middle of the night is definitely not sleepwalking.) After five to 30 minutes of wandering, the child generally returns to bed. He has no memory of the incident the next morning.

What causes sleepwalking?

A tendency to sleepwalk seems to run in some families, and boys, for unknown reasons, are more likely to walk in their sleep than girls. Many sleep experts believe sleepwalking and sleeptalking are related to **night terrors** (see entry) and bedwetting since they all occur during the same sleep transition.

Contrary to popular belief, dreams *do not* trigger sleepwalking episodes. During the dream stage of sleep, the muscles are almost completely paralyzed.

Is medical attention necessary?

Not usually. Only if sleepwalking occurs several times a week or the child becomes quite agitated during sleepwalking episodes. Such agitation may indicate a psychological problem rather than true sleepwalking.

What treatments are available?

Most children need no treatment. Episodes of sleepwalking usually become less frequent as children get older. Occasionally, a child who sleepwalks may benefit from a mild tranquilizer. This treatment is reserved for only the most disruptive cases, however.

COPING WITH SLEEPWALKING

- The only danger of sleepwalking is that the child will fall or bang into something and get hurt. If your child walks in his sleep, arrange the environment in a way that minimizes that risk. Pick up stray books and toys before going to bed. If necessary, place gates at the top and bottom of stairs and use chain locks on outside doors.

- Try to make sure the child gets plenty of sleep and is not overtired at bedtime. Excessive fatigue may contribute to sleepwalking.

- If you must wake a sleepwalking child, expect him to be disoriented. The best method is to repeat the child's name softly several times and, when he is conscious, explain what has happened. The child should go back to bed as soon as possible.

Soiling

For parent and child alike, few problems cause as much shame and frustration as a child's repeated loss of bowel control, known medically as *encopresis*. Although many people (including a few child-care experts) contend that soiling is a result of an emotional disorder, the vast majority of cases are purely physical. Any emotional problems the children have are usually the result, rather than the cause, of the soiling.

By conservative estimates, encopresis (which is generally not seen as a problem until age four) affects about 1.5 percent of children in the early elementary grades. Five times as many boys as girls develop the problem.

What causes soiling?

Soiling is usually the result of chronic constipation, which can, in turn, have a wide variety of causes. In a few cases, harsh toilet-training practices make children reluctant to use the bathroom. More often, however, the problem is caused by painful defecation. Because bowel movements hurt, the child voluntarily tightens the muscles that control the anal opening, holding feces in the rectum. Over time, withholding stool makes defecation even more painful. As the rectal walls are stretched, nerve impulses from the rectum become blunted so that the child eventually feels none of the sensations that signal a need to defecate, setting the stage for soiling.

When a child withholds stool, the rectum becomes distended, forcing the anus partly open and allowing liquid or mushy feces to leak. Such accidents, which usually take place in the late afternoon or early evening, may become a daily occurrence.

Is medical attention necessary?

Yes. A caring pediatrician can help the parents and child put the problem in perspective, separating it from the misdirected guilt and shame that frequently arise. Once soiling is explained as a physical problem with a practical solution, everyone involved can deal with it in a more rational way.

The pediatrician prescribes laxatives or stool softeners to restore normal bowel function. In a severely constipated child, a one- or two-week program of enemas, suppositories, stool softeners, and laxatives may be necessary. Thereafter, gradually tapering daily doses of mineral oil or stool softeners may be needed for several weeks or months. A concurrent program of bowel retraining—consisting of sitting on the toilet for 10 or 15 minutes at regular times each day usually after breakfast and supper —helps reestablish normal bowel habits. Even after symptoms have subsided, however, the parents need to watch that the problem does not recur.

PREVENTING SOILING

Make sure your child does not become constipated. To promote normal bowel function:

- Serve high-fiber foods, including whole-grain breads and cereals; fresh fruits and vegetables; and dried fruits, such as prunes and raisins.
- Encourage your child to be physically active and drink plenty of water.

Coping with soiling

Parents can handle a child's soiling more effectively if they avoid the pitfall of assessing blame for the problem. Let the child know that the doctor can help him stop having accidents. At the same time, let the child know that he will participate by taking the medications prescribed and working on the retraining program.

Dealing with accidents

Children with soiling problems usually feel considerable shame, which can get in the way of effective treatment. If your child loses bowel control:

- Don't scold or shame.
- Do explain that big boys and girls must use a toilet.
- Do have the child help wash out soiled clothing and clean up.
- Do look for signs that the child may need to have a bowel movement, and remind him to go.
- Don't let bowel movements become the focus of most of your interactions with the child.
- Meet with school personnel and inform them of treatment program.

Signs of trouble

Although soiling is rarely, in itself, a sign of a psychological disorder, some children with developmental or emotional problems do defecate in inappropriate places. Your pediatrician may recommend a consultation with a child psychologist or psychiatrist if your child:

- Persistently engages in stool smearing.
- Deliberately puts feces where other family members will find them.
- Shows no signs of distress over the problem.

Getting Help

CALL YOUR DOCTOR IF YOUR CHILD:
- ☐ Complains of painful bowel movements.
- ☐ Is over age four and has one or more bowel accidents per week over the course of a month.
- ☐ Is chronically constipated.

Smoking, Passive

Passive smoking is exposure to smoke from someone else's cigarette, cigar, or pipe. In enclosed places, such as an office, car, restaurant, or home, cigarette smoke builds up enough to expose even nonsmokers to a dangerous array of chemicals, including nicotine, formaldehyde, carbon monoxide, DDT, and arsenic.

There are two types of cigarette smoke: mainstream and sidestream. Mainstream smoke is inhaled by the smoker through the mouthpiece (which usually contains a filter). Nonsmokers are exposed to mainstream smoke when the smoker exhales.

Sidestream smoke is released directly into the air from the burning end of the cigarette. This unfiltered smoke is even more dangerous than mainstream smoke. Some studies have indicated that sidestream smoke contains twice as much tar and nicotine and three times as much carbon monoxide as mainstream smoke. Most of the smoke that a nonsmoker is exposed to is the more dangerous, sidestream smoke.

How is passive smoking harmful to children's health?

Secondhand smoke is listed by the U.S. Surgeon General as a known carcinogen, linked mainly to lung cancer. It also has been linked to heart disease and respiratory problems. People with asthma or allergies may suffer an acute attack when exposed to the irritants and toxins in secondhand smoke.

Passive exposure to cigarette smoke starts during pregnancy, not only if the mother smokes, but also if the husband or other adults in the household or workplace smoke. Exposure to cigarette smoke during gestation can lead to low birth weight, higher risk of respiratory problems, and other health risks to the infant.

After birth, exposure to secondhand smoke continues to harm babies. Children exposed to cigarette smoke (usually due to parental smoking) are twice as likely to suffer from fair or poor health as children who have never been

SMOKING AND BREAST FEEDING

Nicotine and other smoke-related chemicals are passed through breastmilk from mothers who smoke. Infants who are exposed to sidestream smoke as well as to smoke-related chemicals in breast milk have much higher levels of cotinine (a by-product of nicotine) in their urine, which means the chemical is affecting them much the way it affects smokers. Since nicotine constricts blood vessels and has been implicated in the development of heart disease, it is clearly not good for babies. The bottom line, again, is to stop smoking.

exposed to cigarette smoke. Rates of bronchitis and pneumonia are higher among babies under age two whose parents smoke. Children exposed to secondhand smoke are twice as likely to develop asthma, the most common lung disease of childhood.

Children aged five through nine whose parents smoke have decreased lung function compared to children who have not been exposed to cigarette smoke. Rates of acute respiratory illness are higher among children of smokers than in those of nonsmokers.

In addition, at least one study has found that children who were exposed to cigarette smoke have a significantly increased chance of lung cancer as adults—even if they never smoke themselves. The study estimated that 1,700 cases of lung cancer each year are due to exposure to secondhand smoke in childhood. The chances of suffering the effects of passive smoking increase with the number of smokers in the house and the number of years the child

PREVENTING EXPOSURE TO CIGARETTE SMOKE

- Ban smoking from your house.
- Do not permit babysitters or teachers to smoke around children.
- Choose nonsmoking sections in restaurants and other public areas.
- Quit smoking and prevail upon your partner to quit as well.

is exposed. The study estimated that with 25 or more "smoker years" of exposure during childhood and adolescence, the rate of lung cancer doubles.

Stomach and Duodenal Ulcers

These ulcers are raw areas or holes in the lining of the stomach and the duodenum, the segment of the small bowel attached to the stomach. They are relatively uncommon in young children, occurring more often in adolescents.

Ulcers most commonly occur in the duodenum, except in the first two years of life, when they appear with similar frequency in both the stomach and the duodenum.

Ulcers are considered primary if they develop in otherwise healthy children and secondary if they are caused by a disease or treatment with certain drugs, including aspirin. Primary ulcers tend to occur in children with close relatives who have the same condition.

What causes stomach and duodenal ulcers?

Recent evidence indicates that infection of the stomach or duodenum by a spiral bacterium known as *Helicobacter pylori* plays an important role in the development of a high proportion of both gastric and duodenal ulcers. Other factors that may be involved are increased gastric stomach acid secretion or heightened sensitivity to acid in the mucosal linings of the stomach or duodenum. Secondary ulcers are associated with head injuries, severe burns, widespread infection, shock, kidney failure, respiratory failure, abnormalities of the blood system, and prematurity.

When should I suspect that my child has stomach or duodenal ulcers?

In the first two years of life, the most prominent symptoms are vomiting and slow growth. After six years of age, abdominal pain is the most common symptom. Many children with ulcers have two to four episodes of pain a day, each episode lasting less than 30 minutes. Eating sometimes relieves the pain, but it may aggravate it. The pain occurs at night in about one-third of children.

Is medical attention necessary?

Yes. Although not all ulcers are dangerous, some can be serious, so treatment is often necessary.

How can the pediatrician tell if my child has stomach or duodenal ulcers?

The doctor will order X rays of the stomach and duodenum taken after the child swallows

---

PREVENTING STOMACH AND DUODENAL ULCERS

Although there is no sure way to prevent ulcers, the following guidelines may help:

- Never give aspirin and similar drugs such as ibuprofen to children unless a doctor explicitly prescribes them.
- Serve regularly scheduled meals.
- Serve the child small snacks between meals.

a contrast material. Another diagnostic test, called endoscopy is now also commonly performed. In this procedure, a viewing tube is passed through the esophagus into the stomach so that the lining can be examined directly.

What treatments are available?

About half of all stomach and duodenal ulcers will heal without treatment but may recur. However, the pediatrician will probably prescribe medication to relieve pain, speed healing, and prevent recurrence and complications.

Most doctors treat ulcers in infants and children with medications that reduce acid secretion; these have been shown to be very effective for adults with ulcer disease. Although they have not been offically approved for pediartic use, these drugs have had wide application in pediatric patients. Most likely, the first drug used will be cimetidine, although vanitidine is gaining acceptance as well. Treatment is customarily for six weeks. Afterward, parents should be alert for recurrent symptoms which may indicate the presence of Helicobacter infection. Because of the increasing evidence of the role of Helicobacter infection as a cause of ulcers, many pediatric and adult gastroenterologists are now using antibiotics in the treatment of ulcer disease in conjunction with Pepto-Bismol. This should only be done after diagnostic endoscopy.

Surgery may be required for severe ulcers that cause intractable pain, uncontrolled bleeding, or perforation of the stomach or duodenal wall. The simplest surgery involves removing the ulcer or sewing its borders together. In severe disease, more complicated operations may be required. Modern diagnostic and therapeutic techniques have greatly reduced the need for surgery, though.

Strabismus

Strabismus, which also is called lazy eye, affects about one to three percent of children early in life. The condition develops when the two eyes are not fully coordinated, causing double vision. To compensate, the brain suppresses vision in one eye. Unless the condition is treated, vision in the suppressed eye will fail to develop normally, resulting in permanent visual impairment that may be mild or severe. If treated by the age of three, strabismus usually can be cured.

What causes strabismus?

Strabismus has a strong hereditary component. The most common cause is an imbalance of muscle alignment: One eye crosses inward, upward, or outward while the other moves normally.

Is medical care necessary?

Early detection is key to preventing permanent damage from strabismus; the condition does not readily respond to treatment after the age of six. Children from families with a history of strabismus (particularly in a sibling) should therefore be closely monitored.

When should I suspect that my child has strabismus?

An infant's eyes will cross occasionally until about six weeks of age. If a baby cannot focus

properly at that stage, your pediatrician may refer you to an ophthalmologist; the muscles controlling eye movement might be unbalanced or misaligned. Be sure to mention any concerns you have about your child's vision or eye movements to your pediatrician.

How can the doctor tell if my child has strabismus?

To evaluate an infant, the doctor may move an attractive object or light through the field of vision to observe how the baby's eyes follow its movement. The doctor will probably test the two eyes separately, alternately covering each eye.

After diagnosing strabismus, the doctor will conduct more complete ophthalmological and neurological evaluations to rule out some serious eye or nervous system disease.

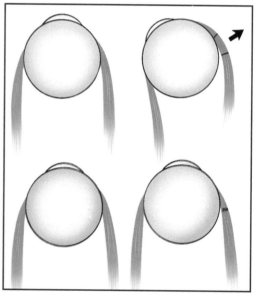

In some cases, surgical repair of strabismus is necessary. In the operation, the misaligned eye muscle is shortened so that the eye no longer turns abnormally.

What treatments are available?

The goal of therapy is to maximize vision in each eye and to obtain, if possible, equal and coordinated vision with normal depth perception. Treatment varies with the child's age, the type of strabismus involved, and the degree of visual impairment. It may include:

- Patching the good eye to force the child to rely on the deviating eye and force the brain to pay attention to images received from the weaker eye.
- Eyeglasses with one corrective lens and one blackened lens if the child has other vision problems (such as nearsightedness).
- Pharmacologic therapy with *miotics,* which constrict the pupil. As a result, the weaker eye will respond to lower levels of nerve impulses and accommodate more readily. Because of side effects, this treatment is used only in selected cases.

- Orthoptics (eye exercises) as an adjunct to glasses, patching, and medication.
- Eye surgery to strengthen and coordinate muscles around the eyes in severe cases, usually before the age of one to two years.
- Subsequent monitoring of the child's vision throughout childhood.

Strep Throat

Strep throat is an infection of the upper respiratory tract caused by bacteria of the *Streptococcus* family. Though streptococci are the most common bacterial causes of respiratory infections, strep infections are much less common than viral respiratory infections (colds), which may have similar symptoms. Strep throat is most common in winter and spring. Children with strep throat also may develop a skin rash known as **scarlet fever** (see entry).

How does strep throat develop?

Strep bacteria spread from person to person in droplets expelled during coughing and sneezing. Usually, however, close contact—such as sharing eating utensils or playing face-to-face—is needed for the bacteria to spread. Outbreaks of strep throat can occur in communities, day care centers, schools, and families.

When should I suspect that my child has a strep throat?

Symptoms of strep throat include fever, sore throat, severe pain on swallowing, tender and swollen lymph glands in the neck, malaise, and nausea. The throat and soft palate are red,

---

Getting Help

CALL YOUR DOCTOR IF THE FOLLOWING SIGNS APPEAR:

- ◾ Deviation in one eye, sometimes making the child appear cross-eyed. Some children show such deviation only when they are ill or tired.
- ◾ Frequently head tilting or covering one eye to see an object up close.
- ◾ Frequent headaches.
- ◾ Difficulty estimating distances, which may show up as an inability to catch a ball.

swollen, and frequently coated with a yellowish-white material. There is usually no cough. Fever typically lasts for one to three days, and sore throat persists for approximately five days.

Strep throat often resembles viral and other illnesses and is not always easy to recognize. Some children develop all characteristic signs of strep throat, but others may have only fever or only a mild sore throat. Children under four years of age can have a runny nose, which is sometimes the only symptom. You should strongly suspect strep throat if the child's fever rises suddenly and the throat becomes sore within several hours after the first symptoms develop.

Is medical attention necessary?

It is necessary to consult a doctor, mainly because strep throat, if left untreated, can lead to serious complications, including **sinusitis, otitis media,** and **rheumatic fever** (see entries).

How can the pediatrician tell if my child has strep throat?

Strep throat can have a dramatic appearance with swollen tonsils covered with white pus. Equally likely, however, the physical findings will be minimal or subtle. Any time a child has a sore throat, the doctor checks for strep throat

PREVENTING STREP THROAT
• Discourage children from sharing eating utensils with siblings and classmates.
• Keep a child with strep throat out of day care, preschool, or school for a full 24 hours after starting antibiotics.

by taking a throat culture, which entails swabbing some material from the back of the throat and placing it in a culture medium. Within 24 hours, signs of the growth of strep bacteria on the culture plate should be detectable. Although quicker tests for strep are available, many doctors prefer the traditional method because it is more accurate.

What treatments are available?

Treatment is usually not begun until culture results are available. Penicillin is the most commonly prescribed treatment for strep, although alternative medications are available

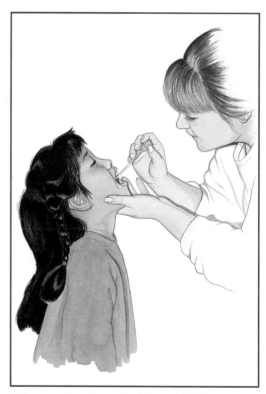

A throat culture is needed for a definitive diagnosis of strep throat. To obtain cells for culture, the doctor or nurse rubs a cotton swab across the back of the throat.

for children who are allergic to penicillin. Oral antibiotics usually must be taken for ten days to eradicate all the infectious organisms.

Getting Help

CALL YOUR DOCTOR IF:
- ☐ Your child complains of a severe sore throat.
- ☐ Your child develops a sudden fever.
- ☐ Your child's throat looks extremely red or is covered with streaks of puslike material.

Stuttering

About five percent of preschoolers have serious problems forming the words they want to say. Such children repeat the starting sounds of words, trip over syllables, or simply freeze up after a tense struggle to speak. It is normal for children to have occasional problems with speech fluency as they start trying to use language in more complex ways. Serious stuttering develops when children in this phase become frustrated and self-conscious about their speech. This can occur if parents and teachers are critical or impatient.

Stuttering can take several different forms, including:

- *Repetition* of phrases, words, syllables, or initial sounds of words. Generally, the longer the repeated unit, the less serious the problem. Speech experts are more likely to be concerned about a child who persistently repeats only the first sounds of words than about one who repeats a word or phrase at the start of a sentence.
- *Interjection* of unnecessary words and phrases such as "um" and "like" when the desired word is not at hand.
- *Pauses* in speech that do not correspond to the context—for example, stopping in the middle of a simple statement.
- *Prolongation* of sounds, such as drawing out the initial sound of a word. This type of stuttering is usually accompanied by signs of frustration and anxiety.

What causes stuttering?

A number of factors can contribute to the development of stuttering. One is confusion about the rules of syntax that help give language its meaning but have no logic for a child who is just starting to put his thoughts into words. Such confusion may lead children to trip over words and phrases or say them in the wrong order. Another is the preschoolers' rapid development of ideas—a development that may outpace word knowledge and vocal coordination. Conversely, children whose vocabularies are expanding rapidly may stumble because they have so many new words from which to choose.

What turns this normal tongue-tied phase into an ongoing problem is the addition of self-consciousness. The harder the child tries, the more difficult speech becomes. The child may start avoiding difficult words or simply clam up in certain situations. Continued problems serve to increase anxiety, which, in circular fashion, worsens stuttering. By the time the child reaches school, the problem may be entrenched.

HELPING A CHILD WHO STUTTERS

- Be patient. Give the child all the time he needs to make a statement. Maintain eye contact and keep your expression neutral. Do not jump in and supply the words the child is groping for.
- Speak slowly and carefully yourself.
- Do not let siblings and other children interrupt the child.
- Acknowledge the problem in a way that does not convey shame or worry.

When should I suspect that my child is developing a stutter?

According to the Speech Foundation of America, the following behaviors may indicate a developing problem. These behaviors are particularly worrisome in children over the age of four.

- Frequent sound or syllable repetitions.
- Syllable repetition in which an "uh" vowel replaces the correct vowel in the word, such as "wuh-wuh-why?"
- Frequent prolongations of sounds.
- Trembling of muscles around the mouth or jaw during speech.
- Changes in voice pitch or loudness during prolongation of sounds.
- Tension and struggle during certain words or sounds.
- A look of fear on child's face while saying a word.
- Avoidance of or delay in saying certain troublesome words.

Is professional attention necessary?

The answer depends on the age of the child and the degree of the problem. If you have concerns, talk to your pediatrician. Your doctor can refer the child to a speech pathologist for testing and, if necessary, therapy. Speech therapy is most effective if it is begun in the preschool years, preferably before age five.

Sudden Infant Death Syndrome (SIDS)

Sudden infant death syndrome, commonly referred to by the acronym *SIDS,* is the term applied to any unexplained death in an apparently healthy infant between the ages of one and 12 months. SIDS is the cause of 7,000 infant deaths in the United States each year, the highest proportion of which occur at two to three months of age. Fatalities attributed to SIDS occur most often at night and on weekends.

What causes SIDS?

No one really knows what causes SIDS. It appears to have multiple causes. In a large percentage of cases, the baby has had a mild cold or intestinal infection, not severe enough to be fatal but possibly capable of triggering breathing difficulty or circulatory failure that could cause death. Another theory is that some victims of SIDS experience episodes of apnea, a temporary halt of breathing which could gradually reduce the amount of oxygen in the system and cause death.

More recently, studies have shown that certain types of soft bedding, including comforters, pillows, and soft or foam mattresses, may create a pocket that traps carbon dioxide so that the baby rebreathes exhaled carbon dioxide, resulting in suffocation. These observations alert parents to be careful about the type of bedding they use. Studies in Australia, confirmed in the United States and Europe, have strongly indicated that SIDS is related to infants' sleeping in the prone (on their stomachs) position. While this may not explain all cases of SIDS, the incidence is strong enough to have led the American Academy of Pediatrics to recommend that babies be put to bed on their sides or backs rather than their bellies.

When should I suspect that my infant is at risk of SIDS?

Scientists have identified a number of characteristics that seem to increase the risk of SIDS. Premature and low birth-weight babies have an increased risk, as do babies born in multiple births. Unexplained death is also more common among male than among female infants. Poverty and crowded living conditions seem to increase the risk as well.

PREVENTING SIDS

Since the exact causes of sudden infant death syndrome are unknown, there are no absolute preventive measures. Precautions you may take include:

- Placing the baby on the side or back for sleep unless specific medical problems such as serious gastroesophageal reflux (backward flow of stomach acids into the esophagus) make stomach sleeping advisable.
- Letting the baby sleep only in a crib, cradle, or bassinet with no extra coverings. Use only a tightly fitted mattress sheet and a light blanket (or a blanket sleeper) for bedding.
- Using home monitoring equipment if recommended by your physician because your baby is at risk for apnea. This type of equipment alerts parents with an alarm if the child stops breathing for a certain period of time.

Certain maternal characteristics also are associated with SIDS. These characteristics include a history of smoking, severe anemia, use of sedatives, or general anesthesia during pregnancy. The risk also is increased if the mother is under age 20.

Styes

Styes, or pimplelike lesions that form at the edge of the eyelid, are extremely common in children. They usually appear in the inner corner of the lower lid. Most styes look like small, red bumps with white centers. There is often a mild swelling and irritation of the entire eyelid.

How do styes develop?

A stye develops when a hair follicle or sweat gland at the base of an eyelash gets infected with bacteria—usually of the *Staphylococcus* family. The bacteria may be present in the eyelash follicle (the tiny passage where the lash is

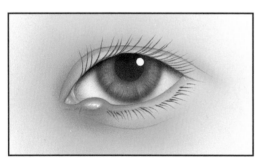

Styes commonly develop on the lower eyelid.

anchored in the skin) and multiply when the follicle is blocked. Bacteria may be introduced when the child rubs her eyes with dirty hands.

Before the stye appears, the child may complain of eye soreness that feels like a foreign object is caught beneath the eyelid. Swelling of the eyelid follows, accompanied by tearing and redness. Soon afterward, the stye itself forms.

Is medical attention necessary?

Only if a stye lasts more than a few days, gets extremely irritated, or enlarges significantly. Persistent styes may be treated with antibiotic eye ointment, but this method is rarely necessary.

What treatments are available?

Home remedies are usually effective. Every three or four hours, apply a warm, wet compress to the eye and hold it there for ten to 20 minutes. Use a clean cloth soaked in fairly warm (but not uncomfortably hot) tap water; a mild saltwater solution may be particularly effective. It is probably not a good idea to use an eye cup (a round container made expressly for soaking the eyes), because they can harbor bacteria and prolong the infection.

Never squeeze a stye. Even if you succeed in pushing out any pus that has accumulated, you risk spreading the infection to other parts of the eye.

PREVENTING STYES

- Discourage eye rubbing.
- Make sure all children have separate wash cloths and towels.

Syphilis, Congenital

In recent years, public concern about sexually transmitted diseases has focused mainly on AIDS. Older sexually transmitted diseases, however, have not gone away. In fact, reported cases of syphilis—a bacterial infection that was one of the first sexually transmitted diseases ever recognized—have steadily increased since the mid-1980s.

Because syphilis is on the rise among adults, an increasing number of infants are being born with congenital syphilis contracted from their mothers during gestation. In the early eighties, for example, fewer than 60 cases of congenital syphilis were reported in New York City each year. Since 1989, the yearly case count has exceeded 1,000.

How does congenital syphilis develop?

The organism that causes syphilis, a spiral-shaped bacterium called *Treponema pallidum*,

passes from an infected mother to the fetus through the placenta. Although maternal-fetal transmission can occur throughout pregnancy, it is most likely if the mother has untreated, active syphilis beyond the sixteenth week. As many as 80 to 95 percent of unborn infants thus exposed to syphilis are born with the congenital form of the disease. In about 40 percent of cases, fetal infection with syphilis results in stillbirth or death within a few weeks after birth. The disease also can be transmitted at the time of delivery if the mother has an active lesion on the genitalia.

How can the pediatrician tell if an infant has congenital syphilis?

If the mother had syphilis during pregnancy, the pediatrician will be alert to the possibility of infection in the newborn. Many obstetricians perform blood tests for syphilis and other infections in all their expectant patients as soon as pregnancy is confirmed. Treating the mother greatly reduces the chance that the fetus will be infected.

All newborns exposed to syphilis prenatally—even those born without symptoms—should be tested for the disease immediately after birth and at regular intervals during the first few months of life. Other diagnostic tests that may be needed include a spinal tap and X rays of the long bones.

What happens during syphilis infection?

A newborn with congenital syphilis may have symptoms immediately after birth or seem normal for the first two to three weeks of life. Symptoms include severe pneumonia, poor

---

PREVENTING CONGENITAL SYPHILIS

To prevent congenital syphilis, pregnant women who are at risk of contracting sexually transmitted diseases should have blood tests for syphilis in the first and third trimesters. Penicillin treatment should begin immediately if the infection is present. Once treatment starts, monthly antibody tests should be done to make sure the infection is eradicated. If an infected woman is treated before the eighteenth week of pregnancy, chances are excellent that her child will escape the infection.

---

feeding, swelling of the liver and spleen, jaundice, fever, and anemia.

After the first week, skin sores develop, and in the second week, some infected infants develop a nasal discharge ("snuffles") that contains syphilis bacteria. Wartlike lesions develop in the mucous membranes, and hair and nails may be lost. The disease also weakens the bones and leads to depression of the nasal bridge. Without treatment, all organ systems are eventually affected.

What treatments are available?

Penicillin will be recommended for the newborn, the dose and duration of treatment depending upon what previous treatment the mother has received.

Teething

No matter when it begins or how long it lasts, tooth eruption causes every baby some discomfort. As a result, teething babies often drool excessively, refuse food, and gnaw on all sorts of objects. Contrary to folklore, teething does not cause high fever, diarrhea, and vomiting. It does, however, frequently coincide with periods of fussiness, which may well be a response to painful gums and other teething-associated discomfort.

The two lower front teeth are usually the first to erupt, sometime after the fourth month and before the tenth. Next come the two top-center incisors and two more lower incisors. The first four molars and pointed (canine) teeth between the molars and incisors generally are in place by the second birthday. Soon after, the remaining four molars and rear cuspids arrive, making a complete set.

Many dentists believe that good dental hygiene can lessen the pain of teething. They recommend cleaning the gums and new teeth with a washcloth twice daily, especially after bedtime feedings. Doing so helps fight bacteria, reducing the risk of infection and tender sores. Begin to teach your child to use a toothbrush when the hard-to-reach back teeth come in, and start regular dental checkups sometime during the second year.

When should I suspect that my baby is teething?

It is usually easy to recognize that a baby is teething: The baby drools nonstop, sucks his fingers, and enthusiastically bites down on hard objects. Sometimes the baby's sleeping and eating patterns become irregular.

Is medical attention necessary?

No; usually a hard rubber pacifier does the trick, easing the pain and even promoting correct jaw development. Avoid plastic objects, which can splinter, and never soothe a teething baby with a full bottle of milk, which can promote tooth decay and set up an unhealthy pattern of using food to soothe discomforts other than hunger.

A cold teething ring, metal spoon, or ice cube wrap can also soothe and properly stimulate irritated gums. If the baby seems to be in serious pain, you may be tempted to use an over-the-counter anesthetic ointment that temporarily numbs the gum. Ask your pediatrician first, and if you get the go-ahead, be sure to follow the directions on the package

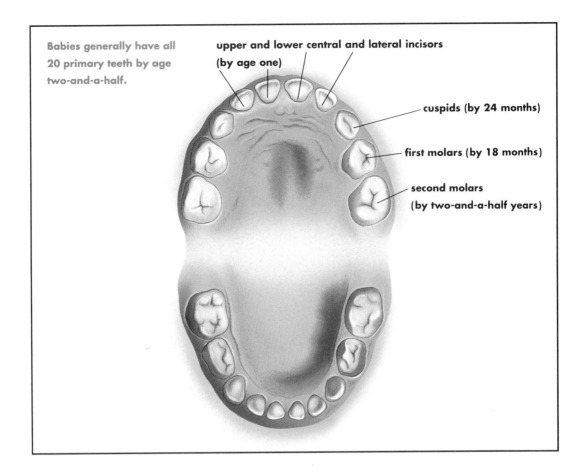

Babies generally have all 20 primary teeth by age two-and-a-half.

upper and lower central and lateral incisors (by age one)

cuspids (by 24 months)

first molars (by 18 months)

second molars (by two-and-a-half years)

label. Keep in mind that such ointments sometimes cause allergic reactions and may be harmful if swallowed.

Occasionally, purplish bruises appear on the gum after molars break through. Although they are unsightly, these cysts are relatively harmless. Bring them to the pediatrician's attention only if they are swollen.

Coping with teething

- Start cleaning the baby's gums before teething begins to prevent bacteria that can cause irritation.

- Provide a hard rubber pacifier or cold teething ring to soothe sore gums. Don't, however, give frozen teething rings, which can injure the mouth.

- A dose of acetaminophen may ease some discomfort.

- Don't rub the gums with aspirin, which can cause irritation and may be dangerous if swallowed.

- Give pain relievers such as over-the-counter anesthetics only as a last resort. They may mask a more serious problem warranting professional attention.

Testicles, Undescended

The testicles are the male reproductive glands essential for fertility and to produce all male (secondary sex) characteristics; they produce sperm and the male sex hormone testosterone from puberty through adulthood. During the male fetus's normal development, the testicles move from the abdominal cavity to their mature location in the scrotum, a pouch of skin suspended behind the penis.

In about two percent of full-term male infants and as many as ten percent of premature male infants, however, one or (more rarely) both testicles fail to migrate to the scrotum; such testicles are termed undescended; the condition, known as *cryptorchidism,* is usually accompanied by an **inguinal hernia** (see entry). Early treatment is important: an undescended testicle will not develop normally, possibly causing infertility and greatly increasing the long-term risk for testicular cancer appearing at age 30 or 40.

How do I recognize an undescended testicle?

An undescended testicle does not usually cause pain, so it may not be noticed unless parents and physicians carefully examine the child's genitalia. Suspect an undescended testicle if the infant's scrotum appears flat and small rather than rounded by the two spherical lobes that indicate the presence of both testicles.

Is medical attention necessary?

Yes. Medical attention is advisable because a failure of the testicle to move down into the scrotum increases the risk of complications such as infertility. In many cases, the testicle will descend spontaneously before the infant reaches his first birthday; consequently, surgical treatment to preserve spermatic development and function usually is postponed until that age, in the hopes that surgery will be unnecessary.

How can the pediatrician tell if my child has an undescended testicle?

Undescended testicles often are discovered in the course of a medical examination at birth or during early infancy. The doctor will perform a careful physical examination to distinguish a true undescended testicle from other abnormalities causing testicular displacement. A *retractile* testicle, for example, is a normally descended testicle that has been pulled out of the scrotum by a strong reflex brought on by pain, touch, cold, fear, or other strong stimuli.

What treatments are available?

Although some physicians try hormonal therapy first, surgical transfer of the testicles into the scrotum, known as *orchidopexy* or *orchiopexy,* is the standard treatment; associated hernias are corrected at the same time. Orchidopexy, if the child is otherwise healthy, is usually performed shortly after age one and allows the testicle the greatest chance for normal development. Hospitalization may not be necessary if the operation is performed in the morning. Within a day or two, the child should be ready to resume most normal activities.

Thalassemia

Thalassemia, which occurs in a number of different forms, is a type of anemia. Children with thalassemia have abnormal red blood cells that are easily destroyed. As a result, they develop classic symptoms of anemia, including fatigue and pallor.

Like many other genetic disorders, thalassemia occurs predominantly in certain ethnic groups. It is most common among people of Mediterranean ancestry, but it also occurs among people of Middle Eastern, Indian, and Southeast Asian extraction.

Children with the form of the disease known as thalassemia major have inherited two copies of the gene responsible for a hemoglobin abnormality—one from each parent. Individuals with only one copy of the gene have a much milder form of the disease called thalassemia minor or thalassemia trait and are usually asymptomatic and can live entirely normal lives.

How does thalassemia develop?

Thalassemia affects hemoglobin, the pigment molecule in red blood cells. Hemoglobin is normally composed of four building blocks, two called alpha and two called beta. In the type of thalassemia classified as beta thalassemia, there are too few beta chains, and as a result, the alpha chains are overabundant. In alpha thalassemia, the reverse occurs. Alpha thalassemia is a fatal condition.

In an attempt to compensate for the shortage of healthy red blood cells in thalassemia, the body speeds production of immature red blood cells in the bone marrow. This strategy, however, results in enlargement of the spleen, which can be quite marked.

When should I suspect that my child has thalassemia?

Symptoms of thalassemia may not be apparent at birth but do appear in the first few months. At that time, weight gain may taper off, and the child may start to develop frequent infections. In addition, the child becomes pale and the abdomen becomes distended due to swelling of the liver and spleen.

PREVENTING THALASSEMIA

Couples with a family history of thalassemia or who know they have thalassemia minor, the mild form of the disease caused by a single defective gene, should have genetic counseling to learn more about the chance of transmitting the full-blown disease to their children. Prenatal testing is also available to identify fetuses affected by the disease.

Is medical attention necessary?

Yes. Children with thalassemia major have a serious, chronic illness. Their bodies are continuously destroying their red blood cells and transfusion therapy is required. Children with thalassemia minor are in a very different situation. Their condition generally requires only periodic monitoring.

How can the pediatrician tell if my child has thalassemia?

The diagnosis is made on the basis of blood tests that show the characteristic abnormalities of the red blood cells.

What treatments are available?

For thalassemia major, treatment consists of transfusions at regular intervals to provide healthy red blood cells. After age five, some children also undergo surgical removal of the spleen. Therapy is also required to remove excess iron from the body. Iron accumulates as a result of the regular transfusions that are required.

With the help of these treatments, children with thalassemia can lead reasonably normal lives. Unfortunately, however, complications requiring further treatment often arise.

Getting Help

CALL YOUR DOCTOR IF:

- You and your partner may both carry the gene that causes thalassemia.

CARING FOR A CHILD WITH THALASSEMIA

- Children with thalassemia major need to avoid excess dietary iron since frequent transfusions can lead to a dangerous iron buildup. Consult a registered dietitian to plan an appropriate diet and learn which foods to avoid.

- Management of thalassemia major requires frequent blood tests, transfusions, and tests of heart, liver, and pancreas function. Children need their parents' support and understanding to cope with these procedures. At the same time, parents should avoid overprotecting such children, trying whenever possible to minimize the role of the illness in their lives.

Thrush

Thrush is the common name for oral candidiasis, a fungal infection of the mouth most frequent in infants during the first six months of life. It appears as white or cream-colored patches, with the underlying tissue red and raw. Children with thrush often have a fungal diaper rash as well.

Fortunately, this common infection can be easily treated. Thrush, however, is contagious, and care should be taken to prevent its spread. Mothers who are breast feeding must be particularly careful if their babies develop thrush because the infection may be passed back and forth between a mother's nipples and the baby's mouth.

When should I suspect that my baby has thrush?

Thrush is usually easy to identify. Irritated white patches inside the mouth are the major indication. The child also may experience discomfort in the mouth and have difficulty suckling and eating. Mothers who are breast feeding may have sore nipples.

What causes thrush?

Thrush is caused by infection with the *Candida* organism, a yeastlike fungus. Oral thrush is most common in newborns, whose immune systems are not yet fully developed and who might contract it during a vaginal delivery if the mother has a vaginal yeast infection. Poor hygiene may also result in the transmission of thrush from person to person at any age. It can be spread through contaminated hands, nipples, bottles, toys, and other personal items.

Is medical attention necessary?

Yes. While thrush is usually not a serious disorder, a visit to the pediatrician is necessary for proper diagnosis, treatment, and prevention of further spread of the disease.

What is the treatment for thrush?

Thrush can normally be cured through treatment with a prescription oral antifungal medication (nystatin), which should only be used according to your pediatrician's instructions.

Breast-feeding mothers must be particularly careful when their babies are being treated for thrush. After nursing, wash the nipples with a baking soda solution (one teaspoon baking soda dissolved in one cup of warm water), then dry and apply a cream such as Vitamin A and D ointment. Make sure all traces of the cream are wiped off before nursing again.

Thumb Sucking

Many babies, toddlers, and preschoolers engage in thumb sucking, a self-soothing activity that was once discouraged but now is considered harmless in the early years. In a baby, sucking the thumb or fingers is not an indication of insecurity or anxiety; it merely satisfies the need to suck, which varies from baby to baby. Therefore, thumb sucking should be regarded as a problem only when it persists into the school years or takes the place of other activities such as playing or learning.

Although many parents worry about the effect of thumb sucking on the teeth, doctors assert that since most children give up the habit before their permanent teeth come in, it causes no dental problems.

When should I suspect a problem with thumb sucking?

For the child under two, thumb sucking is rarely if ever considered a problem, and it may help to alleviate the child's stress or tension. In older children, if the habit interferes with performance in school or is associated with social adjustment problems, it might be a good idea to eliminate it.

What causes thumb sucking in the older child?

Some children are more nervous, shy, or insecure than others, and may use thumb sucking to relieve tension. Others may resort to thumb sucking to alleviate boredom, or to help themselves fall asleep. Sometimes parents unwittingly prolong the habit by getting into power struggles with their child in trying to stop it.

Is medical attention necessary?

Unless thumb sucking becomes obsessive and severely interferes with the child's relationships with others, medical attention should not be necessary in dealing with this problem.

Tics

Tics are repetitive, rapid, involuntary muscle contractions or vocal outbursts that usually involve muscles of the face, head, neck, shoulders, or respiratory tract. They are often exaggerations of normal movements such as blinking the eyes or shaking the head. Children as young as age one may develop tics, although most cases occur later in childhood, between the ages of nine and 12. Boys are more likely to develop tics than girls.

Tics are generally grouped in three categories. Transient tics last more than two weeks but less than one year; chronic tics last longer than one year; and a third category of tics, classified as manifestations of *Tourette syndrome* (a rare, severe tic disorder that may involve multiple tics, lack of muscle coordination, and purposeless muscle movements), may last an entire lifetime or vanish at some point in late adolescence or adulthood.

Most childhood tics are transient. Typical tics in children include involuntary eye winking or head jerking that lasts a few weeks before disappearing or moving to another muscle group.

When should I suspect that my child has a tic disorder?

Several characteristics distinguish tics from voluntary movements such as head banging, which some children engage in as a form of self soothing. Tics are sudden and spasmodic, and the child is unable to control them (and may not even be aware of them). Tics get worse with strong emotions and disappear during sleep.

What causes tic disorders?

The cause of most tics is unknown, although there are a number of theories. In a few cases, the development of a tic or tics may reflect an underlying nerve disorder, but tics of this type are usually persistent and they occur in conjunction with other signs and symptoms. Tics may be associated with changes in the body that occur during normal maturation of nerves and muscles. There seems to be a strong association between anxiety or stress and tics, but it isn't clear what, if any, psychological factors may be involved.

Is medical attention necessary?

Most mild tics do not require medical attention per se, but the child's physician should be consulted to eliminate the possibility that the tic is a sign of some underlying neurological problem. Severe tics that disrupt a child's activities should be brought to a doctor's attention immediately.

What treatments are available?

Most mild, transient tics can simply be left alone. If a tic has remained unchanged at the same muscle site for more than a year, the child's physician may consider treatment, but usually only if the tic is distressing or disruptive. Behavioral therapy—particularly a technique in which the child is instructed to repeat the tic deliberately many times over—is sometimes effective. Only a behavioral psychologist, however, should try to perform this treatment. Tics that are associated with anxiety or stress may respond to other types of psychotherapy, including family counseling.

Severe tics, such as those occurring in Tourette syndrome, generally require drug treatment. Although several medications (mainly sedative, antipsychotic, and antianxiety drugs) are effective in controlling the tics, they do not cure tic disorders, and they may cause serious side effects.

Getting Help

CALL YOUR DOCTOR IF:
- ◼ Your child repeatedly makes movements of the face, neck, or shoulders without seeming to be aware of it.
- ◼ Such movements are repeated regularly over the course of a year.

Toeing In and Toeing Out

Toeing in, or *pigeon toe,* is a common gait problem in young children. Some babies are born with the condition; others first manifest it when they begin to walk. Toeing in often occurs with **bow legs** (see entry). The condition becomes problematic if it makes a child trip while walking.

Toeing out (also called *slew foot* or *duck walk*) is rarer. A slight outward turn of the feet (at an angle of about ten degrees) is common in children and adults while walking. However, toeing out at an angle exceeding 30 degrees is considered abnormal.

What causes toeing in and toeing out?

The most common cause of congenital toeing in is *metatarsus adductus,* an inward bending of the front part of the feet resulting from the fetus's position in the womb. In this condition, the baby's feet are flexible and can be gently pushed to the normal position.

Toeing in that appears after the child begins to walk may be caused by a twisting of the shin bone, which can occur if the child regularly sleeps or sits with knees flexed and feet turned inward. Abnormal twisting also can occur in the hip joint, rotating the entire leg inward. As a result, the child's kneecaps point inward, and the feet whip out to the sides when running.

Conversely, congenital toeing out occurs if the shin bone or the hip bone is twisted outward as a result of an abnormal position in the womb.

Is medical attention necessary?

In most cases, no treatment is required. Many babies toe in or out when learning to stand and walk. For example, toeing in may result when the child shifts his body weight to the middle of the foot to compensate for knock knees, which usually develop during the third year of life and disappear by age seven. Some parents fear that toeing in and toeing out will permanently harm a child's feet and ankles, but these fears are largely unfounded.

Discourage the child from assuming positions that may cause or exacerbate toeing in and toeing out. Avoid these positions:

- Sleeping on the stomach with the knees tucked up under the chest and the bottom resting on inward-turned feet.
- Sleeping on the stomach or on the back with legs in a "frog-leg" position—knees wide apart, heels together, and feet turned outward.
- Sitting on the floor with the knees bent and the lower legs pushed out to either side (the "W" position).
- Sitting with one or both feet tucked under and turned in at the ankle.

What treatments are available?

A temporary deformity caused by an abnormal position in the womb can often be corrected by stretching the baby's feet gently several times a day (for example, when changing diapers); the pediatrician will teach you how. If this doesn't work, a temporary cast or night splint that holds the feet in a normal position may be necessary. Some doctors recommend reversing the baby's shoes for a while—placing the left shoe on the right foot and vice versa—to correct toeing in.

A twisted shin bone often corrects itself, but corrective splints may be necessary if the deformity is great and persists after the child has started walking. Hip abnormalities that cause toeing in and out usually require no treatment, except to avoid sleeping and sitting positions that might worsen them.

Surgery is rarely required unless metatarsus adductus goes undetected until the child attains age two, at which time an operation may be needed to release the tissues holding the feet in the deformed position.

Getting Help

CALL YOUR DOCTOR IF:
- Your baby's feet are bent inward or outward in a fixed manner and cannot be brought to a normal position.
- Toeing in or toeing out affects only one foot.
- Inward- or outward-turned feet cause tripping while walking.
- The feet point out at an angle that exceeds 30 degrees.

Tooth Decay

In 1944, 90 percent of American children between the ages of five and 17 suffered tooth decay; today, that percentage has been cut in half, thanks to fluoridated drinking water and toothpaste and improved dental hygiene. Wider use of fluoride supplements and topical fluoride solutions should reduce the incidence of tooth decay even further. (Consult your pediatrician before using these preparations, especially if your local water supply is fluoridated.)

Many parents mistakenly assume that because a child's primary (baby) teeth are only temporary, they need not be protected from decay. In fact, healthy primary teeth are important for speech development and proper placement of the permanent teeth.

What causes tooth decay?

When normal mouth bacteria attack carbohydrates (such as sugars) on the teeth, they produce acids that can strip and break down the calcium and protein in tooth enamel, producing *caries,* or decay. The most common sites are the biting surfaces of the molars and the places where teeth adjoin. Untreated decay will eventually invade the living inner structures of the tooth.

Infants can develop severe tooth decay if they are allowed to fall asleep nursing or sucking bottles. Liquid from the bottle pools behind the upper front teeth, providing an ideal setting for bacteria to multiply and cause serious decay.

When should I suspect that my child has tooth decay?

Children old enough to talk will complain of tooth pain that occurs on exposure to cold, heat, or pressure, such as biting down. Detecting tooth decay in babies is trickier. Look for altered eating habits (such as chewing only on one side of the mouth) and sensitivity to hot or cold liquids. Looking in the child's mouth may allow you to detect dental problems, but this method is far less effective than a dentist's examination.

Preventing tooth decay

The earlier the child learns good oral hygiene, the better the chance of healthy teeth during adulthood. To promote good dental health:

- Clean an infant's gums with cloth or gauze daily before teething begins. Some dentists believe that this practice will help reduce discomfort and bacterial growth when the teeth begin to break through, usually between the ages of four and ten months.
- Continue cleaning twice a day after the first teeth begin to appear by rubbing them with a washcloth, without toothpaste.
- When the back molars appear, introduce the child to the toothbrush.
- Use fluoridated toothpaste and fluoride rinses. Introduce toothpaste gradually; the taste is strong for small children.
- Use an amount only about the size of a pea; too much fluoridated toothpaste can cause the child's tooth enamel to mottle.
- When the spaces between teeth close up (usually when the back molars grow in), begin flossing the child's teeth or using a water pic at least once a day to clear bacteria from between the teeth.
- Teach the child to brush and floss as early as possible. However, be prepared to help with oral hygiene until the child develops adequate hand-eye coordination, usually by age seven.
- Wean the child from bedtime bottle or breast feeding when the first teeth begin to erupt, or substitute clear water.
- Never put the child to bed with a bottle.
- When possible, brush the child's teeth after every meal and before bedtime. Brushing before bedtime is especially important because bacterial activity often increases during sleep.
- Take the child for twice yearly visits to the dentist beginning at about two years of age.
- Discuss with the dentist the possibility of

applying a sealant (protective coating of a clear, hard material) to the child's tooth surfaces. The sealant acts as a barrier between the tooth's enamel and decay-causing bacteria.

- Prevent your child from developing the habit of eating sweet between-meal snacks.

Tooth Discoloration

Normal baby or primary teeth are off-white or ivory, and they look brighter and shinier than adult teeth. Yellow, brown, or otherwise discolored baby teeth are usually a result of inadequate brushing and tooth decay. Occasionally, liquid medications containing iron discolor the teeth. Sometimes, however, tooth discoloration is a result of an underlying illness or exposure to substances that harm the teeth before or after birth. Fortunately, normal permanent teeth often grow in to replace discolored baby teeth. Even if discoloration persists in permanent teeth, it need not be a serious cosmetic problem, thanks to advances in dental care.

When should I suspect that my child has discolored teeth?

If your child's teeth look yellow, splotchy, or brown despite careful brushing (which requires parental supervision until about age seven), some kind of dental problem is present.

How does tooth discoloration develop?

Tooth enamel forms gradually over several years, during which foreign substances can be incorporated and alter the eventual color of the tooth. Baby teeth can be discolored from about the fourth month in the uterus until the tenth month after birth. Permanent teeth can be affected from age four months to 16 years.

Illness, malnutrition, and other types of physical stress can cause white splotches and bands on the teeth. All children have one such band, known as the *neonatal line,* which results from the stress of birth.

In rare cases, certain childhood infections make a single tooth yellow or brown because the enamel did not grow properly. An injury that causes bleeding in the pulp of a tooth can turn the enamel pink or gray. Also, children who suffered severe neonatal jaundice may have yellow or greenish teeth.

Excessive fluoride can give teeth whitish to dark brown splotches. The antibiotic tetracycline also can be responsible for tooth discoloration in children, causing a brownish-yellow stain that is usually not transferred to the permanent teeth. An infant may have stained teeth if the mother took tetracycline during pregnancy.

Is medical attention necessary?

Yes, but unless your child has a discolored tooth as a result of a very recent injury, the problem is not urgent. Bring it up with your pediatrician during the next well-child visit.

What treatments are available?

In many cases, no treatment is necessary apart from waiting for the permanent teeth to come in. A relatively new process known as *dental bonding* can make discolored permanent teeth appear white and protect against tooth decay.

- Do not take tetracycline during pregnancy or give it to a child under eight years of age.
- Find out the fluoride level in your local water supply. If the water is not fluoridated, ask your pediatrician or dentist about giving your child fluoride supplements. If it is naturally very high in fluoride, consider drinking bottled water and taking fluoride supplements to avoid mottling.
- Clean your baby's teeth with a wet wash cloth for the first year of life, then begin brushing regularly, at least twice a day. Most children continue to need some help with brushing until they are about seven years old.

Toxic Shock Syndrome

When toxic shock syndrome made headlines in the early 1980's, it quickly became known as a potentially fatal, rapid illness that struck women shortly after their menstrual periods. The infection was soon linked to use of certain high-absorbency tampons, which promote overgrowth of *Staphylococcus aureus* bacteria already present in the vagina and which produce a toxin responsible for the symptoms.

Toxic shock syndrome is not unique to menstruating women. In fact, the first cases ever reported, which occurred in 1978, involved children. Although only a few hundred cases of toxic shock syndrome are reported each year, it's important to know the symptoms, since it can develop—and become life-threatening—in a matter of hours.

How does toxic shock syndrome develop?

The bacteria that cause toxic shock can sometimes colonize the skin surface, as well as the mucous membranes (such as the nasal passages and vagina) in perfectly healthy people. It is only when the microbe secretes a toxin that the disease begins. Researchers suspect that there might be more than one causative toxin. Besides use of superabsorbent tampons, deep wounds and surgery have been suggested as possible triggering factors.

When should I suspect that my child has toxic shock syndrome?

Toxic shock syndrome begins abruptly, with a fever greater than 102 degrees Fahrenheit, vomiting, and diarrhea. A sore throat, headache, and muscle aches also may be present. Within 24 hours, a diffuse rash appears all over the body. Then, blood pressure drops, causing

- Avoid packing the nasal passages with gauze to stop nosebleeds.
- Take care to keep deep cuts, burns, and surgical incisions clean and disinfected.

Be aware of and alert to the symptoms of toxic shock syndrome, particularly if your child has recently had surgery or a deep wound. Seek medical assistance promptly.

dizziness and a state of shock. In three percent of nonmenstrual cases, the drop in blood pressure is so severe that it is fatal.

With treatment, it typically takes about seven to ten days to recover from toxic shock syndrome, although the patient may not feel entirely normal again for about three more weeks. During the second week, the skin on the palms and soles often peels, and hair and nails sometimes fall out. In about 30 percent of cases, the disease recurs within three months of the original episode.

Is medical attention necessary?

The three classic symptoms of toxic shock syndrome—high fever, vomiting, and diarrhea—always demand medical attention.

How can the pediatrician tell if my child has toxic shock syndrome?

Since toxic shock syndrome is far from the only possible cause of these symptoms, the doctor will need to rule out other serious disorders, such as septicemia (blood poisoning), Rocky Mountain spotted fever, scarlet fever, Kawasaki disease, and measles. Toxic shock syndrome is distinguished from these other disorders by its wider range of symptoms. A diagnosis is made on the basis of the three classic symptoms, plus involvement of at least three organ systems, which may include the nervous system, digestive system, liver, kidneys, circulation, muscles, and mucous membranes.

What treatments are available?

Children and teenagers with toxic shock syndrome usually need hospitalization for management of low blood pressure and other complications of the disease. High doses of intravenous penicillin are administered for ten days.

Tuberculosis

Tuberculosis (TB) is a serious infectious disease that usually attacks the lungs but can spread to other organ systems, including the skeletal system and the central nervous system, where it can cause meningitis, brain abscesses, and other major infections. Once a leading cause of death worldwide, tuberculosis was almost wiped out in the United States in the 1950s, thanks to improved sanitation, mandatory pasteurization of commercial milk (since one form of the disease is transmitted by cows), and the advent of antituberculosis drugs.

Unfortunately, a serious resurgence of tuberculosis began in this country in the 1980s. At first limited to high-risk groups (such as immigrants from Southeast Asia, the urban homeless, drug abusers, and people with compromised immune systems, such as people with AIDS), tuberculosis has made steady inroads into low-risk populations in recent years. Therefore, screening for the disease, which is done through a simple skin test, is more important than ever.

What causes TB?

The organism responsible for the disease is called *Mycobacterium tuberculosis.* This bacterium is spread almost exclusively by infected adolescents, adults, and older children. As a rule, small children with the infection are not highly contagious.

TB bacteria pass from person to person via moisture droplets expelled when an infected person coughs or sneezes. Inhalation of these droplets can lead to infection in a previously healthy person.

If all people infected with TB developed symptoms of the disease, its control would be much more straightforward. In reality, however, most people with TB infections do not have symptoms. For that reason, screening tests to detect these *latent* infections in apparently healthy people are vital to preventing widespread TB. These tests are generally performed as part of routine well-child care at 12 to 15 months of age, before school entry, and during adolescence. Early detection and treatment of latent infections can prevent their progression to serious illness.

When should I suspect TB?

Usually, the only indication is a positive screening test. (To find out more about screening tests for TB, see page 267.) Signs and symptoms of respiratory illness are the most common manifestations of active infection. These signs include a persistent cough with mucus production, shortness of breath, chest pain, fever (which appears early in the course of the infection and then subsides), and swollen lymph nodes, usually in the chest and underarms. Active infection is most likely to develop if TB exposure occurs in early infancy. Other factors associated with development of active infection include other illnesses and poor nutrition.

Is medical attention necessary?

Yes. A child who develops a positive TB test needs additional testing and, in most cases, medication. In addition, all the child's close contacts need to be tested. It is vitally important to identify the adult or older child who is the source of infection, as well as to treat any other members of the family who may have been exposed. In general, even family members who have negative TB tests should undergo antibiotic treatment to prevent infection from taking hold.

How can the pediatrician tell if my child has TB?

After a positive screening test, the pediatrician performs another, more precise skin test to confirm the result. He also evaluates the child's overall health, with special attention to growth and nutritional status and asks questions about recent or ongoing respiratory illnesses in the child and other members of the household. Chest X rays usually are performed as well. Based on the degree of involvement, hospitalization may be needed.

What treatments are available?

Children with positive skin tests who have no signs of active infection need to receive antibiotic treatment. A single drug (usually isoniazid) usually is prescribed to be taken daily for about a year.

Various combinations of antibiotics are used to treat active tuberculosis. If the child has symptoms, a brief period of bed rest may be needed. Long-term treatment usually has to continue for 12 to 18 months, even though symptoms subside much sooner. In addition, since small children rarely spread the disease, full participation in school and other activities is usually possible.

Screening tests for TB

In the past, routine annual screening using a multiprong skin patch was recommended for all children beginning at one year of age. Although these tests are still available, their widespread use for children with little risk of contracting TB is discouraged because they are highly unreliable, with a large percentage of both false positive and false negative results. Also, parents do not always comply with instructions or fail to interpret results properly. Thus, annual screening is recommended only for high-risk children, such as those Native Americans or minority children who live in impoverished inner city neighborhoods where

TB is prevalent. Children of recent immigrants from Asia, Africa, the Middle East, Latin America, or the Caribbean, as well as those living in a household with a TB patient, should also be screened annually. Otherwise, screening at three stages of childhood—12 to 15 months, 4 to 6 years, and 14 to 16 years—is considered sufficient for low-risk children.

The preferred method of testing uses an intradermal, or Mantoux, technique in which a purified antigen is injected under the skin, and then observed 48 to 72 hours later. Development of a large wheal at the site of injection indicates a need for further diagnostic tests to rule out or confirm TB. If further tests are positive, other household members should be tested, and appropriate treatment or preventive measures undertaken.

Getting Help

CALL YOUR PEDIATRICIAN IF:
- ◼ Your child (or an adult in the child's household) has a positive skin test for TB.
- ◼ Your child develops a persistent cough, shortness of breath, or chest pain.
- ◼ TB has been diagnosed in any of the child's contacts, including family members, playmates, classmates, or babysitters.

Urinary Tract Infection

During infancy and early childhood, both boys and girls are vulnerable to infections of the urinary tract, the system of organs and ducts through which urine is eliminated from the body. The two kidneys filter waste from the blood. By way of two tubes known as ureters, these wastes (now in the form of urine) move on to the bladder for storage. From there, a canal known as the urethra discharges the urine from the body. In boys the urethra runs the length of the penis to its tip; in girls, the urine discharges through an opening found between the vagina and the clitoris.

What happens during urinary tract infection?

Urinary tract infections occur when bacteria begin to multiply in the urethra, causing inflammation. Unchecked, inflammation and irritation will spread to the bladder wall. From there, if untreated, the infection can attack the kidneys, leading to a type of infection called *pyelonephritis,* which is a potentially dangerous condition. (For more information, see separate entry on **nephritis.**) In addition, repeated urinary tract infections, usually caused by some obstruction in the urinary tract, can damage the bladder walls and scar kidney tissue. For this reason, it is important to find and correct the underlying cause of recurrent urinary infections.

What causes urinary tract infections?

Bacteria, primarily from the colon, sometimes gain access to the urinary tract. If these bacteria are allowed to multiply, infection results. During their first four months of life, infants of both sexes are at roughly equal risk for urinary tract infections. The bacteria usually enter directly from the blood at this early stage. Subsequently, however, girls and women are more susceptible than males because the female's urethra is closer to the anus (the source

of fecal contamination) and the females urethra is shorter than the males, allowing infection to spread more rapidly to other portions of the urinary tract. After an infant reaches four months of age, bacteria usually invade the urinary tract from the external genitalia and anal area.

When should I suspect that my child has a urinary tract infection?

In infants, the symptoms of urinary tract infections are nonspecific. They can include vomiting, diarrhea, irritability, abnormal body temperature (either high or low), slowed weight gain, and sometimes even jaundice, a yellowing of the skin. In an older child, abdominal pain and symptoms specific to the urinary tract may also arise. A weakened urine stream, frequent and/or painful urination, unpleasant urinary odor, feelings of urgency, and bedwetting in a child who has been success-

---

PREVENTING URINARY TRACT INFECTIONS

Several precautions can help prevent urinary tract infections from developing:

- Increase the child's fluid intake to help flush potentially dangerous bacteria from the urethra.
- Use careful diaper hygiene.
- During diaper changes, wipe little girls from front to back to avoid fecal contamination of the urethra.
- Provide a healthy diet to prevent constipation, which can contribute to urinary tract infections.
- Avoid bubble baths, which can irritate the urethra.

fully toilet trained may signal the presence of a urinary tract infection.

Is medical attention necessary?

Yes. Since urinary tract infection can spread to the kidney, treatment is essential.

How can the pediatrician tell if my child has a urinary tract infection?

The physician will send a urine sample for culture and urinalysis; the results will confirm the diagnosis and identify the specific bacteria responsible.

The physician will need to perform special X-ray and ultrasound tests to detect possible damage to urinary tract tissues and/or the presence of any congenital abnormalities that may have contributed to the infection.

What treatments are available?

Several antibiotics are effective in combatting urinary tract infections. The medication usually will begin to relieve the symptoms within 24 to 48 hours of the initial dose. If not, notify the physician. To be certain that the infection is completely eliminated, administer the full prescribed course of antibiotics, even if the symptoms have disappeared.

WATCHING FOR RECURRENCES

Urinary tract infections recur at least once in 30 to 40 percent of children; they recur especially during the first three months after the initial infection. Symptoms will not necessarily reappear. To detect recurrence, your physician may check one or more follow-up urine cultures.

Sometimes the physician will prescribe a urinary analgesic to reduce burning or other urinary discomfort. Do not be alarmed if this medication turns the child's urine red. The child should be encouraged to increase fluid intake as well.

In the case of recurrent urninary tract infection, further studies may be needed to rule out obstructions, and long-term antibiotic prophylaxis may be required.

Getting Help

CALL THE PEDIATRICIAN IF:
- ☐ Your child has any signs or symptoms of a urinary tract infection.
- ☐ You notice any change in your child's usual pattern of urination.

Viral Infections, Intestinal (Acute Viral Gastroenteritis)

The sudden onset of diarrhea, vomiting, and abdominal pain usually means a child has contracted an intestinal infection, or gastroenteritis, which is most often caused by a virus.

Intestinal viruses are highly contagious. They can be transmitted through direct contact, water, or food. Outbreaks are most common in overcrowded situations with poor hygiene, but they can occur in any school or day-care setting.

What happens during an intestinal viral infection?

After entering the body (usually through the mouth), the virus multiplies and penetrates

---

the intestines. Viral particles affect the surface layer of cells lining the intestine. Damage to these cells interferes with digestion and causes intestinal upset, which resolves once the virus leaves the body.

When should I suspect that my child has an intestinal viral infection?

While bacterial and parasitic infections tend to start with diarrhea, the first symptom of infection with an intestinal virus is generally vomiting. After a day or two, vomiting may subside, but diarrhea—sometimes severe—then develops. Depending on the virus responsible for the infection, fever may or may not be present.

Is medical attention necessary?

Even if all symptoms point to an intestinal virus, you still should consult a doctor because a number of other, more serious disorders can cause vomiting and diarrhea. Also, it is critical to avoid the complication of dehydration.

How can the pediatrician tell if my child has an intestinal viral infection?

Diagnosis of an intestinal virus usually is made on the basis of symptoms after more serious illness is excluded. If the child is a newborn or has some chronic illness, the doctor will order laboratory tests to identify the infectious organism. In these cases, medical attention is particularly crucial.

What treatments are available?

Treatment consists mainly of preventing **dehydration** (see entry)—the major risk associated with intestinal virus infection. To make sure the child stays well hydrated, the pedia-

---

CARING FOR A CHILD WITH AN INTESTINAL VIRAL INFECTION

- Make sure the child receives sufficient fluids to prevent dehydration.
- Offer extra fluids (diluted juices, weak iced tea, flat soda, and similar drinks) to breast-fed babies, even though nursing continues.
- Avoid giving the child solid food until the symptoms have subsided.

---

trician may recommend a commercially prepared solution such as Pedialyte or a home remedy, such as Gatorade or a flat soft drink. The goal, in either case, is to keep fluid and minerals in the child's system, even if the child is vomiting.

Antidiarrheal drugs are not recommended because vomiting and diarrhea are the body's defense mechanisms against infection and they should not be blocked.

Breast-fed babies with gastroenteritis usually can continue to nurse, but formula-fed infants should temporarily switch to clear liquids such as Pedialyte until symptoms sub-

---

PREVENTING INTESTINAL VIRAL INFECTIONS

The best prevention is to observe good hygiene:

- Encourage hand washing, especially after going to the bathroom and before eating.
- Discourage sharing of eating utensils.
- Promptly dispose of diapers and other contaminated items.

---

side. Some infants develop temporary intolerance to the sugar in milk (lactose) as a result of an intestinal virus infection. To detect such an intolerance, formula should be reintroduced slowly and at half strength (i.e., twice as much water as is normally used) for the first day or so after recovery. If lactose intolerance develops, the baby will need to drink a lactose-free formula for about four weeks.

Getting Help

CALL YOUR DOCTOR IF YOUR CHILD:
- ☐ Vomits repeatedly.
- ☐ Has three or more episodes of diarrhea in a short time.
- ☐ Develops fever and other symptoms along with a digestive upset.

Vision, Impaired

The eye itself and the parts of the brain involved in vision still are developing during infancy and early childhood. Interaction among all the parts of the visual system, including structures of the eye that receive sensory input, cells that respond to light, and the area in the brain that converts messages from the eyes into visual images make vision possible. Disruption of any part of the system, especially in the first year, can lead to vision loss.

How does impaired vision develop?

Loss of vision can happen at any time before or after birth. Certain infections in pregnant women, such as rubella (German measles),

can cause blindness in the newborn. Congenital herpes or gonorrhea infections may damage vision, as may eye infections picked up from other sources.

A condition called *retinopathy of prematurity* frequently causes vision loss in premature infants. This disorder develops when a premature baby's retina is damaged by administration of high concentrations of oxygen—a necessary measure for saving many babies who are born too early.

Some infants are born with congenital forms of eye diseases that generally occur in adulthood, such as **cataracts** (see entry) and **glaucoma** (see entry). Untreated strabismus (lazy eye), a result of the brain's natural tendency to block out images from the weaker eye if one eye is stronger than the other, also can lead to serious vision deficits (see **amblyopia**). In rare cases, vision loss may be a result of a cancer. Blindness may also occur as a late complication of diabetes.

Eye injuries, which are commonly caused by balls, fists, and sticks, often lead to visual impairment or loss of vision. Most of these injuries should be preventable. (For more information, see **eye injuries.**)

When should I suspect that my child has impaired vision?

The signs of failing vision are subtle, particularly in infants. If a baby does not respond to a change in a parent's facial expression or is not distracted by a mobile or toy, it may be a sign that his sight is impaired. In babies over three months old, a cross-eyed appearance may be an indication of strabismus.

Older children with vision problems may avoid activities requiring coordination of sight

Infants with normal sight interact with their parents mainly by focusing on their faces and maintaining eye contact. This type of interaction is not possible with a visually impaired baby, so parents need to learn other ways to foster attachment. Such babies can recognize parents' voices, smells, and movement patterns, and then respond with changes in body language such as becoming still and turning the head. Parents may need some instruction to interpret their babies responses. Help is often available through rehabilitation centers or organizations that serve the blind, which are listed in the "Resource Directory" under "Vision Disorders/Blindness."

and movement, such as playing catch or walking on a balance beam.

Is medical attention necessary?

Yes. If you suspect that your child is not seeing well, a medical assessment is needed. If impaired vision is a result of a correctable problem such as strabismus, treatment should begin as soon as possible. If a child has a permanent vision loss, he should receive rehabilitation so that impaired vision does not interfere with normal development.

What treatments are available?

The treatment depends on the cause and degree of visual impairment. If possible, treatment is aimed first at the underlying cause. Thus, antibiotics are given for eye infections, and eye patching, exercises, and (in some cases) surgery are employed to correct strabismus.

Children with severe and irreversible vision losses generally attend special programs for the visually impaired starting at about age two. Before that, they may receive in-home therapy aimed at providing the types of stimulation necessary for normal development. The therapist can show parents how to play with the baby in ways that depend more on the senses of touch, hearing, and movement than on sight. Parents also may learn how to choose appropriate toys and arrange the home in a way that permits the child maximum independence.

Getting Help

CALL YOUR DOCTOR IF YOUR CHILD:
- Has a yellowish-white mass in the pupil.
- Has an inward turning or wandering eye.
- Has a partially closed. eyelid.
- Does not focus his eyes evenly by the third month of life.

Warts

Few children grow up without developing one or two warts, which are benign skin growths caused by organisms known as *human papilloma viruses*. The most common type of wart—appropriately called a common or *vulgar wart*—is a raised, rough-textured growth that starts out skin-colored and eventually turns yellow to gray. Appearing singly or in clusters, these warts vary in size from a pinhead to a large mass. They usually occur on the fingers, hands, face, knees, and elbows, although they can spread anywhere.

Plantar warts, which are similar to common warts, develop on the sole of the foot and are flat rather than raised because of the pressure from weight bearing.

Closely related to common warts are *juvenile flat warts,* which are smooth, slightly elevated, and variable in color from pink to brown. Juvenile flat warts are usually less than a quarter-inch in size, and they appear primarily on the face and hands.

What causes warts?

Scientists have identified more than 50 different types of human papilloma viruses, several of which are associated with specific types of warts. Like other viruses, papilloma viruses are transmitted from person to person, usually through close physical contact or, less often, sharing of personal items such as towels. The viruses responsible for warts also can be spread from one part of the body to another, which is why warts on the fingers often lead to warts in other locations, including the face. Children's natural tendency to pick at warts also promotes the virus's spread.

Is medical attention necessary?

More than 50 percent of warts disappear spontaneously within two years. However, failure to treat warts increases the risk that they will spread. Therefore, it is desirable to have the pediatrician see the lesions and decide whether therapy is needed, and if so, what kind.

What treatments are available?

The basic approach to home treatment involves peeling the wart off. Consult with your doctor about wart-removal products sold over the counter. The active ingredients of these products can destroy the upper layer of the skin. Therefore, *never allow a child to apply a wart-removal product alone,* and make sure you apply these remedies only to the wart, not to surrounding skin. Follow package directions, which usually recommend twice daily applications. Alternatively, your doctor may recom-

---

Getting Help

CALL YOUR DOCTOR IF:
- ☐ You are unsure whether a growth is an actual wart.
- ☐ Your child is very distressed by a wart that has resisted six weeks of home care.
- ☐ A wart is causing pain.
- ☐ A wart is on the sole of the foot.
- ☐ A wart begins to spread.
- ☐ A wart starts to bleed.

---

mend a prescription wart-removal solution, or plaster that you can use at home.

Never attempt to cut off a wart. This procedure can be performed only by a physician. Wart-removal techniques used by pediatricians and dermatologists include:

- *Cryotherapy,* which uses liquid nitrogen to freeze and kill the wart tissue.
- *Electrodesiccation,* which burns away the wart by means of an electric current sent through a needle.

- *Traditional surgery*, which simply cuts the wart off the skin.
- *Cantharidin*, a powerful chemical that forms a blister underneath the wart and pushes it out. (Cantharidin is derived from the venom of an insect called the *blister beetle*.)
- *Laser therapy*, which is reserved for the most stubborn warts.

Wilms' Tumor

Wilms' tumor (also known as *nephroblastoma*) is the most common kidney cancer in children. The tumor usually appears in children less than five years of age (the median age is three), although it may develop in adolescence. Wilms' tumor is about 90 percent curable. Even if the cancer has spread to distant organs, more than half of all patients survive.

What causes Wilms' tumor?

The tumor sometimes runs in families, indicating a genetic influence which is as yet undefined. One of six children who develop the malignancy has congenital deformities of the urinary tract or the genitals (such as a malformation of the urethra or an undescended testicle; see entry on **testicles, undescended**). Other associated abnormalities include structural deformities of the heart and absence of the iris from the eye. Wilms' tumor sometimes develops in a child who has relatives with these congenital abnormalities.

When should I suspect Wilms' tumor?

Parents are usually the first to detect the tumor, often while bathing or dressing the child.

The first sign is usually a firm or solid lump in the abdomen or side. Abdominal pain and swelling, fever, appetite and weight loss, and blood in the urine also may occur.

How can the doctor tell if my child has Wilms' tumor?

After examining the child and feeling the abdominal mass, the doctor will order blood tests and an X ray of the kidneys. Other tests, including ultrasound, may also be needed.

Is medical treatment necessary?

Yes. Without treatment, Wilms' tumor can spread to the liver, lungs, and other sites.

What treatments are available?

Treatment involves surgery to remove the kidney, along with any cancerous tissue that has spread to other parts of the abdomen. Despite extensive surgery, children usually recover quickly. Chemotherapy also will be used. A combination of two or three anticancer drugs has proven most effective in killing off remaining cancer cells. In advanced cases, surgery is followed by 15 months of radiation and combined chemotherapy with three or four drugs. If the tumor is very large or widespread, or it affects both kidneys, chemotherapy or radiation therapy will be ordered before surgery to shrink the tumor so that the surgeon can remove only cancerous tissue, not the entire kidney.

Follow-up care

Wilms' tumor may recur, most commonly in the lungs. Lung symptoms such as coughing and shortness of breath signal such a relapse, but they are not always present. The physician

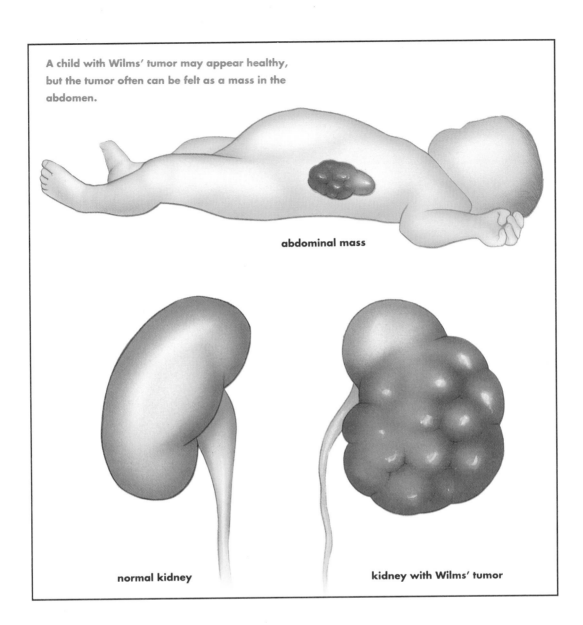

A child with Wilms' tumor may appear healthy, but the tumor often can be felt as a mass in the abdomen.

abdominal mass

normal kidney

kidney with Wilms' tumor

will therefore schedule regular checkups for several years after treatment to ensure that the child remains free of disease. The examinations will involve kidney and liver tests, bone scans, and chest X rays. Chest X rays are ordered every three months during the first year of treatment, then routinely but less frequently for five years thereafter.

Getting Help

CALL YOUR DOCTOR IF:
☐ Your child has any unexplained lump or growth in any part of the body.

Worms

The most common infections throughout the world are caused by intestinal parasites or worms. People of all ages and in all living conditions are susceptible to worms. Small children are particularly prone because they play in the mud and dirt, suck their fingers, eat soil, run barefoot outdoors, and sometimes have less than ideal toilet hygiene. Three of the most common types of worms in humans are pinworm, roundworm, and hookworm.

What happens when a child gets pinworms?

Children become infected with pinworms by swallowing pinworm eggs, which are transferred to their mouths via contaminated food, drinks, or hands. The eggs hatch in the small intestine, releasing immature worms (larvae) to the lower intestine and rectum, where they live. At night, the female worm migrates out through the anus. After laying a large number of eggs, she dies. The entire cycle, from swallowing the eggs to new eggs' being hatched, takes four to six weeks.

In children, the most common symptom is itching in the anal area at night. Girls may also have itching in the vaginal area. Other possible symptoms include insomnia, irritability, restlessness, stomach pain, and loss of appetite.

Infection is spread when the child scratches the anal area, picks up the eggs, then reinfects himself or passes them on to someone else. The eggs also can be spread through the air, when sheets or egg-laden underclothes are shaken out.

What happens when a child gets roundworms?

Roundworm eggs are deposited in the stool of an infected person. Another person can become infected by eating food grown in soil in which contaminated stool has been deposited or otherwise ingesting dirt containing roundworm eggs.

The eggs hatch into larvae in the intestine. From there, they are absorbed into the bloodstream, then carried in the blood to the lungs. They pass up the windpipe and are then swallowed. The larvae mature into adult worms in the small intestine, where female worms produce large numbers of eggs. The eggs pass out into feces, which again enter the soil. Adult roundworms can live in the small intestine for one year or longer.

Some people with roundworms have no symptoms. Others develop wheezing, a dry cough, and difficulty breathing, as well as vomiting, nausea, cramping, or distension of the abdomen. A worm may be passed through the rectum or vomited. Severe infestations can lead to intestinal blockage or malnutrition.

What happens when a child gets hookworm?

Hookworm eggs are spread when an infected person's feces are deposited in soil. These eggs hatch into larvae, which can penetrate the skin.

Once hookworm larvae enter the skin, they travel through the bloodstream to the lungs. They are then coughed up and swallowed. The larvae attach themselves to the lining of the small intestine, where they mature. The females lay eggs, which leave the body in the feces, and the process begins again.

Symptoms of hookworm infection include an itchy rash called *ground itch* at the point where the larvae entered the skin. When in the lungs, hookworms can cause a dry cough, difficulty breathing, a low-grade fever, and sputum tinged with blood. When they reach the intestine, about two weeks after entering the skin, hookworms can cause loss of appetite, diarrhea, and stomachache. Iron-deficiency anemia, due to chronic blood loss in the stool, is a common complication.

How can the pediatrician tell if my child has worms?

Pinworms may be diagnosed by finding eggs in the anal area of a child with a severe night itch. The best method for detecting this worm is to press a piece of clear tape, sticky side down, on the anal region first thing in the morning, before the child goes to the bathroom or washes. If eggs are present, they will adhere to the sticky surface and can be transferred to a slide. Under a microscope, they are easy to identify.

Roundworms may first be suspected when adult worms are seen in the stool or vomit. However, the diagnosis is established through microscopic examination of a stool sample for roundworm eggs. Hookworms are also diagnosed in this manner.

What treatments are available for these types of worms?

Antihelminthic drugs, which kill only worms and not their eggs, usually are effective. Sometimes therapy must be repeated so that the medicine can eradicate larvae hatched after the first treatment.

When a child has pinworms, the entire family should be treated. Depending on the drug, single or multiple treatments may be necessary. In general, only the affected individual needs treatment for roundworm or hookworm.

Coping with worms

- When one member of a family has worms, other members, especially children, should be examined for them.
- In some cases, medication may need to be repeated in two to four weeks in order to kill worms hatched since initial treatment.
- To prevent reinfestation, wash hands carefully before eating or handling food and after using the toilet. Wash bedding frequently and keep fingernails trimmed.

Getting Help

CALL YOUR DOCTOR IF:

- Your child or another member of the family develops symptoms suggesting worm infestation. Particularly noteworthy are bloody stools and an intense perianal itch occurring at night.
- You plan on visiting a country or region where sanitary conditions are poor.

Resource
Directory

Following is a list of many of the organizations that can provide additional information on specific childhood illnesses, as well as on child health, safety, and development.

Acquired Immunodeficiency Syndrome (AIDS)

AMERICAN FOUNDATION FOR AIDS RESEARCH
733 Third Avenue, 12th Floor
New York, NY 10017
(212) 682-7440

CENTERS FOR DISEASE CONTROL AND PREVENTION
National HIVAIDS Hotline
(800) 342-AIDS
SIDA: (800) 344-7432 (Spanish)
(800) 243-7889 (Hearing impaired)

PEDIATRIC AIDS FOUNDATION
1311 Colorado Avenue
Santa Monica, CA 90404
(310) 395-9051

Arthritis

THE ARTHRITIS FOUNDATION
1314 Spring Street
Atlanta, GA 30309
(800) 283-7800

Asthma and Allergy

ASTHMA AND ALLERGY FOUNDATION OF AMERICA
1125 15th Street N.W., Suite 502
Washington, DC 20005
(202) 466-7643

AMERICAN LUNG ASSOCIATION
1740 Broadway
New York, NY 10019–4374
(212) 315-8700

Autism

SOCIETY FOR AUTISTIC CITIZENS
8601 Georgia Avenue, Suite 503
Silver Spring, MD 20910
(301) 565-0433

Birth Defects

ASSOCIATION OF BIRTH DEFECT CHILDREN
5400 Diplomat Circle, Suite 270
Orlando, FL 32810
(407) 629-1466

MARCH OF DIMES BIRTH DEFECTS FOUNDATION
1275 Mamaroneck Avenue
White Plains, NY 10605
(914) 428-7100

Blood Diseases

LEUKEMIA SOCIETY OF AMERICA, INC.
600 Third Avenue
New York, NY 10016
(212) 573-8484

NATIONAL ASSOCIATION FOR SICKLE-CELL DISEASE, INC.
3345 Wilshire Blvd., Suite 1106
Los Angeles, CA 90010–3503
(213) 736-5455
(800) 421-8453

NATIONAL HEMOPHILIA FOUNDATION
Soho Building
110 Greene Street
New York, NY 10013
(212) 219-8180

NATIONAL SICKLE-CELL DISEASE PROGRAM
NATIONAL HEART, LUNG, AND BLOOD INSTITUTE
NATIONAL INSTITUTES OF HEALTH
Federal Building, Room 508
7550 Wisconsin Avenue
Bethesda, MD 20892
(301) 496-6931

Burns

ALISA ANN RUCH BURN FOUNDATION
20944 Sherman Way, Suite 115
Canoga Park, CA 91303
(818) 883-7700

INTERNATIONAL SHRINE HEADQUARTERS
2900 Rocky Point Drive
Tampa, FL 33607
(800) 237-5099

Cancer

AMERICAN CANCER SOCIETY
1599 Clifton Road NE
Atlanta, GA 30329
(404) 320-3333

CANCER INFORMATION SERVICE
National Cancer Institute
Building 31, Room 108
Bethesda, MD 20892
(800) 4-CANCER

Celiac Disease

GLUTEN INTOLERANCE GROUP OF NORTH AMERICA
Box 23053
Seattle, WA 98102–0353
(206) 325-6980

Cerebral Palsy

UNITED CEREBRAL PALSY ASSOCIATION
1522 K Street N.W., Suite 1112
Washington, DC 20005
(202) 892-1266

Child Abuse and Neglect

THE C. HENRY KEMPE NATIONAL CENTER
FOR THE PREVENTION AND TREATMENT OF
CHILD ABUSE AND NEGLECT
1205 Oneida Street
Denver, Co 80220
(303) 321-3963

CLEARINGHOUSE ON CHILD ABUSE AND NEGLECT
P.O. Box 1182
Washington, DC 20013
(800) FYI-3366
(703) 385-7565

NATIONAL COUNCIL ON CHILD ABUSE AND FAMILY
VIOLENCE
1155 Connecticut Avenue, N.W., Suite 400
Washington, DC 20036
(202) 429-6695

NATIONAL COMMITTEE FOR THE
PREVENTION OF CHILD ABUSE
Publishing Department
332 S. Michigan Avenue, Suite 950
Chicago, IL 60604–4357
(312) 663-3540

Childbirth/Maternity Care
INTERNATIONAL CHILDBIRTH EDUCATION ASSOCIATION,
INC.
P.O. Box 20048
Minneapolis, MN 55420
(612) 854-8660

MATERNITY CENTER ASSOCIATION
49 East 92nd Street
New York, NY 10128
(212) 369-7300

Childhood Life-Threatening Diseases
THE CANDLELIGHTERS
CHILDHOOD CANCER FOUNDATION
7910 Woodmont Avenue, Suite 460
Bethesda, MD 20814
(301) 657-8401
(800) 366-2223

THE COMPASSIONATE FRIENDS, INC.
National Office
P.O. Box 3696
Oak Brook, IL 60522–3696
(708) 990-0010

Cleft Palate
AMERICAN CLEFT PALATE ASSOCIATION
1218 Grandview Avenue
Pittsburgh, PA 15211
(800) 24-CLEFT
(412) 481-1376

Cystic Fibrosis
CYSTIC FIBROSIS FOUNDATION
6931 Arlington Road, Suite 200
Bethesda, MD 20814
(301) 951-4422
(800) FIGHTCF

Diabetes
AMERICAN DIABETES ASSOCIATION
National Service Center
1660 Duke Street
Alexandria, VA 22314
(800) 232-3472
(703) 549-1500

JOSLIN DIABETES CENTER
One Joslin Place
Boston, MA 02215
(617) 732-2400

THE JUVENILE DIABETES FOUNDATION
international
432 Park Avenue South
New York, NY 10016
(212) 889-7575

NATIONAL DIABETES INFORMATION CLEARINGHOUSE
Box NDIC
9000 Rockville Pike
Bethesda, MD 20892
(301) 468-2162

Digestive Diseases

CROHN'S COLITIS FOUNDATION OF AMERICA, INC.
444 Park Avenue South
New York, NY 10016
(212) 685-3440

NATIONAL DIGESTIVE DISEASES INFORMATION
CLEARINGHOUSE
Box NDDIC
9000 Rockville Pike
Bethesda, MD 20892
(301) 468-6344

Drug Abuse and Narcotic Addiction

AL-ANON FAMILY GROUP HEADQUARTERS
P.O. Box 862, Midtown Station
New York, NY 10018
(800) 254-4656
(212) 302-7240

DRUG ABUSE CLEARINGHOUSE
P.O. Box 2345
Rockville, MD 20847–2345
(301) 443-6500
(800) 729-6686

NATIONAL COUNCIL ON ALCOHOLISM
1511 K Street N.W., Suite 320
Washington, DC 20005
(202) 737-8122

Epilepsy

EPILEPSY FOUNDATION OF AMERICA
4351 Garden City Drive
Landover, MD 20785
(301) 459-3700

THE EPILEPSY INSTITUTE
67 Irving Place
New York, NY 10003
(212) 677-8550

Family Planning/Sex Information

THE ALAN GUTTMACHER INSTITUTE
111 Fifth Avenue
New York, New York 10001
(212) 254-5656

FAMILY LIFE INFORMATION EXCHANGE
P.O. Box 37299
Washington, DC 20013–7299
(301) 585-6639

PLANNED PARENTHOOD FEDERATION OF AMERICA, INC.
810 Second Avenue
New York, NY 10019
(212) 541-7800
(800) 829-7732

SEX INFORMATION AND EDUCATION COUNCIL
OF THE UNITED STATES
130 W. 42nd Street, 25th Floor
New York, NY 10036
(212) 819-9770

Fertility

THE AMERICAN FERTILITY SOCIETY
2140 Eleventh Avenue South, Suite 200
Birmingham, AL 35205–2800
(205) 933-8494

RESOLVE, INC.
1310 Broadway
Somerville, MA 02144–1731
(617) 623-0744

Genetic Diseases

ASSOCIATION FOR NEURO-METABOLIC DISORDERS
5223 Brookfield Lane
Sylvania, OH 43560–1809
(419) 885-1497

GENETICS SOCIETY OF AMERICA
9650 Rockville Pike
Bethesda, MD 20814–3998
(301) 571-1825

HEREDITARY DISEASE FOUNDATION
1427 Seventh Street, Suite 2
Santa Monica, CA 90401
(310) 458-4183

NATIONAL TAY-SACHS AND ALLIED DISEASES
ASSOCIATION, INC.
2001 Beacon Street
Brookline, MA 02146
(617) 277-4463

THE NATIONAL FOUNDATION FOR
JEWISH GENETIC DISEASES
250 Park Avenue, Suite 1000
New York, NY 10177
(212) 371-1030

Group B Strep Infections

GROUP B STREP ASSOCIATION
2537 Severin Street
Chapel Hill, NC 27514

Growth Disorders

HUMAN GROWTH FOUNDATION
P.O. Box 3090
Falls Church, VA 22043
(800) 451-6434

LITTLE PEOPLE'S RESEARCH FUND
80 Sister Pierre Drive
Towson, MD 21204
(410) 494-0055

Handicapped/Rehabilitation

FEDERATION FOR CHILDREN WITH SPECIAL NEEDS, INC.
95 Berkeley Street, Suite 104
Boston, MA 02116
(800) 331-0688
(617) 482-2915

FEDERATION OF THE HANDICAPPED
154 W. 14th Street
New York, NY 10011
(212) 727-4200

NATIONAL EASTER SEAL SOCIETY
70 East Lake Street
Chicago, IL 60601
(312) 726-6200

NATIONAL INFORMATION CENTER FOR CHILDREN AND
YOUTH WITH DISABILITIES
P.O. Box 1492
Washington, DC 20013
(800) 999-5599
(703) 893-6061

NARIC ABLEDATA
(NATIONAL REHABILITATION INFORMATION CENTER)
8455 Colesville Road, Suite 935
Silver Spring, MD 20910–3319
(800) 227-0216
(301) 588-9284

NATIONAL REHABILITATION ASSOCIATION
1910 Associate Drive, Suite 205
Reston, VA 22091
(703) 715-9090

SCOUTING FOR HANDICAPPED EDUCATION
RELATIONSHIPS SERVICE
Boy Scouts of America
1325 W. Walnut Hill Lane
P.O. Box 152079
Irving, TX 75015–2079
(214) 580-2000

Health Information

AMERICAN RED CROSS (ARC)
NATIONAL HEADQUARTERS
430 17th Street N.W.
Washington, DC 20006
(202) 737-8300

CONSUMER INFORMATION CATALOG
Pueblo, CO 81009
(719) 948-3334

MATERNAL AND CHILD HEALTH BUREAU
Parklawn Building, Room 18–05
5600 Fishers Lane
Rockville, MD 20857
(301) 443-2170

MATERNAL AND CHILD HEALTH CLEARINGHOUSE
8201 Greensboro Drive, Suite 600
McLean, VA 22102
(703) 821-8955 Ext. 254/265

NATIONAL HEALTH INFORMATION CLEARINGHOUSE
"HEALTHFINDER"
ONHIC
P.O. Box 1133
Washington, DC 20013–1133
(800) 565-4167
(301) 336-4797 (in Maryland)

NATIONAL INSTITUTES OF CHILD HEALTH AND
HUMAN DEVELOPMENT
Building 31, Room 2A-32
9000 Rockville Pike
Bethesda, MD 20892
(301) 496-5133

Hearing and Speech Disorders

ALEXANDER GRAHAM BELL ASSOCIATION
3417 Volta Place, N.W.
Washington, DC 20007
(202) 387-5220

AMERICAN SPEECH-LANGUAGE-HEARING ASSOCIATION
10801 Rockville Pike
Rockville, MD 20852
(800) 638-8255
(301) 897-5700

DEAFNESS RESEARCH FOUNDATION
9 E. 38th Street
New York, NY 10016
(212) 684-6556

HEARING AID HELPLINE
20361 Middlebelt Road
Livonia, MI 48152
(800) 521-5247
(313) 478-2610

NATIONAL ASSOCIATION FOR HEARING AND
SPEECH ACTION
10801 Rockville Pike
Rockville, MD 20852
(800) 638-8255 (help-line)
(301) 897-8682 (in Maryland)

STUTTERING RESOURCE FOUNDATION
123 Oxford Road
New Rochelle, NY 10804
(800) 232-4773
(914) 632-3925

High Blood Pressure

HIGH BLOOD PRESSURE INFORMATION CENTER
P.O. Box 30105
Bethesda, MD 20824–0105
(301) 951-3260

Hydrocephalus

NATIONAL HYDROCEPHALUS FOUNDATION
400 N. Michigan Avenue, Suite 1102
Chicago, IL 60611–4102
(815) 467-6548

Kidney Disease

AMERICAN ASSOCIATION OF KIDNEY PATIENTS (AAKP)
1 Dan's Boulevard, Suite LL1
Tampa, FL 33606
(813) 251-0725

AMERICAN KIDNEY FUND
6110 Executive Boulevard, Suite 1010
Rockville, MD 20852
(800) 638-8299

NATIONAL INSTITUTE OF DIABETES,
DIGESTIVE, AND KIDNEY DISEASES
National Institutes of Health
9000 Rockville Pike
Building 31, 9A04
Bethesda, MD 20892
(301) 496-3583

NATIONAL KIDNEY FOUNDATION INC.
30 E. 33rd Street
New York, NY 10016
(212) 889-2210

Learning Disabilities

ASSOCIATION FOR CHILDREN AND ADULTS WITH
LEARNING DISABILITIES
4900 Girard Road
Pittsburgh, PA 15227–1444
(412) 881-2253

Lupus

SYSTEMIC LUPUS ERYTHEMATOSUS (SLE) FOUNDATION
149 Madison Avenue, Room 608
New York, NY 10016
(212) 685-4118

Lyme Disease

NATIONAL LYME BORRELIOSIS FOUNDATION
Box 462
Tolland, CT 06084
(800) 886-LYME
(203) 871-2900
(203) 872-6346

Marfan Syndrome

NATIONAL MARFAN FOUNDATION
382 Main Street
Port Washington, NY 11050
(800) 8-MARFAN
(516) 883-8712

Medical Alert

MEDIC ALERT FOUNDATION U.S.
2323 Colorado Avenue
Turlock, CA 95380
(800) 344-3226
(209) 668-3333

Mental Health/Retardation

AMERICAN ASSOCIATION ON MENTAL RETARDATION
1719 Kalorama Road N.W.
Washington, DC 20009
(800) 424-3688
(202) 387-1968

THE ARC (ASSOCIATION FOR RETARDED CITIZENS)
2501 Avenue J
Arlington, TX 76007
(817) 261-6003

ASSOCIATION FOR CHILDREN WITH
RETARDED MENTAL DEVELOPMENT
162 Fifth Avenue
New York, NY 10010
(212) 741-0100

NATIONAL FRAGILE X FOUNDATION
1441 York Street, Suite 215
Denver, Co 80206
(800) 688-8765
(303) 333-6155

NATIONAL INSTITUTE OF MARRIAGE AND
FAMILY RELATIONS
6116 Rolling Road, Suite 306
Springfield, VA 22152
(703) 569-2400

NATIONAL INSTITUTE OF MENTAL HEALTH
Public Inquiries Branch
Parklawn Building, Room 15C-05
5600 Fishers Lane
Rockville, MD 20857
(301) 443-4513

Muscular Dystrophy

MUSCULAR DYSTROPHY ASSOCIATION
3300 E. Sunrise Drive
Tucson, AZ 85718
(602) 529-2000

Neonatal Death

SHARE (SOURCE OF HELP IN AIRING AND
RESOLVING EXPERIENCES)
St. Joseph Health Center
300 First Capitol Drive
St. Charles, MO 63301
(314) 947-6164

Nutrition

FOOD AND DRUG ADMINISTRATION
Office of Consumer Affairs
5600 Fishers Lane
Rockville, MD 20857
(301) 443-1544

HUMAN NUTRITION INFORMATION SERVICE
Department of Agriculture
6505 Belcrest Road, Room 360
Hyattsville, MD 20782
(301) 436-7725

AMERICAN DIETETIC ASSOCIATION
216 W. Jackson Boulevard, Suite 800
Chicago, IL 60606–6995
(800) 877-1600
(312) 899-0040

Osteogenesis Imperfecta

OSTEOGENESIS IMPERFECTA FOUNDATION, INC.
5005 W. Laurel Street, Suite 210
Tampa, FL 33607–3836
(813) 282-1161

Polycystic Kidney Disease

POLYCYSTIC KIDNEY RESEARCH FOUNDATION
922 Walnut, #411
Kansas City, MO 64106
(816) 421-1869

Psoriasis

NATIONAL PSORIASIS FOUNDATION
6443 SW Beaverton Highway, Suite 210
Portland, OR 97221
(503) 297-1545

Respiratory Diseases

AMERICAN LUNG ASSOCIATION
1740 Broadway
New York, NY 10019
(212) 315-8700

Retinitis Pigmentosa

NATIONAL RETINITIS PIGMENTOSA FOUNDATION
1401 Mt. Royal Avenue, 4th Floor
Baltimore, MD 21217
(410) 225-9400

Reye's Syndrome

NATIONAL REYE'S SYNDROME FOUNDATION
P.O. Box 829
Bryan, OH 43506
(800) 233-7393
(419) 636-2679

Scoliosis

NATIONAL SCOLIOSIS FOUNDATION
71 Mt. Auburn Street
Watertown, MA 02172
(617) 926-0397

SCOLIOSIS ASSOCIATION, INC.
P.O. Box 51353
Raleigh, NC 27609
(407) 994-4435

Spina Bifida

SPINA BIFIDA ASSOCIATION OF AMERICA
4699 Auvergne Street
Lyle, IL 60532
(708) 960-2426

Spinal Injuries

AMERICAN PARALYSIS ASSOCIATION HOTLINE
MONTEBELLO HOSPITAL
2201 Argonne Drive
Baltimore, MD 21218
(800) 526-3456
(800) 638-1733 (in Maryland)

NATIONAL SPINAL CORD INJURY ASSOCIATION
600 W. Cummings Park, Suite 2000
Woburn, MA 01801
(800) 962-9629 (outside Massachusetts)
(617) 935-2722 (Massachusetts only)

SPINAL NETWORK
P.O. Box 4162
Boulder, CO 80306
(800) 338-5412

Sudden Infant Death Syndrome (SIDS)

SUDDEN INFANT DEATH SYNDROME (SIDS) CLEARINGHOUSE
8201 Greensboro Drive
Suite 600
McLean, VA 22102
(703) 821-8955, Ext. 361

SUDDEN INFANT DEATH SYNDROME
NATIONAL HEADQUARTERS
10500 Little Patuxent Parkway
Columbia, MD 21044
(800) 221-SIDS
(410) 964-8000

Vision Disorders/Blindness

AMERICAN FOUNDATION FOR THE BLIND, INC.
15 W. 16th Street
New York, NY 10011
(800) AFBLIND
(212) 620-2000
(212) 620-2147 (in New York)

ASSOCIATED BLIND, INC.
135 W. 23rd Street
New York, NY 10011
(212) 255-1122

ASSOCIATION FOR EDUCATION AND REHABILITATION
OF THE BLIND AND VISUALLY IMPAIRED
206 N. Washington Street, Suite 320
Alexandria, VA 22314
(703) 548-1884

FIGHT FOR SIGHT, INC.
160 E. 56th Street, 8th Floor
New York, NY 10022
(212) 751-1118

NATIONAL ASSOCIATION FOR THE
VISUALLY HANDICAPPED
22 W. 21st Street, 6th Floor
New York, NY 10010
(212) 889-3141

NATIONAL CENTER FOR THE BLIND
1800 Johnson Street
Baltimore, MD 21230
(410) 659-9317

NATIONAL LIBRARY SERVICE FOR THE BLIND AND
PHYSICALLY HANDICAPPED
The Library of Congress
1291 Taylor Street N.W.
Washington, DC 20542
(800) 424-8567
(202) 707-5100

NATIONAL SOCIETY TO PREVENT BLINDNESS
500 E. Remington Road
Schaumburg, IL 60173
(800) 331-2020
(708) 843-2020

RECORDING FOR THE BLIND, INC.
20 Roszel Road
Princeton, NJ 08540
(800) 221-4792
(609) 452-0606

General Resources

AMERICAN ACADEMY OF PEDIATRICS
141 Northwest Point Boulevard
Elk Grove Village, IL 60007
(800) 433-9016
(708) 228-5005

ASSOCIATION FOR THE CARE OF CHILDREN'S HEALTH
7910 Woodmont Avenue, Suite 300
Bethesda, MD 20814
(301) 654-6549

CHILD AND YOUTH SERVICES ADMINISTRATION
2700 Martin Luther King, Jr. Avenue S.E.
L Building
Washington, DC 20037
(202) 373-7225

CHILDREN'S DEFENSE FUND
25 E Street, N.W.
Washington, DC 20001
(202) 628-8787

CHILD WELFARE LEAGUE OF AMERICA
440 First Street, N.W., Suite 310
Washington, DC 20001
(202) 638-2952

LA LECHE LEAGUE INTERNATIONAL
9619 Minneapolis Avenue
Franklin Park, IL 60131
(708) 455-7730

NAEYC (NATIONAL ASSOCIATION FOR THE
EDUCATION OF YOUNG CHILDREN)
1834 Connecticut Avenue, N.W.
Washington, DC 20009
(800) 424-2460
(202) 232-8777

NATIONAL ORGANIZATION FOR RARE DISORDERS, INC.
P.O. Box 8923
New Fairfield, CT 06812
(203) 746-6518

NATIONAL SAFE KIDS CAMPAIGN
111 Michigan Avenue, N.W.
Washington, DC 20010
(202) 939-4993

NATIONAL SAFETY COUNCIL
1121 Spring Lake
Itasca, IL 60143-3201
(800) 621-7615
(708) 285-1121

NATIONAL SELF-HELP CLEARINGHOUSE
33 W. 42nd Street, Room 620N
New York, NY 10036
(212) 642-2944

PARENT ACTION
2 N. Charles Street, Suite 960
Baltimore, MD 21201
(410) 752-1790

PEDIATRIC PROJECTS
P.O. Box 571555
Tarzana, CA 91357
(818) 705-3660

PROJECT SCHOOL CARE
Boston Children's Hospital
300 Longwood Avenue
Boston, MA 02115
(617) 735-6714

SELF-HELP CENTER
1600 Dodge Avenue, Suite S-122
Evanston, IL 60201
(708) 328-0471

SKIP (SICK KIDS NEED INVOLVED PEOPLE)
990 2nd Avenue, 2nd and 3rd Floors
New York, NY 10022
(212) 421-9161

U.S. CONSUMER PRODUCT SAFETY COMMISSION
Washington, DC 20207
(800) 638-CPSC (outside Maryland)
(800) 492-8104 (in Maryland)
(800) 638-8270 (TDD)
(301) 504-0580

Index

Page numbers in *italics* refer to Volume II. Page numbers in **bold** refer to illustrations.

safety of, 82
for six-to-ten-month-olds, 71, 72, **72**
and temper tantrums, 131
for ten-to–24-month-olds, 97
for three-to-six-month-olds, 51, **53**
for toddlers, 120
tracheostomy, *91*
trachial infections, *44*
traction, *130*
tranquilizers, *238*
transfusions, *11, 118*
transient tics, *259*
transitional objects, 98
transplants, *139–40*
bone marrow, *163*
kidney, *153*
transposition of the great arteries, *112,* **115**
travel, 88, **89**
car safety seats for, 27, 30, **30**, **31**, 38, 85, **156**, 188
at high altitudes, *20*
motion sickness in, *177–78*
and preparation of bottles, 19
and temper tantrums, 131
tricycle riding, **150**
trimazole, *220*
trouble signs:
birth to three months, 36–37
three to six months, 61
six to ten months, 77
ten to 24 months, 102
two to three years, 124–25
five to six years, 175
trust, 147
tube feeding, *203*
tuberculosis, 265–67
tumors:
bone cancer, *40*
Wilms', *274–75*, **275**
tunnel vision, *105*
tympanometry, *173–74*
Type I diabetes, *82–83*
tyrosine, *193*

ulcerative colitis, *66*
ulcers:
mouth, *48–49*
stomach and duodenal, 250, *242–44*
umbilical cord, 4–5, **5**
umbilical hernia, *126–27*
underfeeding, 47
Underwriters Laboratories (UL) labels, 224
undescended testicles, *135, 254–55, 274*

United Cerebral Palsy Association, *282*
upper motor neurons, *207*
urate, *20*
ureter, *151*
urethra:
congenital defect in, *135–36*
irritation of, *268*
malformation of, *274*
urinary system, following page 141
deformity in, *135–36, 274*
urinary tract infection, *155, 156, 183, 267–69*
and bed-wetting, *32*
and circumcision, *57*
urushiol, *198*
uveitis, *23*

vacationing, 88, **89**
see also travel
vaccination, *see* immunizations
vagina:
bleeding from, 6
HIV transmission through, *11*
infection in, *201, 257*
vanitidine, *243*
varicella (chicken pox), 118, 279, *54–56, 143, 169, 230*
immunization against, *12, 137*
vectors, *236*
vegetables, in diet, 153
vegetarianism, *172, 218*
ventilation, mechanical, *124*
ventricular septal defect (VSD), *112*
vernix, 5
violence, on television, 9
viral gastroenteritis, *101, 102*
viral infections, 277
chicken pox, 118, 279, *54–56, 143, 169, 230*
conjunctivitis, *69–71*, **70**, *176*
Coxsackie, 277, 278, *89, 169*
croup, 255, *72–75*, **73**
erythema infectiosum, *93–95*
hepatitis, 34, *89, 121–23, 137–138*
influenza, 277, *63, 89, 145–47, 195*
intestinal, *269–71*
measles, *see* measles
molluscum contagiosum, *176–77*
mononucleosis, 277, 279, *143–45, 169*
mumps, *see* mumps
oral herpes, *62–63*
pneumonia, *see* pneumonia
polio, 58, 73, 100, 151, 171, *138, 139, 140–41*

Reye's syndrome, *212–14*
rubella, *see* German measles
shingles, *230–31*
see also immunizations
vision, of newborns, 9
vision impairment, *271–72*
cataracts, *46–48*
from encephalitis, *90*
lazy eye (strabismus), *244–45*, **244**
nearsightedness, *181–82*, **182**
in premature babies, *202*
resource directory for, *288, 289–90*
vitamin C, *18*
vitamin D, *217–19*
vitamin supplements, 153
for breast fed babies, 18
poisoning from, 216, 217
vocabulary, *see* language
voice box, inflammation of, *44*
voices, baby's recognition of, 9, 44
vomiting, 281–82, *210–12*
dehydration, *78–79*
food poisoning, *101*
gastroenteritis, *269, 270, 271*
intestinal obstruction, *147*
and ipecac syrup, 82, 202, 215
meningitis, *169*
motion sickness, *177*, 178
pyloric stenosis, *210–11*
VSD (ventricular septal defect), *112*
vulgar warts, *272–73*
vulva, irritation of, *155*

walking:
with congenital hip dislocation, *130*
duck walk, *260*
with flatfoot, *100*
of mentally retarded, *171*
preparation for, 65
in sleep, *186*
toddling vs., *91*
warts, *272–74*
water:
fear of, 157
fluoride in, *261, 264*
and safety, 38, 75, 155, 224
see also dehydration
water pics, *262*
wax, ear, *85–87*
weaning, 46, 102–3, **103**
well-baby care:
three to six months, 57–58
six to ten months, 73
ten to 24 months, 99–100
two to three years, 118–19